Red Herrings Can't Swim

Red Herrings Can't Swim

A Nod Blake Mystery

Doug Lamoreux

For Jenny

Chapter One

Imagine, if you will, an all-but washed-up private detective chasing a pharmacy technician down a hallway of the Chicago-Loop Memorial Hospital as fast as either of us could run. He was wearing a white lab coat and a look of panic. I was bare-assed for all the world to see. Yeah, I'm the private dick. And, okay, truth be told, I was not completely nude. I was wearing one of those flimsy cotton gowns, pastel blue with an aesthetically pleasing print of tiny tigers, tied in a bow at the back of the neck with a split all the way down and my butt hanging out, running like hell after him. Yeah, we were a sight.

Like I said, I'm a detective. Call it a personality flaw, but I have a hard time minding my own business. Because of that I was wandering the hospital. And because of that, I found the hospital employee in a partially tiled, partially plumbed bathroom on the 'Closed for Renovations' tenth floor, with his sleeve hoisted and a rubber band tied round his bicep, shooting up with narcotics.

He'd just finished giving himself the joy juice when I stuck my head in the room and asked, "Is that in your job description?" He yanked the needle out painting the wall with a spurt of blood. Then, waving the syringe like a modern-day musketeer, came at me in the doorway.

I tripped over my own feet backing up. He did a rabbit over top of me and the chase was on. It continued down the north stairwell, out and across the eighth floor, where ten minutes earlier I'd seen him swipe the drug from a hospital crash cart. There was one on every patient floor in case of cardiac arrest or other emergencies. We continued into the south stairs, down and out again onto seven, past room 708, my temporary residence. No, I was not officially working. I was a patient. But, like I said, a nosy patient. Where were we? Yeah, headed back to the north stairwell. He grabbed the knob on the fire door to the stairs at the same time I tackled him. That was a mistake.

It was also when the fun really started. The pair of us went through the door, onto the floor, and down that flight of stairs like crap through a goose. We bounced off the steps and each other for half the distance and, if you know anything about me at all, sisters and brothers, you will not be surprised to hear I smacked my head along the way. He screamed, I screamed, and the universe had a laugh at our expense. Somehow, halfway down, I wound up on top and rode him to the landing like a five-year-old riding the sidewalk quarter pony outside of the local Venture.

So there I was, a has-been private eye in my nightie, sitting on top of a hopped-up pharmacy tech on a stairwell landing in a major Chicago hospital. He was screaming, calling me names at the top of his lungs, and struggling with muscles fueled by a high-octane mixture of adrenaline and a yet-to-be-determined stimulant. I was wondering if the situation could be any more ridiculous.

I'll never learn. Because that's when *he* burst through the sixth floor fire door, shouting, "What's goin' on here?"

By he, of course, I mean Detective Lieutenant Frank Wenders of the Chicago Police Department, a living and breathing reason for taxpayer outrage. A couple of years short of retirement, but expired and rotten nevertheless, Wenders gave policing a bad name and, assuming there was life on other planets, wasn't doing the universal opinion of man a favor either. My questions just then included: Where did he come from? And what was the tub of lard doing there on the hospital stairs?

"Blake!" he yelled. "What the hell?" The echo repeated his question up and down the stairwell.

I should probably point out that he was yelling at me. My name is Nod Blake, former cop and current decrepit detective. Everyone who knows me knows I go by 'Blake' alone. With a first name like that, who wouldn't? It was a curse cast on me by evil parents. The old man got his ages ago. My mother, on the other hand, looks both ways before she crosses the street. One day I'll have my revenge. But I digress. Wenders was demanding information.

"I'm making a citizen's arrest," I told him. "What about you? Homicide has nothing better to do?"

"Homicide has all kinds of better things to do, wise guy," Wenders barked. "Mason started bawlin' his ass off in the Squad Room, so I brought him in."

I'd had a feeling something was missing and that was it; his ever-present partner, Detective Dave Mason, wasn't present. So rare was it for one to be seen without the other that Wenders looked like a shark without his parasite feeder. Together the pair were a sore on my backside that wouldn't heal. Anyway, the lieutenant was still explaining, "They're doin' an emergency surgery. Gonna remove Mason's appendix."

I made a few comments that occurred to me.

"Yeah, yeah," Wenders said. "Like usual, Blake, you're talkin' but not sayin' anything."

"What would you like me to say?"

"Nothing. I'd like 'em to do surgery on you; remove your voice box. But then you'd just become a pest in sign language."

To show he was right, I offered him the one hand gesture I knew.

He ignored it and went on. "Since you still got your voice, and under the circumstances, I need a few details as to why you're in a hospital stairwell rubbin' your balls on a doctor? I'm Homicide, and I'm not convinced you're murderin' the guy, but it looks a little crime-ish around the edges. Not to mention weird. Want to fill me in? – You shut up a minute!"

That last wasn't for me; it was for the hospital employee beneath me. I forgot to mention, during my short conversation with Wenders, the lab tech had been screaming like a trapped animal the whole time.

"He isn't a doctor," I explained to the curious lieutenant. "He's a pharmacy technician."

Wenders shook his head in mock sadness. "And your mother wanted you to marry a doctor."

"Could you leave my mother out of this?"

"Sure, I got nothin' against the poor put-upon old biddy. So, Blake, sparing me whatever details are so ugly they're gonna put me off my supper, what are you doin' here? On top of that pharmacy guy? And why are you doin' it in a dress?"

There was no way on God's green earth I was going to tell Wenders why I was a patient in that hospital. I told him once, not long ago, that I'd suffered a head injury and confessed the whack had done something to my attic. I'd also told him that, on occasion, I now got random psychic flashes of one sort or another. Yes, faithful reader, I'm as serious as a heart attack. I'll make it more plain to you when I get the chance. But the point then was, I'd tried to explain my condition to Wenders before and he hadn't bought a word of it. There was no point trying again. There was certainly nothing to be gained by telling him I was there, as a patient, for the express purpose of having my injured brain scanned. Why give the guy ammo?

"Why are you here?" Wenders shouted again.

"Hemorrhoids," I said. "I've got hemorrhoids."

"That's a coincidence," the lieutenant said. "Everyone you meet winds up with the same trouble. That said," he went on, smacking his lips, "I was kinda askin' about this situation here on the stairs."

"Oh, that." I took a breath and gave him a shorter version of the story I've just told you. I explained the theft, the illegal drug use, and was midway through the hallway chase, when the stairwell door opened again and the night shift's

7

supervising nurse stormed the scene. And, because I couldn't buy a pinch of luck with a pot of gold, she had to be Nurse Ratched's uglier, meaner sister. She demanded to know what was happening on her stairs.

I raised my voice (the pharmacy tech was shouting again). "You've been losing narcotics from the cardiac crash carts on every floor?"

"Who are you?" she roared. "How did you know that? Nobody knows that."

"I'll take that as a yes," I told her. "Here's your thief. He just hit the cart on the eighth floor, took the drug to the vacant tenth floor, and shot up in one of the rooms on the west wing." The tech squawked louder and I leaned on his head. "Shut up!" Back to the hospital warden and the fat cop. "You'll find a fresh needle track inside his left elbow. You'll find his leavings in the bathroom of room 1020."

Up until that point, faithful readers, it went as I've told it. From then on, it should have gone like this: a quick arrest on several counts for the guy in the lab coat and a pat on the back for me for making the world a better place. Only it didn't.

Because the stupefied supervisor refused to accept the idea that anyone could know something the hospital administrators were keeping quiet. Meaning nobody could know drugs had been vanishing from the floors. Neither would her mind accept the notion an employee under her supervision was responsible. In consequence, she stood there, shaking her head like a ceramic dashboard dog, wishing we would all just vanish.

And the prize package beneath my prize package kept screaming, and the stairwell walls kept echoing, "Get off me!"

I couldn't arrest him. First off, I'm not a cop anymore; I haven't been for ages. Secondly, ah, forget secondly... This is not a police procedural and you don't want to hear it. It isn't a political thriller either, and the workings of a modern-day hospital (this was 1979, after all) and the decisions made by their nursing supervisors were almost entirely political. So I'll cut it short and tell you the pharmacy tech, whose name incidentally was Leon Darvish, did not go to jail. He went to the administrative offices, where he was showered with *tsk-tsk* noises of disappointment, and given a lecture on the hospital's need for a spotless reputation in the community. Then he was quietly *let go*, much like a precious undersized trout is returned to the stream. You see, an arrest for drug theft (let alone use) on duty would have shown a bad light on the healthcare facility. They didn't even slap Darvish's wrist. They didn't want him to go away angry, with things to say and trouble to cause, they just wanted him to go away.

And what, you may ask, of your law-abiding narrator? Me, sisters and brothers, they accused of causing a disruption to patients and staff. I was invited to find a new neurologist. And I was instructed, in no uncertain terms, to get dressed and get out of their hospital.

Chapter Two

"If you're ready… Take the hands of those seated on either side of you. And remember, no matter what happens, do not break the circle."

I'd heard a variation of that line in every Vincent Price movie I'd ever seen. No doubt you have too. And you've seen the set-up; the dark foyer, the inner doorway covered in hanging beads, the darker room beyond surrounded by heavy blood red curtains, the round table (that should have been adorned with a crystal ball but, sadly, was not), the gullible nitwits seated in a circle. I was less than proud, I have to confess, being among the latter. But there I was sitting in at a séance.

If we back up a second I can explain. No, not so that it makes sense. How could it make any sense? But so you see how I got there. Then again, if you know anything about my work and life, you already have a good guess how I got there. In a word, Lisa Solomon. My secretary had an absolute knack for getting me into situations where I didn't want to be.

You may or may not know that Lisa, in her overzealous desire to someday be a detective, recently involved me in a series of murders... I'll spare you a rehash of the details. Suffice to say during that case, while chasing the bad guys, I managed to hit – and hurt – my head... repeatedly. And, as any good friend and confidant would, after we'd pulled my fat out of the fire and put the case to bed, Lisa insisted I go to the hospital. There was real concern, owing to the bizarre symptoms I was experiencing, I had done permanent damage to myself above the neck. What were the symptoms?

Pain, obviously, and swelling of my noggin, tingling nerves, heat flashes, vision problems and, oh yes, hallucinations of visitations, communications, and commiserations with the dead. Huh, you ask? Well you might. But, yes, the dead, specifically the victims in that last murder case had come to me in random psychic flashes and asked for my help in catching their killer. I know. Get a net, right? I was ready for the rubber room; I don't dispute it. I may be crazy. But that was what had happened. In fact, it was worse. I had not only been talked to by the victims, I had relived their violent deaths. Scout's honor. Somehow, and I haven't the slightest notion how, the injuries to my head allowed me, strike that, forced me to repeatedly see – and to feel – their murders. I literally experienced being killed, in a wide variety of ways, over and over again.

After the dust cleared and the killers in that particular case were removed from polite society, and knowing my new and frightening 'condition' would certainly impact our relationship from then on, I sat Lisa down. I had a chat with her about what was happening inside my bruised noggin. I explained, as best I could with my limited knowl-edge, what I saw and heard when these psychic at-tacks came. I told her of the pain in the back of my head, the heat flashes, the blinding colored lights in my eyes. Then I went into the weird parts.

I explained as best I could that my physical sur-roundings actually changed. My location, regard-less of my location, suddenly became the scene of a crime. I was instantly, and painfully, there with the victim. At first, I merely saw them being killed. In later flashes, the victims turned and spoke to me, personally, in the midst of their murders. There was no indication, I could see, that any of the dead heard my replies. But they spoke to me. In later flashes, the experience became more grueling as I began to take the place of the victims. On those psychic trips, I experienced their murders. You can say I dreamed it. But, if I did, they were nightmares repeated over again, one murder after another. I could go on, but why would I? It's too idiotic and unbelievable to believe. So you're either going with what I'm telling you on faith or you've already hollered 'Bull', and have abandoned the idea as fictional crap. Have it your way. For those still with me, no, outside of the brain injuries, I had no explanation for these hallucinations or any idea what brought them on. At times, it seemed the visions were initiated by my touching someone or something, but not always, and no particular person or thing when it did. As I said, they seemed to come at random. And, if you're wondering, the answer is yes, they sucked. Being murdered is no fun at all.

Lisa took in my explanation with wide eyes, made wider by her big round glasses, and a few silent nods (which, for her, was a phenomenally restrained response). I don't know what I'd hoped to gain by telling her what had been happening. I do know what I feared I might lose in spilling the beans. But she was my secretary, and friend, and I thought she ought to know. In the end, she asked a few questions I couldn't answer and we decided to keep on keeping on detecting. We both still needed to eat, after all. The subject of my malfunctioning noggin was filed away.

At least I thought so. Then I found out differently. You see, once I'd dumped the load on Lisa – and this I should have expected – she wanted to help. To that end she soon began needling me, resurrecting the discussion often, with out of the blue questions like, "Did you experience precognition when you were a kid?"

To which I would reply something like, "Outside of sensing the approach of a butt whipping, not that I know."

Or repeatedly asking, "Did your parents have psychic visions?"

To which I'd answer some variation of, "My father could see his future with my mother. As evidenced by the good sense he showed in dying early to avoid it. My mother has no psychic ability. But she is superstitious. She sacrifices chickens to conjure winning Bingo numbers. It never works because she can't hold off drinking the rum before the end of the ceremony. Does that count?"

I agree, I wasn't being helpful. But we weren't going to solve the 'Mystery of Blake's Head Thing' by talking about it. And Lisa was getting on my nerves. She continued to nag and finally dragged me into the hospital to get my busted bean seen to. The plan was simple, scans, x-rays, and a brainstorming session with accredited members of the physicians' neurological community. You saw the hash I made of that. But, if my hospital visit sounded like disastrous fun, you haven't heard anything yet.

After another week of sawing on my last nerve, Lisa forced me into the lair of what she called an "expert at talking to the dead." And so we've come full circle. She'd hauled my cookies to the salon of a spiritual medium in search of a séance.

Two women were already there, in the parlor, when we arrived. The older of the pair was a fleshy, snooty but well-turned out, version of every middle-aged woman that had ever run a shopping cart up my unsuspecting keister. Though the attitude suggested this one had money. No doubt Jeeves or Josette did her shopping for her. She wore a bright orange suit-thing and a matching pill box hat. Neither the flowers pinned below her shoulder nor the pearl baubles around her neck went with the outfit, and the assembled whole returned the favor by refusing to go with her blue hair. The other, a thirty-something brunette giving (or getting) security with a slim-fingered grip on the old hag's arm, was a decidedly sleek looking model, gliding naturally and comfortably from kitten to cougar. The elements comprising her facial features were perfectly measured. Her eyelids, unencumbered by make-up, were lowered in what looked to be an attempt at demure. But they failed. At twice the size necessary for seeing, the eyes knew they were ideal for being seen. (I had an odd feeling I recognized her, but couldn't come up with a name.) What I did know was – if she played her cards right – she could end up as my newest reason for staring sleeplessly at the bedroom ceiling.

The medium, stretching credulity by wearing a turban, and making it worse by calling himself Master Criswell, was no master when it came to scheduling. He'd penciled in both of our appointments for the same time. As the ladies arrived first, and were apparently socially something to write home about, Criswell asked if Lisa and I would mind waiting.

The suggestion didn't appeal to me. I had no clue how long it would take him to do his thing, make his pitch, hook the ladies and reel them in. But I knew I didn't want to wait hours for my chomp at the lure. I strongly suggested Lisa and I go. I may even have suggested the evening was "hog wash" and, if I did, probably too loudly. The old lady was annoyed and the medium appalled. The good looker, on the other hand, seemed mildly amused. She, the good looker that is, suggested we have a session together; one big happy group of strangers talking with the dear departed.

'Mother' baulked at the idea, but 'Daughter Dear' insisted. Resigned, the swami made a sweeping gesture toward the chairs around the table. I wasn't up on my séance etiquette but, as we took our places, Criswell appeared okay with our remaining strangers as he made no effort to introduce anyone.

Mother took the opposite side of the table as far from me as she could get. She wanted, it seemed, to speak with her late son and didn't want me getting in the way. Daughter Dear, who was in actuality daughter-in-law dear, would talk with her late husband if and when Mother surrendered the phone. She took the seat to my right with less enthusiasm than one might expect of a true believer. Lisa pushed her big glasses up on her nose, plunked herself down on my left – between me and Mother – and pushed her glasses up again.

As he lowered the lights, Criswell gave a little speech about those that had crossed over and his special connection to them. It was all I could do not to laugh. I had a few special connections to the dead myself and had half a mind to ask him if he'd like to trade. The guy looked like a magician in a Muscular Dystrophy backyard carnival. The turban was bad enough but, from neck to floor, he also wore a dark blue silk robe decorated with random hieroglyphics sewn in gold thread. They weren't crescent moons and stars but they should have been. If I had to guess, I'd imagine the nearest he'd ever gotten to the orient was the middle east of Chicago, Hyde Park maybe. Still, the show went on. He lit a couple of candles and reminded us, particularly me (though I may have been taking it too personally), of the seriousness of our endeavor. He took his seat between the old biddy and my new heart throb. He stretched his arms, cracked his knuckles, gyrated a bit, did some heavy breathing, then sang a little *a cappella* ditty in a language that was news to me to get himself in the mood.

It was all a bit goofy but, I admit, I wasn't shocked by any of it. Lisa had given me a heads-up. She warned me Criswell would have his own way of conducting his voodoo, that he might have to sing, or chant, or play records, or dance; that he would have to go through some mumbo jumbo in order to contact his *go between* to the other side. To hear the voices of the dead, she said, he needed to enter their plain. It seemed like a lot of work to me. All I had to do was slam my head on something hard.

But my babbling is taking you away from the moment. Criswell apparently found the zone because, suddenly, he was speaking in some other guy's voice. I couldn't place it exactly but it reminded me of nothing so much as a villain from Johnny Quest.

Then all kinds of odd happenings began to take place. The candles somehow snuffed themselves out and the room fell into darkness. Out of nowhere a trumpet blared which, truth be told, I didn't care for a bit. The swami threw his head back, staring wide-eyed at the ceiling, with his spine as straight as an arrow. A light flared, from where I wasn't sure, illuminating a green mist swirling above and behind his head. The Quest villain vanished as, suddenly, Criswell was muttering in what sounded like a Brooklyn accent. I sighed and bit my tongue not to groan.

Then, as reported, in what seemed his own voice, the medium said, "If you're ready... Take the hands of those seated on either side of you.

And remember, no matter what happens, do not break the circle."

Lisa excitedly reached out. I took her hand and got a chill. There was nothing mystic in that, my secretary's hands were always cold. Then I grasped the invitingly warm hand of the lady beside me. Instantly, and without warning, I felt as if I'd been cracked on the back of my head with a hammer.

No, I wasn't assaulted; at least not from without. I was experiencing another of the flashes I'd first encountered on my last case. Apparently, they were with me to stay. I should have told you, that's how the psychic visions came – with a vicious blow. I'd never mentioned it to anyone but, privately, I'd begun to think of it as being 'thunderstruck'. I'd never had the experience, but couldn't help but think that's what it was like to be struck by lightning in a thunderstorm. The nape of my neck was burning. A kaleidoscope of colors exploded behind my eyes. My chair vanished and I was falling through the dark. As I fell, I strained to see anything in the pitch blackness.

I heard it before I saw it. Water! I heard the tumultuous splashing of water that, if it really existed, was as dark as my surroundings. Slowly I made out ripples on a surface far below. But a surface of what? A pool? A lake? A sea? I had no clue. The splashing went on.

Then I heard a great painful gasp. I saw, and could just begin to make out, a familiar shape beneath me. I was still falling through black space, so it must have been beneath me. The bust of a man. No, not a bust, but a live man from the shoulders up. A man sunk nearly to his chin and bobbing in black water. He didn't have a face, not that I could make out. But he must have had a mouth because I could hear him choking, gurgling, spitting mouthfuls of water and foam, trying desperately to catch a breath. He groaned. He cried in pain. But words seemed beyond him. Then he jerked violently and went still.

There followed a pause, pregnant with silence, damp, and cold. My world as I tumbled downward was blackness, the man in the water, and nothing more. Then he jerked awake, or back to life, or back to motion, slapping the surface and kicking in the water. Still he had no face but, finally, he had words as pained and helpless as they were. He screamed, "Help!" Which seemed in order considering his circumstances. Then, weakly, he began to beg, "Help… me! Down… here…"

There was no strength in his voice. The poor guy was drowning. I didn't know who he was, where he was, or how he'd gotten there. But there could be no doubt. The man was drowning. Mind you, all this time I'd been falling through the dark, tumbling toward him. Then I splashed down.

My altered reality was altered again. The first part of the hallucination had been startling. This new change was terrifying. I was suddenly on the edge of consciousness. My head was splitting, in the back as always on these psychic journeys but, now, on the left side of my forehead too. An all new stabbing pain. I was in the black cold water myself. I gagged. I choked. I sputtered and coughed. The drowning man was gone. I had taken his place. And, sisters and brothers, I was drowning.

Then my surroundings changed again. I was still in the dark (though not as dark) but the silence had gone. A horn blared; the blast of a trumpet loud enough to raise the dead. It took a second to recognize it as the same horn we'd all heard at the start of the séance. This was not, however, the fleeting greeting from one of Criswell's dear departed as before. Nor was it a diverting little blast of sound to hide the hiss of a green mist released into the room by a charlatan (a thought that had, I confess, occurred to the cynic in me). The trumpet blare this time was continuous and ear-splitting.

I realized the thunderstrike vision had passed. I was back in the real world. The blaring trumpet was genuine and, as usual, I was to blame. When the psychic attack had come I had fallen out of my chair. Now, as I came back to reality, I found that I'd landed underneath Criswell's table. I had a hold on the solitary center pedestal and was sitting at the medium's feet. Make that the bogus medium.

That wasn't a cynical accusation and it wasn't a guess. I was sitting – painfully – on a panel of foot operated switches wired into the floor. These, obviously, controlled the supposed 'evidences' of contact with those that had passed over. For example, the ghostly blaring trumpet. One of the switches was goosing me sharply and, I realized, it was me blowing the trumpet with my rear end. It was a hustle, the whole séance; one big plastic banana, phony pony show. A second switch, no doubt, snuffed the candles on command. A third, it seemed likely, flooded the ceiling in green light. A fourth, I would bet, sent a cloud of mist swirling above our heads. Disoriented as I was, I moved to kill the horn and rescue my tender derriere. In doing so, I pressed another switch that unleashed what was apparently meant to be a chorus of crying 'dead' children. You can imagine how many friends I was making.

Above the table, the old lady screamed in outraged horror, "Why… I never!"

I agreed. With a face full of her fat ankles it was a first for me too.

The cougar said something, I'm not sure what or to whom. Then Lisa appeared. She dropped to the floor beside me, grabbed me by the arm, and was trying to pull me to my feet. She was a girl of action and it was a nice thought but, in reality, not a good plan. I couldn't stand. I was still under the table.

"Get off!" The medium shouted, kicking me in the back. "Get off me!"

Long story short. The old lady left the place in tears with her pill box hat askew on her blue hair. I felt bad about that. Her daughter-in-law slinked sinuously out after her wearing the same amused look as earlier in the evening, only more so. I felt worse about that. Criswell, his turban unwinding, stood in the entrance – now the site of hasty exits – begging his disheartened customers to come back. It looked to be no use. They appeared to have sworn off his services for good.

The phony medium's plea to Lisa and I was shorter. "Get out," he cried. "Get out. Get out!"

Chapter Three

You're probably wondering if either of those two stories had a point. They did. I'll get to it later. You may be wondering if I'm ever going to put this show on the road. I will right now.

I've mentioned the injuries I suffered on my last case but, until now, haven't said anything about the case itself. Suffice to say it led me through a series of murders of the members of Chicago's famous Temple of Majesty church with a killer leaving cryptic Bible verses like bread crumbs to follow. The whole thing might have been easier to solve if I'd stayed up on my scripture over the years but, like most everything else in my life, it had gotten away from me. That case, though closed, was apparently not completely behind me. It obviously still bugged me because, as I'm telling this, another verse I haven't revisited since childhood springs to mind. If your right hand offends you, cut it off.

Nobody that knows me would be surprised to hear that Lisa is my right hand. She's also my right arm, my brain and, when push comes to shove, most of my backbone. But after nagging me into that hospital stay, where bad things happened, then dragging me to that fraud of a medium, where worse things happened, my secretary was – just then – also a sizable pain in my rear end. I needed a break, time to scream at the cosmos, and told her in no uncertain terms to leave me alone. I tell you this so you'll understand my cloudy mood when, a few short hours later, Lisa called me and interrupted my quiet night. To put it bluntly my secretary was lucky I take that 'right hand' verse figuratively.

In the first minute of her call I had to stop and restart her twice. Lisa has a tendency to talk fast when she's excited and only gains speed as she goes. Whatever she was saying, it sounded like her apartment was on fire. But I was mistaken. When I finally slowed her to a speed I could decode, it turned out she wasn't at her apartment. She was at the city harbor.

When I asked why, she went as closed mouth as Cagney on death row. "I can't tell you on the phone," was all she'd say. That and, "Just get down here!" What could I do? I went.

The harbor is on Chicago's south side, not far from the massive stockyards, but just inland from Lake Michigan itself. It connects to the lake through a short east-west channel.

I no more than pulled up and parked when I spotted Lisa sixty yards away, out on what would prove to be pier 23, doing jumping jacks to get my attention. I haven't described Lisa yet and, it occurs, I ought to for those that don't know her. Lisa Solomon is a tall brunette. It's not over-stating it to say she's brilliant, efficient, and gorgeous. But God has a sense of humor and, for kicks, gave her all the grace of a Bourbon Street wino. Before you can fully take in her long beautiful legs, she's likely to trip over them and fall on her prat. Watching Lisa hop around, as I approached, I was half expecting she'd topple into the drink. But the world is full of surprises and this time she stayed on her feet.

I had almost reached her when she pulled something from her pocket, took a bite out of it, then chewing like a mad cow stowed whatever it was away again. That was not a surprise. I saw Lisa once when she wasn't eating; once. How she stayed skinny remains one of the world's great mysteries. This may have been a cookie, in which case it was probably peanut butter. "You're not going to believe this," she shouted, spitting chewed bits.

"What? What's so unbelievable you couldn't tell me over the phone but you can yell across a pier? While you're at it, why are you on a pier?"

"C'mere." She grabbed my shoulder, leaned in, and whispered, "I came down to rent a boat."

"At this time of night?"

"No! Hours ago."

"Why? What do you need with a boat? What do you even know about boats?"

"I used to date a fishing guy."

"A fishing guy?"

"You know. A guy who fishes."

"A fisherman. You did? I didn't know that."

"It didn't last long. He smelled like fish."

I sighed. Then Lisa sighed, frustrated by my sigh. I could feel her pain. It was probably aggravating to have a boss that wanted information when there was so much to ramble on about.

"Sorry," I said, seeing the situation for what it was. I settled into my gum shoes and grudgingly accepted the fact I was in for the long version. "Go ahead."

Lisa smiled. "It's just that, after what happened to you at that séance, I thought I better come out here and take a look."

I studied her earnest face, owl-like as usual behind her massive glasses, then did a quick study of the pier and harbor beyond. Nothing I saw gave me a clue. Like it or not, I was going to have to ask. "What at the séance led you to the harbor?"

"That thing that happened to you. You know, the head thing."

"The head thing." You, reader, are now up to date on the thunderstrikes, the interactive Extra Sensory movies (visions? hallucinations?) that randomly and painfully played in my head. "Yeah, the head thing. I got it. How does the harbor come into it?"

"The water." She pointed helpfully off the pier.

"I know what water is. What has the water in the harbor got to do with the séance?"

"You almost drowned!" Lisa beamed. "I detected!"

I think I mentioned too that Lisa wanted to be a detective? Yeah. Like Noah scooped pet food, Lisa wanted to be a detective. She was going on, "I added two and two. At the séance, during your head thing, you almost drowned. Where else in Chicago, but the harbor, are you going to almost drowned?"

"The Chicago River," I said. "Or in any of a hundred thousand swimming pools. In a bathtub. A whirlpool in the Bear's locker room." Lisa frowned but I went on. "In Bill Veeck's tears after Disco Demolition Night at Comiskey Park. The fountain at Lincoln Park. A horse trough at the petting zoo. In your cups. In your toilet. A rain barrel."

"All right."

"A puddle. A teaspoon."

"All right," she hissed, angrily digging in her pocket. "I was playing a hunch." She produced her comfort food again and took a vicious bite. I'd been way off. It was a Zagnut bar. "You play hunches all the time," she whined, launching tiny peanut brittle and toasted coconut javelins my direction.

"It's part of my job to play sensible hunches. I'm a licensed private investigator. You are not."

"Well, I'm going to be. Some day."

"Until that fateful day could you just be my secretary?"

"What does that mean?"

"For starters, it means, stop forcing me to chase wild geese. Please! I have no clue what happened at that séance. Neither do you. I don't know what it had to do with water, except I saw a guy drowning. Then I was dropped into it and felt I was drowning. What I did not see, and what I fail to see now, is any connection to the city harbor."

"Well, I did."

"What? What connection? Why are you here? Why am I here?"

Lisa threw out her small but absolutely fine chest, lifted her proud chin, and poked her glasses up off the tip of her nose. "Because of what I have to show you in the boat."

God, the night was never going to end. "What boat?"

"The boat I rented." She turned giving me a view of the water, and of a twelve-foot aluminum craft with a small Johnson outboard to which I hadn't paid any attention, tied to the pier below our feet. She stretched her arm, twisted her supple wrist, and fanned her fingers like Carole Merrill offering a 'Let's Make a Deal' contestant a year's supply of grape Ne-Hi. Then she said (I kid you not), "Ta dah!"

The coat she should have been wearing was spread out across the bottom of the boat, from mid-ship to the bow, covering several inches of dirty shipped lake water and... something else. A pair of soggy boots protruded. It didn't take a genius to see they had people in them. My mouth fell open but nothing came out. What could I say? I stepped from the pier, down into the boat (soaking my own shoes and socks), and lifted Lisa's coat. What I saw ruined my whole day.

There wasn't much to him. He might have stood five-foot-four, back when he used to stand. He weighed maybe a hundred and twenty; a few pounds more with the weight of the water. He was soaked from crown to soles. His work boots were worn brown leather, with the frayed tops of once-white wool socks peeking out. He wore green bib coveralls over a gray button-down shirt, both worn. He wore a suit jacket, brown or tan, it was hard to tell as wet as it was, which seemed a bit odd over the work clothes. Soup and fish maybe? Had he been to an event or meeting it might have been healthier to skip? The coat's gray inside lining featured a tear from the left chest down to beneath the pocket. I guessed him at sixty but it was a guess. What I knew for certain was, he wasn't going to get any older. A sigh seemed in order and I produced one. Then, over my shoulder, I plaintively asked Lisa, "I don't suppose he came with the boat rental?"

"No. He was in the water. I pulled alongside and dragged him aboard."

"Looks like you brought most of Lake Michigan with him."

"I didn't have to go that far. He was actually," she pointed, "right there in the mouth of the thingy."

"The channel?"

She snapped her fingers and nodded. She tried to add something but I cut her off with a sharp, "Wait, don't say anything else. Cripes!"

Down the dock, passing through a pool of amber light cast by one of only three poles spanning the distance, headed our way, was a string bean of a male figure with a decided limp. The combination told me it was George Clay, the son of the old boat renter, and part-time boat renter himself. No doubt the one who'd provided Lisa's conveyance. I'd had dealings in one way or another with both Clay and his father. They were, after all, two ready sets of eyes when eyes were needed at the harbor. They rarely missed a thing and, therefore, came in handy to me on occasion. I wasn't surprised to see George headed our way.

"Time for you to go," I told Lisa.

"Go where?"

"Home. Anywhere. Just get out of here."

"But Blake…"

"But nothing. There's a dead body; it has to be reported. We can't answer the questions that will follow. There's no way they will believe you went looking for a drowned man on the spur of the moment and just happened to find one. And there is no way we are telling the Chicago police you were led here by my psychotic flashes. To put it bluntly, 'This is another fine mess, Ollie.' Wenders would love a chance to bury either one of us so deep in Joliet they'd have to bring us air in paper bags. I don't want you any more mixed up in it than you are. Now I've got to make up a lie about why I rented a boat. And how I found our friend here. And what I've done with him since. I can't do that with you buzzing in my ear."

"Blake, I can help you."

"Don't force me to say, You already have." I stopped there, keeping it to myself that, once again, my secretary had helped me – right into the soup. Why say it? What would have been the point? I might as well start swimming. But there was no time to waste.

"George Clay is headed this way. Don't bother to look, just go, before he gets here. If I get thrown in the jug, I'll need you free to call lawyers, and Large, and God knows who else. Besides, if you don't get home safe, your mother will put out a hit on me."

"What about your mother?"

"She'll take the contract. Go!"

Lisa didn't want to but, bless her heart, she went. George Clay arrived in time to see her fade into the shadows of the parking lot. "Hey, Blake. Was that your secretary? She rented a–" Then it dawned on him where I was standing. "Oh, yeah, there it is." Then it dawned on him what lay at my feet. "Hey, Blake, is that a–"

"Yeah, George, it is."

"Wow. Lisa caught her limit, huh?"

"No. She didn't. You haven't seen Lisa tonight. Got that, George? I rented the boat."

"You rented the boat?"

"Right. I rented the boat. Do me a favor and make your paperwork say so."

"There isn't any. I mean there is, but I... sorta..."

"See, George, we're on the same page. All you have to do is remember I rented the boat. Do that and I won't remember to tell your old man you're skimming customers by not logging the rentals."

"You're a hard man, Blake."

"John Wayne said it. It's a hard life."

"Okay," George agreed with no indication he appreciated the free philosophy. "Who is he? Your dead guy?"

"I don't know. Why don't you hop down here and help me find out?"

George grimaced and threw up his hands. "Uh, uh. No, thanks. He's your corpse. You roll him."

Big surprise, I was on my own.

But George still wanted to be helpful. "You want me to go call the cops?"

"Hang on a second. Let me see what I can see first." I reached down, grabbed the drowned man by his soggy jacket, and instantly regretted touching him. I felt an explosion of heat and pain in my head. Yes, I'd been thunderstruck again. My brain was on fire. Colors flashed in my eyes. The old guy, the boat, George, and the harbor vanished.

Blackness. Nothingness.

Slowly my vision returned; images spinning in my mind like a badly edited montage in a 60's LSD documentary. I saw shadowy crowds of faceless people, walls of stretched canvas, tight ropes on angle, electric cables like snakes on the ground, and brightly colored neon lights above. A roof of red and yellow stripes hid the sky and masked the time of day, or night, in this new unreal reality of mine. I heard a din of human voices, calliope music, shouting and laughter. I heard the shake of ice, bells going off, garbled tones over a loud speaker. I smelled hot grease and, I swear, freshly popped popcorn. I was in the middle of some sort of carnival. Then, as suddenly as they'd blinked to life, the lights were gone.

I was swallowed by the blue of night. And there, in front of me, I saw a fish smoking a cigar. Laugh, kids, laugh. I don't make this stuff up. The visions hurt too much to joke about them. I merely report them. And I'm reporting I saw a gray cartoon fish. Maybe a dolphin? A tuna? What did I know about fish? I saw it through some kind of porthole in a circle of blue. It was smoking a black stogie, blowing smoke rings, and had a big No. 2 pencil tucked under its left fin. You're laughing. I wasn't. My head was splitting. And somebody was screaming.

The screaming wasn't helping my head a bit. This wasn't a scream of delight. It was pain. It was terror. Then, boom, the angle from which I was seeing everything changed. Suddenly Lisa's drowned man was there in front of me, looking the same but different; the drowned man *before* he'd gone for his swim in the harbor. He was the one screaming. He was upright, dry but with a forehead bathed in sweat, his face contorted by fear. Then he fell away into the darkness. I heard a brutal thump and a cry of pain. I heard a splash into water.

As quickly as these visions had come they were gone. I was back in George Clay's boat, leaning over the body of the drowned man, grabbing for the gunwale for balance, trying not to fall into the harbor. George was on the pier above staring down at me like I was nuts. For all I knew he was right.

"You okay, Blake?"

"Yeah," I replied distantly, my mind on other things. George was a distraction. "Never better."

My hallucination had prevented me giving the corpse a going over. There was nothing in the world I wanted to do less than touch him again, but what choice did I have? I hadn't discovered a thing about him. I still needed to know who he was and why he was dead. I took a deep breath and grabbed his jacket again. Nothing happened, nothing otherworldly I mean, and I exhaled in relief. Then I went through his pockets. Sadly, I got bupkis for the trouble. His suit coat came off the cheap rack. The tear in the lining was more than a tear; a piece was missing. He had no identification. Other than a wet wadded dollar bill in the right front pocket of the coveralls, he wasn't carrying a thing. I left the buck where it was in case he needed tip money to get across the river. Yeah, I'm all heart.

George was talking, had been for some time, and finally I gave him my attention. "Did you hear me, Blake? We got to call the cops, don't we?"

"Not we, George," I said, stepping up and out of the boat. "You. Phone away."

"You're not leaving me with this? You're not running out on me?"

"I am leaving. But I'm not running. I've got to find out who this guy is. I've got to find out why he's dead. And I've got to do that before the homicide dicks wrap him around my neck."

"But if you just tell them that Lisa—"

"Lisa wasn't here. Got that, George? Lisa wasn't here and she didn't rent your boat. I rented the boat! Is that too much to ask? To keep my secretary out of this mess?"

"But I can't tell the cops all them lies."

"It's only one lie, George. One! Just tell them I rented the boat!"

"Right. You rented the boat. And… you brought it back… with the body in it?"

"Yes, George. I brought it back, as is, and I left. You don't know nothing from nothing. You can even call me a name in front of the cops, if you like. That will put you in good with them."

I couldn't blame George for being excited. I was a little excited myself. But Lisa had gotten herself in good and, now that I'd taken her place, I had to get me out. That meant tracking down the drowned man and the person or persons unknown who'd pushed him into the pool. All I had to go on was my 'carnival' hallucination. And a fish smoking a cigar. Either one, I was sure, had a ninety-nine percent chance of leading absolutely nowhere. It was daffy. But it was somewhere to start.

"You rented the boat." George repeated aloud on his way to notify the police. "Whatever you say, Blake. You can count on me."

Despite his fading promise, I once again had the feeling I had nobody and nothing to count on but the two idiots I usually hung with; me and myself. I left the pier with a plan consisting of little more than 'Be gone before the cops arrive'. The homicide boys, particularly Wenders, I knew, would flay me alive when they caught up with me. But that would be then.

I jumped into my Jaguar, drove out of the marina, and right into Lisa's homemade soup.

Chapter Four

Other than a lame guess our drowned man appreciated a midnight swim, the only clue the body in Lisa's boat offered had been the visions delivered to my brain on contact. In an instant the din of the midway, calliope music, and the glitter of neon lights (if I was seeing what I saw) exploded in my skull. For some ungodly reason, I'd been transported into the nostalgic world of the carnival. An instant more and that vision had been replaced by the ridiculous sight of a cartoon fish smoking a cigar, by a scream from our drowned man, and by a burst of pain for me and a plunge into cold black water for him. What stew could I make from those ingredients?

Working backwards from where the corpse was found adrift gave me Lake Michigan as a starting place. That was no starting place at all. Marine debris could cover a lot of territory and the body, flotsam or jetsam, could have originated anywhere in Chicago, northern Illinois, western Michigan, eastern Wisconsin, the Great Lakes or, for that matter, the Saint Lawrence Seaway. The pain I'd experienced offered no better clue; it was merely pain. His or mine? I wasn't sure. The fish meant nothing to me. Few cartoons meant anything to me. As a kid, the only 'funny' I ever read was Dick Tracy. I knew Flattop, Mumbles, Gruesome, and the rest, but I didn't remember any cigar chomping fish. I didn't do Saturday mornings inside. Rather than fight my mother for couch space, my weekend days were spent in the streets raising the anxieties of innocent neighbors. The fish was a mystery. The only part of the vision that made any sense at all were the lights and sounds of the midway. But I hadn't been to a carnival in ages.

To the best of my knowledge, which I admit was limited, that year's fair season had come and gone in Chicagoland; in the city and surrounding counties. Midway attractions may have been teeming in the suburbs with corn dog sales out the wahzoo but, if they were, I didn't know about it. Just then, I was aware of only one such attraction in the city; some kind of to-do currently working to lure crowds to Navy Pier. As it was the only carnival I knew of, and it was on the lake, and might have provided a convenient venue from which to chuck a body into the drink, it appealed to me as a starting place. I headed for the near north side and the lake.

Traffic was what it always was on a Saturday night in Chicago. I dealt with it by dialing in a metal station and letting Molly Hatchet warn me I was *Flirtin' With Disaster.* No news flash there. I soon pulled off of Lake Shore Drive, followed the Streeter Drive curve, and turned right for Navy Pier.

Built between 1914 and 1916 at a cost of four and a half million pre-Depression Era bucks, Municipal Pier #2 jutted 3,300-feet out into Lake Michigan. Back then it was the largest pier in the world, handling lake freighter cargo, passenger steamers, and serving as a cool place for public gatherings in a time before air conditioning.

The original plan called for four more like it, but Municipal Piers #1, 3, 4 and 5 were never built. Before construction on #2 had finished, the arrival of mass-produced trucks destroyed the lake freight industry. It might have been a total disaster had it not been for World War One. Wars were always good for business. The Red Cross moved onto the pier, and Home Defense, the Navy, and Army. A pier jail was even opened for draft dodgers.

Following the Great War came the pier's 'Golden Age' when the rich laid claim. There were picnic areas, dining pavilions, a dance hall, a playground, and an auditorium (with WCFL Radio broadcasting from its north tower). It had a streetcar line, exhibition halls, a theater, and its own emergency room. Three and a half million visited every year of the 1920's. Unlike today's post-Vietnam antipathy for the military, these were the days when servicemen were revered. In 1927, in honor of our veterans, Municipal Pier #2 was renamed Navy Pier.

The Great Depression worsened freight and passenger ship activity and New Deal agencies moved into the empty office spaces. Recreational use of the Pier continued, including the 1933 World's Fair (the 'Century of Progress Exposition') but, as Wouk said, the winds of war were blowing again. In the summer of 1941, Navy Pier was closed to the public and converted to a Navy training center with school rooms, drill halls, and barracks to accommodate 10,000 servicemen. Classes began six days before the attack on Pearl Harbor. During World War Two, two converted flattops arrived as freshwater training carriers. Fifteen thousand pilots received their carrier-landing training on Lake Michigan. Over 60,000 servicemen were trained on the Pier before the war ended.

In mid-1946, Navy Pier was returned to the city. The aircraft carriers were sailed out and a submarine sailed in for the training of Great Lakes Naval Reservists. The University of Illinois operated the Pier for the next twenty years, opening it back up to the public for folkloric dances from around the world, international cuisine, and arts and crafts exhibitions. But in 1965 the University moved to their new Chicago Circle campus and the Pier again fell into disuse.

The city tried again to do something with the aging hulk, renovating the east end buildings (furthest into the lake) as exhibition halls for the nation's bicentennial. But they failed to cache any coin for maintenance. Fort Sheridan's 81st Army Band played an occasional concert on the under-utilized tourist attraction. Music and arts festivals popped in and out. A carnival occasionally strayed out over the water. But would the crowds ever re-turn to Navy Pier?

It sounded like a crowd, and sounded and smelled like a carnival, as I drove between the tow-ers, under the massive arch (housing office space), and onto the Pier. Matching towers, on the dis-tant end of that vast municipal construct, housed the old classrooms and dorms. Between stood over 3,000 feet of connected warehouses, running up and down each side of the Pier that, like the walls of a massive fort, created a great open inner rect-angle. Halfway down inside that 'box' a temporary metal fence had been erected and, within that pen, stood – not a carnival – but a neon-lit midway fronting a bright and colorful circus, culminating in a great red and yellow striped Big Top tent!

I found a parking space, locked my Jag, and took it all in.

Even at a distance I could see one of those towering mobile Ferris Wheels, lit against the night sky, inside the entrance. Chicago, you may know, was home to the Ferris Wheel. The monstrous 'Chicago Wheel', designed by George Ferris Jr. and standing 264 feet high, was the largest attraction at the 1893 Columbian Exposition (the World's Fair). I know. I looked it up. The original wheel had thirty-six cars, each able to hold sixty people; 38,000 passengers a day at fifty (19th century) cents a pop. Back then that was not hay. But that massive piece of history was built on *terra firma*. This wheel, though much smaller, was on the Pier. What kind of maniac, with how large a death wish, would put a Ferris Wheel on a pier?

Between the car park and the entrance, depending from or tacked to anything and everything big enough to hold them (the warehouses, fixtures, the cyclone fence), hung flags, banners, and posters splashed with the 'Amazing!' images of the 'Mind Boggling!' entertainments waiting ahead; acrobats, clowns, jugglers, lions, and tigers, and bears. No, it was no carnival. This was the *All New*

Callicoat and Major Combined Circus. So much for my precognitive skills.

As I approached the ticket booth, I saw a sizable share of stands selling food and drink, and rides of every creed filling the allotted space. You name it, corn dogs, cotton candy, fried cheese curds, elephant ears, funnel cakes, ice cream, lemonade, and ice cones and slush drinks in every conceivable flavor. Dotted among them were the live ponies and camels harnessed to travel in ceaseless circles, the mini roller coaster, the mini motorcycles, cars, planes, boats, and trains, for the young, and the Tilt-a-Whirl, the Scrambler, and Spaceship for the tweens, the teens, and up, all unpacked from semis and quickly erected, connected each to another and to junction box hubs by miles of thick black cable crisscrossing the inner Pier. For someone who hadn't walked a midway in a very long time, the festivities were breathtaking, surrounded as I was by barkers, games, balloons, and all manner of stick-skewered foods. But rolling the drowned man, with the thunderstrike and vision that accompanied, had taken away my appetite. And rides had never appealed. My life was a circus ride on its own. And if and when I felt like puking all I needed to do was read a newspaper. I was on the hunt and, with the cops maybe three days or maybe three minutes behind me, I needed to get on with it.

"I'm not 'posed to sell any tickets after eleven-thirty." That's what the acne covered string bean manning the ticket booth told me. "The circus closes at midnight."

"It's eleven twenty-eight," I replied.

"But the final performance is 'bout over. The circus closes at midnight."

"It's eleven twenty-eight."

"You ain't gonna get your money's worth."

"It's my money."

The kid shook his pimples in disbelief. But, unable to talk me out of my stubborn foolishness, sold me the ticket. I nodded my appreciation and headed through the gate into the food and family fun. I serpentined through the midway beneath the glow of thousands of flashing lights that may or may not have been the lights I saw in my vision. How, I wondered, was I to know? If they were, what then? Beyond the midway, moving east toward the lake, I passed through a gauntlet of smaller tents in a wide assortment of colored stripes that, combined, made up the circus Sideshow. Each tent featured a loud and colorful poster highlighting the specific attraction awaiting inside; the Doll Woman, the Tallest Man in America, The Lady Sword Swallower (bless her heart), Omar the Fire Eater, the Strong Man, Sybil the Bearded Lady, Benga the Pygmy, and Oola the Lizard Man. The kid in me was tempted. With the insane childhood my mother had provided, that part of my psyche would have relished an escape to a world of outcasts. But the cynical detective that kid had become dealt with all the freaks he cared for daily and then some. I had no need to pay for extras. A second look took the decision away. The tents were closed and dark, the Sideshow done for the night in favor of the final gala circus performance. The roar of the crowd could be heard from the Big Top beyond.

I passed expectantly into the hippodrome only to discover this circus looked pretty much like every other circus I'd seen in my life. There were three rings, the nearest to the entrance featuring a dark and empty lion tamer's cage, the farthest away featuring dark and idle vaults and teeter-totters of an already ended acrobat act. An audience of several hundred occupied the slanted rows of bleachers to my right, their keen attentions locked on a colorful couple in the brilliantly lit center ring demonstrating the dangers of the Impalement Arts (a knife thrower, to those of us from the projects). But, as I moved into the shadows to my left, circumnavigating the rings on the side of the tent opposite the crowd, I saw the artist was not throwing knives at the moment. He brandished a bullwhip, whirling it above his head like a helicopter rotor, then brought it down with an alarming *crack,* flicking a cigarette from between the lips of his beautiful and courageous assistant. The crowd appreciated the effort and let it be known.

I continued around the rings, trespassing behind the scenes (meaning behind two fat and three skinny clowns, and a seated band of drums and horns), while the artist at center ring discarded the whip in favor of an ax. With fanfare and a flourish he showed the weapon to the crowd then slammed it into a chopping block beside him, leaving no doubts as to its lethal reality. He withdrew it, turned to his target girl roughly fifteen feet away, took aim and threw – depriving her of yet another smoke. At forty-five cents a pack, the budget for the act's cigarettes alone must have been astronomical. The audience, apparently all stock holders in R. J. Reynolds, again, applauded wildly.

A white board was carried out and placed by two huskies in colorful costumes for what looked to be the act's finale. The girl stood before it. The artist, with seven knives clutched in his off hand, stood at a distance. With a snare drum lead-in and appropriately delivered rim shots, one by one the artist threw the knives neatly sticking each blade into the board in a tight outline around the girl.

I'd always wondered about acts of that nature, knife throwers, archers, trick shooters and the like; wondered if they didn't all employ a variation of the same magician's trick? Was he throwing knives at a vulnerable beauty? Or was he somehow palming them while mechanically actuated blades popped up in their stead from the back of the board? The thrills were a given. But did the act feature real danger? Staring on, occupied with that question, I backed without looking into the staging space for the parade finale – and into a perfectly innocent horse. The startled creature leaped back into the three behind it. I tumbled. The horses whinnied in fear and annoyance while their handlers scrambled to rein them in. I found my feet again in a cloud of sawdust. In the instant it took to produce that chaos, in the center ring the distracted artist threw his seventh blade. The knife sailed. His assistant yelped in pain and jumped back from the board. I got the answer to my question. The act was one hundred percent real.

The audience gasped as one. The girl, being only human, lifted her arm to examine the damage from the errant knife. She was bleeding like a pig. But she maintained her composure and, knowing and believing that 'The Show Must Go On', stuck out her chin and grinned. Shouts arose as a midget clown ran out waving a white towel. He looked to be surrendering. Then, with a flourish, he presented the towel to the target girl. She accepted it with mimed thanks and put it to her arm to tamp the blood. The clown cartwheeled away drawing the attention of the kids and all but the most morbid of the adults with him. Just like that the audience was laughing again.

The knife thrower was not laughing. Ignoring the clown and the crowd, he glared past his assistant to me with a red face and an unmistakable message in his eyes; the girl's injury was my fault. Though I didn't entirely buy it, I couldn't say he was wrong either. It had been an accident. In light of the knife thrower's rage (though I'd always used it sparingly and never considered it any part of valor), I tried discretion just this once. I retreated from the parade horses and their scowling handlers, and the lighted performance ring, and headed into the dark again on the far east side of the Big Top. The knife thrower and his assistant took their bows and accepted the applause of a forgiving audience. The girl smiled and ran off holding the bloody towel to her arm. The artist stormed off with blood in his eyes.

The moving finger having writ, the show moved on as the huskies rolled two huge golden braziers into the ring and, sharing a torch, set them alight. A third man pushed a platform out between them stopping it on the downstage side of the ring nearer the audience. Atop this middle construct stood a pedestal, as glittering gold as the braziers, with three thin poles rising six feet into the air, each pole topped by a hand-sized block.

The red-coated ringmaster rumbled into his microphone (in a European accent? German maybe?). Bursting with pride, he directed the audience's attention to the air above the center ring. The floor fell into darkness. The band began to play. A light bloomed at the top of the tent, over thirty feet in the air, on a little blonde pixie suspended in space. I fully expected a muscled partner in a leotard swinging nearby, ready to toss and catch the dainty acrobat (she looked entirely tossable), but saw none. She was alone; a solo act hanging on high. Her hands were stretched above her head, her fingers intertwined in a bright red scarf holding her aloft, running down and around her lithe body. Like the crowd, I stared waiting with baited breath. The music stopped. The acrobat dropped her left hand – and fell.

A collective gasp filled the tent as she tumbled head over heels, head over heels, toward the ground. The scarf, unwinding as she dropped, may have been supporting her but didn't look it and, alarmingly long though it was, had to end somewhere. Unbelievably, as if a hidden brake had been applied, she came to a graceful stop. She hung upside down, smiling at the audience, twenty feet below her starting point, the last few feet of the scarf wrapped in a figure eight about her boyish hips, with the tail end clutched in her right hand.

The audience breathed. The audience applauded.

She righted herself and, kicking her legs like a swimmer treading water, unwound the scarf from her hips without touching it. She slid slowly and sensuously down the tail of the scarf to the pedestal. That was enough for me. My night had left me breathless enough as it was.

Had the city fathers added to my excitement by bringing in the traveling circus? Or had they caused it? Was it the right circus? Or had I seen something entirely different; the carnival I initially imagined? Did the lights of this midway match the lights that had flashed in my dented brain? Had the drowned man Lisa pulled from the lake come from this circus? Or any circus or carnival for that matter? I didn't know. As usual, I didn't know a thing.

I didn't know how long Clay, the boat renter, would hold up under police questioning. My guess was not long. I didn't know how long my shenanigans could keep Lisa out of the soup. I hoped forever. All I knew was I had to learn all I could about our soggy corpse before the sun came up. With nowhere to start but the sights and sounds brought on by touching the drowned man… I had work to do. I found the door flap at the far lakeside end of the tent and left the pixie to her adoring crowd.

Leaving the Big Top, I entered a dark village of supply-filled tents, trailers, and trucks, a Caterpillar tractor, and a maze of stacked materials necessary, I guessed, to get a circus off the ground. All tucked away from the public eye. As was my nature, and mission, I wandered in and out of the shadows snooping behind the scenes and seeing what I could see.

The cyclone fence existed there on the back side of the circus, too, but not so much to keep people out as to funnel them from the Big Top to the east towers and residential block from the Navy days. This was, no doubt, the circus employees' entrance and all were being housed in the old dormitories. Beyond the dorms, a round shadow in the dark, was the roof of the renovated hall on the east tip of the Pier. A lifelong native of Chicago, I'd had no notion of how vast the structure was; a lifelong idiot, I had no idea where in blazes to start. What was I looking for? I hadn't any clue. (Lisa. Lisa. Lisa!) I circled round a flock of strutting seagulls feasting on swiped midway trash; seagulls, and seagull poop, everywhere. I leaned on a pallet of camel food, or monkey chow, or elephant treats, whatever it was… How did I know? I lit a cigarette, listening to Lake Michigan beyond the expanse of warehouses and wallowed in a moment of self-pity. What fool's errand was I on?

Muted musical stings, cries of delight, and applause escaped the back of the Big Top. It appeared the pimpled ticket boy had been correct, the show was drawing to a close. The band struck up a march as the ringmaster, his voice echoing, announced the end of the performers' parade; the traditional end of the circus, muffled by the tent walls, accompanied by the sound of the lake buffeting the Pier.

This could have been the circus in my weird vision; it probably was. So what? If our drowned man had taken a header into the drink there were unending places from which to have done so. Despite the massive 'castles' on each end, or the millions of square feet of warehouse all around, or the short guard rails or loops of drooping chain here or there, not an inch would have been impossible to circumvent and whole sections offered clear sailing to the edge. Anyone could have been chucked over anywhere and it wouldn't have taken a villain; a slight person with a slight push could have made it happen. Even if I knew where, I didn't know who (if there was a who) had helped. I didn't know when. I didn't know why. Murder? Accident? For all that, maybe the guy was a suicide who changed his mind after a couple of laps and started screaming for help?

I stamped out my smoke feeling like screaming myself; a fool's errand indeed. I started the switch from self-pity to self-loathing, wondering why I let me get trapped like this when… my dark thoughts were interrupted.

"What the fuck you lookin' for?"

Make that rudely interrupted. I turned but, to my confusion, saw nobody and nothing. Well, I saw the stacked supplies, trucks, and lots of dark and plenty of shadows, but I didn't see the speaker. Someone might have been hiding anywhere. But why? I didn't know. I wondered if I'd heard what I thought I'd heard? Knowing I had, I asked the night, "Are you talking to me?"

"I asked you a question, numb nuts," came the gravelly voice. "What the fuck you lookin' for?"

Okay, I wasn't crazy. Still I didn't know from where the voice was coming. "I'd be more than happy to whip up an answer," I said. "Where should I send it?"

"What are you? A smart ass?" A red-orange glow appeared in the dark, a floating dot the size of a dime, ten feet away, three feet off the deck of the Pier. It did a crazy eight in the air, brightened, then dulled as it entered a spill of light in front of a stack of hay bales. In that instant, the dot ceased to be a UFO and revealed itself to be the hot end of a cigar.

On the other end stood the midget clown.

Chapter Five

I goggled, watching the little clown stare at me, watching him smoke his cigar, recalling my vision and remembering the pencil-toting cartoon fish smoking the black stogie. I wondered what, if anything, the two had to do with one another? But what could they have to do with one another? This guy was neither a fish nor a cartoon but as equally unlikely. He looked like a kid in a clown costume with the voice (and diction) of a longshoreman. Between the darkness, the shadows, and the white grease paint on his face, his age was impossible to guess. He had blue tears painted on his cheeks, a red rubber nose, and a phony smile drawn over top of a real mouth twisted with a sneer. "I asked you a question," he growled. "Are you a fuckin' smart ass?"

Make that a real dirty mouth twisted with a sneer. *Sheesh.*

"I'm a detective." There was no point flashing my card in that light.

"After your bone-headed maneuver inside," the clown said. "You're goddamn lucky you're not a pin cushion. City?"

"What?"

"You said you're a detective." He sucked. The end of his cigar glowed bright. "City?"

"Private," I said. "The name's Blake."

"Never heard of you."

"Well, give with your name. Maybe I can return the compliment."

"I was right, you are a smart ass." He chucked a white-gloved thumb at his costume. "In this get-up, in the Big Top, I'm Binky the Clown. Ain't that a hell of a thing? In my loin cloth, in the Sideshow, I'm Benga the Pygmy. We used to have a Congolese guy. He croaked. I'm his short-term replacement, no fuckin' pun intended. Don't call me Binky or Benga anywhere else or you'll piss me off. I fuckin' hate being called a dwarf. The Major's always callin' me a dwarf. Some night I'll cut his fuckin' head off. I don't mind little person and I got no problem with midget. Use one of those."

"Quite a speech," I told him. "You don't happen to have an actual name, do you?"

"*Aaahh.*" The midget smacked himself in the forehead. Little orange ashes jumped from his cigar. "Sorry," he said. "Sometimes I rant." He took a hit off his cigar. "When I'm eating, taking a dump, getting a piece of ass, or walking down the street, I'm just plain Alfonso. Alfonso Valencia, that's my fuckin' name. Now, for the third time, what the fuck are you lookin' for?"

"I'm looking for someone who might know a guy."

"You talk like a sausage," the midget declared. He started toward me, bow legs, tiny steps, with a slight wobble from side to side. "Who's the fuckin' guy?"

"I don't know his name. We were never formally introduced."

The midget shook his head and muttered, "Fuck!" under his breath.

Look, sisters and brothers, this story is just started, and you've only been introduced to Alfonso. I don't know how you feel about blue language but, by that point, I was already sick to death of it. I'm warning you, the midget swore every third word, every second I was in his company, for the whole time I knew him. And the F-bomb was an obvious personal favorite. I'm no prude but, as a form of communication, I've found a sparing use of expletives more effective than a downpour. Alfonso was a torrential rain. From here on out, I'll omit the lion's share of his swearing and, as much as I'm able, report *the meat* of the little man's comments. Just know he cussed, every word you might imagine, on average every third word. If you enjoy a steady diet of that – feel free to put it back in yourself.

But I was talking to Alfonso. "Who's in charge around here?"

"You don't want to meet him," the little clown said. "Especially after your contribution to tonight's show. If I know Tommy–"

"Tommy? That the boss?"

"No! Tommy Dagger. The knife thrower. He's probably plottin' your demise. The circus manager, the boss, will be giving him a hand."

I nodded, which was silly as it wasn't at all likely he saw it. "Still, who's in charge?"

"The manager is a guy named Karl Kreis. But nobody calls him that. He likes to be called The Major. I'm the unofficial second in command. In this circus, I got seniority. I make hiring suggestions, for performers and midway staff, the carnies, the ticket sellers. I hire the general maintenance staff myself. I know most everyone here... at least as well as a carny can be known."

"Then you're the guy I'm looking for."

"For what?"

"To help me identify someone. A drowned man washed up near the harbor, south of here, earlier tonight. I have reason to believe he might have gone in the water here at the circus."

"Why? What reason? He could have gone in anywhere. Couldn't he? Why not Michigan? Why not Canada? Something brought you here. What?"

The little guy had a working brain. I made note of it. Then I said, "I'll reserve that for the moment." What else could I say? I couldn't tell him I'd been guided there by a psychic flash. Why ruin a beautiful budding friendship? "But I'd like to test whether or not my reasoning is sound. Did you see or hear anything unusual or out of the way tonight?"

"I see and hear unusual crap every night." He puffed. "People are weird. There are too many to count and they all belong in a circus. If you ask me, Blake, you're fartin' in the breeze. You ain't goin' to find nothin' here to help you."

"Probably not. But you're not opposed to my trying?"

The little clown shrugged. "Knock yourself out."

"All right," I said. "How about I describe my drowned man? You tell me if he rings a bell."

He puffed his cigar, waiting.

"He was small," I began. "Maybe five-four."

"Not a good start," Alfonso said, glowering up at me. "Try it from my perspective, ass hat. He's five-foot-four; a big guy."

I grunted. "Yeah. Huge." God, that's all I needed, a sensitive midget. "Should we pause while I dab your eyes with a hanky?"

"F— you, Blake. Just give me a little respect." His cigar glowed. "Finish your description."

"Gray hair with no clue what it used to be, thin on top. A hundred and twenty pounds–"

"Soaking wet?" Alfonso asked. I stared. He stared back, then growled, "It's a joke. A hundred and twenty pounds... soaking wet."

"That's him to a tee."

"Moving on. What about age? Had he got fifty to look forward to yet?"

I shook my head. "He's got nothing to look forward to; he's dead. But fifty, not a chance. He already waved goodbye to sixty."

Alfonso considered. "What makes you think he belongs here?"

"Like I said, for now you're going to have to call it a hunch." I gave him another minute to think. "Well? Are you missing anyone at the circus?"

The little guy sighed a ton. "That description could fit a million ticket buyers."

"Did you have a million ticket buyers today?"

The little clown sneered. "We had five or six hundred for sure."

"See. That's a lot less than a million, so we're already closing in. How about employees?"

"Your description could fit a dozen guys that work here."

"It could," I agreed. "But does it?" I watched him study the inside of his head. It was worse than I thought. He wasn't merely a sensitive midget with a filthy mouth, he was thoughtful too. "What do you think, Alfonso? You got one like it?"

"Like I said, there's a few older guys around here. There's Ed and Butch. They feed the animals. But it ain't likely them. They're always together, if you know what I mean?" I didn't have any idea what he meant. Alfonso made no attempt to hide his disgust at my ignorance. "They're a pair." I squinted but still couldn't see it. I shrugged my bewilderment. "They got sugar in their gas tanks, Blake. They're light in the loafers, for Chris-sake!"

"Is that what you've been getting at?" I sighed. "What do I care?"

"You're missin' my point, Bulldog Drummond. The point bein', they're always together. So if you only got one body, it prob'ly ain't them. 'Cause they're never apart."

"Brilliant. Unless one killed the other, huh?"

"F—! I never thought of that."

I nodded without enthusiasm. "Anybody else?"

"Yeah. There's Pete, the popcorn ball guy." He was pointing in the air, imagining the midway in his head. "Earl, across the way, elephant ears and cotton candy, he ain't no spring chicken. There's Selma, open shift ride tickets. But you said a guy. Still there's Selma's worthless husband. I don't remember his name right off. Maybe she punched his ticket?" Alfonso laughed. "That'd be great! What does Selma call him?"

He thought about it, remembered, and told me. I'll skip it for you. It was just another example of Alfonso's (and, no doubt, Selma's) colorful vocabulary. The midget went on.

"There's the dart game guy, Tim somethin', he's new. There's Mickey the Geek. There's Vlad in the shootin' gallery. Hell, old guys all over the place, now I'm thinkin' about it, like ticks on a deer's ass. What was he wearing?"

"A worn brown, or tan, suit jacket. It was hard to tell the color for sure; it was wet. Gray button-down shirt beneath green bib coveralls, pretty well worn, work boots, also well worn. The jacket had a tear in the lining. Right there." I mimed it for him. "Inside front left."

"Damn." He hit his cigar and blew the smoke over his right shoulder. "The gray shirt and green bibs make it sound like Mickey."

"Mickey?"

Alfonso nodded. "Mickey the Geek."

"Is that a stage name?"

"No, Sherlock. His middle name is 'The'. 'Course it's a stage name."

"All right, don't lose your shirt."

"Well, you ain't listenin'!"

"I'm listening. You're saying he was your Sideshow geek?"

"No," the midget said. He shook his head. "See, you ain't listenin'. Mickey *was* a Sideshow geek. Back in the old days." Alfonso laughed. "The good old days. You should have seen those guys back then. Grab a chicken. *Snap.* Bite the head clean off. God, did the audience squeal. That was a long time ago. I was young, young, young and the old timers, the real circus performers, were on their way out. The animal rights yobs started poppin' up like weeds and losin' their minds on a regular basis.

They had to give up the chicken routine; you know, adapt. The modern geek, he's a different creature. He's still somethin' to see though. Eat anything. Eat any goddamned thing. Nuts, bolts, toothpicks, coins, jewelry, rocks, toys, anything they can get past their tonsils, and wash it down with lighter fluid. But, no, Mickey was not our Sideshow geek. This crap circus don't have one."

"Wait, what? Then what are you going on about?"

"I was telling you about Mickey, back then."

"Well, what about Mickey, now?"

"Mickey now is Michael Gronchi, his real name. 'Mike' to most around here. 'Mickey' to a few of us. 'Hey You' to our boss. Mickey doesn't perform anymore. He sweeps up and drinks. Mostly he drinks. If the guy you found is Mickey... He could have just fallen off the pier." Alfonso sadly shook his head.

He toked the cigar and blew a gray cloud against the black night. "If it ain't Mickey, I don't know. There's The Major, of course, the boss I mentioned; the manager. He ain't as old as the others, but he ain't young." A light gleamed in his eyes. "We should all be so lucky it's The Major. He'd look great dead. He's part of the reason I'm willin' to talk to you."

"You're willing to talk to me?"

"You're a private dick, right? I got a case I wanna hire you for."

"I'm already on a case, for me."

"We do two shows a day. You can do two cases."

"When we're finished with this," I said, trying to keep him on the tracks.

"We are finished. I gave you the crop. I'm out of old guys."

"I still have more questions."

"Then ask."

"Does a cartoon fish mean anything to you?"

"A cartoon fish?"

"Yes. A cartoon fish, smoking a cigar, does it mean anything to you?"

"Yeah."

"I know it's a stupid question, but I'm... What did you say?"

"You deaf?" Alfonso growled. "I said, Yeah. The smokin' fish. What about it?"

"What is it? What's it mean?"

Alfonso cocked his head, ogling me (quite a sight in full clown get-up), his cigar standing straight in the corner of his mouth. Again the gleam in his eyes. "I told you. I need your help, Blake," the midget said. "I got a case. There's a lady, right here in the circus, is in danger."

"What sort of danger?"

"How many sorts are there?"

"Brother," I told him. "You'd be surprised."

"We're talkin' about a lady needs help."

"No, Alfonso. You're talking about a lady. I'm still talking about a guy, maybe Mickey, and a fish. Remember?"

"I remember. But I ain't tellin' you, or showin' you, one more damned thing until you agree to help me with my problem."

"Okay! All right. I'll listen to your trouble. But *after* I get a handle on the case that brought me here. Not before."

"I want a commitment, Blake. I help you. You help me."

"I said, All right. I'm committed. I will look into your case. After you give me all you have on Mickey. And the fish."

"Come on," Alfonso said, starting away.

"Where are we going?"

"Where do you think? To look at the smokin' fish."

Alfonso led me around the outside of the Big Top toward the foreboding warehouses lining the south Pier. They stood, black and threatening, with a black, green, and white (swirled gray in the gloom) frosting of seagull guano dripping from the eaves. We passed into and through one of the vast empty structures and back out into the night air on the south side. Lake Michigan shown before us. He turned and started up the Pier, headed west, back toward the distant shore. It was a thousand-yard walk, the equivalent of ten trips up and down Soldier Field, with him leading and me taking baby steps not to step on him. We stopped well short of land. The midget pulled the cigar from his mouth and pointed.

There it was, as big as life, exactly as I'd seen it in my… Well, in whatever you call the things that randomly happened to my brain. The image from my hallucination revealed; a cartoon fish, this one drawn wearing a hat, with a gun turret and conning tower on its back in place of its dorsal fin, smoking a cigar, blowing smoke rings, and carrying – not a No. 2 pencil (as I wrongly guessed) but – a yellow torpedo under its pectoral fin, inside a bright blue circle. Suddenly it made sense. We were standing on Navy Pier looking at a moored submarine and, in particular, at the logo painted on its conning tower. What I'd seen in my vision had been a close-up view of the famed World War Two naval vessel, the USS Silversides, permanently moored there as a tourist attraction.

I'd hit pay dirt. Whatever was going on in my head had, as in my last case, led me in the right direction. Mickey the Geek seemed right. Some checking would decide that. But there was no doubt Navy Pier and the Silversides were right. Somehow or other the drowned man had been here. I started for the submarine like a kid for the packages under the tree on Christmas morning.

"Yo, Blake," Alfonso yelled behind me. "What the hell you doin'? You can't go out there."

"Don't sweat it," I told him. "Trespassing and me are old partners. Come on."

I hopped the locked security gate and made short work of crossing the gang plank. But, as I stepped onto the deck of the boat, Alfonso's exaggerated cough made me turn back. He was leaning against the outside of the gate, looking like a baby clown in a playpen, cigar askew in the corner of his mouth, sneering. "Well, Blake?" he barked, and shook the metal fence with his tiny gloved hands. "I'm supposed to fly over this damned thing?"

I hurried back, reached over the fence, grabbed him under the arms and, with a grunt, lifted him over. His size was deceiving. He was small but built solid as a brick crap house. "Blake!" Alfonso growled. "Set me down or buy me flowers." I set him on the gang plank.

I pulled a pocket flashlight and cupped the lens, doing what I could to throw the beam down and invite as few onlookers as possible. I started onto the deck. Alfonso followed in his bow-legged fashion, three steps to my one, down the starboard side of the boat headed toward the bow. I passed the light from the deck, up the conning tower, forward, down the side, and to the water, again and again. I wasn't sure what I was looking for but, owing to the recent workings of my fragmented noggin, I was more than a little curious about whether or not our drowned man had gone into the drink off the deck of the famed submarine. And, truth be told, I was more than a tad nervous walking across her gray metal plates. At any instant, I half expected to be triggered by the location and shoved into another mental nightmare. Still, breathing deeply, I inched steadily forward.

In the bow, I stopped, concentrating. I closed my eyes and tried to recall the details of the visions I'd received. In my mind's eyes he was there before me, the old man *before* he'd gone for his swim in the harbor. Upright, sweating, screaming, his face contorted by fear. Then he fell into the darkness. Over the side of the boat? It must have been. I heard again that brutal thump and cry of pain. I heard the splash into water. I saw him again, the drowned man, bobbing in the water and foam, sputtering and choking in the dark. I heard his pained and exhausted cry, "Help! Help... me! Down... here..." I stared down at the cold black water, ten feet below the deck, and shivered.

I turned away, not wanting to see it anymore, half afraid at any second I'd be living it again. (Wasn't that a stupid way to think of it?) The fact was I was terrified of dying it again.

Alfonso jabbered in a whisper, blowing smoke at my back, and cussing for color. I wasn't paying much attention but, if you took out the F-bombs and boiled the rest down, it amounted to, "Are you findin' what we're lookin' for?" I was more and more certain we'd found 'where' we were looking for. Beyond that I wasn't sure.

I was about to tell him so when I spotted something interesting along the starboard side of the hull. I grabbed the chain rail for balance and leaned to look. It was interesting and suggestive. About five feet down I noted the metal flashing of what must have been an engine exhaust hood jutting from the sub's side. I paused and threw the light on it. I studied it and, more importantly, something hooked onto it, seeing something I shouldn't have seen. I leaned over the rail, ignorantly, as it was too far away. I dropped to the deck, slipped under the chain, and stretched over the side for all I was worth. My guess had been wrong, it was more than five feet away. That blew because, whatever it was, and I thought I knew, I'd decided I wanted it. I inched forward on my belly, uneasily, as the optical illusion created by the angle made the object seem out of reach while the black water beyond seemed dangerously close. That wasn't the only reason for my hesitation. My clothes were drying after my wrestling match with the drowned man's corpse. I had no interest in tumbling into the lake and soaking them again. And, as mentioned, I feared anything that might trigger the head thing. Believe me, I didn't want that. But I had to reach that exhaust hood.

I closed my eyes, took a breath, and chased the fear away. Then, ready to proceed, I shouted in a whisper over my shoulder, "Alfonso. Grab my feet and hold on!"

"Get the fuck out of here!"

"There's something here. Out of reach. I want it."

"Want all you want. I can't hold your weight."

"I said, I want it. I need it."

He swore. His cigar whizzed past my head and into the drink. "I can't hold you." He swore. He pulled his red nose off and stuffed it in his pocket.

He threw his little hat to the deck. Then he swore again. "Switch places. Come on. You lower me down."

That's what we did. And, thank God it was dark, because I'm sure we'd have been a sight for the tourists, a block-headed private dick dangling Binky the Clown by his ankles (just below his big red shoes), bitching and swearing, off the side of that submarine. And I'm telling you, small as Alfonso was, it was no easy chore. Little folks are heavy. But with effort, several nervous and colorfully worded threats from the upended midget, and a bit of luck (probably his as I never have any), Alfonso reached the object of my desire and grabbed hold. On his "Got it!" I hauled him back up onto the deck.

Alfonso jumped to his feet, dancing around his hat, waving the prize. It wasn't exactly Rocky atop the steps of the Philadelphia Museum of Art but I shared his sense of victory.

The prize was exactly what I thought it was, what my intuition told me it would be, a slip of gray material. The piece of fabric torn from inside the drowned man's suit coat. He'd done a swan dive, or been helped to dive, off the bow of the Silversides. In my vision he'd fallen, there had been a thump, and he'd splashed down. The thump had been the old man hitting the starboard side of the sub and catching his coat on the exhaust before he hit water. My throbbing head had led me to the spot.

Great. Now who in the world was the drowned man?

Having done all the damage we could do there, we cleared the deck of the submarine and returned down the gang plank. "My drowned man was here," I told Alfonso as I picked him up again and lifted him over the security fence. Then I hopped it myself back onto Navy Pier. "That's no longer in doubt. Now I need to know for sure who he was. What's chances of looking up this Mickey? Talking to him? If he's here and able to talk, that is. And, if he's not, talking to the rest on our short list?"

"What's chances? Tonight? No chance at all."

"I need to identify this old guy."

"Yeah. You said." Alfonso snipped the end off a new cigar with a beauty of a gold 'Sunday-go-to-meeting' cigar cutter that glinted in the moonlight.

"But you ain't goin' to do it tonight. I mean, how you goin' to know? If he's here, Mickey, that is, he's in bed. The old ones would all be in bed by now, or near all. Those that ain't will be spread out across the Pier or the city."

"Can't we roust them? The ones that are here."

"No. They wouldn't appreciate it... a lot. Besides, The Major would kick my ass. Then he'd kick yours."

"This is important, Alfonso."

"To who? Not to me. Not at this time of night. I need my job. You can come back in the mornin'. Make it early, if you like, old men get up early, take a piss, cough up phlegm, drink coffee."

"Early? And the ticket booth sentry is going to let me in at that hour?"

"Olive? He's no problem. Just tell him you're there to see me."

"His name is Olive?"

"Skinny kid?" Alfonso asked. "Pimples?" I nodded. "Yeah, Olive. It's nothin' hinky. The kid eats olive and cream cheese sandwiches mornin', noon, and night. We call him Olive. I think the acne is olive oil oozing out of his pours."

"Still," I said with a shake of the head. "Olive?"

"Blake. It's the circus. Nobody's name is really their name. You'll be here in the mornin'?"

I didn't like it but it didn't seem I had a choice. I nodded. "You'll be around early to give me a hand?"

"Yeah, yeah," Alfonso said. "I said I'd help. That is, if you'll help me with my trouble?"

"I said I would and I will. But my case comes first. If you don't want to help me–"

"I just risked my neck for you!"

"I appreciate it. It got us closer to where we need to be. But I'll still need your help tomorrow to identify my drowned man."

"If he's even here. You don't know that."

"If he's here," I agreed. "If you don't want to help me, I'll go it alone and take my usual lumps. But that will take longer and that means Homicide will catch up. They'll end up sniffing around your little circus sooner rather than later. And they'll have no interest in your problem at all."

"You're a one-way prick, you know that?" Alfonso blew smoke in my face. Which was no small feat from his height. "Okay, I'll help you go through the geriatric line-up in the mornin'. Then you'll listen to my problem."

Chapter Six

I left the circus with a lot on my mind, headed home, to chew it all over until the sun came up and I could actually accomplish something. As was my habit, I cruised past my office to assuage my natural paranoia. It's always fine and I always keep going. That night, of course, it wasn't fine.

I killed my lights while I was still on the street, shifted the transmission into 'Neutral' and shut the engine off, turned hard and coasted quietly into my own parking lot. I pulled up short of my office. Yes, sisters and brothers, I'm goofy. But I wasn't being goofy. The place had been vandalized. The glass door to the vestibule was shattered; as was the window to my waiting room, Lisa's office, beyond.

Speaking of Lisa... Her car was there, in the lot. I fought the urge to panic. But I'd been with her myself a few hours before and had told her specifically to call it a night. I took a deep breath to calm myself and to realize that, if she'd followed orders, Lisa was home safe in bed. Then it dawned, if my calm demeanor depended upon Lisa following orders, I had better panic. Why was her car there? I slipped into stealth mode and sneaked up on the place, but wasted no time doing it.

I crouched and, without opening it, slipped through the shattered front door into the tiny entryway. In the dim light from the lot I saw a brick lying in the corner. It had done the damage. My brain started ticking off the names of those who might have wanted to hurl brick bats at me. After the first dozen, including two murderers, a blackmailer, and my mother, I gave it up as a lost cause and returned to the moment. Two long steps, taken as quietly as possible, got me across the glass covered floor to the waiting room door. From there I saw the room, the floor around Lisa's desk, and the desk itself, lay in the same condition as the vestibule, covered in broken glass and dotted with the tossed bricks that had done the shattering. Plenty of mess, but no Lisa. I wanted to call out but, again, thought better of it and fought the urge.

The door to my office was ajar. That may not sound sinister, but it was. I always left my door wide open. Lisa always came behind me and closed it. We were creatures of habit and neither did anything halfway. So why was the door to my office ajar? The office beyond was dark. Dark didn't mean empty. I reconsidered the advantages of the stealthy approach and decided, as I was unarmed, there weren't any. I have a gun. I don't carry it. After having been shot, in an event that ended my copping days, I hate guns. Mine was in the office, locked in the safe. The only weapons on or in Lisa's desk were a stapler (probably empty), a letter opener (probably covered in frosting), and a plastic fork (probably covered in cake). Since my only defense was attitude, it seemed sensible to show some. Besides, I was sick of slinking around my own place like an alley cat. I wanted to know who was throwing bricks. I really wanted to know why my door was ajar. It made me mad and I used the anger. I ground the crunching glass into the carpet in a march across the waiting room and kicked the office door open.

By the light spilling in through my broken window, I saw someone in my office, in my chair, behind my desk. The shadowy figure made no move, offensive or defensive, at my entrance. What it did was... belch. That told me it wasn't Goldilocks and, when it spoke, I knew it wasn't Papa Bear either. "You always sneak up on your own office, Blake? Why don't you try payin' the rent like everybody else?"

I'd have recognized that voice in a nightmare. It had only been two days since I'd last heard it in a hospital stairwell. I snapped the light on and blinked until the horrible vision came into focus. There he was, trespassing and laying in wait like a two-hundred-and-fifty-pound spider, Lieutenant Frank Wenders of Chicago Homicide.

You've met him before but, since nobody works to remember a nightmare, let me remind you of the details. Then you can decide, like I had to every time we met, whether to breathe the same air or just kill yourself and get it over with. Wenders was five-foot-nine on his feet and doing everything in his power to create a like measurement around his middle. He was wearing the only threadbare gray suit he owned. His gut bulged like a bale of wool with a cut string. He had a disposition like a tub of acid. His thinning hair, once-red, had gone gray. He had two mean and beady black eyes that drilled holes through you like you were cheap plywood. To be fair to the guy, I did make note of one surprising difference from the norm. His partner, junior detective Dave Mason, usually attached to his hind end by puckered lips, was absent. Then I recalled his appendicitis attack and realized Mason was likely still in the hospital; mystery solved. Wenders was slurping my booze and clinking my ice.

"Did you find everything you needed?" I asked, pointing at the glass in his fat hand.

"Very comfortable. You buy only the best." He took another gulp. Then he pointed at the shattered window. "Your air conditioning is up a little high, but I couldn't find the switch."

"What happened here?" I demanded. "Where's Lisa?"

"You're askin' me where your secretary is?"

"Was she here when you broke in?"

"Like usual, Blake, you got everything ass backwards. I ask the questions, see. You're just the taxpayer. We're going to put the death threat on your answerin' machine–"

"There's a death threat on my answering machine?"

"It's a beaut. But it can't be anything new for you. So we're going to put that, and your secretary, and your new decoratin' scheme, on the back burner for a minute. 'Cause we got somethin' else to talk about." He pointed accusingly at me without spilling a drop. "You left the scene of a murder."

"Absolutely untrue." I grabbed my bottle from the desk and returned it to my liquor cabinet. He'd had enough. "I have no knowledge of a murder. If one occurred, I haven't the slightest idea who might have been responsible. In the middle of a relaxing boat ride, I found a corpse bobbing in the water and, being a solid citizen and friend of man, I hauled it in and brought it to dry land. You're welcome."

"A relaxing boat ride? In the dark of night?"

"Pooh," I said, waving it away. "The sea. The stars. The romance."

"I couldn't care less about the romantic moments you spend alone. Especially in public places. I'm Homicide, not Vice."

I shrugged. "You don't know what you're missing."

"Yeah. So let me see if I got this. You rent a boat, row out under the stars to romance yourself, and are interrupted when you find a body. So you bring it aboard, without riflin' its pockets, cause we all know you got no curiosity, and hurry back to shore because that's what good citizens do." He shook his head. "That, boy, is one large and unbelievable mound of horseshit."

He looked for a reaction. I didn't offer one.

"But to continue… When you got to shore, you changed your mind about bein' a good citizen. You climbed out of the boat and took off without reportin' the body to the police. That, between you and me, Blake, is what's known as *a crime*." He scratched the air putting it in quotes. "When they wad up your detective's license and start shootin' hoops, I'll visit you in the joint with details on how many tries it took 'em to hit the trash can."

I offered a phony chuckle to prove he wasn't funny. "How can you be so wrong so often? The owner of the boat was waiting on the pier when I got there. George Clay? You talked to him? I showed him what I found. I told him all I knew. He immediately called you. Didn't he? There would have been no point to both of us running to phones and reporting it at the same time. I might add that I was under no obligation to guard either his boat or your body."

"You're a cop!" He stopped himself. A mixed look of horror and disgust crossed his fat face. It passed quickly, the usual red returned, and he went on. "I mean, you were a cop, when you had brains! You knew there'd be questions."

"Then ask them."

"Boat boy, who is he?"

"I don't know the guy."

"He was dead in the water?"

"He was dead every minute I didn't know him."

"You're a liar!"

"Often. But not now. He was drowned when we met."

"No," Wenders said. "He wasn't. The coroner gave him a quick look on the pier. You stabbed him in the back before you chucked him in the water."

That was news to me. I wondered how I'd missed it? I hadn't seen any blood. It was dark. I didn't give him a good look. He might have bled internally or bled out by the time I got there. Still I'd missed it and shouldn't have. I tried not to show my surprise.

Wenders was pushing on. "Why'd you run?"

"I didn't. I walked."

"Answer the question. Where did you walk to? And why? What did boat boy tell you or give you before he croaked?"

"Not a thing. He wasn't alive to tell me or give me anything." I feigned a look of shock and added, "Surely you're not suggesting he communicated with me after he died? That's absurd!"

Wenders knew about my... condition. Without knowing about, that is. In a trapped moment of anger, I once blurted the whole thing out to him. He hadn't swallowed a bite. He'd likely put it down as more of my usual jackassery. In which case, he probably hadn't gotten the dig I'd made. If he did he showed no sign. He ignored the comment and charged blindly ahead with his 'by rote' questioning.

"Where did you go when you left the harbor?"

"Not germane." I leaned in on him. "Sorry, Frank, for the big word. It means there's no connection between where I went and what you're investigating, so it's none of your business. That, Lieutenant, is all the help I can give you with your inquiry."

Though it seemed redundant, Wenders again called me a liar... colorfully. He offered to arrest me on several charges, from a misdemeanor 'Mishandling of a Corpse' to a selection of raps under the column 'Felony Murder'. "All I got is your worthless word you found the guy dead. And your empty claim you didn't make him that way yourself. Maybe you were choking somethin' besides your chicken in that boat?" He shook his fat head yet again. "I can just see your poor weepin' mom at your execution."

It was bad enough he'd accused me of murder and masturbation. Now Wenders was getting nasty. Images danced in my head of the Stateville doctor all set to push the plunger on me while my mother sat waiting, front row center, with a tub of buttery popcorn in her lap. It was almost too much.

"All right," I said. "I might have an idea. But I've got nothing to grab. I've got to find the handle."

"Give it to me," the lieutenant demanded. "Let me find it."

"You couldn't find a pregnant elephant in a phone booth. I need a few days to see if it's anything," I told him, "without your bad breath on my neck."

"You're in no position to bargain," he growled. "I could book you as a material witness. I could stick you in a cell."

"What would be the point? If I'm not going to tell you, I'm not going to tell you anywhere!"

Between us, sisters and brothers, I knew then I had him. Wenders knew I knew something. He also knew I wasn't ready to give it to him. I may or may not have mentioned, in the past, the out-sized homicide detective was not averse to letting me solve a case for him; especially if he could get the credit. That being the case, I knew I had him.

"You got two days, Blake." He gulped the last of my stolen whiskey. He crushed the ice in his teeth. "Forty-eight hours. Then you unload everything you got on boat boy. And you better have somethin' or this murder is yours with all the parting gifts that come with it."

"Fine. Now, if you don't mind, Frank, get lost." I looked the office over. "I need to clean this mess up before morning. If Lisa sees it, she'll have a–"

"Your goofy secretary? She's already seen it."

"What?"

"She was here when it happened. Whatever it was that happened."

"She was supposed to be home in bed!"

Wenders shrugged his indifference. "Trouble is, Blake, your secretary is just like you. She can't mind her own business. So, instead of bein' home in bed like a decent citizen, she was here pryin' into other people's lives. One of them didn't like it enough to hit her in the head with a brick."

"She was hit? In the head? And you sit there like a tub of crap, the whole time knowing... Is she all right? How bad was she hurt? Where the hell is she?"

"*Egh*," Wenders said. It was a noise not a word. "She's aw-right. She's been to the hospital."

"Which hospital?" I demanded, headed for the door.

"She ain't there no more," Wenders shouted, stopping me. I turned back to find him ogling me with one raised brow. "Cripes, Blake, what kind of heartless ogre do you think I am?"

"We'll save that."

"One of my men took her to the hospital. He waited; then took her home. She's there now unless the daffy broad made him stop for pizza, Chinese, and ice cream on the way. She was eatin' pretzels when I got here, Blake. Just woke up from bein' unconscious and there she was stuffin' her face with pretzels. I've never seen your secretary when she wasn't eatin'."

"I'm not laughing."

"Oh, dear me, the wise guy's not laughin'. Must not be funny then. 'Cause he only laughs at shit that's funny like the cops and murder." Wenders grunted like a barnyard animal and struggled to his feet. "I told you, Lisa's aw-right. Also like you, Blake, she's got a concrete head. While we're on it, what's your broken building got to do with boat boy?"

"Sorry, your alliteration confuses me."

"My what? What confuses you?"

"Never mind," I said with a sigh. I spread my hands indicating the office. "I don't have the first clue about this mess. Whether it's cause and effect or coincidence or neither, it's news to me. And, if it is related to the drowned man, I have forty-eight hours to find out, remember?"

Wenders twisted his lips, begrudgingly nodded, and lumbered past me out of my office. The glass crunched beneath his size twelves all the way to the vestibule and out.

Chapter Seven

I listened to my messages and Wenders was right. There was a death threat. And it was a beaut. But I didn't know the speaker from the man in the moon. And, with real problems to think about, I reset the tape for new messages and put it out of mind.

I picked up broken glass until sunrise. Then I threw cold water on my face, scraped my face and, finally, gave up on my face in the closet-sized bathroom in the corner of Lisa's reception area. I wanted to check on Lisa; to see how badly she was injured and make sure Wenders was right when he guessed she would be okay. I usually keep a change of clothes in the office but nothing that day had been usual; I didn't have one. I didn't want to go all the way back to my apartment for one. But I didn't want to risk Mrs. Solomon's ire by showing up looking like a hobo either.

Have I mentioned Lisa's mother doesn't like me?

Anyway. Before I could head their way, or do anything else, I had to call the window repair people and get someone to babysit my vulnerable office until they arrived. The question was, who did I know with a life so empty that playing watchdog for me would seem like an adventure? Luckily, the question answered itself. I called Willie Banks.

If you joined me on my last case, you already know Willie. (I've probably already apologized for bringing him into your life.) If this is the first time you're hearing his name, I apologize now for what you're about to experience. Willie Banks is a slug of a human being, a small criminal, a sometimes informant (though everything he says must be taken with a salt lick), a sometimes gopher, and an unending irritant. His mother is a neighbor and, to her credit, a bitter enemy of my mother. Anyone who agrees my mother is off her rocker can't be all bad. In light of that, I've done an odd investigative job or two for Mrs. Banks and, on occasion, take pity on her wastrel son by giving him grunt work for peanuts on the shiny side of the law. There's no question of reforming him; it won't happen. I just feel bad for his old lady.

The last time out, Willie took a bullet in the left shoulder saving my life. The jerk. I'm never going to live that down. Still I needed a warm body to watch my unprotected office and it seemed a job even a crippled Willie could handle. Yes, it was like asking a mouse to keep an eye on your cheese. But, if necessary, I knew how to kill a mouse. Besides, don't think for a moment I trusted him. I didn't trust him any further than I could throw the pip-squeak. But I doubted his criminal friends would tag along. If they did, I doubted they'd cause me a problem. If they tried, I doubted they knew how to crack a safe. Willie, by himself, knew nothing at all.

Hiring Willie seemed to solve the problem and allow me to do a good deed at the same time. He'd be all right, I told myself. Knowing, of course, he probably wouldn't. But he was better than nothing. God, I needed better acquaintances. Or a friend, I could have used a friend.

On second thought, knowing I couldn't afford it if something did go haywire, and in case my idiot guard did go snooping, though I despised the thing and usually pretended it didn't exist, I removed my gun from the safe and slid it beneath my suit coat into an uncomfortable shoulder holster I wasn't used to wearing to take with me. That left the safe empty save for a few business papers, some personal papers, and a mummified brownie I'd hidden from Lisa and forgotten. Theoretically Willie couldn't hurt himself with any of the three.

Willie arrived, with his arm still in a sling, whining through his nose (all his vocal communications annoyingly arrived that way) about how much pain he was in. He probably did hurt, and probably still needed the sling; it hadn't been that long ago he'd been shot. But I hated hearing about it, and worse seeing it, because it reminded me how guilty I felt about the whole thing. Who told him to come save my life anyhow? It didn't help that he was gingerly cradling the arm and milking his injury for all it was worth. It made me want to shoot him myself.

I gave Willie his instructions; watch the place and, when they got there, make sure the glass repair people had all they needed to do the job. Otherwise he was to keep his nose in the middle of his face where it belonged, to not invite his friends over, and to keep his feet off the desks. I hit the road.

The only way to check on Lisa, and make certain myself she was all right, was to go to her. That meant visiting the apartment she shared with her mother. That meant getting past her mother; never a happy proposition. Like I said, Mrs. Solomon doesn't like me, meaning she hates me (not entirely without reason).

Our relationship, let me tell you, had not improved since I'd ruined the esteemed Reverend Delp as her source of inspiration and entertainment. If you missed that case, Conrad Delp, the famed Chicago-based televangelist had been exonerated of the jeopardy of murder charges when I'd tied them onto someone else. But the affair had damaged Delp's reputation and had definitely soured the minister for Lisa's mom. An elderly Jewish woman can only worship a Gentile religious leader so much and then she has to reel it in or become the talk of the ladies at the Community Center. My investigation had pushed it over the edge. Mrs. Solomon didn't actually growl when she opened the door and saw me on her stoop, but you couldn't have fed a parking meter on the difference. The old dear reluctantly led me to Lisa's bedroom and, even more reluctantly, left me alone with her daughter to talk.

Lisa was eating when I got there; always a good sign. She said she was all right but had a goose egg on the side of her head that would have done Muhammad Ali proud. She offered to let me touch it but I begged off. I wasn't particularly squeamish about head injuries, mine were still plenty tender, but ever since the Delp nonsense I'd grown more and more paranoid about making casual, or even pointed, physical contact with anybody. I described for you what happened in the boat with the drowned man. That same thing could happen again, I was discovering, at any time. I never knew who or what was going to send me into La La Land for either a conversation with the dead or to share a lethal ass whooping from a complete stranger. I was trying to avoid both. Don't think I'm hollering 'victim'. If it was my turn to go nuts, okay, it was. But it would be nice, when your brain gives up the ghost, if they'd give you a manual on how to operate the damaged remains. The point was, on the previous night Lisa had hooked and landed the drowned man. Touching him had sent me splashing and sputtering into cold dark water for the second time in as many days. With two trips into Lake Michigan already under my psychological belt I think you can understand why, when Lisa offered, I didn't give her boo-boo a rub.

In no time at all I learned Lisa knew nothing about the attack on our office. She couldn't tell me a thing about the vandal or vandals. Her head had taken a glancing blow by the first brick through the first window and she'd been knocked cold as a mackerel. I rarely saw Lisa angry. But she was mad about the office and the goose egg. The more I questioned her about it, the madder she got.

To cool down, she switched subjects, taking the conversation to the boat and the drowned man she'd found. I cut her short. I told Lisa I was looking into the drowned man, but reminded her she *did not* find it. "I found the body. You need to remember," I said. "If anyone asks, particularly a cop, you know nothing of it."

Fact was, I was still shocked by the whole setup. What possessed Lisa to rent a boat and row out into the harbor? How did she find a drowned man in the dark? How did she get his carcass into the tiny craft? It was all beyond me. I sometimes doubt her sanity. I never doubt her humanity. But I have on occasion questioned her human-ness. Lisa is, I'm certain, some otherworldly being sent to constantly amuse, frequently annoy, and occasionally bedevil me. Once in a great while she'll mail a letter.

"Speaking of which," I asked, "how in the world did you land him? He's small but, still, I don't see how you got him into the boat. Along with everything else that isn't tied down, you must have been eating your Wheaties, huh?"

Lisa nodded. "I don't think I could have done it if he hadn't helped."

That was it. No warning at all. She just dropped that bomb and stared at me.

"If he hadn't helped? What are you telling me? He was alive when you found him?"

"Yeah."

"You didn't tell me that last night."

"You didn't give me a chance. You ordered me to go, so I went."

I would have sighed but to what end? I kept my frustration to myself. "Give."

"I was motoring out, down the channel thingy, 'cause I knew something was out there waiting for me. I believe in your head, Nod, even if you don't. I thought I heard something, so I shut the motor down and started rowing. I heard him calling for help, pretty weakly. I rowed that way and found him floating in from the lake. I tugged him in. You're right, it was a chore. And I leaned him against the..." She waved her hand.

"The gunwale," I said.

She nodded. "It was dark. I couldn't see very well at all. But he looked like he had blood on him."

"Blood?" I asked. "I don't remember seeing any blood."

"There wasn't much to begin with. By the time you got there, he probably ran out."

I shrugged. "Probably."

"I asked him what had happened to him and, I couldn't believe it, he was rude."

"He was rude?"

Lisa nodded. "I asked what happened. He groaned and, you're not going to believe it, he asked me if it was my business. That hacked me off. So I pretended I was you and told him, 'No. It's your baggage, pal. Carry it!'"

I almost laughed.

"Then I felt terrible," Lisa continued, "because you're meaner than I am. I wouldn't have said that to someone that was hurt."

"God, give me strength," I mumbled. Lisa was still talking.

"I asked him to pull his feet in so I could step past him to the motor and, you won't believe this, he said, 'Don't let me stop you.' That really cheesed me off. You know, Blake, I see now why sometimes you're a wise guy. Though I don't know why you're a wise guy to me? Still he was being a jerk and I was thinking it would be an okay world if it weren't for all the people in it."

"Could we get back in the boat, please?"

"Yeah. Like I said, he ticked me off, so I told him, 'Look, mister, if I'm annoying you, feel free to jump back in and finish your swim.' Only I didn't really want him to because he was the reason I was out there in the boat, right? Anyway, he changed his tune and said, 'You gotta help me.' And I said, 'Help you? If you hadn't noticed, I already did.'"

I don't know about you, but I was getting a headache. "Lisa!" I shouted. "Does this boat ever reach the pier?" She stared wide-eyed. I felt bad, but criminy. "I know you're on a roll," I told her. "And I hate to interrupt. But get to the point. Before he stopped paying taxes, did the drowned man do or say anything to answer the question, 'Hey, mister, who made you dead?'"

"I have no idea. What he did say was, 'The canary. The canary. The canary.'"

"The canary... what?"

Lisa shrugged her skinny shoulders. "He just said, 'The canary' over and over again."

"That's it?"

"No. Finally, he said, 'Didn't die when she fell from the sky.'"

"The canary, you mean?"

"I don't know. If he was trying to finish a sentence, then, yes. It was probably the canary. If it was a second thought, then I don't know."

"The canary," I repeated. "Didn't die when she fell from the sky."

"That's what he said. Then he died."

"Great. That's just great. What am I supposed to do with that?"

"That's pretty standard, isn't it? A romantic obscure final sentence for a clue."

"Clue to what?" I asked. "You and your romance!" I took a short walk around her room. "Well, if you like your final messages cryptic, that's a crowd pleaser."

"Yeah. It meant nothing to me. Does it to you? Anything?"

I shook my head. "How could it?"

"Hey," Lisa said, brightening. "I got an idea. Grab me."

"What? Are you crazy? Your mother's here."

"No, Blake, not like that. I mean, touch me." She held out her arm. "We don't know what causes your head flash thingies. I helped the old man into the boat. Maybe something rubbed off." She shook her arm. "Grab me. See if you can spark one."

"When I spark one," I objected, "I get killed. I don't want to!"

She glared. "I'm right here with you."

Even without the pain that always accompanied the event, the idea did not appeal. But Lisa was insistent. And we needed to know all we could know. Finally, hesitantly, I agreed. I leaned over her. I reached out, took a breath and, with both hands, took hold of her arm.

Nothing happened. I released her, faced her, took another deeper breath, and grabbed her shoulders instead. Nothing.

I swore, too loudly. Lisa shushed me.

It was aggravating. And left us where we'd begun, with a drowned man and a cryptic clue. If murder victims survived long enough to be chatty, why the heck didn't they spill it? Why not come out and say, 'My name is Joe Blow and the name of the guy who killed me is–'" Before I could finish that thought the bedroom door came open.

Mrs. Solomon barged in to see me still leaning over her daughter's bed holding Lisa by the shoulders. "What's going on in here?"

"I touched your daughter," I told her. "Nothing happened!"

Mrs. Solomon stared for a cold long time. Then she sneered. Then she said, "I'm not surprised." She shook her head at her fallen daughter, turned and, muttering to God, vacated the bedroom.

"Did she want something?"

"Probably. But seeing you molest me so mortified her she forgot what it was."

I nodded. "It happens."

"Well," Lisa said, getting back to business. "Our attempt to goose your ESP didn't work. What's our next step?"

"We don't have a next step. I've got work to do. You've got to rest."

"I can't rest," Lisa exclaimed. "You've got to find the drowned man's killer. I've got to track down the vandals who ruined our office."

"Oh, no, you don't."

"Yes, I do."

"No. You don't. You're not recovered from your injuries. You're not a licensed detective. And you're not going out into the streets to chase violent anonymous vandals. Forget it! Rest and nothing else. That's an order."

Lisa was not happy. But she saw I was immovable and let the subject drop.

"So, what are you going to do about the drowned man? Where are you going to start?"

"I've already started. I'm going back to where our drowned man went into the drink."

"You know where that was?

"Yes. Navy Pier. But I don't know who he is, or who helped him in, or why. I'll go back to the Pier first, then I'll widen the search. Chicago can't have but eight, ten million doors, tops. All I've got to do is knock on each and, when it's opened, sing out, 'The canary didn't die when she fell from the sky.' It's too easy. You get some rest. Your mother will show me out."

"I'm sure," Lisa said with a laugh. "Her favorite part of your visits."

Of course I wasn't going to knock on eight million doors. I was going back to talk to Alfonso and his promised menagerie of circus performers. But I wasn't going to tell Lisa. She had enough on her bruised mind. As to what I'd learned... Lisa's cryptic quote about a falling canary may have been the clue that exploded the case but I was hanged if I could see it. Not a glimmer.

What I could see, when I returned to the street outside Lisa's apartment, was that some person or persons unknown had flattened all four of the tires on my Jaguar. And, because I have no luck, the air had not merely been let out. They'd used a knife and stuck each and every tire like a pig. They were destroyed. Staging a terrorist attack on my office and making death threats was one thing, but going after my Jag was too much! And, with the incidents within hours of each other, they were more than coincidence. Who, I demanded of the heavens, had it in for me, was following me, and wrecking my property? The situation warranted cussing and I obliged! I screamed until I ran out of air. Then I took a breath and looked around. I was alone. Whoever paid my Jag the visit had gone. All right, I needed to line up my ducks.

The quickest solution to my acute transportation problem would, obviously, have been to go back inside, borrow Lisa's phone, and call for assistance and a ride. But Lisa had had enough excitement. And the thought of Mrs. Solomon and me ogling each other again... I cringed. Then I vetoed the idea. The relationship I had with my own dear mater, unbalanced to say the least, left me leery of middle-aged females in general and mothers in particular. Having to admit I'd suffered vandalism by unknown enemies in front of their residence would have only given the woman another reason to distrust and despise me. I gauged the humiliation and decided it wasn't worth it.

Instead I hoofed it to a Spudnuts Coffee Shop in the next block that, sadly, had a full counter but, happily, had an empty phone booth. I searched my pockets for dimes, dialed the roadside assistance folks at 'Triple A', and started singing the blues.

Chapter Eight

With the shoes on my beloved Jaguar repaired, I went back to the circus. I hoped, with Alfonso's help, to talk to the performers I'd been unable to interview the night before. I hoped we'd discover which circus employee, if any, was our drowned man. And, if any luck was to be had, I hoped we'd decipher the meaning of Lisa's cryptic clue, 'The canary didn't die when she fell from the sky.'

I met Olive as expected, at the entrance lining up his ticket booth for the day, making ready to open. Between bits of business, he chomped massive bites from his breakfast of champions; the sandwich that had given him his name. He returned my stare, chewing olives and cheese, trying to recall where he'd seen me before. I stepped up, mentioned Alfonso's name and, like magic, found myself inside the fence and freely wandering a very different midway than I'd seen the night before.

Alfonso hadn't come down to meet me. Not that I expected he would. I'm merely stating he hadn't. The performers, I imagined, were housed in the old residential areas of the Pier (formerly used for Navy trainees), in the south section of the arched superstructure on the far east Lake Michigan end. That put the midway and Big Top between me and Alfonso's likely location. Meaning I had a built-in reason to snoop my way across. As I did, I saw several carnies oiling their respective rides, several sweepers giving the grounds a once over, and several fellows collecting and emptying the trash. None showed any resemblance to our drowned man. The Sideshow was quiet, the tents closed, but shouts and laughter could be heard in the Big Top beyond. As I am by nature nosy, and it was on my way, I slipped inside the hippodrome to see what I could see.

What I saw was a pair of elderly gents, most likely the two Alfonso had called Ed and Butch, laughing at a private joke as they wheeled a barrow of raw meat through a row of hanging stage curtains to disappear beyond. Based on the noises emanating from the depths, they were about their jobs feeding the animals. The midget had been right, Ed and Butch were accounted for. As the pair were busy, I made a mental note to look them up later for an interview.

I saw a sleepy looking young girl taking an orangutan for a walk. I thought the monkey's antics funnier than she did. I saw a pair of electrical gaffers atop a scaffold wrestling a set of lights in the rigging. I saw a woman in curlers walking, and making kissy noises at, six leashed poodles.

I saw the knife thrower and his assistant. From his shoulders up the artist, Tommy Dagger, was perfectly coiffed and performance ready. From the shoulders down he'd taken the morning off, baggy gray sweats and tennis shoes. His assistant, still the target girl to me, looked fresh from the shower. Her hair was towel-tossed. She wore none of the stage makeup from the previous night but was naturally lovely all the same in quickly pulled-on shorts, tennies, and a Houston Oilers' jersey (Earl Campbell, of course). Her right arm bore a clean white bandage.

They looked to be rehearsing a new act. Tommy Dagger stood verbally setting the stage (in what sounded a French-ish accent). "The ringmaster will announce us. The audience will take in my brilliant authority, your unequaled beauty. The trumpets will sound, the kettle drums begin their march, spurring excitement in the crowd, stimulating you, my dear, to courage and me to confidence." He spun in place, pointed, and a couple of sleepy looking stage hands, the huskies from the night before without their costumes, hopped to.

"The Wheel of Death shall be revealed." The carnies pulled an ornate and colorful cover off of an impressive prop piece set atop a massive platform. Beneath stood a giant circular target board painted in pie slices of red, white, and blue, set up to spin about its middle. They rolled the platform on casters into the center ring.

"As the audience reacts in awe and building terror," Tommy said. "I escort you to the wheel and surrender you into the hands of–" He sneered at the lackeys. "Them." He turned and walked away, declaring over his shoulder, "While I ready my knives with the appropriate flourishes, they will quickly secure you to the wheel." Tommy turned to see the lackeys standing uselessly on each side of the wheel staring at the target girl. She stood ten feet off, arms crossed, face set on 'Don't touch me', staring at the knife thrower. "What are you doing?" Tommy demanded.

"Isn't it obvious?" she replied. "I am doing nothing. After last night can you blame me?"

"*Pah!*" He pointed with one of his keenly sharpened knives. "Get on the wheel!"

"No."

"Don't be stupid. Get on the wheel."

"No. Why should I?"

"Why should you do what you do? Ridiculous. We must rehearse the new routine."

She displayed her arm. "After last night–"

"It was not my fault! That fool… That whoever! He had no business there. He broke my concentration. Last night was a mere nothing."

"Nothing to you. It was something to me. Where were you? What happened to your concentration? What happened to your head?"

"It was nothing!"

"Nothing. Your response is to add five times the danger? Requiring ten times the concentration?"

"Your arm was scratched. *Pah!*" He tossed the bundle of knives on their table. "My reputation was deeply gouged. I must mend it."

"Not with me," the girl declared. "Not until you govern your anger and regain your head."

His reply was instant fury. "How dare you?"

And, of course, that's when he spotted me – and rerouted his fury. He stopped the (already halted) rehearsal with a shout, and grabbing a knife back up from the pile on the table, turned to face me. "How dare you," he screamed, raising the blade above his head. "How dare you return here?"

I reached beneath my jacket, laid fingertips on the grip of my holstered gun and, hating my life, stared warily at the circus performer.

"You ruined our performance. You humiliated me. You were responsible for my injuring my beautiful assistant. I ought to cut your throat. I ought to pierce your heart!" Speaking of hearts, his face was red as a valentine and he shook so that his head genuinely looked as if it might explode. He screamed, "*Pah!*" He threw the knife back down, clattering atop the others on the table, and disap-peared behind the curtains to the tent's backstage area in his own private storm.

The target girl approached me. "Who are you?"

I took a badly needed breath. "The name is Blake. And you?"

"Sandra. Assistant to the great Tommy Dagger."

"Is that Sandra Dagger?"

She laughed; a charming sound. "The answer to the question I believe you are asking is, yes. That is my excitable husband. Thomas Lacrosse." She stretched a hand. Despite the injury she shook with a firm grip. "I'm Anita Lacrosse." She laughed again at my arched and questioning brow. "In the circus, Mr. Blake, no one's name is their name. Call me Sandra."

Sandra was as pleasant as her husband and partner was disagreeable and she was willing to answer my questions. Willing, but not able. She didn't know Michael Gronchi or, for that mat-ter, any of the older fellows Alfonso had men-tioned. She didn't enjoy the midway, the food had no place in her diet and, she confessed, she was frightened of the Sideshow. She performed, she rehearsed, and, between, she read romance novels in her room. She said, without saying, Tommy kept a tight leash. Speaking of which, Tommy was no doubt waiting, and wondering where she was, and getting angrier as a result. Sandra accepted my apology for the part I'd played in her being injured. She wished me good day. And she said hello and goodbye to Alfonso, entering the Big Top, as she passed him headed away to find her husband.

Alfonso was a surprise. I'd heard him plenty but had never seen him without his costume or makeup. His language led me to believe he was a native of the Bronx, or maybe South Chicago, but his accent hinted – like many around there – he was European in one way or another. What I didn't imagine was he was black (really an attractive tawny brown). Last night I guessed, without a thought, he darkened himself to perform the Pygmy in the Sideshow. Now I knew he actually laid the Clown White on thick to do Binky. Mind you, none of it mattered. I have as many prejudices as anyone, but I'm too lazy to be an -ist and too contemptuous of society in general to form specific -isms. I take folks, clerks, clients, and criminals, as they come. I'm just telling it so it dawns on you, like it was dawning on me, that nothing is as it first appears in the circus. But the real surprise was still to come.

I'd made a rough start of the morning. Seeing the midget brightened my day as I had high hopes he could smooth the path between me and those I wanted to question. So much for my hopes. Alfonso had come down in a surly mood and with a chip on his shoulder. Before I got a serviceable word out he growled that he'd changed his mind – and our bargain.

"I've been thinkin' it over," Alfonso said. "You're not gonna get anywhere without my help. And I ain't showin', or tellin', you one more thing until you listen to my problem and promise to help."

"I already said I'd help."

He jammed what must have been his breakfast cigar into the corner of his mouth and folded his arms over his chest. He was serious. He wasn't moving.

"Okay," I told him. "Tell me your problem."

He jerked the cigar back out, leaving a satisfied sneer, and jutted the thumb of his smoking hand toward the tent's east opening. "The canvas has ears. Let's take it to my room."

Again I found myself helplessly following the midget.

Alfonso's second floor room was your standard run-down dormitory digs, mixed and unmatched furniture, some of it held over from the 40's, built the right size for someone like me but miles too big for the diminutive circus performer. A worn dresser, table, and chair. A bed with a bad mattress. Four coat hangers, impossible to steal, hung in the closet niche. A faded area rug lay in the corner with a surprisingly hairy gray chihuahua prostrate upon it. I'd always understood that breed of dog to be hyper but this example of the species looked as run down as its surroundings. The dog not only didn't jump, or yip, or nervously skitter, it showed few signs of life. It merely looked at us with eyes as big as its head and sighed. (I mean it. It didn't yawn, it sighed.)

Alfonso closed the door, shutting us in. He offered me the chair, then climbed up and perched himself on the foot board of the bed like a rodeo performer on an arena fence. There he sat, deep in thought. I waited. The dog did it again. "Did your dog just sigh?"

"Don't mind him. He gets depressed."

It was my own fault. I had to ask. I gave the situation a few more minutes and, finally, blurted, "Can we get the show on the road?"

Alfonso took what, for him, was probably a big breath, and said, "There's this girl."

Now I was ready to sigh. "Yeah. There usually is."

"I got no sense of humor about this."

"I'm sure you don't. All right. Tell me about the girl, but do me a favor and skip the romantic parts if you can. It's too early."

"There ain't no romantic parts. She's engaged; not to me." He stewed for a few seconds, as if convincing himself of what he'd said, then went on. "The guy she's engaged to ain't no good and I want you to check him out. Maybe if I can prove he ain't no good–"

I held up a hand. "You ever met a woman before? She's probably after him because he's no good."

"Not a woman like this. And she ain't after him. He's after her."

"I thought you said they were engaged."

"So they are."

"Then the chase is over, Alfonso."

"This is the circus, fer Chris-sake. Nothin's over until the fat lady sings."

I would have pointed out he had the circus confused with an opera but it would only have prolonged the argument. He was in no mood to see reason. I had a case I wanted to get back to. "Okay. Tell it."

"There's a lady, right here in the show, she's in danger and needs help."

"I've already got that much memorized," I told him. "Move it down the track."

The midget frowned. "I'm just introducin' you to the characters."

"Good. I need more characters in my life."

Alfonso hopped down from his perch and squared off on me, all three feet and a few inches, looking half-mad and half like he couldn't decide what I was. "You're so tough I gotta take that from you?"

"Keep your shirt on, Alfonso, and tell it."

"The lady," he said, forcing the words out through clenched teeth, "I'm concerned about, her name's Alida Harrison."

A bell rang but I didn't know why.

"She's only been with us a short while; our new star aerial acrobat."

That was why. The pixie from the night before. I'd heard the ringmaster's introduction. 'Alida, Lady of the Air'. What had he called her? 'The world's most astounding aerial acrobat and contortionist'. I'd heard of a contortionist but had always imagined it to be a skinny Indian guy who could twist himself up like a pretzel then screw himself down into a wicker basket. Not that I'd given performers of that sort much thought, but a sexy blonde pixie had never occurred.

Alfonso was going on. "The guy, I already mentioned, is Karl Kreis."

"The show's manager," I said, proving I did on occasion listen and remember. "The guy you'd like to behead."

"He calls himself The Major. Supposedly 'cause of some great military career. But you could have fooled me. I don't think he could fight his way through the poodle act. I doubt he's ever been on the water. I'd be surprised if the son of a bitch bathes reg'lar."

"I got it. You don't like The Major. But what's he got to do with the lady?"

"To hear him tell it, they're engaged. But that shouldn't ought to be 'cause, they say, long before he was The Major, back in the real circus days, he was already married."

"So? Lots of people marry more than once."

"Hold your horse. I'm gettin' to the so. The so is... There's rumors. Lots of rumors. There's somethin' hinky about that first marriage. He's divorced. He's a widower. She disappeared. Rumors live and breathe in the circus but, when it comes to Alida, I don't like rumors. Where's the first wife? Who is she? Where is she? Why isn't she anymore? Same goes for The Major. Who is he? Where'd he come from? Where'd he get his job? His dough?"

"Does any of that matter?"

"I don't like him. I don't think he's good for Alida."

"Is that it? You want a background check? That's simple enough. But what's Alida to you? Are you her guardian?"

"No, I ain't her guardian."

I studied him. "Oh that." I may have added an unnecessary, and unnecessarily smug, nod of the head. "You're in love with the girl yourself."

"It doesn't matter what I am. I'm a nice guy with a big heart of gold, ain't that enough?" (I hope, sisters and brothers, as you're listening to Alfonso you're still inserting random cuss words and plenty of F-bombs along the way. He certainly was.) "I'll take care of what I am and what is. I want you to find out what was. Will you do it, Blake? I don't know how you find out about people. I wouldn't know where to go; who or what to ask. You do. Find out about this guy."

"What do you know about Alida Harrison? You said she's new. How long's she been here?"

"Just long enough for The Major to get his hooks in."

"Where's she from? Is there any family to look after her interests?"

"I don't know much about her. The Major doesn't let her out among us peons. I was hopin' to get to know her, if you get my drift. But that ain't goin' to happen if she marries The Major."

"All right. I'll check their backgrounds." I stood. "Now... can we get back to my case?"

Alfonso didn't like it. But he couldn't object. I'd listened and promised to look. He nodded his agreement. "Where do you want to start?"

"Left field," I said. "If you know, what does the phrase, 'The canary didn't die when she fell from the sky' mean to you?"

Alfonso stared. He smacked his lips. "Nothin'. Should it?"

"I don't know. I'm asking. The canary didn't die when she fell from the sky."

Alfonso shook his head. "Nope. Not a damn thing."

"Okay. Let's get back to our search for the identity of the drowned man. You named the possibles last night, the old timers here at the circus. Let's start with them."

"Start how?

"We question as many as we can lay hands on at this hour of the morning. We waylay them in the hallways on their way to the showers, the can, or breakfast. We rap them out of their beds. If they can lean against door frames and rub the sand from their eyes, we'll know they aren't dead and the body isn't theirs. We then ask if they saw or know anybody fitting the description of the drowned man. We ask if they saw or heard anything out of the ordinary last night. As we eliminate, we ask when was the last time they saw... whoever we can't find. We find anybody who knows anything. Eventually, through the glamorous work that is detection, we'll identify our drowned man."

"If he came from here," Alfonso said. "If he had anything to do with the circus."

"Don't forget our hard-won piece of evidence," I reminded him. "The fabric from the jacket lining. He came from here."

"I can tell you right off your dead guy ain't The Major," Alfonso said. "I already seen him up and about, so he didn't drown in the harbor. More's the shame. Besides, after I thought about it, it was stupid to even have mentioned him. You saw him last night."

"I did?"

Alfonso nodded. "He doesn't just run the circus. He's the ringmaster."

That was that. "What about the others you mentioned?"

"It ain't Ed or Butch. I heard 'em arguin' on their way out to feed the animals this morning."

"Not dead," I agreed, "either of 'em. And have no fear, they made up. When I passed them, they were laughing and hauling meat to the carnivores."

Alfonso nodded, opened the door, and gave the hall a look. Then he ducked back and quickly and quietly closed the door again with the two of us still in his room. His facial arrangement suggested a whiff of bad cheese.

"What is it?"

"The Major," Alfonso said, "headed upstairs. And the circus owner is with him."

"He rates a visit from the owner at this time of the morning?"

"He rates a shove down the stairs."

"I'm asking why the owner is here this early?"

"Business meetin' I imagine. They've had one or two since she took over."

"She? A woman owns the circus?"

"The better part of it. How the hell would I know why they're meetin'? It could be on a million subjects from aardvarks to zebras or anything in-between. On-hand stock of toilet paper? The nutrition in ostrich feed? The going price for granulated sugar and fresh lemons?"

He had a point.

"Besides," the midget went on. "What's the difference? Neither of them is your drowned guy."

I couldn't argue with that either. But I was nosy by nature. "The Major have a room upstairs?"

"Yeah. But I doubt they're headed for it. Now I think about it, they're probably goin' up to see Alida."

"Why?"

"Why not?" Alfonso asked defensively. "She's their new headliner. She's a rising star and will soon join the elephants as the reason people are comin' to the circus. Why shouldn't the manager introduce her to the owner? Nothin' suspicious about it. No hint they're discussing a recent murder."

I had to admit it didn't look it from my angle either. With no compelling reason to wonder further, my brain let go. We had enough work to do.

"I guess they'll be a while," Alfonso said. "You want to knock on doors or peek in rooms right now, we can. Might as well start on this floor." He checked the hall up and down, found it clear, and led us out. He pointed and, whispering, said, "Selma, from ride tickets, and her worthless old man have the room at the end of the hall. Simon, that's his name! Selma and Simon! Why can't I remember that? Anyway, they're down there. They're in 'cause I heard him go for a pee an hour ago. That good enough or you want to go knock?"

I shook my head. "We can question him later. If he's peeing, he isn't dead."

"S'what I thought." Alfonso took a moment to think. "There's Tim – whoever – the dart game guy..." He turned and started down the hall, pointing. "He's down here on the opposite end. Rooms with Vlad from the shootin' gallery." We listened at the door to Tim and Vlad's room and heard nothing. I tested the knob and found it un-locked. Alfonso stood guard while I stuck my head in. The geezers, as my miniature guide called them, were safe, dry, and softly snoring in their beds.

Alfonso pointed to the stairs in mid-hall. "Pete, the popcorn ball guy, sleeps one floor up. Old Earl, the elephant ears and cotton candy guy, has the room across the hall from him. Mickey, the guy we were talkin' about, the geek, he's downstairs, first floor, across from Sybil, the Bearded Lady." Alfonso swore. (I know you're surprised.) "This is goin' to take all day." He looked at me with pleading eyes. "You said last night Mickey sounded about right. Maybe we should start down there. If Mickey is it, I can get the bad news over with and we can save bothering everybody else."

It sounded like a plan to me. We headed for the first floor and slipped quietly into Michael Gronchi's room. It was empty. The bed showed no signs of having been slept in.

Alfonso was glum. "Does this mean Mickey is your guy?"

"Not necessarily," I said, wandering the room. "But it's another tick in the 'probably' column."

Alfonso hopped onto the bed and sat dejected. Seeing that made me glad we'd waited until morning to do this rather than assaulting the dormitory for witnesses and information the night before. Alfonso was one sad sight. But at least he was wearing jeans and a shirt. The thought of him, depressed and defeated on Mickey's bed, wearing last night's clown costume, a frown beneath his painted smile, and shoes half the size of the rest of him, would have been too much too take. Norman Rockwell would have bawled his brains out.

"Tell me about him."

"Mickey?" the midget asked. "What do you want to know?"

"You said the day of the circus geek was over. So what was he doing here?"

"I hired him." I looked the question. Alfonso nodded and said, "Remember, I told you. The Major hires the talent. I hire the slaves. The slaves aren't people, they don't have names, as far as The Major is concerned. To him they're all 'Hey You'." The midget was thinking and, suddenly, he was smiling. "Mickey was big in the heyday of the circus. But that was a long time ago in a different world. His gig fell out of favor. The ballyhoo of the Sideshow faded. The big circuses got smaller. The small circuses disappeared." The smile faded again. "The way I heard it told, Mickey crawled inside a bottle and disappeared too. No one heard from him. Then a couple of weeks ago, out of the blue, he showed up here. Said he wanted a job."

"In the Sideshow?"

"Nah. He knew better. Any job. He wasn't particular. I told him I had nothin' but undignified slave work and he jumped at it. So I hired him. He swept, picked up trash, shoveled elephant shit, did odd jobs, ran errands. As far as I could see, he mostly drank and stayed out of The Major's sight. I didn't give a damn. Like I said, I came into the circus when a lot of the acts were retirin' or dropping dead. I got a soft spot for old circus performers. To most everybody around here Michael was a burned out drunk but, to me, he'll always be Mickey the Geek."

"Anyone else feel strongly about him?"

"What do you mean?"

"Did he have enemies or, other than you, friends around here? See, Alfonso, when you're murdered, unless you're being robbed, that's who murders you, your enemies or your friends."

"He couldn't have been robbed. Mickey didn't have a pot to piss in. Look around. Doesn't look to me like he took a thing and still he left nothin' behind. As for enemies... He was an old man with a broom and a shovel. I can't imagine him having a real enemy; not someone wanted to kill him."

"What about friends?"

"I was his friend."

"Did you kill him?"

"F— you! No, I didn't kill Mickey the Geek."

"Right, so let's skip you. What about other friends?"

"Real friends?" He shrugged. "Sybil. The Bearded Lady. Sybil knows Mickey as well as anyone. She knew him in the old days; the real days of the circus."

"Where do we find Sybil?"

"Right across the hall." Alfonso led the way. He rapped on her door, waited a beat, rapped again and called out, "Sybil, you decent?" Then, either certain she was, or equally certain no amount of waiting would make her so, the midget reached up, grabbed the knob, and pushed into the room.

Make that... the empty room.

Chapter Nine

Sybil's bed, really two decrepit twin beds jury-rigged into one with C-clamps binding the inside legs, was still made up. Alfonso took the sight in and, with a firm grasp of the obvious, proclaimed, "Don't look like she slept here last night."

"Any chance she got up early, made the bed, then went for a walk down the midway?"

"No chance at all."

"How can you know?"

"Because makin' the bed would constitute exercise. Exercise was against her religion. And walkin' the midway would involve walkin' which let's Sybil out." The midget scanned the room. "Besides who takes everything they own for a walk?"

He had a point. The bureau had been cleaned out, empty as a frat house keg, without anyone having bothered to push the drawers closed.

Empty clothes hangers lay dropped on the floor in haste. The room was without a closet but the tiny alcove meant for hanging apparel was as empty as the drawers. There was no sign of a suitcase and a quick check of the john showed neither tooth-brush nor any tools for taming a money-making beard. The Bearded Lady had taken a run out powder.

"Makes no sense," Alfonso said. He pointed to the bed. "She ought to be right there, watchin' the boob tube and scarfing chocolates." The midget opened the drawer on the bedside lamp table and scanned inside. It was a sign of his desperation. I'd seen a poster of Sybil outside of the Sideshow tent and, at well over three hundred pounds, she couldn't possibly have fit. "She even took the Bible," Alfonso shouted. "Who leaves the towels and steals the Bible?" He slammed the drawer. "She'll need it, and all the prayers she can muster, if she ran out on us. I'll kill her."

"Any idea where she went?"

"Not the least in the world."

"Wherever it was," I said, feeling a little desperation myself. "It looks like she went fast and for good. Any idea why Sybil would take off in the middle of the night?"

Alfonso hesitated, enough that it made me suspicious, then crossed his arms and answered with absolute certainty. "No. I got nothin'."

I didn't believe him. But I could see he'd said all he intended to say. Pushing him, I was sure, would only create an angrier midget. I left that go for the moment. "When did you see Sybil last?"

"Last night," he said. He considered it. "Come to think... That was kind of hinky."

"What?"

"After I left you on the Pier and come up here, Sybil came to my room. She was all nervous and fidgety. I knew something was up 'cause she wouldn't have climbed them stairs for money. She'd seen me with you earlier, after we'd come off the submarine. She wanted to know who you were and what you wanted. I've known Sybil a long time and didn't see the harm, so I told her. Said you were a private dick lookin' for a name to stick on a body."

"What else did you tell her?"

"What else did I know? Nothin'. Besides, I didn't have time. That's when she cut our talk short. Said she had to go."

"Go where?"

"I assumed she meant to bed. But I guess that wasn't it."

"It didn't strike you as weird?"

"It was weird. That's what I said. But it wasn't weird enough to keep me from hitting the sack. Like I said before, everybody's weird around here, so what?"

"Do you think she knew something?"

He cocked his head at me. "Everybody knows somethin', don't they Blake?"

"Not in my experience," I told him. "I know plenty of people don't know a thing."

We started for the door but, before we made our exit, Alfonso stopped and studied the empty room shaking his head. "How're we goin' to replace that fat bitch?"

We stepped from Sybil's room. That was it, one step, then Alfonso grabbed the side of my shirt and tugged me back in the doorway. "Shit!" he said in a whisper. "We're nabbed."

He jerked his head to the stairs and, in specific, to a man and woman talking as they descended. He was right, we were caught. The man was heavy-set, middle-aged, mean-looking, and German-sounding. I recognized him as the ringmaster and knew that made him The Major. The woman, therefore, had to be the circus owner. She was lovely and moved like a cat – and I couldn't believe my eyes. I recognized her as well. I'd not only seen her before, but had touched her. One of the more memorable, if painful, moments in my life.

Just like that, sisters and brothers, I'd found a connection. A connection to what exactly, I had no idea, but an undeniable connection. The circus owner descending the stairs was the lovely daughter-in-law from Master Criswell's lunatic séance (to which Lisa had dragged me). The woman whose warm hand had sent me tumbling into cold water. She'd seemed familiar that night but I'd been unable to come up with a name. Now, surrounded by her circus, her name and situation flooded back to me.

Private dicks, being the bad men they were, doing the filthy job they did, needed all the information they could get. That meant they read newspapers. I'd read a few myself. The cougar on the stairs had made an appearance or two in the daily rags, usually in the Society section. But about six months ago, May, if I had to guess, she'd crashed onto the Front page. Actually, her husband had done the crashing. She was Danita Callicoat. Her multimillionaire hubby, Reginald Callicoat III, had gone out in a blaze of glory – with 297 other passengers and crew – in the deadliest air disaster in the history of American aviation. He'd done it before a home town crowd at Chicago's own O'Hare International Airport.

If I remembered correctly, Mrs. Callicoat had been safe at home at the time. Good on her, as the airliner's take-off had gone pear-shaped and, in under a minute, the plane returned unexpectedly and violently to earth. The crash, in an open field at the end of the runway (by a trailer park in the next-door suburb), left no survivors and even killed two on the ground.

The death of a spouse couldn't have been any fun. But facts are facts and, when the grieving ended, there was a bright spot for Mrs. Callicoat. She came out of the affair with bundles and, if she wasn't now Chicago's richest widow, she was certainly a member of the club. Maybe that's why she'd joined her former mother-in-law at the séance; to cross over and thank Reggie for the loot. Now here she was. It appeared that, along with dozens of other businesses, factories, warehouses, and apartments, the Widow Callicoat was now the majority owner of the Callicoat and Major Combined Circus.

The drowned man, if he was Mickey the Geek, and that looked more and more the case, was Danita Callicoat's employee. Without meaning to she'd shown me his murder. Without meaning to she'd led me to her circus. But what had it to do with her? And what had it to do with me? How could the fates have known Lisa was going to stick in her thumb and pull out a corpse? Questions. I had nothing but questions. But would I get the chance to ask them?

The pair descending the stairs had reached the first floor. Mrs. Callicoat was staring at The Major because her circus manager was staring at us. "Alfonso!" The Major, forgetting the owner, barged our direction. "Who is that?"

"His name is Blake," the midget said. "He's a... freelance writer. Doing a story on me for 'Little Folks' Magazine." I had to admit, for a lie cooked up on the spot, it wasn't bad.

Whether or not The Major was buying it, I wasn't sure. He ogled Alfonso like he was a piece of rotted meat. But that may have been the way he always looked at him. "A story on you? Who wants to read about you?"

Alfonso beamed. "Little folks. That's why 'Little Folks' Magazine is asking."

The Major's sneer remained unreadable and I remained unsure he was buying it. To sweeten the pot, I pulled out a card case, without showing the holster under my jacket, passed by my detective's ID and driver's license, dug into a clutch of calling cards – each bearing a different name and claiming I was a plumber, an electrician, a broker, a real estate agent, a green grocer, an employee of the

Illinois State Lottery, and others – and selected one that insisted I was a Freelance Writer. I handed it to The Major.

"Blake?" he asked, more convinced, but not any more impressed. "Just Blake?"

"Professionally, yes."

"No first name?"

"Not that I confess to in public."

He turned to look down at (and on) Alfonso. "What's a story about you got to do with Sybil?"

He hadn't missed our coming out of the Bearded Lady's room.

"Blake wants to talk to the people I work with. I suggested Sybil since our booths are next door to each other in the show. But she ain't here."

"She's... probably rehearsing," The Major said without conviction. Then he repeated the insult. "Who wants to read about you?"

"I think it's marvelous," Mrs. Callicoat said step-ping up. She glowed in Alfonso's direction. Then she turned staring at me at least as hard as I had earlier stared at her. "Publicity is always welcome. As long as the investigative reporting isn't too hard-hitting. We are, after all, a fun family entertainment." The comment had me wondering. But she said it with a smile and no indication she knew who I was or that she recognized me from my humiliating performance in the medium's salon.

Changing the subject, Mrs. Callicoat told The Major, "I'd like to see those invoices" and, without waiting for an answer, disappeared into a room on the other side of the first floor stairs.

The Major ignored Alfonso to lock his mean eyes on me. "Do I know you from somewhere?"

I shook my head. "We've never met."

He nodded. "Do your story on the dwarf. But don't get in the way." He turned on Alfonso. "The minute he's in the way, he's out on his ear. Understand?"

"Absolutely," I replied. He hadn't been talking to me, but he'd been talking about me which made it more imperative I butt in. I could've added that I was used to landing on my ear. I did add an offer for him. "Perhaps you and I might get a chance to talk, Major? Maybe there's a feature article in you, eh for a different publication, of course."

The manager sneered. "That will not happen. I have work to do. I do not like people in the way.

I do not like people in my business." He started away, then turned back. "The others have their work also. Talk to them in the car park when they are finished. Alfonso has work now."

I took the hint and headed for the front door. Behind me, The Major told Alfonso, "Get Alida's breakfast. Take it to her."

I heard Alfonso shuffle away. I heard The Major shout after him, "Knock! Then leave it by her door. You hear me!"

Outside sat a white Dodge Tradesman van wildly splashed with the name and colors of the circus, parked against the grain, before the dorm entrance. Behind it, as out of place for its classiness as the other was for its garishness, sat a new shiny black Cadillac Fleetwood Limousine.

Waiting with the limo, leaning heavily against the rear passenger's door was a character right out of fiction. Which fiction I couldn't quite decide; perhaps he'd stepped from The Great Gatsby or, just as likely, the Arthurian legend. Like the evil knight of old, this guy was decked in solid black; knee high riding boots, jodhpurs, uniform jacket (fronted by a gauntlet of silver buttons), and driving cap. He even wore embossed Gucci leather gloves that, by themselves, had to have set somebody back a couple of C's. He was the most crisp, clean, and serious looking chauffeur I'd ever laid eyes on. I didn't like him on sight. Nobody with a service job that cushy, wallowing in that level of luxury, had any business looking as above it all and as ridiculously bored as he did.

I was thinking of a question to ask him when Mrs. Callicoat exited the dormitory alone. The chauffeur ushered her into the limo with too big a smile. He gave me a fleeting glance, with too big a scowl, then climbed behind the wheel. He drove his lovely employer away.

I watched them go. Then my mind started doing pushups. Questions. Questions. Minutes later, I don't know how many, my calisthenics were interrupted by a familiar gravelly voice. "Blake! Hey, Blake, you deaf? I been standing here talkin' to you."

I followed the voice down to Alfonso beside me. "I'm sorry. I had something on my mind."

"What'd you think of The Major?"

"It wasn't him on my mind. I told you, Alfonso, I'll look into The Major and your acrobat when I've got a handle on the drowned man."

"God, you're a one-way prick."

"My mind is on Mickey and the circus. And, until I find out why she ran, on the elusive Sybil. I need to find the Bearded Lady. I need to be sure our corpse is Mickey the Geek. And, if it is, I need to find out why somebody wanted him turned off."

"Why do you think I came out here?" Alfonso asked. "Because it dawned on me, assuming you're right and Sybil boogied for reasons other than she was fed up like all of us, then I think I know where she went."

Chapter Ten

My plans changed in an instant. Instead of going on a dull document search, digging into the lives and loves of a good many of the fun souls I'd met that morning, I went to the circus. Meaning, I stayed for the noon performance of the circus already at the center of my universe. I needed Alfonso's idea concerning Sybil's whereabouts. He wouldn't cough it up until I promised he could go with me in search of the Bearded Lady. He couldn't go until, you guessed it, after the noon show.

You've been to a circus. There's little to be gained from a moment by moment description of this one. Ballyhoo was the word. And music, laughter, thrills, and lots of noise. Oh, and clowns, all sorts of clowns, girl, boy, tall, fat, crazy, and crying clowns. And, let us not forget Binky, the shortest clown with the foulest mouth this side of the Ringling Clown College. Clowns running randomly in from entrances on all side of the bleachers, or piling out of a little car, or racing through the crowd, throwing confetti, spritzing water, shouting and causing hilarious havoc. The Major, as the ringmaster, played straight man and chased them off. Then, to trumpets and drums, he brought the acts on in their turn, the jugglers, the dancers, the trick riders, the human cannon ball. With animal acts interspersed throughout, the orangutans, looking like a troupe of hairy orange Frank Wenders as they danced, pulled their lips over their own heads, and made lewd gestures. A pack of poodles yipping and chasing their own tails that reminded me of Wenders' mutt, Dave Mason. Horses, camels, ostriches, and the huge but graceful elephants that put me in mind of my friend and snitch, Large.

Finally came the dangerous, the heart-stopping, the death defying.

Cedric, the courageous tamer, entered his cage with whip, and chair, and pistol commanding the lions and tigers to do his bidding. The act had me, if only for a moment, thinking again of the sleek feline circus owner. (Could a cat really be tamed?) The performer escaped the cage triumphant and alive. That's more than most of us accomplish.

Trumpets sounded and kettle drums beat a march as the lights came up on Tommy Dagger and Sandra. With her usual grace and his indomitable bravura, they moved effortlessly through their preliminary routine, ruining cigarettes with whips and axes. Then The Major reentered, mic in hand, and asked silence of the audience. The knife thrower's covered prop was rolled into the ring and, to a threatening fanfare, the stage hands revealed the giant wheel I'd seen earlier that morning.

"The Wheel of Death," the ringmaster intoned.

Tommy led Sandra onto the platform. This time she went willingly. He turned her over to the huskies, then prepared his knives, while they strapped her – spread-eagled – to the wheel.

"This, ladies and gentlemen, is one of the most dangerous feats under the Big Top," The Major warned. "But that is not danger enough for Tommy Dagger or the fearless Sandra."

The trumpets blared. The drums pounded. The stage hands hustled back on carrying a large paper screen which they maneuvered to center and stood on the sawdust near Tommy. "In a performance," The Major went on, "attempted only three times before in all of circus history…" Tommy readied himself, squaring off, steadying his nerves, gauging the range to Sandra and the wheel. A snare drum rolled. The wheel began to spin and the immobile and helpless Sandra began doing cart-wheels in place. The crowd gasped, *oohed* and *aahed*. Kettle drums replaced the snares as tensions in the massive circus tent began to rise. Cued into action, the stage hands moved the screen into place between the knife thrower and the spinning wheel, completely blocking Tommy's view of Sandra.

"The Callicoat and Major Combined Circus," The Major boomed, "is proud to present Tommy Dagger, Sandra, and The Veiled Wheel of Death."

Like the paying crowd, I watched breathlessly (and unmoving) as Tommy did his thing. Executing rapid, consistent, and carefully timed throws, he hurled seven knives through the blinding paper veil and into the wheel alarmingly close to – but never touching – the courageous Sandra. Thomas Lacrosse may have been a mad man but Tommy Dagger was one hell of a performer. All I can say about Sandra (or Anita, whichever you prefer) was that I'd never seen so gorgeous a woman with a bigger set of balls. Based on the applause, the crowd agreed.

Then came the ringmaster again. As he introduced Alida there was something more in his voice than vigor and showmanship. Personal pride and braggadocio welled as he announced "The pièce de résistance" and directed all eyes to the peak of the Big Top. The aerial performer may have been the girl of Alfonso's dreams, but she was more than a dream to The Major. It was a relief, bound by circumstances, to see her act in full without having to battle urges, feel guilty, or cut out early.

Alida made her stunning entrance as before, dropping from the sky on a rope made of fabric, undulating free, and alighting on a pedestal before her audience. This pedestal featured only one post, upon which, in a glistening purple leotard, the pixie did a handstand and – upside down – rotated before the crowd as the post slowly turned. She gracefully dismounted, plucked the post from the pedestal, and tossed it away, then did seven back flips in place atop the empty podium. I was dizzy.

She stepped backwards to where a ring, three feet in diameter, attached to a slack cable, lay on the platform. She took the cable in one hand and the ring in the other. As she touched it, the ring lit from within and glowed white in her hand. She spun in a circle. She released the ring, but held her grip on the cable, and continued spinning. The glowing ring circled her, faster and faster, to the delight of the crowd. The cable grew taught in her hand, lifted, and carried Alida spinning into the air. Thirty feet up the lithe acrobat came to a stop and floated as the ring orbited her like a glowing moon.

Alida hooked the cable with one leg. She hooked the ring with the other. She spun above the crowd, her glistening purple leotard, her glitter, and the lighted ring becoming one blurred arc of beauty as she picked up speed. She released the cable, taking the ring with both hands, shifting the orbit of the whole, and was suddenly spinning in the center of the ring.

She let lose, dropped, and fell across the ring at her stomach, spinning, but now dangling on either side. She took a slender ankle in each hand and became a blur of purple and light again. The audience went wild with applause. She came out of the spin and righted herself as the ring dropped. She was good, very good in the heights of the Big Top, and as good and easy on the eyes once she'd touched safely back down on her platform.

I had yet to meet or speak with Alida. I wanted to for a number of reason and hoped to after the show. But it was not to be. Immediately after the final gala parade, as the boisterous crowd made its collective exit, the tent flooded with carnies, animal handlers, and maintenance crew, returning everything to its starting place for the night show. In the organized turmoil, the performers vanished. There was no time to speak with Alida or anybody else.

Alfonso, stripped of his red nose and floppy shoes, his face cleansed of grease paint, back in his civvies, was suddenly at my side and raring to go. He had a lead, or at least a guess, on the destination of the lamming Bearded Lady and, finally, he laid it out.

I had to hand it to him, it sounded like the trail to follow. I certainly had no better suggestion. But it meant leaving the city. And gave us a thin window through which to follow it. The midget was needed back in Chicago for the evening performance.

We hit the road but, on the way out of town, I stopped at my office first. I had to. I needed to know Willie had not burned the place down or stolen me blind. I needed to know how Lisa was doing. I needed to see how the repairs were coming. We didn't have the time but I took it all the same.

As we entered the lot I saw the glass remained broken out of my front door. But there was no reason to panic. I also saw the vestibule had been swept and the door frame prepped for a replacement. On the opposite end of the building, the window in my office had been replaced and gleamed like a lake in the summer sun. The glass crew were in the waiting room easing the pane for the picture window into its new home. They secured it and I had a word with the foreman who promise they'd be done and dusted by mid-afternoon. Score one for the good guys!

Lisa was not there. That made me happy and disappointed me. We'd argued about it and I had insisted she stay home, rest, and recover. And I'd meant it. But I would also have been secretly de-lighted had she come in. I have difficulty finding my hind end without her. I would like to have told her where Alfonso and I were headed, just so she knew.

Willie was still there, looking sad and pathetic, hugging the sling supporting his arm and shot shoulder. That made me happy and disappointed me. I appreciated his coming to my aide, said so, and meant it. But I wasn't overjoyed to have needed him in the first place and secretly held it against him. What? I can't be complex?

"We'd better get on the road, Blake," Alfonso said. (That's the redacted version, he cussed three times getting that sentence out. It was a perfect introduction for Willie.)

"I want to give my secretary a call at home first," I told him. "See how she's feeling."

"She ain't home," Willie said.

"How do you know?"

"She came in. Then she said she had things to do."

"What things?"

"She didn't say."

"Was she all right?"

"She looked aw-right to me," Willie said. Then he grinned like an ape. "Then, Lisa always looks aw-right to me. Ya know, Blake, if she really wanted to help a guy out–" I slapped his shoulder. Yes, the one in the sling. He jerked, howling like a mutt, and accidentally smacked his own chin.

"Does your mom let you eat with that dirty mouth?" I asked.

"What?" he cried, cradling his arm, dabbing his shoulder, cradling the arm again. "I was only say-ing! Ya sweet on your sec-r-tary or something?"

"That was a slap," I warned him. "Next time I punch you on the bullet wound."

"Aw-right, aw-right!"

"Now get back to Lisa; and keep it clean."

"She looked fine to me." Willie raised his good arm in defense. "She looked… healthy. What word won't get me punched? All I'm saying is, if she was sick or hurt, it didn't show."

"Where did she go?"

"I don't know. She didn't say. She didn't say what she was going to do. Said she had things to do and asked if I'd mind staying and keeping an eye. I told her I already told ya I'd stay. Then I told her I'd stay. So I stayed."

"Good. Thank you. Continue to stay. Continue to not have your friends here. Continue to not put your feet on my desk."

"Okay, Blake, okay. But how about a little something for the effort?" Willie pinched, then rubbed, the fingers of his good hand. "I'm starving."

I patted myself down… to no joy. I looked to Alfonso. He swore at me, without saying a word, then shook his head.

"We're destitute," I told Willie. "I haven't been to the bank yet." I pointed at Lisa's desk. "Try the lower drawers on either side. Lisa stocks more food than the Piggly Wiggly."

Alfonso and I beat it out of there.

Chapter Eleven

Our destination, to hear Alfonso tell it, was just over two hours from Chicago.

Just.

One hundred and ninety minutes in a two-seat Jaguar with a grumbling, cigar smoking, bad tempered midget incessantly changing radio stations was, I'm telling you, not "just" anything but a slice of hell. I took I-90 west toward Rockford with Cheap Trick covering *Ain't That a Shame*. But before Robin Zander got a chance to tell me why... *click*. Crossed the state border into Wisconsin while the Blues Brothers bounced a *Rubber Biscuit*. Before it landed... *click*. Continued north for the famous Wisconsin Dells resorts with Billy Joel griping about a *Big Shot*. His tale was half told when... *click*. Near the Dells, I took the WI-33 exit while Rickie Lee Jones strained to *Chuck E's*

In Love... click. At Barrelton, I turned onto Washington Avenue with The Knack's drummer trying to get *My Sharona* started... *click.* Each time I demanded he pick a station and leave it, Alfonso swore at me. At last I turned onto Water Street and, as the World Circus Museum rose before us, Rod Stewart whined *Da Ya Think I'm Sexy* in my ears. That's no way to travel.

But we'd reached the hunting grounds. The World Circus Museum, in Barrelton, Wisconsin, the National Historic Landmark and original home and winter quarters of the famous Parker Brothers' Circus (not the game board family, the circus clan). That was Alfonso's brilliant intuitive guess and our destination in the search for Sybil.

At the turn of the 20th century, three of the world's largest circuses, one originating there (the others, from European old countries, adopting it), made Barrelton their home and returned there following each tour to repaint and repair equipment. The shows spent the cold winter months sewing wardrobe, building props, auditioning new acts, rehiring returning performers, and planning the itinerary and travel routes for the up-coming season. They also cared for their animals, hundreds of horses and ponies, dozens of elephants, camels and other hay eating creatures, tigers, lions, birds (including ostrich), and monkeys. Of the original twenty-five Parker Brothers' structures, ten winter quarters buildings still remained while the entire facility had been made into a museum and theme park. This was home to the old-time circus folks and to performers like Sybil.

The Main Entrance, off Water Street, crowned by a sign reading: 'The Grandest Show on Earth', took us into the museum's largest building. Adult tickets were ten bucks, kids got in for half. I'd stopped for folding money en route and, as I was paying for both and my humor needed stretching, I suggested we pass Alfonso off as a child. The notion was received with the same attention-grabbing diction you've come to expect from my miniature companion. The midget's ticket cost me ten bucks too.

The Grandest Show Hall housed exhibits on all aspects of circuses from around the world, circus history and, in particular, the history of the Parker Brothers' show. But we weren't there to see that. I had a case to follow and Alfonso had a friend and co-worker to find. He knew the place and I did not. Without needing to be asked, the midget led the way on a bee line through the crowd and the building, past the costumes, the banners and flags, the props, past the pics of the Parker Brothers, and the Stronk and Witte Combined, past the John Whipple Circus, and on out the northeast exit into the park. Despite my having legs three times longer than his, I had to run to catch up.

Beyond the door, running the length of Water Street, was the historic Parkerville portion of the park. To our left was the Wisconsin River, bisecting the grounds and, on the far side of the river, the kids' playground, Sideshow, and the Hippodrome. Yes, they had a permanent full-sized Big Top tent where the museum staged a full-fledged circus every day.

A sizable crowd stood gathered on either side of the river. Above their heads, balanced on a wire stretched from one bank to the other, a Tightrope walker slowly made his way across. With a childish glee, I pointed him out. Alfonso followed my stare without enthusiasm. "That's Tight 'wire' walker," he said, correcting me. "But he isn't a Tightwire walker. He's over twenty feet above the water, so he's a Highwire walker."

I couldn't argue. But I didn't care either. The guy was far enough out and high enough up that, as far as I was concerned, he could call himself anything he wanted. He wore leather slippers, carried a long sagging balance pole (rotating it to check his sway), and looked the part to me. The crowd agreed.

"He's good," I said.

"Yeah," Alfonso allowed with a shrug. "But he's no Karl Wallenda."

"Right," I conceded. I wasn't an expert but knew the name from the papers. One of the most famous wirewalkers, from the most famous circus family, of all time. The founder of the Flying Wallendas, aged 73, had fallen ten-stories to his death the previous year while trying to cross between the towers of the Condado Plaza Hotel in San Juan, Puerto Rico. "He's no Karl Wallenda. But neither is Karl Wallenda anymore."

Alfonso ignored me, snipped a new cigar with his fancy cutter, and lit it. "I'm surprised they're still putting on the full show. It's getting late in the season."

"August is late?" I asked. Alfonso nodded and puffed.

The wirewalker teetered, drew a gasp from the on-lookers, recovered his balance, and continued across. "You ought to add something like that to your act," I told the midget.

He swore, of course, then added, "I couldn't do that high balancing crap. Even if I could, my act's too tame. People like imminent danger. That ain't me." Alfonso smiled. "I'm Frankie Avalon. I can't work without a net." I gave that the groan it deserved. "That's a joke," Alfonso said. "That's funny shit."

I waved for the midget to shut up. By then, the wire walker had arrived safely and was waving from the far side of the river. "Yippee," Alfonso said. "He made it. Big surprise. Can we go now?"

"Absolutely. Let's find Sybil."

"It would be better if we split up," Alfonso said. "Cut the place in half to look. Be faster."

"How faster? Wouldn't she be at the... Whatever they call it; the Sideshow."

"She might. If they put her to work. Then again, she might not. Be faster if we look and not waste time guessing."

"I wouldn't know where to start."

"You start here in Parkerville," Alfonso ordered, indicating the row of old buildings before us. Then he pointed over the bridge. "I'll cross over and take the circus."

"But I've never seen Sybil."

"What, are you kidding me?" The runt stood, arms akimbo, staring like I was an idiot. "How you gonna miss a three-hundred-pound lady with a full black beard?"

He had a point.

I was being ridiculous, I knew. I was a grown detective, wearing my own long pants, and didn't need a chaperon. But I felt as out of place as a whore in church. And, I admit, I didn't fully trust Alfonso. I didn't know him. I didn't know anything. He may have been Mickey's killer for all I knew. He was so insistent on coming to Wisconsin with me and so adamant about our splitting up, it struck me wrong. It might have been my paranoia, God knew I had plenty. Then again it might not.

It didn't matter. Alfonso was on his way.

Not only was I suspicious but my inner child wanted to kick up a fuss. Alfonso had taken the circus on the far side of the river, and all the fun, for himself; the play area with swings and slides, blown up bounce houses, a carousel, and something called the Double Wheel of Destiny I could only wonder at. East of the playground, he'd have the Circus Wagon Restoration Center (featuring, I'd learn later, a gargantuan handmade miniature circus) where, obviously, tourists were entertained by seeing old circus wagons refurbished. Beside it, the Wagon Pavilion housed a collection of two hundred antique wagons from circuses and carnivals around the world. On the opposite end, to the west, were rail trains on truncated tracks (the object of which I didn't quite see), the penned live animal rides, the caged wild animals, and the Sideshow tents leading to the Hippodrome. I was jealous watching Alfonso cross the bridge. But I wasn't there to play and neither was he. We'd come to find Sybil.

He'd given me this side of the river, the Hall through which we'd entered and Parkerville, the original winter grounds buildings. I started my search at the Office. Not in it, at it. A sign on the door promised someone would return soon. I re-started my search at something called the Ring Barn and, from there, hit each of the old buildings in succession, the Elephant House, Animal House, Baggage Horse Barn, and the Wardrobe Depart-ment looking for, and asking all I met if they'd seen, the Bearded Lady. I got a fascinating glimpse behind the scenes of a circus. Beyond that, I was chasing a wild goose.

We were looking for Sybil in connection with the murder of Mickey the Geek. Not as a suspect, merely to ask what (if anything) she might know about it. We had no clue as to the killer or the mo-tive. We had no sense of a sinister conspiracy. At no time did it occur to me we were wading into deep dark waters. It never dawned our questions would be of interest to anyone but us. Or that those ques-tions might spook someone to kill again.

I made the rounds, without progress and with-out a return of the office staff, and was more than ready to abandon Parkerville for the circus side of the museum. But, as there were so many bodies in motion, before crossing the bridge, I thought I'd better give the Hall a second quick look.

I wandered into a vast room of old circus posters. At nearly 10,000, the world's largest collection, if the wall placard was on the level, from circuses large and small; Ringling Bros and Barnum & Bailey, Clyde Beatty, Gentry Bros, Circus Clemons, Kelly Miller 3 Ring, Snyder Bros, Russell Bros, Cirque Pinder, the Funfair, the Carnival, the Burlesque Circus, the Wild West Circus, the Grand Water Circus.

And, apart from those, a separate collection of posters highlighting headlining acts; trained wild animals, African lions, Bengal tigers, camels, the world's largest hippo, the world's smallest horse, and dog acts galore. All you could conjure from Poodles to Great Danes. Posters of trained exotic and trick animal acts, the Flying Pig, 'Big Bingo' the giant two-story elephant (The Biggest Brute that Breathes), 'Gargantua the Great' the Largest Gorilla Ever Exhibited. Banners of people billed as animals, Ferry – the Human Frog, Dezano – the Man Serpent! Over there was a poster of the Dog-Faced Boy and, over there, a flier for the Dog-Faced Man (no relation). There, in all her inky glory, hung the Amazing Tattooed Lady and, there, from the other side of the world, her male counterpart, L'Homme Tatoué. Here was May Wirth, the 'Greatest Bare-Back Rider that Ever Lived', and there Mister Misten Jr., the Child Wonder of the World. Mistic Skidmore Master Magician, Ethardo the French plate spinner, Deadeye Danny 'Greatest Trick Shot Artist of Them All' headlining the bill over The Great Rudolpho (with no hint what it was Rudolpho was Great at), and every imaginable entertainment in-between from the towering Amazing Amazon Woman ('Every Man's Worst Nightmare') to the oddly benign-looking Kilpatrick, the trick bicycle rider.

On another wall hung the posters dedicated to the artists of the air. The history of aerial acrobats in splashes of once brilliant, now faded, yellows, reds, greens, and blues. The Great Wallendas, Princess Victoria the 'Fantastic Wire Dancer', M'lle Beeson the 'Marvelous High Wire Venus', Gaspary the Equilibriste, described in a smaller font as 'The Only Aerial Gun'. (I wasn't certain what that meant but, with my attitude toward guns, I have to admit, it didn't appeal.) The posters went on. There hung Emma Jutau, a French damsel suspended from the rafters by her teeth. There The Flying Dillons. There Miss Antoinette and the Flying Concellos. And there… I caught my breath.

Taken by surprise, I moved closer to soak in the details. I was amazed to have found it and more amazed at what it was, or at least what it might have been. A poster from the Kessler Traveling Circus featuring what promised to be 'Elegance in the Air' performed by an aerial acrobat called – The Canary. The final words of Mickey the Geek, as delivered to my excited secretary, rang in my ears: "The Canary didn't die when she fell from the sky." There she was. But could she be? Was this canary, The Canary?

I turned to consider the find. But, before I had a chance, found more to contemplate. For not far from The Canary poster, hung a black and white photograph every bit as surprising and interesting: a group picture taken at center ring, beneath a circus Big Top, of a band of smiling performers. There, in the front row, stood our drowned man, Michael Gronchi, identified in the small type beneath as

'Mickey the Geek' and, beside him, a planet-sized lady in a light-colored moo moo sporting a bushy black beard. Though she may have been any Bearded Lady among all the Bearded Ladies of time, I couldn't help but believe this was Sybil in her younger days. Mickey and Sybil together. I was so glad to have stumbled upon the image that, without thinking, I reached out and touched it.

Thor's hammer hit my head. Heat. Pain. Then the circus disappeared and I found myself in a distorted nursery rhyme. I saw Little Miss Muffet sitting on her tuffet eating her curds and whey. Or did I? How would I know? I had no idea what a tuffet was. The lady I saw might have been anyone in the world except a Little Miss. She was huge. Humpty Dumpty? Mrs. Humpty Dumpty? Even that was wrong. She wasn't the nursery rhyme's egg-headed headliner or his wife, but something akin. I saw her from the rear, her dress a bulging tea cozy over a gigantic body, sitting on an ottoman. She turned, grabbed up a massive bowl of porridge, scooped a tablespoon full, and stuffed it – beneath her thick mustache, above her trimmed beard – into her gaping mouth. It was Sybil from the photo, the Bearded Lady. I'd been thunder-struck and was in another vision.

My first impression, the nursery rhyme thing, had been in error. I was still at the museum, or a circus at least, as I could hear calliope music distantly playing. I was in a dressing room; I could see bare light bulbs encircling a mirror over a makeup table. Sybil sat, eating, gesturing between bites, frantically telling a story (with her mouth full) to someone I couldn't see. Then she squawked in pain and tossed her porridge into the air. Suddenly a knife was buried in her back. It had been thrown so quickly I missed seeing its flight. But Sybil felt it. She leaped up and immediately went down.

Flashes went off behind my eyes and my perspective changed. I was in the same room but, now, on my knees on the floor. My right hand was hot and wet (and probably delicious). It had landed in the spilled porridge. That wasn't a problem, merely an annoyance. The problem was behind me. Through the magic of my psychic (or psychotic) head, I had taken Sybil's place and the thrown knife was now buried in my back. I could feel every cold inch of the keen blade. That was only the beginning of my new nightmare. From there, I was off to see the wizard.

Someone took me by the throat from behind. Strong hands, choking me. I fell on my face on tacky linoleum which, in itself, was hard to comprehend. I'd been standing on concrete in the circus museum gallery. I hadn't taken a step. But then... I was no longer me.

I fell, gasping for breath, sucking up dirt from the floor. My back burned with pain, my throat was on fire, and it was all I could do to take in air. Something rolled past my face. One, two, three... four little pearls glinting in the amber light as they raced across the floor. My body jerked and I yelled as the knife blade was yanked from my back. I felt myself being rolled.

I saw something odd beneath Sybil's bed. I couldn't make it out and had no time to try. My murderer was moving again. A lamp with a butt ugly shade, on a table above me, had turned him into a shadow. A film noir killer who hated Sybil's guts. He came with the knife again, stabbing my chest. I felt the blade glance hard off my sternum and sink home. Incredible pain. My breathing went to hell as my lung was pierced. The knife was pulled free but the attack continued.

Now... even more targeted. The blade sank into my crotch. Yes, stare wide-eyed, sisters. Cringe, brothers. I swear I (and by that I mean Sybil) was being stabbed in the groin. Right in the package. But Sybil shouldn't have had a package. Yet I'll say it again; viciously stabbed in the meat and two veg over and over again.... More loose pearls, soaked now in blood, rolled past me. Tears filled my eyes and blinded me.

I came to on the cold concrete floor of the museum poster gallery. Alfonso stood over me, tugging on my arm, trying to rouse me, in a panic. "Blake! Blake! Wake up! Come out of it, fer Chrissake!"

"I'm awake."

"Blake, get up. Get up, boy!"

"I'm awake. Stop jerking my arm. It isn't a pump handle."

"We got to go. We got to get the hell out of here!"

Apparently seeing my gyrations had scared the living crap out of Alfonso. He was as ghost white as I imagined a man of color could become. Still.

"We're not going anywhere," I told him. "We've got to find Sybil. Something bad has happened to Sybil."

"You aren't just shitting."

"What? Why?" Maybe my flopping around like a landed fish hadn't been what scared him. The midget was terrified, but he'd arrived that way. "What's happened? What do you know?"

"I don't know anything. We have to go."

"Where's Sybil? Alfonso, where's Sybil? I'm afraid she's been hurt."

"Hurt hell!" Alfonso realized he was shouting and stopped. He looked around, scanning the gallery like a lookout expecting the enemy. He whispered, "She's dead." He helped me to my feet and started for the main entrance. I grabbed him and spun him around.

"Sybil?"

"Dead," Alfonso insisted. "I was talkin' to her. Then she had no more to say. Let's get out of here!"

I refused, of course, insisting on Sybil's whereabouts. We'll skip the swearing and arguing that followed. What mattered was I forced it from him. The Bearded Lady was across the river, on the circus side of the museum. Under further duress I forced him to lead me to her.

We crossed the bridge and veered left, west, past the animal rides. We passed the Sideshow tents and their promised wonders, the 'Fantastic Feats and Live Physical Oddities' of the Armless Wonder, The Rubber Girl, Dynamo Dan the Electric Man, The Wolf Boy, The Fire Breather, The Strong Man and, you betcha', the Bearded Lady. Alfonso hurried on by and I followed.

Had we continued down the paved midway we'd have come to the Big Top. Instead, we left the path behind the Sideshow tents and headed for another short section of rail track, supporting a row of old coachman cars. These were, I was about to discover, the Sideshow dressing rooms. The midget led me to the last of these and wasn't happy doing it. "She's in there."

I climbed the three steps and opened the door. What I saw was both stunning and, I'm sure you'll understand, no surprise at all. Sybil, the Bearded Lady, lay like a bizarre island, one huge mountain surrounded by a sea of blood (and spilled porridge and scattered pearls). Even Lisa would have had trouble labeling the scene romantic.

Despite the fact I'd seen it, felt it, in my waking nightmare, despite the fact I saw her now, freshly stabbed and newly dead, still the idiotic question escaped my mouth. "What happened here?"

I didn't see, or know it at the time, but behind me Alfonso was shaking his head, trying to decide what to do next. Decided, he turned and beat feet, running away as fast as his small bow legs would carry him. All I knew was, when I turned to question the midget, the doorway was empty and Alfonso gone. To where I hadn't a clue.

My mind turned to other things. I considered grabbing a couple of the pearls off the floor. I had a habit of swiping little pieces of evidence (in violation of the law) for my own investigative purposes and possible comparisons later should they come up. I decided at the last instant not to bother. Pearls were pearls were pearls, weren't they? And I was too far from home to be caught with the valuable property of a murder victim on my person.

It ended up being a good decision. But I'd taken too long in making it. Because, just then, someone hit me on the back of the head. Everything went black.

Chapter Twelve

There I was again, sisters and brothers, in a bleak and barren interview room – being stared at by, not a bored city bull but, for a change of pace, a bored county sheriff's deputy – in the sleepy community of Barrelton, Wisconsin. Well, sleepy until now. The stabbing, strangulation, and bloody mutilation of Sybil had awakened it. At least that part of it that represented the law. A full bottle of aspirin stood in the middle of the otherwise empty table – untouched. I would have loved to imbibe but, being allergic to most pain killers, couldn't. I sat holding a bag of ice on my splitting (and nearly split) head waiting to die, hoping to go to heaven, while a humorless sheriff somewhere in the building prepared for his return and another round of questioning designed to drag me through hell.

No more had I thought the thought when the door came open and Clayton Cobb rejoined us. If you're picturing a sheriff from an old western, cheeks stuffed with chewing tobacco, cowboy hat tipped back on his head, one pant leg riding inside a boot, forget it. If you're thinking of a good ole' boy, a hick from the sticks, with a gut like chewed bubble gum hanging over an outsized belt buckle, forget that too. Clayton Cobb looked like nothing so much as an investment banker or perhaps a high school principal. In his mid-fifties, with a full head of neatly coiffed white hair, a wide mouth that, you imagined, could smile pleasantly but didn't, and a pair of pale blue eyes that caught you off guard with their ability to go from Mother Teresa to junkyard dog without blinking. Instead of the traditional accoutrement, he wore an inexpensively cut medium brown suit. The only thing about his dress that suggested he was who he claimed to be was a small gold star pinned to his left lapel.

The sheriff closed the door. He nodded at his underling. He placed a stack of file folders on his side of the table and retook his chair across from me.

He started again, demanding answers to the same questions he'd already repeatedly asked about the murder of the Bearded Lady. Pausing for the waves of pain in my bruised head, the ringing in my ears, and for the occasional breath, I answered in the only way I could; the sum total amounting to... "I know nothing about Sybil's murder."

Speaking of murder, I could have killed Alfonso. He'd left me in a pickle. There was no way I was telling this Wisconsin law man about our investigation into Mickey's murder, or any part of it. The truth would automatically link our murdered geek with his murdered bearded lady. There was a link, a huge one, but he wouldn't learn it from me. To empty the bag, would have complicated the matter beyond all reason. I would not be believed and I'd be in the stew over my aching ears a long way from home. Refusing to talk was also out. To do so would have immediately got me chucked into the dungeon as a hostile material witness. Neither appealed. No, I needed to be co-operative without doing any silly co-operating. I needed a simple solid lie. Mickey's murder was off the table, I didn't know Sybil from Adam, her murder couldn't have been more shocking.

The lie that would have worked best went like this: Alfonso and I drove up from Chicago together to coax his co-worker Sybil back to her Navy Pier gig. They, Sybil and Alfonso, had a spat, like good friends did, and Sybil had gone away mad. I convinced Alfonso to cowboy up and apologize. So we'd headed north. But what difference did any of that make now? I needed Alfonso for that lie to work and he'd flown the coop.

Any mention of the midget now would have put the cops on him. I wanted to find him, but wasn't keen to find him that way. Bottom line was, it left me nothing to offer the sheriff but a tale of an innocent tourist (yes, me again) alone in the wrong place at the wrong time. I was a poor slob who knew nothing and saw nothing. What choice did I have?

Sadly, something about my face, my eyes, my voice bugged the sheriff. He wasn't buying my innocence in any flavor. The crack on the head that someone, probably the murderer, had given me at the scene didn't help any. "If you had nothing to do with this," the sheriff barked. "Why were you unconscious beside the victim?"

"I've told you six times."

"Tell me again."

"I was passing the Sideshow. I heard a commotion in the train cars behind. I knocked, heard nothing, and entered. I saw a bloody mess. I bent down to see if the person... I thought it was a lady, then I saw the beard and thought it was a man in a dress. Then I didn't know. I bent to see if the victim was still alive. Someone hit me over the head. Here I am."

"Who hit you?"

My head hurt. I was tired. "I told you. I didn't see," I said with a sigh, "whoever it was."

"How did you know Sybil?"

"I didn't know him. All I knew was..." I stopped talking because the faces of both sheriff and deputy made it clear they'd stopped listening. They'd heard something and had honed in on it.

"You didn't know him?"

"What?"

"I asked how you knew Sybil. You said you didn't know him."

Oops.

The law men drilled holes through me with their eyes. "What do you mean," the sheriff asked, "you didn't know 'him'?"

Great. Again I'd allowed a head injury, and weariness, to distract my thoughts and loose my big mouth. You'd think, with as many enemies as I'd made over the years, I'd take it easy on myself. But, no. Every chance I got I stepped on my own penis. And I'd done it again.

Speaking of the male member, the master of ceremonies, the sword of love, pleasure, and pain, the cause of and solution to all of life's problems... As I'd already let the cat out of the bag to the county cops, it seems as good a place as any to make it crystal clear to you, faithful reader. Sybil, the Bearded Lady, wasn't a lady. She was a fraud. He was an anatomically correct, far from rare, good ole' bearded man. Whether or not the World Circus Museum knew, I don't know. Whether the Callicoat Circus, or The Major, or Alfonso knew, I don't know that either. But I knew. I'd learned it in a way no one should learn anything. I'd suffered the Bearded Lady's death. She, and there we make it 'he', had been stabbed in the back, garroted to the floor, stabbed in the chest, and viciously stabbed in the twig and berries by someone in a fury. I'd gone along for the ride and knew Sybil was a man!

But seeing the gleam in Sheriff Cobb's eyes, I should have kept it to myself. I wasn't supposed to know Sybil. Nobody at the circus had told me she was a man. There was too much blood at the scene to have been able to distinguish anything in the short time I claimed to have been conscious and looking. The cops hadn't mentioned it. And I wasn't supposed to be able to see dead people, or experience their murders. So I shouldn't have known and I shouldn't have called her 'him'.

I was shaking my head, even as I considered it, so I'd already decided. My only hope was to continue to lie and play innocent. Good luck to me. "Sorry," I said with a smile. "Slip of the tongue. Obviously, I meant to say 'her'."

"Oh, obviously," the sheriff said, his voice thick with sarcasm.

"I misspoke."

"Bull. You knew she was a he. Yet you claim you didn't know Sybil. How did you know?"

"Know what?"

"That the bearded lady wasn't."

"Wasn't what? Bearded?"

"No, wise guy. That she wasn't a lady; that Sybil was a man."

"Sybil was a man?" I asked in mock surprise. "Really? I didn't know! For the third time, my slip of the tongue was just that. Sybil really was a man? I had no idea! But maybe you're right. Maybe I'm psychic? No, I don't believe it." I looked at the sheriff in all sincerity. "That I'm psychic, I mean. I don't believe it. But, now you've told me, I have to admit I'm not surprised by the Sybil thing."

"You're not surprised the bearded lady was a man?"

"Yes. I'm not surprised. All these carnivals and circuses are scams, aren't they? Fat men with high voices are probably easier to come by than real bearded ladies. Especially on a budget. That would be my guess. So I'm not surprised. I wouldn't be at all surprised if their strongman was a ninety-pound weakling in a muscle suit."

"Did you know Gerald Lapinski?"

"Never heard the name. Who's he?"

"Sybil!" It was clear the poor sheriff had had all of me he could take. I can't say I blamed him. He was fed up. I was worn down. And Sybil, the Bearded Lady, her act over for good, as famous as she was ever going to get, was plain old Gerald Lapinski again.

Cobb wasn't buying my lies. I smiled to show I sincerely thought he should. He didn't smile back. He merely changed the subject and kept on grilling. "What do you do in Chicago."

"I already said. I'm a private investigator."

"And you're up here on a case?"

"No. I am not working a case."

"What case?"

"Are you deaf?"

"No. Neither am I stupid. Why are you snooping in Wisconsin? What brought you up here? And how did it get Sybil killed?"

"I understand," I said, with genuine compassion. "You're a cop. You're naturally nosy but you're also a cynic. I used to be a cop; I got the same chronic conditions. But your questions are out of bounds.

I have no case. Even if I did, it would have nothing to do with the crime you're investigating. So it wouldn't concern you and no answer would be forthcoming." I adjusted the ice bag. God, my head hurt. "I came up to see the circus museum. I'm a Toby Tyler fan ever since my days as a Mouseketeer. I've always loved the circus."

"A spur-of-the-moment road trip to the circus? What kind of jerk do you think I am?"

"You never wanted to join the circus when you were a kid?"

"Your story stinks, Blake. No, I'm not any fun. I'm missing all the comedy in this murder. But I'm willing to try. So let's examine the whole hilarious situation in which you now find yourself. You are most definitely a material witness to a vicious homicide. For that alone, I can stick you in the slammer and leave you until long after all the funny wears off. You are absolutely a suspect in that murder. You have no reasonable excuse for being here in Wisconsin, let alone the scene of the crime, and your story is a pack of lies. You might stop with the jokes and build a defense. You're going to need one."

"You have diddly-squat," I informed him. "I went to the circus museum like a thousand other tourists today. While wandering past the Sideshow, I heard a scream. I entered the train car to see if I could help. I saw a bloody murder scene and, before I could back out, got hit over the head and knocked unconscious. End story. I did not see who hit me. I did not know Sybil. I recognize your authority to arrest me as a material witness. But I'm a witness to nothing and it would be a waste of your time and my life. There's nothing else to tell you. If arrested, I will sit quietly in your cell, watching the rats scratch their fleas, until my mouthpiece arrives with a writ of *habeas corpus*. What's the point?"

"Why is your wallet crammed full of ID's, all in different names?"

"Come on, Cobb. We both know the game. If I was Joe Citizen, you'd have me flummoxed. I'm not. I used to be a cop. All you're doing is wearing out your chairs and both of our butts. Do we really have to keep going back to square one every half hour?"

"The ID's?" the sheriff repeated, tapping the table.

"I'm a private investigator. I can't get a warrant; the courts don't grant me information. I have to be a lot of different people to a lot of different people to get them to tell me things. There's no law against having aliases. Now would you please move on?" I regretted the shouting. My head felt as if it was coming apart. Whoever hit me, and whatever with, they'd done it with care.

"Who was the midget?"

"What?" I'd been too busy with my pity party to hear the sheriff's question. "What did you say?"

"The black midget," he repeated. "When you got to the museum, you bought a ticket for yourself and you bought a ticket for a little person. Who was he?"

That one caught me off guard. It was the first hint they knew about Alfonso. I had to do some quick thinking – and keep a poker face at the same time. Should I reconsider emptying the bag? If they knew about Alfonso... Then again it was possible they didn't know about Alfonso at all. They might just have stumbled upon the naked fact I'd been seen with a midget. Surely they...

"We talked to the girl in the ticket booth," the sheriff barked, interrupting my thoughts but helpfully filling in the blank for me. "We know damn well you bought a ticket for a midget! Now who is he? And where is he?"

Make that blanks, plural. Johnny Law had given me all the answers I needed. They didn't have Alfonso. They didn't know about him specifically. They knew I bought two tickets to the museum, one for a little person in line with me. They had no details. That left me free to lie with impunity.

"I didn't know him," I said with a gloriously straight face. "I don't know him. I haven't the slightest idea where he is."

"The ticket girl remembers you."

"Well she may. So what? I'm standing in line, minding my own business, waiting to buy a ticket," I explained. "I heard a voice ask if I had the price of a second ticket. I turned and didn't see anyone. Then I looked down. I was a little confused because I thought it was a kid, but the voice was clearly that of an adult. Then, sure enough, the little guy asked again if I could go him a ticket. I thought I was being had. You know, like Candid Camera? Then, I thought, maybe it was part of the circus show. I didn't know. I started to laugh but, the midget, he said he was serious. He wanted to see the circus and didn't have ticket money. Well, who am I to stop the forward momentum of a serious little person? Or to deprive him of the joy of the circus you turned your back on? I love the circus; I already told you that. I was at the circus. I was in a circus mood. I bought a midget a ticket. Trust me, after years of scratches and dents, my karma needs all the buffing I can give it."

"Blake," the sheriff said staring me down. "You are a liar."

"I can hardly deny that; you've seen my business card collection. But I only lie when it's necessary for business."

"You knew the midget. You tried to get him in on a half-priced kid's ticket!"

"It's my sense of humor does most of the damage to my karma," I confessed. "The midget didn't laugh either. There's no accounting for taste."

"Empty your pockets."

"We already did that."

"We're doing it again."

I stood, shakily, and did as requested. He surveyed the pile, wallet, card file, keys to the Jag, folding money, a couple of coins. Nothing seemed to shock him but, why should it, he'd seen it all before.

"Take off your jacket."

That required my setting down the ice bag first. I doffed the coat and tossed it down. He felt it up, from collar to cuffs, giving special attention to the insides of the pockets and the seams of the lining. "Take off your shoes."

I sat, paused for the dizziness the square dance he was calling was giving me, then untied and pulled off my gum shoes. He stared into each and shook them for good measure. No rabbits fell out.

"What in God's name," I asked, "are you looking for?"

He considered me for a good long while. Then he pulled a photograph from a file and slid it in front of me. It was a picture of Sybil, in the Sideshow, with a group of tourists, grinning at the camera and saying "Cheese." I stared, trying to find the sheriff's point but, with my head spinning and the image going in and out of focus, was having a time of it.

"Sybil's necklace," he finally said.

Oh, yes. The pearl necklace. There it was in the picture.

"It was broken during the murder. We collected the scattered pearls as evidence. But, using this photo as a reference, and doing the math, it's obvious some are missing and all but certain the killer left with a handful." Then, because he either recognized my impairment or thought I was stupid, he summed the situation up. "There weren't enough pearls at the scene to recreate the necklace."

I was trying with all my might not to react, while thanking my stars I had fought the urge to slip a pearl or two into the side of my shoe for later use. Had I done so, I'd already be cooling my heels in a cell with a murder charge hung around my neck. I was also arguing with myself; wondering whether Alfonso was, not only a murderer but, a thief? Wondering how I could even think such a thing about Alfonso? Wondering why I was being so sappy? What the hell did I know about the midget? He'd known both victims, hadn't he? Of course he had. None of it made any sense. If the lovesick little guy wanted someone dead, why would it be Mickey or Sybil? Surely, if he had murder in his heart, he'd have used it up on The Major. Hell, now I had The Major on my mind, without even knowing a motive, it made more sense he was the murderer. But if not, if Alfonso was the killer... How could he have possibly reached the top of my head to hit me?

I was confusing myself, going in dizzy circles and coming back to where my racing thoughts had begun, I was again quietly congratulating myself on not having copped a pearl. To be caught with one at this juncture would have been bad. I had no sense but, at least on this, my senses had not failed me.

The sheriff was staring a hole through me again.

"So you think robbery might have been a motive?" I asked, trying to be helpful. "Seems odd the killer didn't scoop them all up but, maybe. Are you checking your local fences and pawn shops?"

"Thanks," the sheriff said with a sneer. "What would we do in the sticks without helpful tips from ex-cops visiting from the city?"

The interrogation continued to not go well. But as they really had no evidence I'd done anything, ultimately it didn't go that badly either. I spent the whole night and the morning into the wee hours convincing the sheriff of Barrelton County it wouldn't do him or me any good to put me in the slammer; and promising on my mother's grave (fingers crossed) I'd return when summoned. Finally, amazingly, I talked myself out of an arrest and, with a "Pretty please," even got my gun back.

Early next morning, the door to the Interview Room of the Barrelton County Sheriff's Department opened for good and one used up big city shamus, little ole' me, passed through and out. Having squeezed the turnip for hours, and found it bloodless, Cobb and his deputy finally gave up. I'd convinced them I knew nothing. Which was an odd experience for me; with most of my acquaintances that fact was a given. I was granted leave of their county, and the State of Wisconsin, with a clearly stated warning that failure to respond to a summons to return for questioning or a trial of the murderer, if and when caught, would result in an assault on my investigator's license and my future liberty. I agreed and the deputy kindly dropped me back off at my Jaguar in the museum parking lot.

I had to get while the getting was good. But I confess I felt bad leaving. I had no clue where Alfonso was and, despite feeling abandoned by the little squirt, was half afraid I might be abandoning him. Had my former companion left the museum? Assuming he had...

Even that was a guess. For all I knew, by now, he may have become a murder victim himself. Was he? Had he already been hidden in a circus wagon? Or been fed to the lions? It wasn't doing my humor any good to think along those lines. So, assuming he left the museum, it was anyone's guess how he'd made his getaway. The museum grounds were in the middle of nowhere; meaning he needed to get somewhere in order to go anywhere. Assuming the escaping midget was headed home, and by that I meant his home circus, then he was headed back to Chicago. So he walked, or hitched, or caught a conveyance east to the Wisconsin Dells, from where he could take a bus to the Windy City. All guess work but I was following my nose. What I couldn't guess was whether I was chasing a frightened Alfonso in need of help or a murderous midget on the lam from justice.

It took twenty minutes to reach the Dells and, once there, another ten to locate the Roadway Cross Country Bus Company. Add another fifteen minutes in their parking lot for typesetting in bad light, printing with the doohickey from the 'all purposes illegal' ditty bag in my trunk, and letting the ink dry on my new calling card. It was almost three a.m. when I headed inside the bus terminal with questions on the tip of my tongue.

"I'm Agent Taft," I told the ticket clerk, in my most serious tone. "Immigration and Naturalization Service." I opened my leather case and flashed my card as proof. ('Qui Pro Domina Justitia Sequitur,' don't you know.) The only lesson of value my mother had ever taught me was, 'If you're going to lie, lie big.' Or, as I'd adapted it for this particular situation, if you're going to impersonate an officer, impersonate a Fed. Despite the abuse I'd taken at the hands of Sybil's killer, my aching neck and still throbbing head, it seemed the Fates were with me. The ticket clerk melted like butter in the summer sun. And, as an upstanding American citizen and helpful Roadway employee, he hustled off to the back room to "do some checking" as fast as his legs would carry him.

Then came unexpected assistance from the peanut gallery. A nosy, but equally helpful, eavesdropper hanging out in the terminal's waiting room for a morning bus to Nevada, volunteered the information that the little 'person of interest', with whom I'd told the clerk I wanted to speak, had boarded their tour bus at the circus museum and had gotten off there, at the Dells. How the midget had managed passage wasn't known; it was a chartered tour. But he'd definitely been aboard. In fact, though the trip lasted only twenty minutes, the little guy had spent the time entertaining the passengers, pulling whistles, candy, and colored balloons from his pockets like a magician. The balloons he'd blown up, tied into animals (he took requests), and doled out to the kids. She, the nosy informer, added, "The children loved him." Alfonso may have been a murderer but God bless Binky the Clown.

The nosy informant's story, as interesting and gap filling as it was, was made mute a moment later with the return of the clerk. Happy to do his part to protect the homeland from sinister foreign midgets, he produced a receipt confirming Alfonso's purchase of a Roadway bus ticket. (He'd had money, the little liar.)

As it did not feature his name, I had to ask, "You're sure of the passenger?"

"Absolutely." He hadn't sold the ticket himself; he'd come on at eleven. But the clerk he'd relieved had done so and had made mention of the passenger, in particular. The ticket had been sold to a balloon twisting, candy handing midget who, when he wasn't messing with the kids... "Stood right out there," the clerk said, pointing through the glass to the bus bay sidewalk, "smoking a cigar, almost as big as he was, and pacing back and forth like an expectant father in a Labor and Delivery waiting room. In fact," the ticket clerk went on, "the p.m. shift I replaced said it was kind of weird. The little guy was yucking it up, when the kids were around then, when he was alone out there, went all nervous and sullen and cussing to himself under his breath. Like he was two different people."

Wasn't that really the question I had to answer? Was Alfonso two different people? Was one of them a killer? I waved the receipt he'd handed me. "You're sure he was on this bus?"

"Yes, sir. No doubt. The ten p.m. bus for Chicago."

That, as they say, was that. Alfonso had abandoned me. It made me sore. But I wasn't burning up about it either because it also made me curious. Why had he abandoned me?

Chapter Thirteen

I wasted no time heading back to Chicago from my mission in central Wisconsin. Make that my failed mission. Outside of verifying the identities of what were now two murder victims (which I admit was something) and another pounding headache (which, I'm here to tell you, was also something) – I brought back nothing at all.

No, the trip wasn't a complete waste. I'd wanted to verify our body in Chicago as that of Michael Gronchi. I'd hoped Sybil could do that for me. A picture on the wall of the museum photo gallery had accomplished the task instead, but at least it was done. The drowned man was Mickey the Geek. But knowing that didn't bring any joy to Mudville because, in one way or another, learning it had led to Sybil's murder. Now that her (or his, if you're thinking of him as Gerald Lapinski) body had been added to the stack and Alfonso had gone missing, I wondered if this 'second sight' crap was worth anything at all. Looking at murders that already occurred is not a great way of preventing them. So, if you're keeping track, score this trip as one step forward and two steps back. Some detective I was. The take away was nothing but a basket of questions.

Who was Mickey's stabber? Where was the knife with which he'd done the deed? An obvious suspect was Tommy Dagger. I mean the guy was a knife thrower and had proved himself to be a maniac. But I knew nothing about him or his courageous assistant Sandra. What was the real story behind Thomas and Anita Lacrosse? Did Tommy have a reason for flipping one into the old geek and then giving him a shove out to sea? If yes, what had it to do with Sybil? If not Tommy who else, knife expert or no, might have wanted Mickey dead? And why?

Gronshi was an old man who swept the midway, followed the exotic animals with a pooper scooper, emptied the Big Top trash cans, and drank on his free time like God's own fish. He was a nobody. So who wanted him dead? Someone he'd hurt? Someone he could hurt? If that was the case, it meant he knew something. And, maybe, had tried to do something with the knowledge. Or had threatened to. Had Mickey been too big a risk to allow to roam the circus? Had he done something to make it worse? Sweepers got around; sweepers saw things. Could the old boozer have known something, or seen something, and been using it to blackmail somebody?

Alfonso had hired Mickey; according to him, he hired all the drudge help. So it followed the midget had little or nothing to fear by the old man's presence. At least not at first. Had Mickey seen something at the circus soon after coming aboard? Had he found the ingredients for a blackmail stew so quickly? Alfonso claimed there were hinky things going on under the Big Top. But hadn't the midget just been talking about romance, guys and dolls? Hadn't he been bitching with his penis? Likely, Alfonso's problem wasn't *the* problem. So the blackmail, if it existed, stemmed from something else. If it had, then that meant history. Who at the Callicoat Circus had a history with Mickey the Geek?

Alfonso did. That I knew. But it was only in passing. Had he known Sybil was really Gerald? Did it matter? Was Sybil's being a Sideshow fraud a bone of contention for anyone? Why should it be for Alfonso; he was a Sideshow fraud himself. Benga the Pygmy. *Sheesh.* Besides Mickey, to hear it told, had once been the genuine article. Maybe there was nothing to Alfonso knowing either of them. He'd known a lot of the old performers. How had the midget said it, he'd been coming in while they were all going out. Alfonso was a yes (but with a lower-case *y*). Sybil? Yes, of course (capital *Y*). Mickey and Sybil had worked together somewhere back in the day. I'd seen the picture that proved it. There was no doubt that, no sooner had the Geek been killed than, the Bearded Lady beat swollen feet and waddled out of there. No! That wasn't true. She hadn't gone immediately. She didn't leave at the murder. She'd paid Alfonso a clumsy visit. She'd asked about me sticking my face in and then she took a powder; when she learned someone was looking into the murder. Was that on purpose? Or had my appearance merely brought the murder to her attention? Which was it? Did the facts make her a frightened runner? Or did they suggest Sybil had done the deed? The former held water. The latter leaked when you added the pesky fact that Sybil had become the second victim.

But was she the second victim? Of the same murderer? Her murder, too, had been initiated by a knife in the back. A second circus worker? In two days? An acquaintance? Too many coincidences. No. It had likely been the same killer. Probably for the same reason. The same guilty knowledge? The same threat of blackmail? Someone else, the killer, may have had a history with Mickey the Geek *and* Sybil the Bearded Lady. Who?

The Canary? I'd seen the poster. But was the bird on the poster the same as the bird in Mickey's cryptic final sentence? If it was one sentence; one complete thought. Lisa didn't know for sure. Thinking of Lisa… How was she? Where was she. What was she doing? I didn't have time for that now. I had two bodies to worry about.

"The Canary didn't die when she fell from the sky." Was The Canary a trapeze act? It was almost too cute to buy. Then again, what had been the likelihood of my seeing that poster among 10,000 posters on display two hundred miles away? In a museum I shouldn't have known anything about? Was I, Nod Blake, finally able to claim a little luck? I knew better than to count my chickens. Nothing had been hatched but more questions. There were a lot of birds in the sky. Who was The Canary? What was her story? When did she fall? Was she Mickey's canary? And, if so, where was she now?

I was on a roll. I didn't know if I was accomplishing a thing, but the miles were disappearing beneath the new tires of my Jag, Wisconsin had vanished in my mirror, and Chicago was inching closer. I may not have been learning a thing, but I was on a roll, so I kept at it. Who remained? The Major...

Who was Karl Kreis? What was his deal? Other than those few minutes in our chance meeting in the performers' dormitory – when the midget and I had told him a whopper – I hadn't spoken with The Major at all. Yet, based on Alfonso's assessment that "something hinky is happening around this circus" (and the corroborating fact the circus employees were dropping like flies), I had to admit I seriously suspected The Major of the murders. But I also seriously suspected that notion was stupid. All I had to do was back up a step and take a good look. When I did, with the exceptions of Mickey and Sybil, I still suspected everybody.

What about the Callicoats, the late owner and his good lady widow? Anything to be sifted there? Or had they merely owned the playground? The slay ground? I reminded myself of the first rule of detecting, 'When you begin to wax poetic, move on.'

Alida Harrison? While I'd heard a lot about her from the lovesick midget, he hadn't really told me a thing. Hell, I got the impression that, other than the fact she made his heart beat faster, Alfonso didn't know a thing about her. I'd never met her or even seen her up close, so I had no way to guess. What was her deal? Did the aerial acrobat hold any cards? Was it a coincidence Alfonso had dealt her in? Or was the midget sticking knives in people?

Speaking of that little twerp… Where was he? Why had he run out on me in my hour of need? What did he know? When did he know it? Where was Alfonso while Sybil was getting her murder and circumcision? Had he been there? What part, if any, had he played? What had he seen? Or heard? Was Alfonso the killer? Was he in line to be killed? I looked at the dashboard clock, did the math, and realized the midget's bus had long ago reached Chicago. That brought another worry. Now he'd reached home, with no notion who or where the murderer was, was Alfonso still breathing?

None of my questions offered any obvious answers; at least not to me. All contributed greatly to my already throbbing head. That brought up one more query to which I was champing at the bit for an answer, who hit me over the head?

On my return to Chicago, I wanted to go immediately to my snitch, Large, to learn all he could find about the victims, the circus owner, the performers, and The Canary. The timing made that impossible. I may have been able to roll Large out of the sack, and he may have been willing to start the wheels of progress rolling, but his usually delightful wife would have taken one look at the clock and chased me north swinging her jumbo gumbo ladle at my already aching head. The investigation would have to wait until, at least, early morning.

I considered paying a visit to the circus performers' dorm on Navy Pier to check on the whereabouts and the vital signs of Alfonso Valencia. But I nixed that stop over for the same reason. It would have to wait until the sun came up.

Hosed in both directions and unable to proceed, I returned to my office instead. As I pulled into the lot, I was delighted to see the windows were all repaired. I found the bill, front and center, on my desk blotter and – while it wasn't chopped liver – it wasn't anywhere as bad as I had imagined it might be. Depending how the wind blew, I thought I might pay it out of pocket and take away the insurance company's opportunity to raise my rates. Something... Something had finally gone right.

I took the gun from my shoulder holster, glad to be rid of it, and locked it back in my safe.

I made myself a well-deserved drink with a few fingers of 'this' from my liquor cabinet, a splash of 'that', and a twist of 'one of those' from my tiny refrigerator. I jury-rigged a bag of ice from the freezer. I applied the latter to the back of my abused head and the former to my parched lips. I slipped into my desk chair with a relaxing sigh and gave the repair bill another glance. For a guy whose life had been stood on end by the murders of two people from a circus he hadn't heard of three days prior, who'd taken several good whacks to the noggin, whose office and precious Jaguar had been vandalized, who was still under the real threat of being charged (and maybe convicted) of homicide, it was nice something good had finally happened. I sipped myself to sleep.

I woke to sunlight streaming through my new office window and to the raucous sounds, streaming through my door, of Lisa rummaging through her desk. Pulling my feet from my desk, I accidentally kicked over my half-finished drink, creating a puddle on my papers and a situation that asked for cussing. Request granted. Putting my feet down, I accidentally stepped on and popped my fallen bag of water (formerly ice), creating a larger puddle on the floor beneath my chair and a situation demanding more of the same. It was a colorful start to the new day.

I called Lisa's name as I stepped from my office, then stopped in my tracks. It wasn't Lisa. It was Willie Banks rummaging in my secretary's desk with his working arm. "What are you doing here?"

He looked confused. "Ya called me here."

"When did I call you?"

"Yesterday," he said, looking even more confused. "To watch the window guys. Don't ya remember?"

"Of course I remember. Who called you here today?"

Believe it or not, Willie managed to look more confused yet. "Nobody. I'm still here from yesterday."

"You didn't go home?"

"No. Ya didn't tell me to."

"You stayed all night?"

"Yeah. Wasn't I supposed to?"

"Where did you stay? You weren't here when I came in?"

"I was. I slept upstairs."

Upstairs was one room, a small one, filled to the rafters with unpacked boxes of only God knew what. It was a running gag that some day I would hire a detective to discover what was up there. The slug had used it as his flop house.

If that wasn't bad enough. "Hey, Blake, it's a mess up there. If yer going to stay, ya ought to unpack and move in sometime. Just sayin'."

Great. Now I was getting life advice from a societal reject. "What are you doing in Lisa's desk?"

"What do ya think? I'm looking for breakfast. I'm starved."

"Didn't Lisa pay you, or feed you, when she came back yesterday?"

"She didn't come back yesterday."

That got my attention. "What do you mean she didn't come back yesterday?"

He cradled his arm and ogled me. "Blake, did ya hit your head or something?"

"Never mind my head." I sighed. Lisa's recent activities, her comings and goings, seemed out of character. I couldn't decide whether they were odd and a result of her head injury, or whether they merely seemed odd and were a result of my head injuries. Consequently, I didn't know whether to be worried by her absence or just annoyed. It would have been simple enough to call and check on her. But all thoughts of calling her place, at that hour, were out. Her mother would answer, then I'd have to answer to her mother. I moved my curiosity, and my concern, to a back burner.

"I've got some running to do," I told Willie. I dug in my pocket, fingered the cabbage I owed him for the help, but didn't pull it out. Fact was, I didn't know what the morning would bring. Instead of paying him, I asked, "Is there any way you can stick around until Lisa comes?"

I hated the idea, and myself for getting it, let alone asking the question. But I had no other choice. I wasn't secure in leaving the place alone yet. After all, someone had broken out the windows and fixed my car tires. Besides, I still thought I was doing the slug a favor.

You couldn't have told by the look of fear on Willie's face. "I'm broke," he whined through his nose. "I'm hungry. My shoulder hurts. Ya remember, Blake, I took a bullet for–"

"Yeah, I know. Lisa will be here any minute. When she gets here, tell her I said to make us square on what I owe you. Then tell her I said to buy you breakfast before you take off."

"Okay." Willie shrugged his acceptance. I turned to go. "Hey, Blake, ya want your messages?"

"I thought you said Lisa didn't come–"

"She didn't. I took 'em. If I can take a bullet for ya, Blake, I can take a message."

Would it never end? I sighed again and, for the first time, noted two stacks of messages on Lisa's desk. The first stack sat beneath a paperweight with an attached note, written in Willie's broad chicken scratch, reading 'Not Important'. The other sat under a paperweight with a note reading, you guessed it, 'Important'. I didn't want to know what criteria Willie had used to make his determinations. I quickly browsed the 'Not Important' collection and was happy to find I agreed. Then I moved to the other pile, to find four messages from Lieutenant Wenders – each one a sliver nastier than the one before.

"That cop, Wenders," Willie said, rolling his eyes. "He was insane trying to get a hold of ya."

"Put it down to his lack of a sense of humor."

"Whatever ya say, Blake. But after the four calls." He pointed at the notes. "Ya see there. Then he sent a prowl car. No, two cars. No, wait, it was one car, twice." Willie shook his head, reshelving the books in his mental library. "He wanted to know what I was doing here. I didn't think it was any of his business, but ya know the lieutenant. He kind of has a way of making ya answer. Maybe it's the way he offers to arrest ya every other sentence."

I nodded, fully able to relate.

"So," Willie went on. "I told him I was watching the place for ya. He called me a liar. Then he said something nasty–"

"About you or me?" I asked.

"Both."

Wenders' insanity was a given and his threats entirely expected. It was like the fat slob to give me forty-eight hours to find something, and then start hassling me after only twenty-four. Well the lieutenant could wait.

The other important message, out of the blue and completely unexpected, was from Mrs. Callicoat. Our rich widowed circus owner had also called, twice; the first time to say she wanted to see me as soon as possible and the second to say she needed to see me "urgently". With all the unanswered questions about her little circus, and after what I'd been through behind the cheddar curtain, the summons was more than I could resist.

But morning had come and, before I even thought of doing anything else, I made a trip to the south side. I needed help to dig deep. That meant I needed the biggest, fastest shovel in Chicagoland. That meant Large, my snitch, my researcher, my grounded brain. He was the only human being on whom I could off load my thousand questions and know he'd do something practical with them and waste no time about it. You'll meet Large later in the story, sisters and brothers. For now know I was handing The Major, The Canary, Alida Harrison, Tommy Dagger, Sybil, Mickey the Geek, and Alfonso, off to an expert. I roused him from his slumber and put in my request for information. I ended my portion of the quick visit apologizing for my obvious desperation but reiterating my fear that sloth might add more bodies to the pile. He ended his by promising to loose his locust upon the field. (That's how the big man talked.)

Afterward, I found a phone booth and called Mrs. Callicoat. Despite the early hour, she was terribly, awfully glad to get my long-awaited return call. I was invited to join the rich widow for coffee on the grounds of her palatial estate. How grand.

Chapter Fourteen

"Blake," I told the intercom. "I have an appointment with Mrs. Callicoat."

A female voice, made tinny by the speaker, agreed I was expected. The heavy iron gate hummed and swung open like the mouth of a leviathan preparing to swallow me. The voice instructed me to follow the drive around to the rear of the estate. Her mistress, the voice went on, awaited me in the carriage house. I thought carriage houses disappeared with the horse and buggy. What did I know? I didn't have two nickles to rub together. Salivating as I passed the mansion, I followed the long curving drive through unending immaculate lawn and into the estate's back forty.

Turned out I had been right. Carriage houses, functioning ones, had disappeared from America's residential landscape with the loss of horse drawn conveyances. What the intercom voice should have told me was her mistress was waiting for me in the Wagon Pavilion, or warehouse, or barn. That's what the carriage house was, a huge pole barn standing like Oz in the distance. I parked, took it in, and entered through wide open sliding doors.

The place was filled front to back with gorgeous wagons from the glory days of traveling circuses. A mini version, I imagined, of the pavilion at the circus museum. I hadn't had the opportunity to visit that one. I'd been curious but Alfonso had hogged that side of the river for the search. Sybil's murder had hogged the attention thereafter. With my psychic replay of the killing, my brief unconsciousness, and my hours at the mercy of the county sheriff, I'd never gotten back to see the wagons. This may not have been the real circus pavilion, with its two hundred wagons, but it was impressive all the same and as close as I was likely to ever come again. Here there were, perhaps, a dozen wagons. But gorgeous and numerous enough you couldn't see them all at once. What do you want for nothing? I followed the sounds of splashing water between the wagons and cages, cut the corner around a sleeping steam driven calliope, and came upon the rich widow at center ring.

That's what it was. In the middle of the barn, in the midst of the wagons sat a circular concrete pad, roughly twelve feet in diameter, six inches above the pea gravel floor, a patio and symbolic center ring surrounded by circus history. The pavilion's walls were decorated in posters, specific to something called 'The Major's Major Circus' and the Callicoat & Major Combined Circuses displayed, not merely to champion quantity as at the museum, but to be seen individually. There in splashes of yellow and red, Cedric, whip in hand, faced his big cats. There in green and yellow the elephants danced. There in an explosion of color clowns fell laughing from a pocket-sized Pontiac (could have been a Chevy). In dramatic blue, a cartoon Tommy hurled paper knives at a cartoon Sandra. And there, on a new poster, Alida the pixie hung in the air – happy as a clam to be dangling upside down. Two of these one-sheets hung between each space separating the barn's doors and windows. Almost that is; a gap showed. By the sun-bleached plaster, and rectangle of bright paint, it appeared, one wall recently lost a poster.

From her place, lounging – coffee in hand – in one of two long sun chairs on her private patio, the lovely rich widow had a swell view of the heart of the pavilion. She seemed, however, to be eying only one item – her chauffeur. Shirtless, his chiseled chest beaded with water, Chicago's stand-in for Surfer Joe stood manipulating a garden hose (with a pressure nozzle) at one of the wagons while his employer had him for breakfast. It's probably the pig in me but, for my money, he looked to be simultaneously blasting the suds from one and lathering up the other.

I watched for a moment unobserved. When it was clear nothing of note was taking place, or about to, I coughed and made my presence known. "Pardon me." I got a smile from the lady of the house and a humorless glare from the buff wagon polisher. "I'm Blake. Mrs. Callicoat?"

"Of course." She rose in one smooth move, catlike as ever, and stepped from her circular pedestal offering a hand. I hesitated only an instant, remembering the last time we'd touched, then told myself I was being stupid. What, after all, were the odds of triggering another flash? I took the hand. All went well, even better. Most of the women in my life had cold hands (and hearts). As before, this one was warm with a firm pleasing grip. You don't get that every day among the debutantes. "Danita Callicoat," she said. "You probably don't remember me."

"Certainly, I remember," I said, noting her friendly greeting came with a glare from the hired help. "Yesterday morning in the Navy Pier dormitory–"

"Oh, come, Mr. Blake. Neither of us did anything memorable yesterday." She smiled, enjoying herself. "I was speaking of the evening in Master Criswell's parlor."

"Ah, yes. Only a select few have heard my trumpet solo."

She laughed. It was a nice laugh. "It lives in infamy," Mrs. Callicoat said. "My mother-in-law is still in shock. And desperately looking for a new medium to replace the one you despoiled."

"My talents are endless. Offer your mother-in-law my apologies, will you?"

She turned to the sweating chauffeur. "That's all, Rudy."

He didn't look a 'Rudy' to me. But, as I no longer take my shirt off in public, I admit my prejudice. Rudy, the chauffeur, released the trigger on his spray nozzle killing the water flow. He swept the two of us with his eyes; not a happy camper. Mrs. Callicoat seemed okay with that. Still smiling, she told him, "You can finish that later. I'd like to talk with Mr. Blake alone." She gave him a moment to respond and, when he didn't, still smiling, raised the volume and lowered the tone. "You can go."

Rudy didn't like it. But he dragged his hose past the wagons to the near wall, tossed it in a pile, and turned off the tap. He grabbed his shirt, bowed slightly to his mistress, and went without giving me another look.

"Rudy Ace, my chauffeur and valet," Mrs. Callicoat said. "He's rather protective." I nodded my understanding and that took care of Rudy. She returned to her concrete stage and her silver break-fast set up. "Would you care for some coffee?"

"Thank you. Black."

She poured and brought it to me on a saucer. I took it awkwardly, proving what we both already knew, that socially I was out of my league. Then she stated a simple undeniable fact. "You lied to my circus manager yesterday. You told him you were an author."

"A writer, actually, for 'Little Folks' Magazine."

"It was a lie?" she asked. I nodded. "Then do the details matter?"

"Certainly; especially with a lie. In my business, it's vital to keep your lies straight."

"So... you are a liar?"

"Absolutely. I already said, it goes with the busi-ness."

"That night in his salon Master Criswell said you were a detective. But he made it stronger. He called you a snooper, I think?"

"We started so nicely," I said with a smile. "Cof-fee and all. Then it went downhill fast. That's your second nasty crack. Maybe I should call your chauffeur back to protect me?"

The rich widow frowned.

"Don't get me wrong. I'm sure I'd benefit from a discussion of my character – or lack thereof – but coffee won't cut it. We'd need cocktails, a meal, and after dinner cigars. And we'd only scratch the surface."

"I didn't mean to offend you."

"Yes, you did. If only as a test. But it was a waste because I'm not offended. I'd love to have the conversation. After, we could do you. Without knowing a thing about you, Mrs. Callicoat, I'm already convinced still waters run deep. I wouldn't mind taking a peek at all. Let's schedule it for when our current affair is wrapped up. In the meantime, let's save time. We'll agree, I'm a cad. I wouldn't trust me any further than I could throw me. Now... Why did you want to see me? Or should we skip to why I agreed to see you?"

"You have been... detecting... around my circus. I want to know why. That's reasonable, isn't it, to know what it is you're after? Why you're there pretending to be someone you are not? What is it you're looking for? I want to know what your game is?"

"Don't you know?"

"I do not."

"If that's true… Then, yes, you have a right to know why I'm sticking my nose into your affairs."

"Oh?" She looked shocked. It could have been baloney but one gets a feel for these things. Her reaction seemed real enough.

"If it's true," I repeated. I took a sip of my coffee. It was good coffee. "Are you aware a number of your employees have gone missing?"

"I know one of the Sideshow performers left suddenly. The Bearded Lady. The Major told me that yesterday."

"Left for where?"

"I don't know. He didn't say. I don't think he knew. He was annoyed, that's all. I don't blame him. I doubt bearded ladies grow on trees. But he didn't seem surprised. There's nothing notable in circus performers appearing or disappearing without notice. As I understand it many are, by nature, gypsies. They come and go like the tide." She sipped her coffee. "You said a number of employees? The Major didn't mention others. What others?"

She seemed taken aback. That took me aback. Was I being played? Or was it really news to her? That in itself would have been informative. But the interview was going backwards. I was either slipping or the head injuries were catching up with me. A good detective never gave more information than he got. I was giving away the farm. But I needed some place to start so I continued cautiously forward.

"Do you know Michael Gronchi?" I asked, watching for a reaction.

"No." She shook her head. "The name means nothing to me. Was he–"

"Employed by you? Yes."

"And he's gone missing?"

"For a short time. Actually, he's gone dead."

"Dead? How did he die?"

"He was attacked two nights ago at your circus and given a hand off the Pier into Lake Michigan."

"That's horrible."

"He thought so too."

Unsure what to do with that, she decided to ignore it. "He drowned?"

"No. Do you know anything about him?"

"No, of course not. I already said I didn't know the man. He was an employee? Doing what?"

"Sweeping up spilled popcorn and horse poop."

"I don't know the maintenance workers. I'm sorry."

"In the old days he was a performer, a circus geek, but that was long ago and far away."

"This may sound cold or distant but my connection with the circus is tenuous at best. I inherited one. That's all. I have little to do with it. I'd love to sell it. But people aren't buying circuses these days."

"No one has mentioned Gronchi's name or his absence in the last two days?"

"Are you asking if anyone has confessed to killing him? Not to me. I repeat, Mr. Blake, until this moment I've never heard the name. Besides, who could have mentioned it? I don't know anyone at the circus but The Major. My only contact with the show is to occasionally discuss needed business with him, as on yesterday morning when you saw us."

"Where we you two nights ago?"

Mrs. Callicoat paused. Then she gasped. I thought she might spill her coffee but she got it under control. Anger flared in her eyes. She opened her mouth, closed it again, then she took a deep breath and the fire disappeared. It was quite a show and I saw it to the credits. "When you're born rich," she finally said, reddening. "People go out of their way to avoid annoying you. On the rare occasion they do, it's unforgivable. When you're born poor and fall into riches, as in my case, people who used to annoy you stop. You forget what it was like to be annoyed. When you finally remember, you also recall you can handle it." She smiled and the blush faded from her cheeks. "Where was I two nights ago? I was fighting desperately not to yawn at a charity gala in downtown Chicago; a dinner and silent auction that lasted just short of forever. I'm certain all of the cringe-worthy details can be found, with pictures, in the Society pages of the World's Greatest Newspaper."

"Thank you. Just to tie all of the bows, where were you yesterday? Late afternoon and into the evening?"

"Yesterday? Why?"

"Humor me."

"I was..." She put her brain on it. "Here." She reconsidered, then nodded her agreement. "Here. I didn't go anywhere at all yesterday."

"Rudy can vouch for you?"

"My chauffeur?"

"And valet," I added.

She gave me a twisted look, frowned, apparently decided I wasn't worth the argument, and turned her thoughts to the question. "No, Rudy can't vouch for me. He was off. My maid was here. If necessary she can, what's the phrase, 'Give me an alibi'. Why do I need one for yesterday?"

I considered again my rule about not handing out information. If she was innocent of the diabolical doings at her circus, and it was certainly possible she was, she had a right to know what I wanted and why. She might even help me to figure the mess out. If she was innocent, that is. But was she acting? If so, she should have been a performer instead of an owner. Because I was buying it. I might have been wrong, but I didn't think she had killed Mickey. I didn't think she had killed Sybil either. I didn't know if I trusted her, but I trusted me. Feeling the way I did, it made sense to, not necessarily dump the bag, but to give her a peek inside.

"There's been a second murder."

I was still watching her reactions. And still saw only what I read as real shock.

"Another employee of the circus?" she asked. I nodded. "But The Major has said nothing–"

"It's the missing employee you and he discussed."

"The Bearded Lady?"

I nodded again. "Killed yesterday afternoon at the circus museum in Wisconsin."

"Our Bearded Lady?"

"Sybil. Yes." I decided to really test the waters. "Her real name, his real name, was Gerald Lapinski."

For an instant, I thought she'd drop her cup and saucer to shatter on the concrete like they do in the movies. She didn't. Again she got a hold on herself but, shaken badly by the news, set the coffee down not to drop it. She was still ringing true. "Our Bearded Lady was a man?"

"All three hundred pounds of him," I said. "But every ounce a lady."

The widowed circus owner didn't laugh. Nor did she meet my stare. In truth, she looked a bit green about the gills. The revelation of Sybil's gender, and the fraud her circus had been perpetrating upon the paying public, seemed a greater shock than the revelations of the murders had been. I didn't deduct points for it; human minds processed information differently. What mattered was I was more convinced than ever the shenanigans at the circus had occurred without her knowledge.

"Are you all right, Mrs. Callicoat?"

"Yes, I'm… It's all so…" She finally managed to look up. "Please, call me Danita."

"All right, Danita."

"You were Mr. Blake last week at the séance. And, yesterday you were, if I remember right, 'just Blake'. Have you a first name?"

"Yes. But Blake will do." I handed her my cup and saucer and strode away. It was time to change the game up and push. "What do you know of the acts working for you?"

"Very little. I–"

"Tommy Dagger?" I pointed to the poster.

"The knife thrower?"

"It's a reasonable question."

"Yes. I suppose it is. I wish I could give you a reasonable answer. But I don't know the acts in the circus; not in any personal way. My husband was the circus fanatic. It was his toy. You're aware I recently lost my husband?"

"I am. My condolences."

She nodded, accepting them, without thanks. Then she looked past me to take in the wagons, wheeled cages, banners and posters surrounding us. She set down my cup, paced a bit, then laid a hand on the sculpted molding at the corner of the nearest wagon. "Reginald came here to escape the world."

"Would seem to do the trick," I said, following her lead and looking around. "A fantasy world of make believe. The artwork, the wagons, fun and exotic but hardly functional."

"You have a good eye, Blake," Danita said. "And a reasoning mind. The real circus wagons, the everyday functional wagons, were that; work wagons. A few of those exist as collectors' items. Most were dismantled, ages ago, stripped of their steel for war."

"Which war?"

"Name one," Danita said with a sad smile. She returned to rubbing the gold painted surface. "Most of these were street models, built for show. Their only function was to roll slowly in parade, to make the crowds gasp, and make the people follow them to the Big Top. Beyond that," Danita said, turning. "I don't really know much about it. As I said, it was Reginald's world."

"Yet you take your coffee in this gallery?"

She stared trying, it seemed, to decide how to take the question. I waited with a curious, but innocent, expression. Let her take it how she would. She softened and looked away. "When I want to be near my husband, I come here."

Uh huh, I thought. Thinking of hubby with morning coffee and chauffeur cheesecake. I know, I'm a cynic. Hoping for something on Reginald and Danita a bit closer to reality, I dove back in. "Kindred spirits, your husband and you?"

"Nothing of the kind. As a matter of fact, we were virtually opposites. My husband was a dignified middle-aged prude. I was fighting to hold on to my youth. He feared and agonized over the future like an anxious child. I dwelled in – and ran from – the past like a tired and depressed old woman. We weren't kindred spirits at all. We were a mess. But we were in love... once upon a time. That's how fairy tales begin, don't they, Blake? And fairy tales are filled with ornate coaches."

"I'll take your word for it. I'm no expert."

"Nor am I." Danita returned to her 'center ring' patio and reclaimed her chair and cup. "I have my own pass times. But when I want to be near Reginald, I come here."

She shook away her reverie, showing ire, whether at me or herself, I wasn't sure. "What are you, Blake? A second-rate detective who's let me steer you off the subject to garner your sympathy? Or are you better at what you do than I gave you credit for? Have I bared my soul to a heartless cop?" She smiled her patented amused smile and sipped her coffee.

"Back to the present," I said.

"Yes. When it comes to the circus, Blake; the circus operating on Navy Pier... If you have questions, you'll need to ask The Major. I was aware our Bearded Lady had left us. I knew of no other missing employees. I knew, I know, nothing about any murders. I know only what he tells me. He tells me only what I need to know for the show to go on. I own the circus. I sign checks." She paused. "Speaking of which... who hired you?"

"A client's name, if there was one, wouldn't come into it. Confidentiality. But this time around the question doesn't apply. I haven't got a client nor have I been hired. I'm snooping for me." To show her how at ease I was in snooping for me, I raised a hand to one of the wagons intending to lean like the confident private eye I was. When I made contact with the wagon, the psychic flash came so quick I had no time to formulate my regret. The Callicoat pavilion disappeared.

You know the story from there, sisters and brothers, the pain, the heat, the ringing in my ears, the colored lights, the temporary blindness. The oh-so-familiar feelings that were absolutely impossible to get used to. Finally, the blackness as I arrived wherever the vision had taken me.

That too was familiar. I heard splashing water, coughing, sputtering, and… Over there, though I had no inkling of distance or direction, I made out the head and shoulders of the drowning man. Still he had no face. But he had a voice and, weakly, struggling for breath, he used it – this time to call me by name.

"Blake. Blake. Help! Help… me! Down… here…"

Then the world, at least the world I was in, stood on its head – while I took a blow to mine.

I was lost, completely disconcerted. I don't know if, in the telling, I can make it make sense. I was in the same place, the same dark water but, suddenly, the drowning man was gone. He was gone and I, as suddenly, was choking, gagging, and could not catch my breath. I heard an explosion and, an instant later, felt a sharp blow above my left temple. I disappeared into oblivion.

I have no notion how long the unconsciousness lasted. When I came to there was no doubt – I had taken the place of the drowning man. My forehead ached, but that was the least of my troubles. I had a mouth full of filthy water. I spit it out, choking. I gasped. I gagged. I bobbed to my chin in foaming freezing water. It was dark as pitch and I strained but saw nothing; nothing but the dirty black water and churning white foam flooding over me, dragging me to my doom. I fought it. I splashed. I kicked trying to hold the surface. I ached all over, the injury (whatever it was) split my skull, and I was dead exhausted.

"Help!" I cried weakly, in another man's voice. Then I choked and gagged and swallowed more filthy water. "Help... me! Down... here..."

The vision passed. Still gasping, I got a breath. I took one, then another, filling my lungs. I flailed my arms, trying to stay afloat, but soon saw it wasn't necessary. I was kneeling on gravel on solid ground. I grabbed the wooden spokes of the painted wagon wheel beside me and leaned heavily until I had my balance. No longer dying the death of the drowned man, I saw the hallucination was gone and I was back in the Callicoat wagon pavilion.

But the embarrassing truth was I had never left. I found immediate proof when I looked up to see Danita Callicoat standing nearby, mixed horror and shock on her face, staring down at me as if I were a mad man. "Blake? Are you... Are you all right?"

"Do you know Michael Gronchi?" I shouted.

"I... I... I've already told you. I don't."

I'd scared her. I didn't care and demanded again. "Think! Michael Gronchi? Mickey? Do you know him?"

"I don't!"

"Do you know," I shouted. I paused and caught my breath. "Did you ever know anyone who died by drowning?"

"Did I... What? Drowning?"

"Yes! Who do you know that drowned?"

"Nobody! Never!" she said, shouting back at me now. "I don't know anyone who drowned!"

I stopped shouting questions. The rich widow stopped shouting answers. We caught our collective breaths in the vast silence of the pavilion. Still on my knees, I felt suddenly vulnerable for I sensed another presence nearby. I turned to see Rudy, the protective chauffeur, looking unhappily on from a walk-in door in the far wall. He didn't get any happier as he came my way.

"Are you all right, Blake?" Danita asked again.

I nodded and, when I found the air, said, "Yes. I'm... I'm all right."

"Do you need...?" She didn't know what to offer. I couldn't blame her. She didn't know what had happened. I couldn't tell her. Still she was trying. "Shall I call...?"

I waved away her calling anyone. "I'm all right. I have a... condition."

"Rudy..."

The chauffeur took my arm with a solid, not friendly, grip and helped me to my feet. For him it was no chore as he had me by four inches and forty pounds. He held the grip once I was up. Dizzy, I was in no condition to wrestle free or argue the point.

"Would you like some water," Danita asked, frightened and still trying to help. "I can have some brandy brought out."

"No." I reached to balance myself against the wagon wheel, but stopped short. I studied it for a moment. I took a breath and laid my index finger on it. Nothing happened. I released the breath and took hold of the wheel. It made a good crutch (now I knew it wasn't going to bite) and I steadied myself on my feet. "I'm all right, really."

At a nod from his mistress, Rudy the ape let go of my arm.

"It's a... seizure. It comes out of nowhere sometimes."

Danita breathed more easily. "Can I do anything?"

"Yes. You can ask your man if the names Michael Gronchi or Mickey the Geek mean anything to him?" I turned, looking up to take in the chauffeur. "You've been to the circus, Mr. Ace, standing guard over that lovely Fleetwood. The acts come and go around you. Did you know Michael Gronchi or Mickey the Geek?"

Rudy turned to Danita and got her nod. He turned to me and shook his head. He knew nothing and he said nothing.

"How about Sybil? Or Gerald Lapinski? Any bells going off?"

Again the silent shake of the head.

"You're sure you're all right, Blake?" With my assurance, the rich widow dismissed her chauffeur again. He didn't like it before and taking seconds did nothing to cheer him up. But he went.

"He doesn't talk?" I asked after he'd left us.

"He has a beautiful voice," Danita replied. "When he has something to say."

The dizziness had passed. There was no way to apologize for the embarrassment the episode had caused, for either of us, so I dove back in to get the meeting over with. What else was there to do? "What can you tell me about Alfonso Valencia?"

"The little clown? The subject of your article?" She enjoyed a laugh at my expense. "Him I know. I don't mean personally, but I know about him. Everybody in the circus knows Alfonso. He's quite the character." She paused as she realized I was studying her. "Oh, Blake, he's not..." She tried to find the words. "Are you telling me Alfonso's been killed?"

"I don't know. He's missing – without explanation. I want to find him before he ends up like the others."

"Of course. Yes, you must. I'll pay for your services myself."

"I'm not looking for a client."

"If I can help you solve these horrible crimes in any way, you need only ask."

I cannot say I completely trusted Danita Callicoat. With the sole exception of my secretary, I don't think there was anyone on the planet I completely trusted. What I can say is I no longer suspected her of murdering the performers in her show. I believed her when she said she knew nothing about the killings. She seemed bothered by them. She said she wanted them solved. And when I asked for her official sanction, she replied, "Yes, of course. Go back to the circus. Dig. Inquire."

Chapter Fifteen

I raced through the drive-thru of the chain burger joint that promised I could have whatever I wanted, *My way, Any time of day*. What I wanted was a half-dozen plain hamburgers. "No. No fries. No. Nothing to drink. Right. Nothing on them. Plain." The kid on the other end of the intercom sounded disappointed. He might as well get used to it. It was a long life. I collected my burgers and turned the Jag for the north shore.

I pulled onto Navy Pier, parked, grabbed my burgers, shanghaied Olive from his ticket booth with a plea for help (he found a replacement), and headed around the Big Top and into the performers' dormitory on the far east end of the Pier. Pinned waist-high (my waist) on Alfonso's dorm room door was a note reading: *What the Hell? See Me!* It wasn't signed. It seemed a likely bet the midget had missed the evening performance. That left little doubt who'd written the note.

Inside the room, Olive and I found Alfonso's personal effects untouched. There was no sign the little clown had come or gone. His depressed mutt was there, as I feared, no more or less active than before, giving a blink, a sad slow gaze, an occasional heartbreaking sigh to prove he was alive, laying on his rug between several pools and piles unavoidably left on the surrounding floor. I unwrapped the 'plain' burgers – then spent five minutes scraping the ketchup, mustard, and pickle from each. Damned drive-thru employees.

"What's his name?" I asked Olive.

"The dog?" The pimpled youth shrugged his shoulders. "Don't think he has one. I'd say, 'Mornin', Alfonso. How's the dog.' He'd say, 'Depressed.' That's all was ever said 'bout the dog."

I broke the burgers into his empty bowl while the dog sighed. I filled his water bowl from the bathroom tap while he hungrily ate. I assured the pooch – though it did nothing to cheer him up – that Olive would keep an eye on him until Alfonso returned.

"Me?" Olive asked. "Why me?"

"Alfonso said you were a good kid. So be a good kid." I offered Olive a five spot for a promise he'd walk the dog until the midget came back. He countered that feeding the dog wouldn't be free. I made it a sawbuck and he was on board.

I asked the kid where I might find either The Major or Alida Harrison. Both were main players – in their show and in mine – whose interviews had been too long-delayed. It was about time we talked officially. At mention of the boss, Olive lifted his brow sharply, asking (without asking) why anyone would want to meet that man willingly. "The Major is already stalking the Big Top," he said. "Laying down the law, making the early risers sorry they bothered. The acrobat…" He blushed around an idiotic schoolboy grin. "Alida is prob-ly still in bed."

"Where's her bed?"

"O-one flight up. Room 304." Youthful lust shown in his eyes. "I'll show you!"

"I've got it, son, thanks," I told him. "You cheer up your dog. I'll see what I can do with Alida."

I left Olive to his adopted mutt and his wondering imagination.

I climbed the stairs and discovered immediately that the image of the blonde pixie buried in soft sheets had been wishful thinking on Olive's part. Alida Harrison was not in bed. She was anything but at rest. As my head topped the landing above, I got my first close up view of the little acrobat, hurrying from her room, pulling the door quickly closed behind her, red faced and breathing rapidly as if she'd just... Well, let's go with 'ran a marathon'.

She was a short-haired blonde with black roots but I never hold that against a lady. She didn't have the curves that normally invite male urges but had instead one of those hard, athletic bodies that guaranteed a full evening of satisfying contact sport. In fact, the more I looked, the more I take back my comment about male urges. She was a few inches over five feet, somewhere in her mid-twenties, wearing an open pink bathrobe (that heightened her rosy blush) over shorts and a T-shirt cut off just below her pert breasts. She wasn't Mae West, but she'd have fit in fine on the dessert menu and plenty of guys would have ordered seconds.

She saw me and froze in place against the door. I did my full share of staring back. "Alida Harrison?"

Her black eyes widened, for an instant, then she brought them under control. The silence was good and pregnant. Then she gave birth to a smile. "Who are you?" Like many around the circus, she too had a slight accent. But from where? Your guess is as good as mine.

"The name's Blake. I'm a private investigator."

It was like watching a magic trick. In an instant, the little blonde's smile went from Cheshire Cat to kitten. She closed her robe, slowly, issuing an invitation not taking one away. Then she moved my direction like a hundred and five pounds of warm smoke crossing the landing. "Whose privates are you investigating?"

I wouldn't have given a penny for the joke or her delivery. But I'd have emptied the wallet for the giggle that followed, then asked what she wanted for a tip. I was on foot and kicking myself for not wearing a seat belt.

The acrobat's eyes lit up. She darted forward and snatched my arm as if she feared I might get away. Then, steering me to the stairs I'd just come up, she started me down again, rambling aloud in an odd little stream of consciousness. "Private investigator. Alpha male. Man of action. Decisive. Strong. Knows his mind. Knows what he likes. Come see my new act."

Her excitement was genuine. But, in anticipation of what, I couldn't tell you. She claimed she wanted to show me her new routine but, to me, she seemed headed away from – not toward – whatever was on her mind. Of course I had no basis. I'd just met the girl.

"You can watch me," she was going on. "Tell me what you think. Then investigate me. Ask me questions. Anything comes to mind."

On the way out, she paused on the first floor to bang on a door. "The muscle behind my magic," she explained, the sing-song stream of consciousness gone. When the door came open she issued orders to two semi-comatose roughs within. (The pair I'd already seen at work with Tommy and Sandra.) They were needed pronto for a rehearsal in the Big Top, she barked. They hopped to, grabbing for clothes, as if they were her private slaves. That's how she treated them. Without waiting,

Alida led me away. "I'm Tinkerbell," she said, all smiles again. "They make me fly."

We hit the lot outside of the performers' dorm like we were on a mission. Considering she'd never heard of me, I was surprised to find myself so high on her 'To Do' list. Then again, we weren't going out to watch my act.

I did have to pause for a second – not related to the blonde pixie. Coming out of the building, I saw Danita Callicoat's limousine parked nearby. That set my mind to racing. What was it doing there? Had the rich widow sped from her estate to the circus after our talk? If so, why? I'd all but crossed her off my list because I'd gotten the impression the murders were a shock to her. Now I was wondering again. Could I have been that wrong? Where was Mrs. Callicoat? What was she doing? But my questions were fleeting; my urge to investigate the situation overruled by the pushy little acrobat. Alida wanted to show me her act; she wanted her turn to be interrogated.

I'll digress for a moment more to mention that with Mrs. Callicoat's limo in the lot and its owner on my mind and with Alida Harrison on my arm, I couldn't help but compare the two. The rich widow was a sensuous cougar who felt dangerous but read innocent. The acrobat was a smoking kitten who felt cuddly but read evil. Both were pure feline. But where did they prowl? For what did they hunt? In the night, I'd already seen, the circus was a world of lights, shadows, and lots of places in which to slink without discovery. Now I saw even in daylight there were plenty of nooks in which to hide and from which to spring. Who or what was I dealing with? House cats? Alley cats? Hell cats?

We followed the fence toward the employees' entrance at the rear of the Big Top. On our right, on the north side of the hippodrome, a reserve engine from the local Fire House had been coaxed into service. They'd pulled a hose line and were gleefully assisting circus staff in washing three elephants. The massive beasts, in turn, trumpeted their delight. To the distant left, on the far south side, I made out a shape that looked to be The Major standing near his white van. Beside him were two others in dark suits (not far from a green sedan) that could only be city detectives. They'd finally found their way to the circus. That wasn't surprising, they were bound to eventually even if only on a fishing expedition. Neither shape was round enough to be Wenders. And, as there was no boss, there were no hard clues. They were merely one of many teams following potential leads on the Lieutenant's orders. No need to panic yet. That said, I still wasn't ready to talk with the cops. This was my first opportunity with Alida and I wanted my interview. I replaced the acrobat's grip on my arm with my grip on hers, and hurried her into the Big Top, anxious now to see her act as much as she wanted to show it to me.

Her muscled stage hands showed up on our heels rubbing sleep from their eyes. Alida ordered them to "Get everything ready," and they dutifully disappeared backstage. The pair reappeared rolling out a four-by-eight pedestal platform with two posts rising four feet from its center, then disappeared again. Alida dropped her robe and ran her hands from her breasts, down, to rest on her thin hips. "Imagine it, Blake," she purred. "See an all silver leotard covered in silver sequins reflecting the changing color-gelled lights splashing over me." She ran to the backstage curtain, turned back and shouted, "The band strikes up 'A Gift for Caesar' from the film Cleopatra!" She disappeared.

A moment later the huskies entered the performance area at a steady march, carrying a litter, bearing an acrylic glass box that couldn't have been more than two feet square. I looked on. I stared. I did a double take. Somehow, some way, Alida was balled up inside the box, contorted backward over herself, smiling at me through the translucent side. They laid the box on the platform and left the ring.

Alida unrolled upward from the box like a charmed snake, thighs, pelvis, stomach, breasts, and head, until she was standing. I could imagine it in silver; glistening diamonds and light. With an all new smile, neither Cheshire Cat nor kitten, she did a back flip out of the box, spun in a pirouette, and – as if there was nothing to it – ended up in a handstand atop the posts above the pedestal.

In that position, she performed what amounted to a dance, gracefully contorting her body in all manner of ways, backward and forward, supporting herself on one hand, then the other, adjusting her balance by extending a limb, by spreading or closing her legs as the situation demanded, upside down all the while rotating slowing in place. How in the world a human body could twist itself so, I had no clue. Alida dismounted, bowed, then pulled the posts from the pedestal and tossed them aside.

A silver ring, three and a half feet in diameter, dropped from the sky (compliments of the stage hands), and a light came on inside of it making the ring glow. "Now the theme music changes," Alida called out as she took hold of the supporting cable. "To Cleopatra's 'Love and Hate'." I wasn't up on my soundtracks but, with this second allusion to the Egyptian queen, was beginning to question the score playing in the acrobat's head.

She spun on one foot, turning on the podium, whipping the ring ever more rapidly in a circle about her. The ring jerked and lifted, carrying Alida, still turning, into the air. She reached the heights, dangling thirty feet up, with the glowing ring in orbit about her. In a blur, she and it became one. Still spinning, the ring slowed to show the acrobat inside sitting on the lower curve. "See it in lights!" Alida cried. Then she let herself fall.

The lower arc caught her spine, supporting her, as she hung backwards from the waist on either side of the ring. Her head hung even with her feet, her heels touched the nape of her neck. She reached behind taking hold of her own ankles, still spinning. The ring sped up again. Alida became a blur. With little trouble, I imagined it in lights. The blur became the pixie again. The girl was upside down, her feet alone in contact with the ring, dangling from her flexed arches. She did a sit up in midair, took the ring in both hands, and was lowered spinning to the floor.

I applauded. But she wasn't finished.

The spinning ring rose again with Alida dangling beneath it. She pulled herself up with the lower arc at the nape of her neck. She dropped her head back as if she'd fallen asleep, and let go. She spun high above the floor with no visible means of support. The effect was startling. She was holding on with only the muscles of her neck. She lifted her legs, grabbed her ankles, and spun. Then, slowly, returned to earth and took a final bow. Alida rolled her tiny body (and her evident self-satisfaction) into a ball as she slipped back down inside the glass cube. The huskies carried her out again.

I followed her like a pet schnauzer.

Backstage, out of her box, Alida invited me to gush over her new act. It was hard to blame her. For a rehearsal, it had been a hell of a performance. I told her so. She dismissed her team of muscle, took me for a walk and talk past the cages and pens of exotic animals, and invited me to perform. She wanted her interrogation. That was when the circus really began. I asked questions. She flirted and answered questions I wasn't asking. Nothing I asked, and certainly nothing she answered, got us anywhere near the murders. Here's a sample:

"No. I did not know Michael…" She looked the question.

"Gronchi. Michael Gronchi, the grounds sweeper. Mickey the Geek."

She waved it away. "I didn't know him. I don't know the grounds sweepers. I spend so little time on the ground."

"Sybil?" I asked. "The Bearded Lady?"

She grimaced. "NO! That disgusting fat woman with the beard? No. I did not know her. I don't know any women. Why would I?"

"Alfonso? You know Alfonso?"

"Of course I know Alfonso. He's everywhere, playing the little boss, when he isn't playing the clown. He's a pest."

"He's very fond of you."

"Of course he is." She purred, honest to God. Then she leaned seductively back against the corner of a tiger's cage and traced a circle around her navel with an index finger. The tiger growled at her. She gnashed her teeth at the big cat. "All male creatures are fond of me." She ran the same finger down my lapel. "For a lucky few, I am very fond in return."

I wondered how the lucky few were selected but decided against asking. Without missing the question, she'd moved on. "Tell me, Blake." She moistened her lips. "Do you ever interrogate suspects in bed?"

"I go where the suspects are."

"I'm not asking about location. I'm asking if you've ever questioned a suspect while making love?"

"Sounds risky."

"Risk makes sex incredible. Don't you think?"

"You have a point," I agreed. Then I shook my head. "But where would I keep my notebook?"

She was the kind of girl where, if you stared too long, you got ideas. As the only ideas I wanted then concerned murder, I found myself needing to look away. The only thing to look at were animals and I looked. She was the kind of girl who demanded attention. Not happy with what I was giving her, Alida stepped between me and the cages.

"You're blocking the view."

She purred again. "I don't mean to block it; merely to replace it."

"Yeah. We were talking about Mickey the Geek, the Bearded Lady, and Alfonso."

"You were talking about them, Blake. I have nothing to say about them. I spend my time in the air, not on the midway, and certainly not in the Freak Show. I have my own way of getting freaky."

Poor Alfonso. He'd swallowed this baby's lure all the way down to his toes. He hadn't merely been hooked, he'd been boated, gutted, and was already sealed in the can. All that remained was for Alida to open him up with her key and eat him on crackers. Her shapely keister ought, by law, to have been placarded with a skull and crossbones. Everything about her screamed 'Poison.' The mind boggled wondering what exactly the love-struck midget thought she needed protection from.

The longer I asked her questions, the less interest she showed in answering them. The only thing she wanted me to know was that she had *tastes*. Like other people's tastes, but more so; lots more so. Alida was a tart. Don't get me wrong; don't think I was being critical. I wasn't. I love tarts. They're delicious. They're sweet and sticky and can do delirious things to your pleasure centers. But, boys, they're no damned good for you. And this one was no good for my murder investigation.

She may have been a perfect match for The Major, I'd yet to really talk with the guy, but I had no idea what the midget saw in her. Alfonso, wherever he was, was in for disappointment at best and likely a painful fall. Sure, Alida and a bottle of vodka could have turned any slob, including me, into Gene Kelly dancing the horizontal mambo. But the midget's repeated demands she was a 'lady' required rose colored glasses with lenses as thick as Mama Cass.

And there, in the midst of the circus animals, Alida was still talking drivel. "Do you ever get the urge, Blake."

"I'm getting one now," I replied. I wasn't lying. I had an overwhelming urge to head for the exit. I was ready to cross Alida off my list as being too self-absorbed (and too horny) to concentrate long enough to kill a man. But I was interrupted by a shout that even startled the tigers.

"You!"

It had to be the cops – and they had me. I raised my hands and turned to accept my fate. But before I came fully around a keenly sharpened knife whizzed past my bruised head and stuck – with a *thwack* and a frightening quiver – in the side of the tiger's cage behind me. It missed me by inches.

Unfortunately, it wasn't the cops. They would only have dragged me to Wenders and chucked me harmlessly into the jug. This was something far more lethal.

Tommy Dagger stood on the other side of the animal enclosure, glaring, his throwing arm cocked above his head, ready with a second knife. He clutched a half dozen more in his other hand, apparently in case he missed again. I wasn't exactly sure why I raised his hackles but I did. Sandra, his assistant, wearing Band-Aids on her arm and alarm on her face, stood nervously looking on behind him.

The tiger and Alida were frozen in place, behind me, watching intently. Both smelled blood and, in my mind's eye, I saw both lick their lips. The situation, in my humble opinion, was ripe for getting out of hand. Coupling that with the knowledge I was the outsider, that murder had already been done on the premises, and that my gun was again securely stored in my office safe, it occurred to me that some de-escalation would do no harm. With that in mind, I said, "Hi!" and asked Tommy, "Was that necessary?"

He lowered the knife. He cocked his head. "Necessary?" He swore, making a hash of the English with his accent (I'm still guessing French). Still I gave him points for passion. "Why do you torment me?" he barked. "Why are you here again? Who are you?"

I admit, I was getting sick of that last question. The owner had by that time, no doubt, informed The Major I'd be 'snooping' around. He, in turn, would have done well to warn them all. The performers needed a team meeting. That was it; a soiree, during which I could be introduced. Following the dance, one of the attendees could then save the rest of us the hassle and confess to the murders. Case solved. Brandy anyone?

"What are you?" I demanded of the knife thrower. "Circus security? If so, wouldn't a gun be more intimidating?"

"Only to the ignorant." Tommy raised his hand, threatening again. "I assure you, at this moment your life is in my hands. Now who are you? Why are you here again?"

"Blake. I'm a private investigator."

"Investigating what?"

"When I get to you, you'll know."

"You're not investigating me?"

"I'm looking into several missing employees. Michael Gronchi. Sybil, the Bearded Lady. And I'm looking for one of the clowns, Alfonso. Can you account for any of them?"

"We mind our own business," he said defiantly. "You were here yesterday. Wandering backstage where you do not belong. You were here before, during our performance, sticking your nose where it did not belong. You are the one who shall be called to account... for Sandra's injury."

"You're too generous, Mr. Dagger, and you're selling yourself short. I created an accidental ruckus, I confess. It was clumsy of me. I've already apologized to your wife. But you're supposed to be a pro. I'm not allowed to shoot a suspect because somebody coughs next door. I'm supposed to know my deadly business. I'm afraid it's on you. You drew blood in your act." I pointed past him to Sandra. She returned a frown and covered her arm self-consciously. Tommy didn't see her response. He continued to stare at me without giving his wife a glance. "That a habit of yours?" I asked. "Drawing blood?"

His knife remained unwavering. "Should we put your question to the test?"

"I'll take a rain check on the knife demonstration. After cutting your partner, you seem a bit shaky."

"You are the one who will shake… if you do not stay away from us."

"I'm here under Mrs. Callicoat's authority. Will you answer my questions?"

"You are not investigating me," he insisted. This time it wasn't a question. It was a command.

Between you and me, the knife thrower had anger issues. I probably should have been afraid. With two knife killings already on the scoreboard I should have been very afraid. But I'm not smart enough, braggarts bore me, and the danger part is how I earn my bones. So I dove back in instead. "I said, I'm investigating missing employees. Did you know Michael Gronchi? Or Sybil? Do you know Alfonso? Can you account for yourself for the last three days and nights? Your interactions with any of the three? Your whereabouts?"

"I will not answer." Tommy jammed the knife into the bunch in his hand, eliminating the immediate threat of my murder, for which I breathed a sigh of relief. Then he screamed, "I do not know you. I owe you nothing."

Who knows where the situation might have gone had it been allowed to continue? But it was brought to a close in a spectacular circus sort of way. The white Dodge van, painted with splashes of circus ballyhoo, roared into the tent, between the animal cages, and growled to a stop beside us throwing sawdust into the air. The animals ran, paced, panted in wild circles within their cages, growling, meow-ling, screeching, and generally going ape. The Major leaped from behind the wheel, riding crop in hand, growling in his own fashion, "What is going on here?"

He had apparently, at least temporarily, rid himself of the city detectives and was making one of his 'tours of the grounds' that Alfonso had spoken of with such disdain. He'd come upon us in time to see Tommy Dagger and I at odds. "I asked you," The Major boomed, "what is going on here?"

"Your knife thrower and I were having a talk," I said. "He doesn't like the way I talk."

"If you cross me again," Tommy cut in, yelling. "You will be talking without a tongue." The threat made no sense. (But then many threats don't.) He must have realized it as he quickly offered another option. "Or perhaps I will give you a second mouth; a wide one from ear to ear." He passed his fistful of knives across his own throat to demonstrate.

"I'll handle this, Tommy," The Major said. "You and Sandra enjoy your day off."

Tommy shouted, "*Pah!*" He grabbed Sandra by her injured arm. She winced, but didn't make a sound, as the knife thrower stormed away dragging her with him.

"You are too ignorant to understand," The Major told me. "I may have saved your life. When Tommy is all there," he pointed at his own head, "he's very good. But he isn't always all there."

Done with Tommy and Sandra, he glared past me to his aerial contortionist and, rumor had it, fiancé. His cold stare was loaded with accusation. Alida took it without flinching. He passed the look on to me, got nothing for the trouble, and made one last try on the pixie. He was being bit hard. The many jealous bones in the circus manager's body didn't like the scene his eyes were taking in. Blood wasn't exactly pouring from his tear ducts. But that may or may not have meant anything as the jury was still out on whether or not he had any blood in him. It would be fair to say, without guessing, The Major was unhappy with the personal guided tour I was getting. "You," he said, pointing his riding crop at my nose. "Let me guess. You are now doing a story for 'Little Girl' Magazine?"

"No," I said. "I wouldn't say that."

"What would you say?" The Major asked, his face reddening. "Before I lash you within an inch of your life?" He was six feet away, and waving a riding crop instead of the whip he apparently wished he had, but I gave the old boy high marks for intimidation.

"There's no need for that," I assured him. "I'm here on business."

"Yes? What is your business? Who in hell are you?"

"You've already got the name, I think. Blake. I'm a private dick on a case. I've spoken with Mrs. Callicoat and have her blessing to inquire. I'm quite certain she has spoken with you."

He strode toward us, lowering the riding crop but puffing up his chest. He seemed bent on putting a scare into us (or at least me). Though I wasn't looking at her, I sensed no fear from Alida. I'd already put the little acrobat down in my book as a card-carrying tart. It was no great leap from there to a girl who thrived on conflict and chaos; one of those dames who loved men fighting over her, who couldn't wait to paw the victor. Poor Alfonso. She was a peach.

But I'd gone off into my head again; a dangerous habit with a jealous lover within striking distance. The Major was growling again. "What does a private detective want with my fiancé?"

"The same thing I want everywhere. Answers. I came looking for Michael Gronchi." The Major carved holes through me with his stare. "Did I say something wrong?"

"Wrong? No. But interesting. Why would anybody on God's earth be looking for him? A homeless booze hound who sweeps for a cot and the price of a bottle. Why would you be looking for Gronchi?"

"At the time, I was concerned something had happened to him."

"What could have happened to him?"

"Aahh," I said. "The mind runs riot. Anything could have happened."

"Nothing happened. He's here, somewhere, pushing a broom, tipping a bottle, taking a nap."

"Is that what you told the cops?" I shook my head. "I said I *was* concerned; I'm not anymore. Gronchi is dead, murdered, here at your circus." I watched his face, hoping a reaction would tell me something. If one came, I missed it. The Major merely stared. "You have nothing to say about the death of one of your employees?"

"Not to you."

"Oh," I said, with a shrug. "Then how about two? Sybil, your Bearded Lady is dead as well. Or did you already know that?"

"If what you're saying is true, why–"

"Why is that the first visit you've had with the cops? Why so short and sweet? Why haven't you and your show been swarmed? Okay, let's pretend you don't know. It's because the bodies were discovered elsewhere. The cops and scientists are snapping pictures, bagging evidence, and questioning the wrong people." I started away. "I'm telling you the signs are there to be read and they will soon get around to questioning the right people."

The Major didn't like me. He was mad as hell I'd lied to him the day before and madder yet I'd gone over his head to the owner. Worst of all, he was jealous of finding me with Alida. He apparently knew Alida better than Alfonso did.

"I have already told the authorities everything I know."

"About?"

"Everything they asked."

"But you won't tell me?"

"Mrs. Callicoat, my partner–"

"And major shareholder," I helpfully put in.

The Major tried to adjust his face. But, unable to decide what to do with it, went on. "My partner has asked me to allow you access to our facilities. I do so. I am under no obligation to speak with you or answer your questions." He smiled like, I imagine, a cannibal smiles at his dinner. "I say this to you. As you pry, go for a long walk down the Pier." He pointed east. "Stop when your hat floats."

I wasn't wearing a hat. But it was a dandy exit line all the same, so I made my exit.

I headed west out of the Big Top and through the groggily waking midway. I passed Olive's ticket booth where, I'll be hanged, the kid and Alfonso's dog were together wolfing down an olive and cream cheese sandwich. That was it for me. I wanted my car and to be away from the circus.

Other than the warm and fuzzy feeling I got from knowing the midget's sad mutt now had two meals in him, and a friend to take him for an occasional walk and pee, I hadn't learned a thing or advanced the investigation one step. Unless you count adding suspects as an advance. From my point of view, I was dead in the water, if not drifting backwards. Then again, I had made a few acquaintances and formed several personal relationships. Despite my status as a complete stranger, Alfonso's pixie acrobat was ready and willing to booger my body bone. Her fiancé, the ringmaster and circus manager, was ready and more than willing to horse whip me with his riding crop. And the knife thrower was ready and eager to spin me on his Wheel of Death and hurl cutlery at me until my working parts stopped working. The morning hadn't been a total loss.

Chapter Sixteen

I passed by my office but didn't stop. Make that couldn't stop.

I'd underestimated Wenders' desire to catch up with me. He had a patrol unit staked out in my lot, watching the place, and apparently intended to grab me the moment I showed my face. It was enough to make me wonder whether or not the lieutenant was serious when he threatened to pin Mickey's murder on me? I decided not to test him and, as I said, drove on by. But I must confess, two near misses in one morning renewed my enthusiasm for finding the real perpetrator.

A few blocks away I found a delicatessen with a phone booth instead and gave my office a call. Staking me out was one thing but he couldn't have been tapping my phone. He'd need a warrant and, "I'm lazy, Your Honor, and need Blake to solve a murder for me," isn't a legal reason to secure a judge's order. But back to the phone. I wanted to touch base with Lisa and pick up my messages. It wasn't likely but maybe, just maybe, I'd get a shove in the right direction.

Lisa didn't answer, Willie did. We repeated the idiotic verbal dance we'd done before. Why are you still there? No Lisa! Where's Lisa? No idea! Here's your messages! Why are you taking messages? I'm starving! I hired an office sitter, when did I adopt you? I'll spare you the remaining details and skip to the bottom line: The cops were glued outside my place waiting to drop a net on me. My secretary was MIA. A low-class criminal was guarding my livelihood. There had been one message, from Wenders, and my goodness he sounded annoyed. I was annoyed myself, and worried. Where was Lisa? Had her injury been worse than we all thought?

Against my better judgment, and without any measurable delight, I called Lisa's home and spoke with her mother. No, Lisa wasn't home. She was out working. Didn't she work for me? Didn't I know where I'd sent her? Maybe I should tell her

(Lisa's mother) where Lisa was! I apologized for the trouble. I told her not to worry. I thought Lisa might have stopped home while doing her running. I wished her a good day, got called a "schlemiel," and heard the slam of the phone.

I hadn't learned a thing and I'd lost an inch of hide doing it. Lisa told her mother she was going to work, so she was recovered. To what extent I had no idea. She wasn't in the office, so she wasn't working for me. Where was Lisa? What was Lisa working on?

Pinched for a next move, and not wanting to be pinched by Chicago's finest, I decided the time was right for a return visit to my researcher and snitch, Large. He'd had little time. I didn't expect much. But, like Sinatra's little ant, I had high hopes. And, as the visit might be extended this time, you'll need a quick tour of Large's place so you're comfortable in the telling.

There were a few blues, jazz, and rhythm and blues clubs on the Gold Coast, where monied Chicago dabblers could get a taste of the old-world bayou culture without getting their figurative hands dirty. And, of course, there were real blues joints on the city's south side where, by leaps and bounds, the majority of the transplanted Louisiana (and Mississippi, and Carolina, and Georgia) blacks made their homes. But if you wanted to hear blues, real "Whoo-eee" Louisiana blues, then Large's 'Taste of New Orleans' was the only place to go. It wasn't a theater or a club. It was a restaurant and, by its looks when you first drove up, only just that.

The Taste of New Orleans, and now I'm talking about the physical building, had started life as a full-service gas station in the 1930's. The small concrete block building sat on a lonely south side street corner. The lot out front, with both pump islands long removed, could park ten cars if the last four parked the first six in. Four newspaper boxes, chained to the building, stood guard in front of the wide glass windows (iron bars permanently in place). The face of what once had been the two bay service garages had been covered in barn board and white washed; over top of that, in bright splashes of blue, from one end of the building to the other, had been painted the business hours and the restaurant's menu. I don't know if you've read any good restaurants lately but this place made your mouth water. Behind the building, and above, stood an even older wood and concrete railroad trestle. Time had marched on and the six inter-city rail lines that once used it had been consolidated into one (Amtrak) eight years before as mass passenger travel went the way of the dinosaur. Still cross-country goods needed to be moved and the line, taken over by Burlington Northern South Bend was still heavily in demand. Day and night trains shunted noisily by.

A monstrous two-story residence to the west of the restaurant housed Large's brood of children, nine in all, and was ruled over by his wife, Estella, a woman of both indomitable mettle and precious metal (a heart of gold, a fist of iron, a soup ladle of steel). But the restaurant was Large's kingdom.

One of the old gas station's service bays had been converted into the restaurant's cutting and mixing kitchen, larder, and walk-in cooler. The former lobby and office had been transformed into the cooking kitchen and dining area with a six-stool counter and three tables with three chairs apiece. As outside the interior was simple, white wash, with blue brush paint listing and championing the delectable virtues of New Orleans' Gumbo, Blue Bayou Burgers, Hot Burgers, and Oyster Po-Boys.

Red Beans, at 19 the middle-aged of Large's five sons, was in his usual station at the stove and grill, stirring a kettle of red beans, and watching over the black beans, dirty rice, and the sizzling pans of blackened fish, off to one side from the monstrous and ancient oven where a succulent dripping "P-i-g, Hog!" was all set to come home to Papa. Lizbet, at 17 Large's eldest of four daughters, was fending off a come-on from a customer on a stool at the end of the counter and, without missing a beat, drying a mountain of dishes and shelving them neatly on the wall above her head.

I barely crossed the sill before Lizbet saw me and, toweling her hands, hurried my way. "Blake! Daddy said I missed you earlier." Her hugs, which used to encircle my thighs, now wound round my waist. Time marched on. Those same hugs would soon be forced, by the natural order of things, to come to an end. Another sad day to which I had no choice but to look forward. Red Beans hadn't given me a hug in nearly a decade. But he waved big from where he stood and smiled bigger.

Before I got a word out, the door to the mixing kitchen came open and a four-hundred-pound black man with an intellect, heart, and soul twice that size appeared from his lair. "I thought," Large said, "I heard your appellation." He turned to Lizbet. "Shouted in the too-excited-to-be-good-for-business voice of my eldest angel." She twisted her lips in a loving frown. "To work," he told her, raising a huge ham hock of a hand, glinting rings on every finger, and waving her away. "To work."

Lizbet smiled at me and returned to her dishes.

Large looked past me to ogle the customer at the end of the counter who'd been giving Lizbet the business. "You again?" he asked. "And more of the same?"

The fellow flexed his jaws like a landed carp. No sound emerged.

"Would they were edible," Large told him. "I would twist you in half like a Louisiana Crawfish and suck out your innards. Sadly, I'm convinced your entrails are as tainted as your thoughts and I fear—"

It should come as no surprise to you, it came as none to me, the young man did not wait to hear the details of Large's fears. Having a few of his own, he vacated the stool and the restaurant toot sweet. Without giving the running cock's rear a second glance, my mountainous associate waved me toward the door to the back rooms. "Now Brother Blake, to work."

The outer service bay was now Large's office and fortress. This inner sanctum was a world unto itself and not unlike, it always seemed to me, visiting a giant's lair. There were two huge chairs, a gargantuan couch, and a massive desk. Those were necessary. Large was a giant, but a gentle giant, a well-spoken man, an artist, and a connoisseur of music. Not any music. As I already mentioned, this was the place in Chicago for real Louisiana blues. And New Orleans blues, and Cajun music (the old French sounds), Dixieland Jazz, Ragtime, Zydeco (the Creole music), Swamp blues, and the Afro-Caribbean rhythms. The walls of Large's lair testified, wall-to-wall-to-wall shelves of vinyl LPs, and a fourth of 7-inch 45 single records, each in his words, "A chariot bearing glory upon the wind."

Professor Longhair's piano played me in, to a chair and (thanks to Large) a gin, with the happily raucous 'Tipitina'. We sipped slowly while Moses 'Whispering' Smith gave us the 'Mean Woman Blues' on his harmonica. We commiserated with the magical guitar of Lightnin' Slim while he shared his 'Bad Luck Blues'. Then, despite my desire to say to hell with it and keep spinning records, I asked Large what he'd been able to ferret out concerning my cast of circus characters. His minions had had the assignment for mere hours, yet the answer appeared to be plenty. We got down to business.

"This was, and is, an infinitely interesting group of individuals you named for inclusion in our search," Large said. "With whom among them shall we begin?"

"I always start with the client. But, as this time I haven't one, I'll take the next best thing. Alfonso."

"Your diminutive clown. Yes." Large selected a manilla file folder from a stack on a nearby table and settled back. "A fairly straight-forward case lacking anything sinister to sink the teeth into. Alfonso Valencia. Thirty years of age, born Queens,

New York, 1949, to average-height adult parents (a Polish mother, an Egyptian father, both naturalized). Diagnosed with Achondroplasia, a form of short-limbed dwarfism. Outside of the genetic disorder an otherwise healthy individual who joined the circus in his teens. Has been with six circuses of various sizes throughout his career," Large waved a paper. "The list is here. No incidents of note bringing him to the attention of law enforcement. Currently, as you know, employed by the Callicoat and Major Combined Circus."

"All right," I said. "If you were able to find anything, let's move on to The Canary."

"If I was able to find anything?" Large shook his head in dismay and picked up another folder. "The Canary. An excellent choice." He took a deep breath. "If – and I emphasize *If* – The Canary of your drowned man's quote is the performer you saw featured on the circus poster in Wisconsin," he shook the file, "and it is possible, even likely, though I'd put little faith in her being billed as 'The One and Only', then your drowned man was in error and his dying declaration faulty. The Canary," he shook the file again, "did, in fact, die when she fell from the sky."

"You have my attention."

Large chuckled with a childish glee, an infectious sound and sight. Whether it was food, music, or information, he loved unveiling tastes and tidbits to virginal reactions.

"The name of our 'One and Only' Canary was Aurelia Marx Herman. She was the premiere aerial performer and trapeze artist of the Kessler Traveling Circus. There isn't a lot known about her but, I can tell you this, she did die during a performance, three years ago in Cape Girardeau, Missouri."

I raised a brow. How could I not?

"Now to her limited background," Large said. "Aurelia Marx joined the Kessler troupe the previous year, from where it is not known. Hired to replace an injured acrobat, she joined the remaining half of that couple act, a competent and moderately successful, but obscure, trapeze artist and aerial catcher named Gunther Herman. Aurelia's new partner was considerably older, eh, twenty years, but still a marvel of physical strength and prowess. Their act was initially billed as The Hawk and The Canary and they were an instant hit. Such a hit the injured performer was let go. The Hawk and The Canary became Kessler's star attraction. Behind the scenes, the couple got on famously and soon married.

"But the spotlight shined far brighter on The Canary than it did her husband. In no time, the act was introduced simply as 'The Canary'. Gunther Herman remained, as partner and husband, but the cheers fell only on The Canary. I'll add, Brother Blake, as I know your cynical mind, there is no suggestion the change in billing or the shift in audience adoration bothered the husband in any way. It was merely show business and Gunther appears to have handled it as such."

Large coughed a throaty cough and continued. "On the fateful day in Cape Girardeau, a fire broke out inside the temporarily erected hippodrome during the performance of their headlining act. Details, even at the time, were naturally sketchy owing to chaos and excited memory. The intervening years have brought nothing new to light. What is known is that the fire got quickly out of control, a good number of circus goers and performers were injured in the tumultuous escape from the Big Top, a trick rider, eh, one Luna Blaženovic, went missing and, in the panic, The Canary fell to her death. Your informant, Brother Blake, your drowned man was in error."

"So much for cryptic clues."

"Indeed. The results were, of course, a legal nightmare. No sooner did the smoke clear than the Kessler Traveling Circus disbanded and its displaced performers scattered to the four corners of the world. There remains one item of interest; a fact discovered in cross-checking the employee lists. Among the displaced acts was a Sideshow performer billed as Mickey the Geek and payed as Michael Gronchi. This lends gravitas to your hypothesis that this Canary was The Canary. Beyond that…" Large shrugged his meaty shoulders.

Michael Gronchi was there, on hand, or at least in the show, when The Canary fell from the sky. But it made no sense because he'd been wrong. The Canary died.

Large was going on. "A fact worth noting is that, following the fire and the death of his wife, Gunther Herman appears to have vanished. There's no record of his moving on to another circus."

"He quit the business? Well, his wife was dead. I'm sure he was heartbroken."

"Yes," Large agreed. "But neither you nor I are classical romantics, Blake. A fact takes it deeper."

"And the fact?"

"Following the dissolution of the Kessler Circus there is no record of Gunther Herman, that particular Gunther Herman, anywhere at all. He didn't merely stop performing. He vanished."

There were facts and there were facts that made you think. That one made me think.

Large picked up another folder. "Shall I proceed?"

"Don't let me stop you."

"Michael Gronchi, your first victim. Gronchi worked in a number of small circuses, before and after the Kessler Circus fire, in their Sideshows, as Mickey the Geek. Cross-referencing again gives us one item of note. Fourteen months after the Cape Girardeau fire, Gronchi joined the 'Buckets and Barns Circus' traveling the U.S. southern circuit. In addition to Mickey the Geek, the Sideshow of the Buckets and Barns Circus featured a Bearded Lady named–"

"Sybil."

"Indeed. Buckets and Barns folded its tent after one season. Sybil moved on to another circus. But Gronchi with, if you'll excuse the vulgar slang, Geek-work going out of vogue, appears to have taken up imbibing adult beverages as a full-time endeavor. Before you ask, he has a colorful history of Public Intoxication, Vagrancy, and Drunk and Disorderly arrests in his recent past."

"Did you have any more on Sybil?"

"Yes." Large cleared his throat. "Gerald Lapinski. Lithuanian by birth. Began his circus and carnival careers, he had a number in both, as a carnival barker, roadie, circus ticket salesman, and maintenance man. He was not originally a performer. On this side of the pond, he routinely spent the off season working for the circus museum in Barrelton, Wisconsin; his American home. The first appearance of Sybil, the Bearded Lady, and Lapinski's first position as a Sideshow performer was in the Great Garland Circus, where we find he worked for the first time with Alfonso Valencia, the diminutive Sideshow performer. This was before his Kessler days and his association with Michael Gronchi."

"Gerald. He's been Sybil to me for so long," I confessed, "the names and pronouns are making me spin."

"We can refer to him by his circus persona if you'd prefer. There is no record of who originated the notion to put Sybil in a dress and pass her off as a Bearded Lady. There is no record, though I'm not certain there would be, of Sybil having been a transvestite or a cross dresser. Logic suggests it unlikely with the positions she held. The disguise seems to have originated solely for monetary reasons. The ruse worked. The act was a success with Kessler and led to her immediate hire by The Major's Major when they premiered their show."

"Never having met Sybil, I can't say whether or not I would have been fooled. She certainly fooled many," I said. "All I know is I was painfully awakened to the truth in the end."

Large offered no comment. A tenacious digger, he nevertheless never dug at me. He merely switched files and continued with his presentation.

"The venue of your current inquiry, The Callicoat and Major Combined Circus, came about as its own entity under two years ago when the majority of The Major's Major Circus was purchased by a holding company owned by Reginald Callicoat III. Karl Kreis, known to all as The Major, remains a minority owner. There are several interesting historical side notes. I recommend you peruse them."

"Something significant?" I asked.

Large smiled with a glint in his eye. "Not for me to say. I beat the brush, Brother Blake. You are the keen-eyed hunter."

I nodded, silently reminding myself that, one, the big man's having made special mention of it made it significant and, two, having brought it to my attention he'd said all he would say on the matter. I took the file in one hand, and my refreshed gin in the other, and carefully examined the histories of both circuses and both owners. I did my best to soak up the raw information like a sponge.

There was plenty there to file away, in case, and much there to consider in general.

I couldn't help but marvel at how fast Large and his pack of snoops had met my request, and told my friend so. "How do you always come through with so much, so quickly?"

"Give you my secrets and cut my own throat?" Large asked with a laugh. "But this time, as you were there and the answer should prove embarrassing, I'll tell you. The World Circus Museum has a library and research center on grounds. The world's largest collection of circus-related newspapers, magazines, books, and photographs. Open to the public."

"Why didn't I know that?"

"Perhaps," Large said, "you were too busy killing the Bearded Lady."

"Perhaps." I returned his file. "You offered nothing detailed on the widow Callicoat or Alida Harrison. I'm pressed but would a little more time help?"

"More time? Yes." Large smiled. "And a look at your bank balance before I begin. A records search to the ends of the earth may be needed and likely will be a laborious and expensive endeavor."

"Oh?"

"Indeed. But that doesn't mean the vault is empty. Let me tell you, Brother Blake, what I've learned about Reginald and Danita Callicoat, Karl Kreis, and Alida Harrison." He proceeded to do just that.

Chapter Seventeen

I'd been right about the lovely Mrs. Callicoat. In her case, still waters did run deep. There were curious things to learn about all four, in fact, the late circus owner, his junior partner and manager, his widow, and their star attraction. Unfortunately, that's all there was so far – curious discoveries. There were no smoking guns (or thrown knives), no signs directing me to a murderer or their motive. But my big snitch had given me plenty of human drama to think about.

After my visit with Large I headed north again, into the heart of the city and the loop, and made a stop at the City Hall building on North La Salle. Specifically, I visited Room 107, the Clerk of the City of Chicago, in an effort to see for myself any and all permits issued to The Callicoat and Major Circus to perform their dog and pony and tiger show at and on Navy Pier. My curiosity was soon satisfied, though I had no idea as to what end.

Finished there, and while I still felt nosy, I detoured to West Washington for a repeat performance at the Cook County clerk's office. My goal there was slightly different. I did some, probably completely wasted, research on the details of the history of the Callicoat Estate and holdings. I'd like to report specifically what I was after, and what I found, in my hunt. But, the fact was, I had no idea. I merely wanted to know all I could know.

Like I said, Large hadn't handed me a murderer but he'd given me food for thought. And knowledge gained in my trips to his Taste of New Orleans always made me hungry for more.

Speaking of hunger, I'd seen to Alfonso's mutt and visited the best Louisiana restaurant in the city but had forgotten to feed myself. I needed grub, and a place to down it, and a place to quietly sort the head full of facts and rumors I'd collected. My office was out, the cops were covering it like a cheap suit. I imagined the same might be true for my apartment but, as it featured several points of access, I decided to give the homestead a look. I sneaked home.

Well, close to home. I parked the Jag on a 'Used Car' lot two blocks away (the owner and I had an understanding) and I darted from phone pole to dumpster to discarded refrigerator box up the alleys to the rear of my apartment building. No bulls in the back. I hopped the rear fence, low crawled the yard, and slipped into the basement through a window secured with a trick latch for just such occasions. As quietly as I could, I maneuvered the cellar and climbed to the ground floor. I eased a crack in the door and found the hall empty. I slipped off my shoes, slipped into the hall, and peeked through the front door window. Sure enough there sat an unmarked, but obvious, city unit with a nodding copper at the wheel. Whatever Wenders wanted, he wanted it bad.

I climbed the stairs as noiselessly as I was able to my second-floor apartment. I reached the landing puffed with pride at having outsmarted the law. I unlocked the door, and was pocketing my latch key when – for no reason I could see – I was thunderstruck. That increasingly familiar searing pain tore through my neck. I lost my balance, dropped my shoes, and tumbled like a sack of rocks backwards down the stairs. So much for pride or a silent entrance. My head hit a step, my ankle hit the rail, my wrist hit the wall, over and over again all the way down. You get the picture. A week later, it seemed, I hit the hardwood floor at the bottom of the staircase.

I'd felt every smack of the tumble but saw none of it. My mind and senses were busy. Following the waves of heat, pain, light, and darkness you're coming to expect as much as I, and for some ungodly reason of which I couldn't even guess, I found myself back in Sybil's train car at the circus. I don't mean merely that the vision had put me back in Sybil's place. I was back in her bulbous body as well. Both place and person were instantly recognizable by the distant calliope music, the long room, the lighted mirror, the crap furniture, me on my knees, my hand wet again with Sybil's spilled porridge, oh, and the knife. I shouldn't forget the keenly sharpened throwing knife again plunged into my back.

In the time it took to set the scene for you, the shadowy phantom killer behind me had moved into the room and was upon me. Ignoring the knife he'd thrown for the moment, he grabbed me, no, he grabbed my pearl necklace and began choking me. The knife hurt make no mistake. But there's nothing on earth to match the outright terror of not being able to breathe. I, by which I mean poor dying Sybil, couldn't get a breath. I had quite a murderous metaphor building in my boiled brain. Amid my thunderstrike, the killer was strangling me so hard the necklace snapped under the pressure. The loosed pearls scattered like hail stones and I dropped to the linoleum like a tree felled by a storm.

An instant later I yelled (how could I not?) as the killer pulled the knife from my back. It was not an altruistic move on his part; I knew, I'd already died through it once. He was about to play butcher and was rolling me onto my back to get the game started. It was then, as the murderer turned me, I saw it again. The same something tucked beneath Sybil's bed I'd seen before but could not recognize. I saw it, saw him, clearly now. Alfonso!

In that instant, I had one answer at least. The midget was not the killer.

But the little twerp had lied to me. He'd seen Sybil catch the knife in her back, as he'd said. But he hadn't hightailed it out of the room and away to find me. He'd stayed for the show. I knew because I was in it, in the starring role of doomed Sybil. There he was, less than five feet away, hiding under the bed. It didn't appear he could see me – or my murder. He had crammed himself in, probably in one hell of a hurry, with his head pointed in the opposite direction. Once there, he couldn't turn. The space proved too confining to move. Facts were facts and Alfonso's head was the biggest part of his body. From his hiding place, a few feet away, he couldn't look at the dying Sybil or see the murder. But he heard it – and he heard the murderer. No wonder he'd split; got while the getting was good.

Alfonso was innocent. He was on the run, in fear for his life. But I had no more time or thoughts to devote to my miniature associate. I was still Sybil! The killer's knife was flashing again in the amber lamplight, into my chest and through my lung, into my groin again and again. Blood splashed pearls rolled past my eyes.

I went blind. Colored lights flashed in my mind.

I was burning with fever as the flare in the back of my neck worked its way around my face. My head felt ready to explode. My sight returned; but what I saw was not in my world. I was still in the midst of the thunderstrike but my perspective, my location, and my sensations had changed. I was flying or floating, I didn't know which or the difference between the two, above a room completely foreign yet somehow oddly familiar. I'd been there, or somewhere like it, before. But where?

I saw movement in the room, turned in the air, and was able to make out the form and face of my buddy Alfonso. He stood gesticulating wildly like a lawyer pleading for his client. Then he dropped his arms in resignation and turned in defeat. I saw his danger, too late to help. Too late even to holler a warning. Not that it would have helped. Nobody in my visions had ever heard a word I'd said. But I wanted to help. A shadow crept up on Alfonso, raised an arm, and blasted him over the head with a green bottle. The bottle broke and shattered glass flew. The midget growled and went down.

Then, in a loop, I saw it again. Alfonso on his feet, the bottle flying in a roundhouse arc, crashing down on his crown, Alfonso sprawled on the floor. And again. Alfonso up, bottle down, Alfonso down. Again. And again. I wanted off that bloody merry-go-round.

Then, sisters and brothers, I was reminded why they warn you to 'Be careful what you wish for'. My vision switched again. I was in the same room but no longer hovering – and no longer seeing Alfonso. You guessed it. I had become Alfonso. My head, already sore from the ravages of my last case, injured again in a hospital stairwell, injured again by an unknown attacker in Sybil's dressing room, slammed seconds before in a fall down my own stairs, hadn't felt anything yet. I was Alfonso. And I'd just seen the little guy–

Something smashed the top of my head. I didn't see it but I knew what it was. I fell in excruciating pain. Blood rained down my neck, down my face, into my eyes. I was the midget clown and, unless this was all a fantasy inspired by a bruised brain, a deftly swung bottle had crushed my skull.

Maybe it was the head injury, perhaps it was merely my consciousness slipping away, all I know is everything went from horror to goofiness. Out of nowhere, as he had at the circus museum, suddenly Alfonso appeared standing over me. I expected him to tug on me as he had before. I expected him to shout, in his own colorful way, "Blake, wake up! Come out of it, fer Chris-sake!" But he didn't. This time something was different. Something was wrong. The midget's eyes were flat and dull. His skin was ashen gray and waxy as if he'd come through a couple of years' worth of cosmetic surgery. It was worse than that. The little guy looked as if he was…

"Alfonso!" I screamed. "You were there. You were there when Sybil was killed. Why didn't you tell me? You were there. You saw… You heard the murderer! Why did you run? Why didn't you say something to me?"

"Dames!" Alfonso shouted, in my face, so loudly and bitterly it scared me. "Fuck!"

Sorry, sisters and brothers, but that time he dropped the F-bomb like an H-bomb. I'm just reporting. And, if the experiences gleaned from this chronic head thing were any indication, he'd said it from the other side of the barrier between life and death. I didn't know what it meant. I don't mind confessing I was terrified of what I thought it meant. As if to underline my terror, an alarming crimson eructation bubbled up from between the midget's lips and ran down his chin. Alfonso swore, spitting an arc of blood through the air. Then he vanished.

It was then I realized I hadn't 'come to' at all. I was still in the middle of my vision. And I was the midget performer again. The pain in my head was intense. Which made sense as I'd received what had to have been a lethal blow. Everything went black. But the experience went on. I knew that because blood was again pouring from the top of my head, as if over a waterfall, down my neck and face and into my eyes. Seconds (or a month) later, I didn't know, I felt an incredible compression of my chest and stomach as if all the air had been suddenly and violently squeezed from me; as if my body had been crushed. It was surreal. Somewhere beyond my brain, I heard Alfonso scream again, "F—!"

"Blake. Blake." I heard my name being called. Over and over, in a muffled voice, as if the speaker stood behind a wall of cotton. "Blake. Blake!" I came to again – this time for real. It had to be real because no psychic vision, no matter how horrible, could be that horrible. Frank Wenders stood beside me, over me, breathing on me like a malevolent dragon and calling my name. "Blake. Blake!"

"Yeah," I groaned, trying to find my head. "Yes!"

"Blake? Did you fall down the stairs?"

Yet again, Homicide's fattest lieutenant had a firm grasp of the obvious. And don't think for an instant he'd asked out of concern for my welfare. He was merely curious. I grunted and fought to a sitting position.

"You okay?"

The question was loaded with contempt. He wanted something and was ordering me to be okay so he could get on with it. He hadn't found me to give himself more work by having me re-paired. It made no difference. My head was splitting, but I wasn't dead so I kept it to myself. "Never better," I muttered. "Where did you come from?"

"I was drinking tea with your landlady."

Despite the pain, I took the time to gawk. I couldn't believe my ears but, sure enough, he looked sincere. More, we were on the ground floor of my apartment building, outside the landlady's door. The door was open and there, standing behind Wenders, was what's-her-name, my landlady. She wore her usual tattered bath robe, her usual curlers, and her usual puckered expression. She peered past him, taking me in, banged up on the floor on my keister. The questions – and a contempt rivaling Wenders' – lit up on her face like a neon 'Good Food' sign outside of a Skid Row greasy spoon. She looked to the top of the stairs, probably for whoever had thrown me down from the floor above, only to find the hall outside my door empty. I swear, she looked disappointed. I considered explaining the situation to her but to hell with it. She thought likewise as she vanished back inside her own apartment and closed her door without a word. Why Sherlock Holmes got kindly old Mrs. Hudson while I got her was another of those nasty unsolvable mysteries. The only thing I knew for certain was… Truman was right. If you want a friend in this life, get a dog.

"Sorry to interrupt your tea," I told Wenders. "What are you doing here? Stealing?"

"Fat chance. I've seen your apartment. I've been in abandoned buildings with nicer furniture."

"So you're just lying in wait? What do you want?"

"What do I want? I've been scourin' the city for you, wise guy. You've been avoiding me. You and that voracious secretary of yours. Speakin' of which, where is she? It can't come as a surprise to you I talked to George Clay. I squeezed the little creep and he babbled like a brook. You lied, Blake! Your secretary rented that boat, not you. Meanin' your secretary found that body, not you. Meanin' you're both in a lot of trouble. Now where's your secretary?"

"I don't know."

"Why have you got that retard criminal watchin' your office? Where have you been? Why am I wastin' time and manpower posting men at your apartment and office? These are a sample of the questions currently making me itch. What I want, Blake, is, when you're done playin' on the stairs, to hear everything you know and everything you've learned about a certain murder I'm peering into. That talk of ours is now overdue. I got a bunch more questions you are damn well going to answer. That is what I want. Unless you got nothin' to talk about, in which case I'm going to pin these murders on you and call it a day."

I started to rise, realized what he'd said, and halted.

"That's right, bright boy," Wenders said. "I said 'murders' with an 's'."

Someone had told him about Sybil. I finished climbing shakily to my feet, took a needed breath, then climbed slightly less shakily to the upper landing. Wenders waddled closely behind, up and into my apartment. Me and my shadow.

Chapter Eighteen

"What the hell was that?" Wenders asked entering the apartment on my heels. Not having been home in a while, I passed in, leaving him to close the door and bark at my back. "How come you fell down the stairs?"

I had no idea what was coming. I didn't know why he'd been searching for me with such zeal, why he was taking tea with what's-her-name, or what bad news he had for me. But I knew what we weren't going to discuss. My head condition and my journeys into the land of the dead were off limits and none of his business. I already had a world of trouble and a headache. I saw no need to add to either. "It's a new medication I'm on," I lied. "I'm not supposed to operate heavy machinery or walk up stairs."

"A new medicine? With the allergies you're always whinin' about?"

"Never mind my allergies. Why are you hounding me? Stake outs on my office and apartment? Ten phone calls? Threatening messages? You gave me forty-eight hours to snoop around. Before twenty-four have gone by you're harassing me. Why?"

"Why do you think? Because I'm bein' harassed. The newspapers got wind of boat boy and started printin' colorful headlines. That made the Mayor unhappy. She chewed on the Commissioner. Now he's unhappy and chewin' on me. This ain't your first day in long pants, Blake. Crap slides downhill."

"Yeah. Crap slides downhill. But I just got started."

"Don't give me that! Don't bother with the lies; they're wasted. You been holdin' out on me. You found something. And kept it to yourself."

"What are you talking about?"

"I said 'Don't' and I meant it! You're going to spill, Blake, now, everything you know about this case. And you're not going to leave out a thing."

"Let me make a phone call first."

"What the hell? Are you already in so deep you need a mouthpiece?"

"I'm not calling a lawyer."

"You're not callin' anyone. Now spill."

"The drowned man was Michael Gronchi," I said. "That's as far as I've gotten."

The lieutenant made a noise that might have come from any number of barnyard animals. "That's not news. We already know who he was. We got a kickback on boat boy's prints and identified him. As to your claim you got no further, as usual, you're lyin' through your teeth. We know Gronchi was a circus performer. We know you know it too. We know that, until he quit payin' taxes a couple of days ago, he was working for the little circus currently leaving lion poop all over Navy Pier. We know you know that too. You've been annoying all the circus workers. I don't care, I just mention it to show I haven't been sittin' on my duff. But you and I had a deal, Blake, and you've been holdin' out on me."

"What else could I possibly tell–"

"How's the weather in Wisconsin this time of year?"

I paused. First rule of detection, when you're too tired to think, tap dance. "Wisconsin?"

"You are really pissin' me off," Wenders growled. "Is your head that damaged? Are you so stupid that you actually think we're that stupid? Why do you think the Barrelton Sheriff let you go? Because he liked you? Because he believed in your innocence?"

Wenders shook his head in disgust. Then he wagged his fat finger at me.

"Sheriff Cobb called to check on you. When he did, they passed him to me. You were not only aware of Gronchi's identity and background, you were chasing that circus lead without informin' your old friend, Frank." He jabbed his chest with his thumb so I'd get it he was the Frank he was talking about. "Now what sort of mood do you figure it put me in to learn you ran up there without tellin' me? That you connected yourself to another circus murder without tellin' me? The answer, Blake, is 'a bad mood'. You put me in a very bad mood. For that, I considered throwin' you to the wolves." He held up a hand. "Before you crack wise, give the situation a moment and a brain cell, Blake, and relish as I did the supreme power I held over your worthless life. All I had to do was tell the Sheriff you were already wanted for murder down here. That you seemed to have it in for circus people. That maybe he should chuck you into a deep hole until your trial."

I nodded wearily. "But then sense took over."

"Yes, it did," Wenders agreed. "I realized I want to be there when they give you that last injection and send that lethal juice racin' through your veins. Barrelton is out of our jurisdiction and you ain't worth the drive. So I told him you were too small a fish to bother cleanin' and to throw you back."

He waved off my attempt to thank him. "Don't even. Now you're home, I've got Gronchi to pin on you and I'm slobberin' all over my shirt to send you to Death Row."

"Sorry," I told him. "Didn't recognize it. I assumed that was your normal everyday slobber."

"Give me what you got, you prick," Wenders yelled. "On the Pier. In Wisconsin. Give me everything you got on these circus murders."

"After I make a call."

"To who?"

I'd forgotten how much my head hurt. Wenders' barking reminded me. I waved him back into the saddle. "Who else?" I asked in a quiet voice. "I'm calling the circus." He squinted, trying to figure out who or what I was. "After I call, I'll tell you all I know, everything. Maybe you can make more of it than I've been able to."

Wenders grunted, unimpressed with the compliment, but grudgingly nodded his consent. I lifted the receiver and started dialing. He waddled around the island separating my living room from the kitchen headed, I was willing to bet, toward my booze.

Waiting for someone on the other end of the line to answer, I had nothing to do but watch Wenders ham-hand the bottles on my counter top. "That's good scotch," I told him. "You wouldn't know what to do with it." I pointed past him. "There's a Mickey

Bigmouth in the refrigerator. You can drink that. Or, better yet, you can go buy your own."

The lieutenant snorted at the suggestion and lumbered for the fridge.

Someone finally answered the phone in the Navy Pier offices. I told her I needed to get a message to one of the Callicoat Circus performers. She didn't seem to care but, once I'd insisted it was urgent, agreed to pass it on. I gave her Alfonso's name. When she showed no sign of recognition I explained that he shouldn't be hard to find. He was the only half-pint employee on the Pier.

Confession, sisters and brothers, I didn't know what had happened in my head. If the past was prologue, I knew someone had been done to death. With the images, the voice, and the saucy diction in my vision, I greatly feared it was Alfonso. I wanted to be wrong, as wrong as wrong could be. I refused to surrender hope. I didn't know and, sure as hell, wasn't going to say a word about it to Wenders until I knew. Maybe I was full of raspberries? I wanted to talk to the little guy to prove it.

A five-minute wait got me no satisfaction, just the same tired female voice back on the phone to say they'd do what they could to get the message to him. But, she warned, they couldn't promise anything. I gave her my name and number and asked her to ask Alfonso to please call as soon as he could.

"What's that all about?" Wenders hollered from the kitchen when I'd hung up.

"I don't know, for sure," I said. "I've got a weird feeling I'm trying to get rid of."

"Don't give me anymore hogwash about your bein' a psychic because, gee, haven't I had enough of that."

I frowned but said nothing. With an immovable object like Wenders what could you say that would do any good or make any difference? "I'm going to throw some water in my face."

I detoured on the way to the hall as, for the first time, I noted one of the living room windows open. It was odd. It should come as no surprise Chicago detectives do not, as a rule, leave their apartment windows open. I looked out on the roof of the connected garage, the back yard, the alley. All seemed normal, save for a ladder laying in the unmowed grass. It was out of place but not particularly sinister. Many tenants offered many possibilities. I noted it and started for the bathroom again.

Cold water splashed in my mug revived me. Warm soap and water on my aching neck felt marvelous. I didn't know what had happened in my latest vision. I didn't know if it really was Alfonso I'd seen and felt getting his ticket punched. Plenty of dead guys must have gone to their graves with filthy mouths. All I knew was my head was screaming and my body used up. I turned the tap off, stared at the mess in the mirror, and toweled off. It would be an exaggeration to say I felt refreshed. But I'd managed to kick exhaustion, hospitalization, and death down the road for the time being. I could concentrate again.

Then I was concentrating on, and growing annoyed by, the sound of Wenders banging my cupboards. His snooping was no surprise. Wenders was a born thief. I had no doubt, following judgment, as they led the fat bastard through the fiery portal, he'd swipe the condom from Satan's wallet just to stay in practice. It was a bigger surprise when the slamming sounds stopped. I returned down the hall to find the lieutenant, still in the kitchen, standing motionless, staring in silence into the cupboard beneath the island. He looked up and followed me back into the room with mean eyes. He sneered. He returned his stare to the cupboard. "Been to the store lately, Blake?"

"The store? No. Why?"

"Why?" he shouted, aping me. "I'm just wonderin' if this midget is fresh."

How could I resist that line? I entered the kitchen, circled the island, and looked where Wenders was looking. He stepped aside giving me a view of the cabinet's lower cupboard. I couldn't believe my eyes. There, folded at the waist and stuffed onto the lower shelf like a ventriloquist's dummy in a suitcase, was the body of Alfonso Valencia. His forehead was touching his knees. The back of his head was a riot of blood. Blood covered what little of his chin I could see. His cigar had been jammed back into his kisser, the tip jutting to his right ear. Both he and the cigar were completely snuffed out.

Chapter Nineteen

I grabbed hold of Alfonso and pulled him from the cabinet onto my kitchen floor. His cigar tumbled. A bit of blood spattered. It wasn't to be helped.

"What the hell are you doin'?"

I ignored the growling lieutenant and felt Alfonso's carotid artery. That told me for certain what I already knew. To cement the idea, I said it aloud. "He's dead."

"No shit, Sam Spade. You needed to disturb the evidence to figure that out?"

"You don't think it's something you ought to be sure about?"

"I *was* sure. You killed him good and dead. It was obvious."

"I didn't do this."

"Your little buddy. Your cupboard. Your apartment." Wenders yawned. "You have the right to remain silent. Anything you say can and sure as hell will be used against you in a court of law."

"I didn't do this, Wenders, come out and look at the sun." I pointed to the living room. "A window I left closed is gaping wide open. There's a ladder in the yard should be hanging up in the garage. Somebody went to a little effort to put him here – and put me in the frame. A blind man could see it without his cane."

Wenders started around the island, into the living room, heading for the phone. "I'm callin' this in. Don't touch that body again."

I paid the lieutenant the compliment of waiting until he'd turned his back before I crouched back down and gave Alfonso's corpse a once over. He'd been hit hard over the head from behind, exactly as I'd seen in my vision; the hair on the back left of his crown was coated in largely dried blood. As mentioned, blood marred his lips and chin. I had no time, with Wenders screaming at his subordinates so nearby, to check for further injuries. It wasn't necessary. The head wound would have killed a giant.

A quick search of Alfonso's pockets produced forty-two dollars in folding money (and I'd paid for the museum tickets, *sheesh*), some loose change, and his wallet with ID. Too bad the killer hadn't been as generous with Sybil and Mickey; identifying both would have been a lot simpler. I considered the personal effects again and paused. Something – I couldn't think what – was missing. The thought was interrupted by Wenders yelling again.

"Damn it, Blake! I told you not to touch the body. This is a crime scene! Get away from it."

"I was just–"

"You were just... nothin'. There's a dead guy, murdered circus performer number three, found in your cupboard. Now get away from it. Take a seat on the couch, smart guy, and start cooking up answers to the questions you know are coming."

And they came, the questions and the police scientists.

The photograph snappers, the measurement takers, the fingerprint lifters all did their things. The place was gone over, in minute detail, from the kitchen cupboard, to the living room window, to the garage roof, to the back yard fence. Meanwhile, an Assistant County Coroner examined Alfonso's remains, jotted a few preliminary notes, then ordered him bagged and removed. Such a little corpse, such a big plastic body bag.

Throughout, Wenders beat me with his breath (worse than a rubber hose) demanding answers to an unending parade of questions. Questions that, coincidentally, gave him repeated opportunities to insult me and accuse me of murder. "Your bein' such a great detective," he said, going back over well-trodden ground. "How is it the midget was able to lose you?"

"He didn't lose me. I told you, I went into Sybil's train car to see what had happened and he stayed behind. He'd apparently seen all he wanted. After I saw it, I couldn't blame him. No sooner did I bend over the body when I got hit from behind. I came to with a volunteer ambulance attendant holding ice to my head and spent the next five hours with the Barrelton Sheriff yelling at me. You all go to the same school where they teach you to holler as loud as possible around head injuries."

"Yeah, yeah. Back to the midget."

"From then to now I never saw him again."

"This Alfonso... He ran because he killed Sybil?"

"No."

"How do you know?"

"Next question."

"He ran because he was afraid? He—"

"Not for himself. He may have been afraid for his life, I don't know, but he didn't leave me in the lurch to save his own bacon. He came to the same conclusion I have; The Major is looking an awful lot like a killer of circus performers. Alfonso didn't run for himself."

"For who, if not himself? And to where?"

"I told you. I've told you three times. I'll give you any odds you like he came right back here to Chicago. He saw what happened to Sybil and he was afraid for Alida Harrison, the aerial acrobat he thought he was in love with. He thought she was going to be next and wanted to protect her."

Wenders snorted. "He should have protected himself."

"He probably agrees with you. But his being dead shouldn't count against him. It suggests he may have been right. If he was right then Alida might still be in danger."

"From who?"

"Follow the bouncing ball, Frank. From The Major."

"You think The Major is our man? Out of jealousy alone?"

"I don't know. All the victims were men."

"An old alchy used to bite the heads off chickens? A guy wears a dress and defrauds suckers into thinking he's a bearded lady? And a midget clown? Is that what you're sayin'? Jealousy – over those three – gives the circus manager motive to kill everybody in his circus? It's thin, Blake. Even from you it sounds like hooey. How does the guy see where he's going lookin' through eyes that red?"

"He had all the means and opportunity in the world and then some," I said. "As for motive, I don't know. The clink is full of criminals with undisclosed motives. We've got to grab a hold of The Major and shake. We've got to dig into his closets, find the skeletons."

"Whoa," Wenders said. "Just put a hold on that."

"What do you mean? How many more people do you want this guy to kill?"

"You never learn. Do you? It ain't been a month since you were screamin' for Reverend Delp's head on a stick. And we're you wrong about that! You got a bad habit, Blake, of stompin' all over the toes of your betters. You ain't gettin' me to do it with you. Before you dig into any of this Major's closets, you better be sure. Does the circus manager have skeletons?"

"I don't even know if he has closets. For God's sake, haven't you even been to the circus? Haven't you looked at all?"

"Yeah, bright boy, we've looked. And we're still lookin'. But we ain't finding a thing." He started across the room.

"Where are you going?"

"I'm going to the can, Blake. You have that effect on me. While I'm gone, don't move a muscle."

"To where would I move?"

I considered praying for divine intervention, that Wenders might accidentally flush himself into the Chicago River, but gave it up with the certain knowledge nobody up there owed me a favor, let alone a miracle. I tried to rearrange my brain, to sort my worries, but that too seemed like an impossible task. Beyond any and all belief, Lisa had rowed out in the middle of nowhere and found my drowned man. Since then I'd been on one continuous slide down Skid Row.

Thinking of Lisa, where the heck was she? I'd had no choice over the last two days; I'd had to shove her to the back of my mind. But now I had nothing to do but stand in place and think, where the heck was she? That's probably why I was so deep in do-do again. I'd spent two days running around the country writing checks with my mouth. But I'd had no choice, my right arm was MIA.

The scientists and the questions had used up the rest of that day's sunshine. I turned on a table lamp and pushed back some of the darkness without any measurable effect on the suffocating gloom. I was starting to feel good and sorry for myself when Lisa, my lovely but awkward and long time absent secretary, walked alive and well into my apartment.

I goggled, finding it hard to believe my eyes. "Lisa!" That was all I got out, her name. Then I grabbed her, hugged her, and held on. I probably scared the life out of her but I didn't care. The hug was for me. A full minute later, sated but with the trembling in my hands still visible if you looked, I released her to breathe again. "Where have you been? Are you all right? How did you get past the sentries?"

"It's a long story and I'm fine. As for getting in... Who do I work for? I lied. I told them Wenders called me and told me to get over here."

"How did you know Wenders was here?"

"The first time I went by I saw the Coroner's wagon. Where there is a body, there is Homicide." She looked the place over, took in the organized mess, the print dust in various shades, and her disheveled boss – me. Lisa shook her head. "Look at this place. What's happening?"

"It's a longer story."

"I stopped at the office first, looking for you, before I came here," Lisa said. "Good heavens, Blake, what made you leave Willie there all this time?"

"Willie?" Again I'd forgotten about Willie.

"He's a wreck. He's living like some kind of homeless guy in the upstairs room. He was smart enough to leave your liquor alone, but he's eaten all the lemons, limes, and olives out of your fridge. He's eaten everything in my desk except the pencils. I'm not kidding, he tried the eraser. He's starving to death. He's also frantic and he's getting paranoid. Did you know the office is being watched by the police? And they're not being sly about it. There is a squad car in the lot. Now I come here and find this? Nod, what's going on?"

"Alfonso was murdered. And his killer decided to plant the body here in my apartment."

"That's terrible," Lisa said. "Who's Alfonso?"

"It's been a while since we've seen each other. Which brings us back to the question, Where in the world have you been?"

"You!"

The shout came from Wenders, returning down my hall from the bathroom, directed with a fair amount of venom at my secretary. The cop was spitting fire. "I've been looking for you. Where have you been?"

"Hold on," I said, raising a hand.

"Hold on, nothin'," the lieutenant yelled. He stared past me as if I wasn't there, then pushed past me, to confront Lisa. "You found a body in the channel to Lake Michigan two nights ago."

Lisa looked my way.

Wenders stepped between us. "Don't look at Blake. Answer the question!"

"Did you ask a question?" There was brass in her voice. "It sounded like you made a statement."

"Don't give me any of your 'Blake junior' attitude. I get more than enough of that from your boss. Did you rent a boat at the Chicago harbor two nights ago? And take it out? And find a body in the lake? Yes or no?"

"Don't yell at her," I said, stepping around the fat bastard to Lisa's defense. "She found the body. I told her I'd take care of it. Your complaint is with me. You don't need to abuse her."

"The two of you think you're both so funny. The law don't mean a thing to you, either of you. It's just a big trampoline for you to jump up and down on! Well, no, it isn't. And you're done with that." He shot me his coldest stare. "Get out of the way, Blake!"

I considered the request, stifled my initial response, and stepped to the side.

Wenders turned the stare on Lisa. "You will answer questions. You will make a formal statement and you will sign it. You'll be at my office at nine o'clock tomorrow morning, ready to tell the truth and nothin' but. It makes no difference what your criminal boss tells you. Do you understand?"

"All right," Lisa said. "Nine a.m. I'll be there."

"Fine," Wenders told her. He pointed. "Now go down, and out, and sit on the stoop until I tell you differently." Lisa ogled him in disbelief. "I got more to say to your employer. Not for your ears. Go down and wait; or get lost."

"I'll be on the stoop," Lisa said with resignation. She disappeared out the door like a student headed for the principal's office.

When it was only Wenders and I again, he turned his glare on me and, after a minute of hard staring finally stated the obvious. "I'd like to break your neck."

"Honestly put," I told him. "I'd enjoy pushing your 'Off' button as well. See, we can find common ground."

"Ignoring our personal feelings for the moment..."

I nodded my tentative agreement.

The lieutenant went on. "There's something else we seem to agree on. As a place to start, The Major looks good for these killings. I'm willing to send him to prison forever for murder. But I got nothin. He's giving nothin'. All I can get him to say is, The show must go on. That means we need something on The Major. I need something on The Major."

"Then get something on him!"

"I've got no evidence, so I've got no reason, so I've got no warrant, so I've got no right. Meanwhile, though she may be either an accomplice or as innocent as the driven snow, the circus owner, Mrs. Callicoat, complained to her monied friends, who complained to the whoop-de-dos above, that my detectives were rude. She won't take my calls. She too wants the show to go on. You know the game, Blake. The same city breathing down my neck that the killer must be caught is also breathing down my neck that Mrs. Callicoat and The Major must not be upset."

"It all sounds like your problem to me."

"No, Blake, it's your problem. See, as far as I know, The Major ain't been within a mile of a corpse. Right? So one way of lookin' at it is, I can live without The Major because I got you. Without breaking a sweat, I can prove you were found with not one, not two, but all three of the murder victims. You went for a romantic midnight row with drowned Mickey. You took a nap beside Gerald, the Bearded Lady. And it ain't been an hour since Binky the Clown tumbled out of your kitchen cupboard. If you add all that up, you ought to kill yourself and save the Illinois taxpayers the expense."

"You know I had nothing to do with any of these–" I stopped.

Wenders wasn't listening. He was shrugging his shoulders, whistling silently, and waiting for my lips to quit moving. When they did, he said, "A difference that makes no difference is no difference. As soon as someone goes to jail for murder, everybody above me shuts up. It don't matter who it is; the real killer or a big mouth with a private snoop attached."

"What do you want me to do?"

"What I can't do, dumb ass. What comes as natural to you as breathing; lie, cheat, steal, and break the law to get the evidence we can't get. Then figure out a legal way to use it, tie a bow around it, and give it to me so I can be a hero – and quietly and graciously tear up your death warrant."

"You ought to be in a museum," I told him. "You are a genuine piece of work."

"It's okay by me, Blake. You'd rather hear me recite Miranda, I know Chicago's version by heart. You have the right to remain silent–"

"Shut up! I'm going."

Chapter Twenty

Wenders made a last call, on my demand for breathing space, removing the cops he'd had staking me out. All except one beat cop on duty outside my apartment. We fought about him, in front of him on the stoop, for several minutes but it was no go. "Your apartment is a murder scene. The sentry stays!" We parted company as we usually did, fuming at one another.

Lisa reminded me I looked like 'death warmed over' and offered me a ride to the hospital of my choice. I declined without thanks, reminding her I had work to do. A trooper, she offered me a ride to my car instead, then confused me by walking me to a vehicle that wasn't hers. She drives a speck of a car; a 1970-something Volkswagen Cabriolet. I call it her electric-yellow roller skate and tease her it's fueled by lead-free gas and pretension. She

wasn't unlocking her Volkswagen. She was unlocking a rust brown two-door Ford Pinto, with
seating for two up front and a rear seat in name
only that could carry either long spaghetti or short
snakes. Anything wider would have had to hold its
breath.

"Where's your car?"

"At a shop in Des Plaines. That's part of the long
story. I can't wait to tell you!"

But she would have to wait. There were many
things I wanted to do that minute, all with Lisa.
I wanted to know how she was after her injury?
I wanted to know where she'd been? What she'd
been doing? I wanted to run over the details of my
case, the case she'd put into motion. I wanted a
thousand things. But I had no time. There'd been
three murders, including Alfonso. The killer was
still out there. Despite the killer being at large, the
lead homicide detective was ready to arrest me for
the murders. And Alida, or others at the circus,
might at that moment be in danger of their lives. I
had no time and told her so. I told her she needed
to drop me at the car lot hiding my Jag and asked

her if, after, she would run through a drive-thru for starving Willie.

"Feed the little rat," I told her. "Relieve him, give him something – not too much – for his trouble, then send him on his way. Make sure when he leaves he doesn't take anything that isn't his."

"Wait. You're going back to the office, aren't you?"

"No. I've got corn to plow."

"You can't. I've got something to tell you. I solved the case!"

I did a take. I goggled. Then, without meaning to, I initiated one of the word games Lisa so enjoys playing. Stunned, I asked, "What?" She repeated herself. "I know what you said," I told her. "What are you talking about? What case?"

"My case."

"Lisa, what case?"

"I caught the vandals."

"What vandals?"

"The ones who were ruining your stuff and your life. The vandals who destroyed your office. The ones who trashed the tires on your car. The ones who threatened your life."

Oh, I thought, that. I didn't have the heart to tell Lisa that, with everything that had been going on, I'd forgotten about the vandals. I didn't have the energy to tell her, yet again, she wasn't a detective and as a standing rule I'd like to kill her for pretending she was. But if she had discovered the identities if the idiots breaking my stuff... Well that was great and I didn't want to deflate her ego.

"Don't you want to hear about it?" she asked, busting.

"Of course I do. I'm dying to hear every detail. But you're going to have to save it. I don't have time to listen right now. I've got a couple of murders to solve."

Lisa looked like a popped balloon. The first action I'd taken, after not having seen her for days, was to yank the V out of her victory. I felt like crap. Lisa looked deflated. Then she looked angry. Then, to my complete stupefaction, Lisa refused to do as I'd asked. More, she poked her glasses back up on her nose, crossed her arms, and informed me the offer of a ride to my car had been rescinded... because she was quitting as my secretary.

"You're being a terrible boss. And you're being a worse friend. There are things I need to tell you and if you don't want to hear them, I don't want to work for you anymore." I raised an eyebrow. She raised two at me (not a good look). Then she added, "You can give me a few minutes."

"Yes, I can," I agreed. "Of course, I can. Drop me at my car. Get food. I'll meet you at the office."

She beamed. I shoehorned myself into her loaner Pinto and we were off.

I beat Lisa back to the office (Wenders had kept his word, the prowl car was gone) – and got my first look at Willie in over twenty-four hours. He sat at Lisa's desk looking like hell's own mess. He was unshowered, unshaved, unfed, and under watered (apparently the doofus didn't know how to operate a tap). Even his sling was sagging. Still the slug had the nerve to tell me, through his sinuses, that I looked awful. *Sigh.*

I promised Lisa I'd hear her exciting detective story, and intended to. Beyond that, on the trip back to the office, I'd see-sawed back and forth between 'Discuss my case with Lisa' and 'Skip it for now and get to the circus' so many times I'd lost count. I was back to 'Get to the circus' when Lisa pulled in. Food in hand, already chewing fries, she hurried inside.

Willie nearly took her fingers off wrenching the bag of burgers from her and, one-handed, tore into them like he'd never eaten before. I did my best to ignore him, plopping down in one of two waiting room chairs that seldom saw paying customers, and gave Lisa my attention. "Okay. While Willie serenades us slurping shakes and swallowing cheeseburgers whole, give me the short version of your story. Save the details for later."

She lit up again as happy as a pig in poop.

"The short version," I repeated. "You promise?"

And here, sisters and brothers, is something I promised you many chapters ago: that part of the adventure where I – meaning Lisa, of course – tie in and tie up the two rambling stories I told you at the beginning of this case.

You probably remember as well as I do the morning after Lisa received her injuries; her excited determination as she declared her intent to track down the vandals that had damaged our offices and her head. I demanded she forget it – and thought that was the end of it. But I know Lisa and I should have known better. I should have guessed once she'd made up her mind to solve the mystery she wouldn't stop until it was solved. Especially after she'd gone to the trouble of giving it a file name right out of Perry Mason. I was an idiot not to realize that, unspoken and outside of my knowledge, she'd assigned herself 'The Case of the Vicious Vandals'. God help us all.

"Do the names Leon Darvish or Norman Narque ring any bells with you?" Lisa asked, spitting masticated potatoes in her excitement.

"No," I told her. "Should they?"

"Yes. You've met both. More than met them. But you're busy and you've met a lot of people and I won't hold it against you." I followed Lisa as she paced the room because, one, her channeling Philip Marlowe was kind of cute and, two, the only other thing in the room to look at was Willie scarfing his meal and he was making me sick. "Leon Darvish," Lisa said, "was a pharmacy tech at the Chicago-Loop Memorial Hospital. You caught him stealing narcotics and shooting up on the job. You tackled him in a stairwell and got him fired. You also got yourself kicked out of the hospital."

"Yes. I remember."

Lisa nodded. "Norman Narque, with a 'q-u-e' not a 'c', you may remember better as Master Criswell, a small medium – if that's not too confusing – whose séance you disrupted with your head thingy and who, as a result, lost his best paying customers and his business. You got us both kicked out that time."

"Yeah, yeah. Now I remember. What about them? Are you telling me they're the vandals? Both? Together?"

"Yes. But I'm telling you more than that. They're brothers-in-law. Leon recently married the younger sister of Norman's wife."

"How do you know that? How do you know these people?"

"How do you think? I know them because I met them. I met them because I detected them!"

Alfonso was dead and Lisa was a detective; it was turning into one of those days. Rarely did I want one of Lisa's stories to go on but, this one, I had to confess, I wanted to hear. She obliged.

"While I was lying in bed," she said, "my head throbbing from the brick I took for you."

I glared at her. I glared at Willie in his sling behind her. I sighed. She went on.

"I determined I would solve the mystery of who attacked our office."

"My office," I injected to keep her in her place. "You're not a detective."

"Our offices. I have a desk."

"Have it your way."

"I was going to detect the culprit. But I didn't know how to start. Then you visited, finally; it took you long enough."

"Wenders occupied my time. Besides, he said you were all right and you needed to sleep."

"You didn't want to face my mother, did you?"

"Not a lot. You said this would be the short version."

"Anyway. After I told you what I knew about the drowned man and what he said about The Canary, and after you left, I got my first clue. Mother brought me something to eat and told me she saw the guy who slit the tires on your Jaguar. She got his license number."

"Your mother..? She got the..? Why didn't she tell me?"

Lisa cocked her head, staring at me like I was the stupidest creature on God's green earth. "Would my mother tell you, Blake? She hates you. She only told me to share her joy with someone."

"But you digress," I said urging her on.

"I detected. I called a friend at the PD. She ran the plate for me and came back with Leon Darvish. So I had, potentially, the name, address, and the employer of the culprit. But I didn't have any evidence or opening. So rather than go there and give away the game, or spook him, I did as you do and started asking myself questions. Was Darvish the suspect? Why had he done this? Did he act alone? Was the vandalism to your car connected with the vandalism to our office? What was his likely next move? So I called a friend in the Security Department at the Chicago-Loop Memorial Hospital–"

"Where did you get all these friends?"

"I'm secretary for the world's greatest detective, aren't I? I have sources too, you know, and they're not all in Homicide. He got me a copy of Darvish's

ID photo. Then I knew that I knew him. He was the pharmacy tech with a great reason to hate you."

"I just don't... When did you do all this?"

"You ordered me to stay in bed, which was silly. But you didn't expect me to be in the office."

"I held down the office," Willie whined between bites of what, by then, had to be either Lisa's or my sandwich.

"Yes, you did, poor thing," Lisa told him. She turned on me. "You haven't exactly been checking in regularly on your case, you know. So I took a few days away from the office to stake out Darvish's place. I noticed a visitor I recognized, a frequent visitor; namely Master Criswell, the medium. I ran his plate and got his real name, Norman Narque; 'q-u-e' not 'c', and I found he lived right down the street from Darvish on the same block. I was going to take pictures of their meetings. But I didn't have your equipment or a budget."

"You're not–"

"A detective, I know. Turned out, after I checked, it didn't matter. Narque used to drive for Checker Cab. The city had a photo on file. There you go. Darvish and Narque are brothers-in-law. Together they decided to get back at you for ruining their lives. That's what the vandalism was about."

"I ruined their lives? So they decided to ruin mine." I stood, shaking my head. "Unbelievable. Little did they know card-carrying experts work to ruin my life on a daily basis. Those poor slobs couldn't hold a candle to the real villains I know."

"Wait," Lisa said. "Where are you going?"

"I've got to get going."

"But you haven't heard the end."

"I want to. I will. And I'll have a million questions when I do. But right now, I've got to go."

I shouldn't have waited that long. The Major was out there. He had buried motives or was plain crazy. Alida Harrison might well have been in danger. If I screwed up and let him kill Alida, I knew Alfonso would never forgive me. He'd haunt me for eternity, swearing at me and blowing smoke in my face, from beyond the grave.

"I'm going with you," Lisa said.

"No," I said with meaning. "You're not. If you're feeling up to it, you're three days behind in your work here. Or..." I pointed at Willie, all ketchup and grease, with a bright pink strawberry shake

mustache. "If you're really champing to do something, clean that up!"

Chapter Twenty-One

I headed back to Navy Pier with my foot heavy on the pedal and The Major heavy on my mind.

The employees had the night off and the show was dark. Whether or not that would work for or against me had yet to be seen. Getting onto the Pier and into the performers' dorm was no trouble; not for an old trespasser like yours truly. And, after slinking in, getting a look at The Major's room was easier than anticipated because he wasn't there. My only worry was he might appear unannounced. I took the chance.

There wasn't much there. I'd come to the conclusion that traveling light was the way of all circus lifers. The bathroom contained the usual toilet accoutrement, including a safety razor, but nothing with which to stab or evidence he'd done so. The clothes niche held several worn but serviceable suits for managing in and several sets of jodhpurs and red long coats to don while acting the ringmaster. Two top hats and three pairs of white gloves rested on the shelf above. One pair of business shoes and two pairs of black riding boots stood against the wall by the door. If he was a killer, he was a rather dull one. The drawers of the lone dresser held the usual, socks and smalls, until I reached the back of the bottom drawer and hit a gusher. Beneath an out of place T-shirt lay an oddly lonesome cigar box. I'd never seen The Major with a cigar. I took hold of the box – and a kaleidoscope exploded in my head.

There followed the familiar heat, pain, and blinding flashes of light. Whatever the box contained, it must have been the mother lode, as I found myself back at the start of the case. Meaning I found myself on the fore deck of the USS Silversides. I must have been Mickey as I was stabbed in the back. I fell to the deck. The knife was pulled free and I was shoved over the side. I didn't fall cleanly into the water because, of course, I wasn't me and Mickey hadn't. I hit the side of the boat, above the sharp metal flashing of the engine exhaust port. The flashing caught my coat. I hung there a second, then the lining tore and I fell with a cold splash into the water.

The heat and pain again. Another flash of light behind my eyes and suddenly I was in Wisconsin, in the Sideshow train car, the Bearded Lady's temporary digs, at the circus museum. I was stabbed from behind. I was suffering Sybil's death again. The murderer had me by her necklace and was choking me to the floor. The necklace ruptured and came apart in the killer's hand. I got a fleeting glimpse of Alfonso under the bed, then loose pearls rolled past my blood-filled eyes like shot marbles.

Heat. Pain. Another flash of light. Before I had time to see or identify where I'd gone, I was sorry I was there. Something heavy and blunt smashed my skull. Broken glass rained on my head. I screamed, swearing in Alfonso's gravelly voice. I kept swearing until my mouth filled with blood and gagged me. I swallowed more than I wanted. It went down like bad medicine, touched bottom, and bubbled within me. It started to return climbing my gullet like a furious snake. It poured back into my mouth and erupted from between my lips. Blood painted my chin and chest. At once I was Alfonso, Benga the Pygmy, Binky the Clown, and Blake – the biggest clown of all – rolled into one and dying all over again in Alfonso's stead. One by one, The Major killed them all and I was along for the ride. Sick and dizzy, I held on, waiting for the horrendous vision to come to its end. But it didn't end.

It didn't end at all. Out of the blue, I was in a new vision. I was suddenly on the run, past canvas and poles, past circus wagons and animal cages, running for my life... through the backstage area and into the dimly lit center ring of the Big Top. That was new!

There was no crowd. The seats were empty. There was no show. The ring was silent. I saw no one but I felt a presence behind me. I was being chased. I wanted to turn, to look, to face my tormentor, but I couldn't. I was not in control. I was living someone's experience; meaning someone else had died violently. I was in their shoes and they either didn't want to know, or they knew already, who was at their heels. So I ran breathless, terrified, and completely ignorant of my pursuer.

But fully aware of what was about to happen. Any instant I would feel it, as Mickey the Geek had, as Sybil had; the cold razor steel would be launched and land in my back.

But it didn't come. What came instead was brutal and merciless physical force as I was tackled from behind. I went down like a felled tree. Sawdust blinded me, filled my nostrils and mouth, and the air was blasted from my lungs as I hit the ring floor with my attacker on top of me. Gasping for a breath that wouldn't come in a cloud of sawdust, I didn't waste a thought wondering what was happening to me. I already knew. My only questions were: Who was I? And why was The Major killing me?

My attacker raised himself off of me and, still gasping, I fought to rise. I felt the dull kick of a leather boot in my side and went down again. Any second I expected the murderous blade. But it didn't come. Instead my head was jerked up off the floor by my hair. The sawdust swirled as a rope was thrown about my neck, cinched tight, and my head left to fall. I heard the crunch of my attacker's boots as he walked away.

I couldn't believe I'd been left alive. More, I couldn't understand it. I knew nothing about my crazy mental affliction except for the single fact all of my hallucinations had come to me via the dead. Whoever I was at that instant had to have been dead. But my attacker had walked away!

You may have guessed before I did, sisters and brothers, I spoke too soon. The killer, I was about to learn, had walked away with a purpose. A moment later the rope tightened. The slack in the line was pulled up. Suddenly I was being lifted by my neck, off the ground, to my knees, to my feet – and into the air. I clutched at the rope, strangling, rising above the center ring. I was being hung in the heart of the Big Top. No calliope music, trumpets, or drums. No fanfare save a few work lights. No ringmaster to champion the victim's name. No audience to appreciate the final performance. Somebody had died in the hippodrome. Now I was dying in their place. Damn The Major!

The lights changed. The heat vanished. I woke with a gasp on the floor of The Major's dorm room. I had dropped his prized cigar box but, otherwise, hadn't moved an inch. I was on my stomach trying to breathe and rolled to my back to ease the effort. I was hurting, more than you can imagine, and I was crying. But, thank God, I was no longer dying.

Still I couldn't shake the knowledge that somebody had. I fought to sit up. I held my breath, grabbed the cigar box again, and exhaled in relief that this time nothing happened. I opened the box.

It took a moment to realize what I was looking at. Once I did, it took a moment more for the weight of the contents to strike me. The box held evidence; all Wenders would need to send Karl Kreis to Death Row. But it was more. It was a half-assed collection; all a psychiatrist would need to prove a nasty habit on the part of the ringmaster and to keep him on meds for the rest of his days. The items inside, innocuous enough looking at first, were on second glance easily identifiable as personal items stolen off of the murdered bodies in the case. It was a collection the sickest creeps in the world would have relished, the killer's personal mementos. There was Michael Gronchi's money clip with the worn but readable name 'Mickey' engraved with a flourish across the front. There were eight missing pearls, sought by

Sheriff Cobb, loosed from Sybil's necklace when the life was strangled out of her. There was the 'something' I recognized as missing from Alfonso's personal effects without being able to name it, an item he'd carried, used, and was to no ends proud of, his fancy gold cigar cutter from his glory days under the Big Top.

On top of the aches and pains, the physical sickness that accompanied the visions, I suddenly felt dirty and ashamed. Looking at the pearls, and remembering I'd nearly swiped a few myself (as evidence), I felt pathetic and creepy. What kind of mind took pleasure in that sort of remembrance?

There was another item in the box, an odd item, that meant nothing to me; a class ring from a renowned northeastern university. Its presence offered nothing but confusion for me. None of the departed circus performers had, as far as I knew, been Ivy League material. From what I'd seen, they were better than that. So who the hell did it belong to? The recipient of the nasty hanging I'd just experienced? All right, but who? Who had The Major killed? Where was the body?

Forget the box. It may have been eerily interesting but it wasn't a key to the case. It wasn't opening any doors. At least not yet. It pointed to The Major as the man behind the murders in his own circus but, otherwise, seemed less a solution than another complication.

The main question it didn't answer, Where was The Major?

Now I knew my quarry, the hunt could begin. But that always presented a personal problem. I needed to find the murdering Major without, if at all possible, his adding me to his list of victims. I had to get out of his room. I had to search the dormitory. Or, if he wasn't there, search the circus. I had to do so with dispatch as Alida's life was still likely on the line.

I lifted The Major's mattress, tore a hole in the fabric of his box spring, slid the cigar box inside, and covered it again. There was no sense in giving him a chance to eliminate the evidence before I could return for it. Then, seeing the hall was clear, I got out of there to start my search.

I began in the flying acrobat's room. She wasn't there, as expected and feared. Neither were most of her things which, I admit, was a surprise. The few items of clothing that remained were either hanging haphazardly in her closet or strewn across the floor. I dropped down to take a quick gander under the bed (thanks to the midget, I was suddenly paranoid in all sorts of new ways). I saw nothing and got nothing for the trouble but a small cut on a finger by a stray shard of broken green glass nesting amid the distant dust bunnies. I rinsed the tiny wound in the sink, wrapped it in a toilet paper bandage, and took note of the fact Alida's toiletries were still there. Back in her room, I saw what little there was of her jewelry was still on the dresser. She'd gone, but not completely.

That opened a whole new world of questions. Had Alida been rushed out by The Major? Voluntarily or not? Had she flown the coop on her own? Was she in real mortal danger? Or was I as big a sap as Alfonso had been?

I saw no advantage to continuing the search of the dorm. Alida could be anywhere but most likely wasn't. The killer could have been around any corner but probably was elsewhere; probably with the acrobat. Had there been a kidnapping as prelude to another murder? Were they partners in crime on the lam? Or was I reading everything wrong? I was suddenly overwhelmed with the realization of what I didn't know. I was a bigger mutt than Alfonso's dog. The dog slept quietly while I chased my own tail.

I abandoned the performers' dorm for the Pier and some badly needed night air. From there I had the choice of three thousand linear feet of warehouse on my right, another three thousand on my left, or the monstrous and oh-so dark Big Top straight ahead. Or, I could have said to hell with it and headed home. Of course, then Wenders would wrap the murders around my neck with extreme prejudice and not a little delight. I chose the Big Top.

It goes without saying the dark inside that massive hippodrome tent was a real 'no stars, no moon' kind of dark one doesn't experience in the city of Chicago. Not even tying the tent flap back helped a whit. You couldn't see your shaking hand before your face. Now add the low distant, but distinct, grunts and growls of brown bears, the trumpet of an elephant, camel snorts, and the meow-ling of lions and tigers. I was feeling groovy. Country dark, jungle noises, and the knowledge The Major, a multiple murderer, was likely somewhere within. Perfect. I advanced slowly, to the first performance ring on the lake side of the tent, giving my eyes a chance to find what little light was stealing in and to adjust.

Slowly, like a Polaroid picture developing, the shadowy outlines of empty animal stands and resting acrobats' vaults came into focus beside me. Then appeared the outline of the curtains to the backstage area on the far right. Then came the outline of the empty seats rising into the heights on the far left. Then, above the center ring, came the outline of a body hanging by its neck from the high wire rig.

"No. No!"

I flicked my lighter to life and lifted it. That was stupid. The background disappeared entirely and I blinded myself with the flame. I returned the lighter to my pocket, where it couldn't hurt me, and waited again for my eyes to adjust – terrified the whole time for Alida. She was a crazy little mess but she hadn't deserved this. And Alfonso, even on that side of the grave, would never forgive me for letting it happen. Finally, I could see again.

I could see the body was too big to be Alida. I could just make out who it really was; and couldn't believe it. I literally couldn't believe it.

All signs had pointed to the ringmaster as the killer. But there he was dead and dangling above my head, The Major, now Karl Kreis again; a hanging trophy to my failure to solve the case. My two reasons for being there had been, one, to rescue Alida and, two, to purloin enough evidence against The Major to triumphantly hand him over to Wenders. Now both goals were in shreds. The trinkets, now hidden in his mattress, had been planted by someone else. I had nothing. No wonder the seats were all empty. I was putting on 'The Worst Show on Earth'.

I was so busy vacillating between vilifying and feeling sorry for myself it took a long moment to dawn that I'd better lower the guy and make certain he was dead. I hurried to the ropes to do that and found, pinned to the pole, his suicide note. Make that his supposed suicide note. Supposed because... Well, sisters and brothers, you know why. I dragged you through it with me. I'd experienced The Major's death, his murder, and knew the note and the suicide it proclaimed were lies.

The note made the whole thing stink to high heaven. I knew it wasn't true. It hadn't happened that way; he hadn't died by his own hand. If any of the undamaged parts of my brain doubted the damaged parts, it didn't last long.

Just long enough for a brilliant light to snap on behind me. I turned into it; which was a mistake as I was instantly blinded. I blinked repeatedly, jerking my head, throwing my hands up, to shield the white flare and somehow see past it. Impossible. Something *thwacked* menacingly into the upright pole beside my head and stuck there vibrating in place. I blinked again to make it out.

A knife… right beside my head. Somebody was throwing knives again.

Being nosy and stupid is a dangerous combination. Instead of diving for cover, as a sane person would have done, I turned to look. This time I made out the barest outline; a soft silhouette twenty feet away. "Tommy!" I shouted, and ducked as another knife flipped over my head.

My brain finally made the effort. I hit the dirt, crawled, rolled, and dived for cover on the other side of the center ring. I followed the ring around on my hands and knees, not sure at all from where the knife had come, or where the killer was. How could I know? Until three minutes before, I'd believed the fellow dangling above like a piñata was the killer.

Then, as if things hadn't gone haywire enough, someone took a shot at me.

Great, a gun! Until that moment, the killer had made do with knives, strangulation, and blunt instruments. Now they'd introduced a damned gun. Yes, guns were part of the game. Yes, I had one of my own, locked in my safe, in my office. But none of that changed the fact I hated guns! Now my killer was intent on using one – on me.

Or was it a different killer? Different weapon, check. Different *modis operandi*, check. Different victim, check. (My life was a circus, but I was not a professional performer.) Were there two killers? One who liked knives and one who appreciated diversity? It could easily have been any of the above.

Facts were few and far between but there was no end to the suspects.

Another shot hit a nearby chair and ricocheted. I rose and took off running. The shooter was to my left and above. They fired again and I dove for cover on the back side of the ring. That shot missed by a country mile and started the wheels turning in my head. Either the shooter was playing with me or they weren't any good with a gun. I'd have paid real money to know which.

I raised my head, to spit the mouthful of sawdust I'd collected in my dive, and saw a massive electric box on a pole above my head. I took a breath, counted three, and jumped to my feet. I threw the door open, grabbed the main lever with both hands and yanked. The center ring was plunged into darkness. I hit the floor and scrambled on hands and knees, in the dark, heading nowhere in particular, away from where I'd been. But the expected shot didn't come. The silence matched the darkness.

Behind me, outside the main entrance of the tent, I heard the whine of a small engine and saw the glare of equally small headlights. Silhouetted by the lights from the Pier, whatever it was I saw was coming on, with no slowing down and no indication the tent flaps were a barrier. What in the name of... God only knew. It raced through the opening, bouncing, revving harder, headed for me. It blew its horn, an embarrassment to horns everywhere, and flashed its little lights. Dear God, did they really intend to run me over with a clown car?

Chapter Twenty-Two

Speaking of the Almighty, was He really going to allow it? It was bad enough being killed in a circus. But was I really fated to be wiped out beneath the wheels of a clown car? How, I wondered, would I ever recover from the shame?

My whining thoughts, and impending doom, were interrupted by a crash and the sound of running on the opposite side, the lake side, of the Big Top. I glanced up to see an empty teeter-totter in motion, as if someone had banged into it in the gloom. To the right I caught sight of a shadow (or two?) exiting the massive tent for the Pier. The killers escaping? I didn't know. But if they were the killers... I turned back to the racing car. Who in the hell–

The mini car was nearly on me. I thought of the only clown I had ever known, the late Alfonso.

Though he occasionally dropped by to swear or let me share his murder, I had no reason to suspect him of haunting me or to think his spirit might be behind the wheel of a toy car about to smash me. But enough rambling; I was done.

Or thought I was. But, now the little vehicle was upon me, it looked a tad larger than I'd first imagined; not a full-sized car by any stretch, but a subcompact maybe. Instead of running me down, the little car skidded to a stop in a cloud of sawdust beside me. The tinny passenger's door flipped open and an amber excuse for an interior overhead light came on. "Nod, are you all right?"

I couldn't believe my ears. I couldn't believe my luck. It was Lisa, crying, "I heard gun shots!"

It wasn't a clown car, not one owned by the Callicoat and Major Combined Circus. It was my secretary's rust brown two-door Ford loaner. Lisa, so long absent from both the case and my life, was at the wheel saving the world – and my bacon – with her clownish gas saver. God bless her!

But back to business. Lisa wasn't the killer. Nor was she working for the killers. Meaning the figure, or figures, that had done a runner out the far east flaps of the Big Top was, or were, the criminals I was after. Now I could take chase. I jumped in, tucked my knees under my chin, and pulled the door closed with a hollow *bonk.*

"Hey, Blake!"

The exclamation didn't come from Lisa. It came from behind, from the mail slot that passed for the back seat. It came in a familiar, but horrible, nasally whine. I couldn't believe it and was afraid to look for fear it was true. Of course I had to. There across the seat, bad arm and sling balanced on bent knees, grinning like a baboon on fermented banana juice, lay Willie Banks. Why me?

"Are ya sure you're aw-right, Blake?"

"Never better," I told the whiny slug. Then I did myself a favor and forgot he was there. I turned and pointed through the windshield, inches in front of my face, to the slim exit ahead and shouted to Lisa, "Follow those shadows."

We were headed east as Lisa raced us out of the Big Top. All well and good for a few hundred feet but then we'd be swimming with the fishes. I was about to tell her to turn us around when she did just that. She took us west again, around the hippodrome, between a line of parked cars and the inside of the southern row of warehouses. She cut back into the circus grounds through a parted section in the temporary fence and cranked the wheel hard, turning back west zig-zagging through the dark midway.

"There!" I shouted because I saw what had to have been our shadowy killers. They'd commandeered a vehicle, had spun back out of a parking stall, and were racing west intent on using the entrance as an exit. How, you're wondering, did I know? Trapped in a miniature hell car, with Lisa insanely working the wheel, my put-upon mind switched to Dr. Seuss' method of detection, Calculatus eliminatus. The escaping vehicle was the circus manager's white van. Nobody drove The Major's van but him. He was hanging by his neck in the center ring behind us. Therefore–

"Who are we chasing?" Lisa shouted, interrupting my thoughts. Her eyes were intent on the windshield, her knuckles white on stick and wheel as she avoided by inches taking out a darkened elephant ears stand.

"We're running out of suspects," I told her. "It's not The Major, Sybil, Alfonso, or Mickey the Geek. It is a circus employee. He throws knives. And he's got a homicidal temper."

"Who's that give us?"

"Tommy Dagger," I said with conviction. "It gives us Tommy Dagger and his lovely assistant Sandra."

No sooner had I got the accusation out then Lisa rounded the ticket booth at the entrance, down shifted, and punched her breaks hard. "Look out!" There were two new shadows, pedestrians, in the way. The Pinto skidded. The innocent pair threw packages into the air and dove for safety. We spun out.

The Major's borrowed van disappeared under the Pier arch, turned hard right for Grand Avenue and, presumably, headed west again making for Lake Shore Drive and a getaway.

Lisa tried to restart her stalled engine. I climbed out, searching for the pair we'd almost hit, and hoping we hadn't committed vehicular homicide in our haste. We'd done a hundred-and-eighty degree turn before coming to a stop. I saw the shadowed pedestrians had landed atop one another outside the sweep of our headlights. One, a man, was helping the other, a woman, back to her feet. Thankfully both were able to stand. He was swearing to beat the band. Who could blame him? He was outraged. Then it dawned – he was outraged in a very familiar voice.

The irate man stepped into the beam of light shaking his fist and screaming. I couldn't believe my ears. I couldn't believe my eyes. I absolutely couldn't believe what I saw and shouted, "You've got to be kidding me!" The disheveled pair in our headlights, the couple we'd almost hit and damn near killed, were Tommy Danger and his lovely assistant Sandra.

Whatever they had been carrying, and wherever they had been coming from, they'd just returned to the Pier. They hadn't been on the grounds. They were not responsible for the violent death of the circus manager. Whoever had been trying to kill me in the Big Top, whoever had killed The Major, whoever had stolen his van and was, at that moment, racing away from the Pier was not the hot-headed knife thrower. This case was fast becoming a boil on my butt.

The Pinto's engine roared back to life. (Roared might be a bit strong; it was a Pinto.) With Tommy still shouting curses at us, I jumped back into the car and told Lisa to burn rubber. For the second time in an hour my certain conclusions about the identity of the murderer of the drowned man – and his circus cohorts – had been blown to smithereens.

"At the risk of asking a stupid question," Lisa said. "If that was Tommy Dagger back there, then who is it again that we're chasing?"

"I haven't a damned clue. Which means we'd better catch them or we're sunk."

You'd have thought by then we were so far behind we had no chance of catching them. But the fates hadn't finished teasing us yet. The traffic on Lake Shore Drive was thick, nasty, and slow. As a result, the white van had only just merged from Grand Avenue and, thanks to the bold circus colors of its paint job, was still easily visible as we left the Pier.

"There, Lisa," I shouted. "Heading north!"

She popped the clutch and stomped the gas. She squealed her tires intruding onto Grand and nearly sideswiped a checkered cab. A thousand yards further on she cut a sports car off stealing into the right lane. She banged the bumper of a yellow cab merging onto Lake Shore Drive. Willie screamed in the back seat, hugging his sling and wounded shoulder. I hugged my knees, trying not to scream, up front. My mind took a nerve-wracking trip around our current situation.

The oil crisis of 1973 (coupled with the oil crisis of 1978) made our pursuit vehicle, the Ford Pinto, the perfect car, not only for an indigent tree-hugger like Lisa, but for chasing a crappy old van. Speed was less important than the ability to sneak in and out of tight traffic. And the sub-compact got great gas mileage if you could only find a station with gas. On the down side, the fuel system of the Pinto (responsible for the largest recall in auto history owing to its potential fire hazard) made it the less-than-perfect vehicle to have wrapped around you during a bumper-smashing breakneck car chase.

Every working brain cell told me to tell Lisa to slowly pull over and forget it. As usual, the owner and rag-tag employees of the Blake Detective Agency were on a fool's errand. We were going to wind up dead if we kept up the chase. Worse, we could end up being murdered ourselves if and when we caught the killers. Having reached that conclusion, I shouted, "Step on it, Lisa. We've got to catch them!"

"Hey, Blake?" Willie squeaked. "Too bad we ain't got my car, huh? The ole' Mustang would catch 'em with no trouble, huh?"

Dear God, perish the thought. It was bad enough being pinched into Lisa's borrowed Pinto. I could see the three of us jammed into the criminal slug's car with the bald tires, shattered left headlight, dented green left and rusted blue right quarter panels highlighting the faded Madagascar Orange body, racing through the streets of Chicago, burning oil, the engine coughing huge clouds of black billowing smoke. That's assuming he could have gotten the engine started. But Willie wasn't wrong. In his car we'd have had a better chance of survival. Unable to catch the van, we'd have safely finished the pursuit by pushing his ole' Mustang back home.

The honk of a car horn – or three – shook me from my reverie. Lisa was zigging and zagging up North Shore Drive keeping the van in sight, if not exactly closing the gap, and infuriating dozens of drivers around us in the process. She was having the time of her life. Riding her new high, she said, "As long as you're a captive audience, Blake, you can hear the end of my story."

"What story?"

"My detective story. The Case of the Violent Vandals. I didn't tell you the end."

"What end? Didn't you turn them over to the cops?"

"What good would that have done? Misdemeanors for everybody. *Whoopee!*"

"I'm afraid to ask." Only Lisa could make me grip the dashboard with white knuckles and sigh in despair at the same time. "Well... what did you do?"

"I confronted them. I barged into their house... Well, Norman's house. His garage really. They live a couple of houses apart in the same block in Des

Plaines, did I tell you that? That's why my car's there. That's where it broke down. Anyway, the two of them, Leon and Norman, were in Norman's garage and I walked up and confronted them."

"Geez, Lisa, they could have killed you."

"You don't know those two."

"Neither did you!"

"But I did! I did what you taught me. I didn't just find these guys, I studied them, got to know them. Despite the dumb death threat they left on your answering machine, they weren't going to kill you."

A horn honk interrupted. Lisa veered hard left, accelerated, then veered right again. My stomach did the same an instant behind. "They weren't going to kill me either," she continued. "Neither of them could hurt a fly. Anyway, I took them by surprise. Walked right in. Watched Norman suck in his gut, and Leon runs his hands through his hair, and both of them lick their lips, like men do when they see a woman they don't know. They thought I was lost or had a flat tire or, who knows, maybe they–"

"Lisa!"

"Anyway," she said. She honked her horn (I mean the Pinto's). "I told them who I was and why I was there. You should have seen their faces. They denied everything, of course. But that did them no good."

"You laid the evidence on them?"

"I was going to," Lisa said. "But after all they put us through I decided to be nasty instead."

"What does that mean? What'd you do?"

"I got their wives. Madge, Norman's wife, and her younger sister, Jeannie, who married Leon. I brought them out. There in the garage I accused them of vandalizing the office and your car, and leaving that horrible threat on the phone, in front of their wives."

"And?"

"They tried to deny it. But their wives could tell they were lying. Women know, Blake. Leon held out the longest. But it did him no good. When I offered to produce the proof I'd collected, Norman broke down. He cried like a baby–they took the ramp!" Lisa shouted, interrupting her own story. Sure enough, the van was headed into the north suburbs. Lisa fought her way to the same exit, eliciting as many honks, banging as many bumpers, and infuriating at least as many drivers getting off Lake Shore Drive as she had getting on.

The traffic pattern changed in the uppity residential streets of the far north side but we soon picked up the van again. Lisa found her groove tailing it and, at the same time, eased back into her story as if she'd never left. "They tried to blame you."

"Who?"

"Leon and Norman. Said you ruined their lives, so their vandalism was your fault. I didn't let them get away with it. I said, 'Yeah, Blake did it. Tomorrow he's going to make it rain.'"

I shook my head at the thought of the fired lab tech and shamed medium in tears – again. The poor guys. Maybe I had ruined their lives?

"Don't get me wrong," Lisa went on. "I don't use that kind of sarcasm. But I figured that's what you would have said, Blake. Or something worse. So I said it. Right?"

"Probably. Finish your story."

"The bottom line is they're both repentant."

"Repentant?"

Lisa nodded. "Leon phoned in your death threat before they attacked the office. Then they attacked the office and hit me with a brick. Then they felt sorry. They didn't want to hurt anyone, especially me. In fact they followed me to the hospital and home because they felt bad. They were outside my place, trying to decide what to do, when you showed up to check on me. As soon as they saw you, Leon got mad again and slashed your tires."

"Nice guys, Lisa."

"They're impulsive."

"To say the least."

"Anyway, they promised Leon would get help for his addiction. They promised to pay for the damage to our office, your tires, and my Emergency Room visit. And they promised to leave us alone."

"Yes. With their wives breathing down their necks."

"You really are a cynic."

"For these promises, you offered them what?"

"We will not sick the cops on them."

"That's where you left it?"

"Pretty much. I gave them a Jack Webb 'Jesus speech' to make them feel bad. Then I forgave them."

"Goodie."

"And told them you forgave them too."

"I don't forgive them."

"Yes, you do."

"No, I don't. You might as well learn, Lisa. In this business, we detect. That's it. We find the bad guys and gals. We turn them over to the cops. We do not negotiate their penalties."

"This is a special situation. We were the only victims so we can decide their fate. I turned them over to their wives and I forgave them. You will forgive them too, because they're going to be better people. And you're going to be a better person. While you're at it–"

"What now?"

"You should congratulate me on solving my first case."

"I would," I said, smiling. "But you're not a detective."

I apologize for the rambling, sisters and brothers, but now that part of the tale is told. If you're wondering, yes, we were still in a chase trying to catch the Callicoat Circus killers. It probably should be said that we were lucky they were driving The Major's old van, a vehicle that had seen better days. Whoever we were after was an experienced driver; if they'd also had a good car we'd have been lost.

"Where are the murderers leading us?" Lisa asked.

I didn't want to admit I'd traveled the same route only that morning and had a good guess where we were headed. With The Major dead, and Tommy out of the frame, the facts I'd gleaned over the last three days were sorting themselves, finding places in several new theories. Frankly, I didn't want any to be true. So, pretending I had no guess, I answered Lisa's question by stating the obvious. "We're headed for the monied side of the tracks."

"But who are we following? Do you know?"

I shook my head. It wasn't a lie. I thought I knew, but I didn't know for sure, so it wasn't a lie. "I don't want to think about what's in front of us," I told her. "Any more than I want to think about what's behind us."

"You mean all the murders?"

"No. I mean what's behind us."

"What are you talking about?"

"Don't you ever use your rear-view mirrors?"

Lisa checked hers and saw what I'd seen. Our high-speed chase had picked up several outriders. A block behind, but gaining rapidly, were two police squad cars. I wasn't sure who they represented, the City of Chicago or the suburb through which we were currently jetting, but they'd evidently taken notice of our tiny parade. If their red and blue flashing lights were any sign, they didn't approve and wanted to tell us in person.

"Oh, God!" Lisa exclaimed. "What should I do?"

"You have to ask?" I pointed forward. "Catch that van!"

I hated what was happening. We were only in this sickening mess because of my original desire to keep Lisa out of a mess. Hadn't that worked out just peachy? Now, unless we caught our quarry, and pinned the works on them, I was going to end up tagged with four murders instead of one. And Lisa, and maybe even that hapless slug, Willie, might well end up tagged with me as accessories.

Trust me, I was hating myself. Little did I know my favorite obnoxious homicide detective, in his vehicle listening in on calls, had heard the curious traffic reporting a white circus van being pursued at high speeds by a rust colored Ford Pinto. Wenders wasn't the sharpest knife in the drawer but, able to add two and two, had chimed in to say he was joining the chase. If only I'd known, I'd have hated myself harder.

"It's turning," Lisa shouted.

I'd seen it already and was shaking my head, without being exactly sure why. A little confusion? Perhaps at first. Disbelief? That all depended upon who was behind the wheel. A lot of disappointment? Same answer for the same reason. Either way I let it slip, "They're home."

"What?" Lisa asked. "Who's home?"

"That's a good question."

The late Major's white van squealed its tires as it turned into the drive of the Callicoat Estate. The huge security gates were wide open as the van passed in. Those same gates began immediately to close. There was no way we would get there in time. Lisa didn't say a word. She just kept going.

We'd only started through when the gate halves came together with a tinny crunch on each side of the Pinto, behind our front tires, pinching us like tweezers. The car lurched. My knees racked my chin. Willie screamed. Lisa bit her bottom lip, redoubled her grip on the steering wheel, and floored the pedal gunning the engine. It felt as if the car would be crushed and sounded like we'd driven into a chipper shredder. Lisa yelled but didn't stop. The gates bit into the metal of both doors, Lisa's and mine, and shaved them. The amputated tin cartwheeled to either side of the drive as the Pinto squirted through. The shaking gates slammed shut behind us. We must have been a sight, with both doors missing their skin, the tinny ribs showing nakedly, as we passed onto the estate and around into the dark after the van.

"Nice digs," Willie whined.

"Don't even think about it."

In the distance, the van skidded to a stop on the gravel drive near the pole barn; Reginald Callicoat's wagon pavilion and altar to the memory of the circus. A shadowy figure jumped from the van.

"The driver's out," Lisa shouted.

"Stop here. Don't get any closer!"

Lisa hit the brakes and, even with her clown car, managed to throw a fair share of gravel. Willie yowled. I did too as my knees almost broke my nose.

The shadow ran into the pavilion. "It's not The Major," Lisa said. "It isn't Tommy. So who is it?"

"It has to be Rudy."

"Who?"

"Rudy Ace, Mrs. Callicoat's chauffeur."

"How do you know?"

"He had a control to the front gate, he's male, and we're here. There's nobody else it could be. Stop missing staff meetings." I grabbed the door handle. "You two stay here."

"I'm not staying here."

"Me neither."

"I don't want to argue. This is real detective work, the dangerous part, and you're both staying here." I opened what was left of the door on the passenger's side and freed my cramped legs.

"Nod," Lisa said. "You can't leave me behind when you're going after a murderer."

"Don't be thick. That's why I'm leaving you behind."

I stood outside the car, considering the fastest safest route to the pavilion, when I heard a metal *bark* that could only have been the compartment doors on the far side of the van coming open. An indistinct shape appeared at the boxy corner of the van's rear and stooped to the tail light. I goggled because I'm an idiot. I was still goggling when I heard the *crack* of exploding powder. On its own, my face switched to arched brows and a wide O mouth as a bullet sailed through Lisa's windshield.

Chapter Twenty-Three

I should have ducked. Anyone with a brain would have found cover in the midst of incoming fire. But I'd heard the howl of a kicked dog erupt from inside the Pinto and my mind was occupied. "Lisa!"

"I'm all right! It wasn't me!"

The front windshield had only a small hole in it but had cracked into a massive spider's web. Lisa appeared to be unhurt. Willie, on the other hand, had disappeared into the dark back seat.

"Willie! Willie, are you all right?"

"I'm shot," he screamed.

God, not again! "Is it bad?"

"It's terrible!"

I strained to see him in the dark and was well rewarded; what a sight. He'd let go of the left arm he'd been supporting in the sling and, with his bad hand, was holding what had been his good right shoulder. As was becoming the new norm for the little creep, he was leaking red through his fingers.

"Who told you to get shot again!" I hollered.

"I only came to help," Willie bawled through his nose.

Lisa was bawling herself. "This isn't my car! Don't bleed on the seat!"

The bullet had passed between Lisa's and my empty passenger's seat, into the back, straight through Willie's right shoulder, and out the rear window. That wasn't a guess. The window had completely shattered and Willie lay covered in broken glass. Like I said, he was a sight.

Though I have no clue how she managed it with those long legs, Lisa slid under her steering wheel and dropped to the floor. From that position of questionable safety, she screamed the patently obvious, "Nod, he's shooting at you!"

"Yes. I know." Having concluded that, one, Willie's wound was not life threatening; two, under the circumstances there was nothing I could do to help him anyway; three, I couldn't assuage the guilt I felt at his having been shot again in my company; and four, Lisa was right, someone was shooting, I dropped to cover beside the car. "Did you see Rudy leave the barn?"

"No," Lisa replied from below the dash. "I didn't see anyone."

"It must be his partner, the second shadow. The same one who shot at me in the Big Top." My mind was racing. "But that doesn't make any sense."

"What are you arguing with yourself about?" Lisa demanded. "Someone is shooting at you! Does it matter who?"

"Of course it matters. Every time I'm ready to name a killer I'm wrong. It just happened again."

"It's not Rudy?"

"Yes, it's Rudy! I'm talking about his accomplice. Whoever that is," I jerked my head in the direction of the van. "They're a lousy shot. That's the second time tonight they missed me by a mile."

"A mile!" Willie screamed. "A mile my–"

"Shut up!" I shook my head – at my life. "It can't be who I thought it was."

"What does that mean?" Lisa asked.

I gave it another thought and nodded. "It means I finally know who it is."

I scanned the distance but could no longer see the shooter at the rear of the van. They may well have used the moment I'd taken with Lisa and Willie to follow Rudy into the pavilion. Or they might have merely taken a step back and were patiently waiting to take another shot. Not knowing which made me unhappy. So did the remains of the tin foil door I was using as a shield. "I'm going to put an end to this. Please, stay here."

"Nod," Lisa cried. She reached from beneath the dash, fumbled on the passenger's side and, finally, opened the glove box. She contorted herself further, grabbed something from the compartment, and stretched it my direction. "You can't go into another gunfight unarmed."

Sure enough she'd brought my gun.

"I don't want that."

"Take it!"

I stared hatefully at it, ready to argue, when a question exploded in my head. "Where did you get it?"

"Where do you think? From your office safe."

I shook that away. "How did you get it? How did you open my safe?"

"Blake!" Whether owing to my ingratitude or her cramped position under the dash, Lisa was frustrated. "The first four months you owned the safe, until you finally memorized it, you had the combination written on an envelope in your top desk drawer."

"You've known the combination all along?"

"Of course. I'm not a dolt."

"But... the brownie..."

"What brownie?"

"The brownie in my safe. Why haven't you eaten it?"

"If I'd eaten it, you would have known I had the combination to your safe. Now take the gun!"

My hatred of and refusal to carry a weapon was no secret, especially to Lisa. But we both knew we were dealing with a couple of crazed killers and, she knew me well enough to know, my love of life was stronger. If you'd like to debate the ethics involved, we can, that's why they invented bars. But for the moment, I took the gun. "Stay here."

Lisa took her small victory. "All right. We'll stay here."

I went commando, from one tree to another, in the direction of the killers. I looked and saw nothing but the quiet pavilion, the darkness, and the van. If the shooter was there, I couldn't see them. I took a chance and ran for the van. I made it safely to the rear, edged around, saw the far side doors standing open and eased up on them. Gun foremost, I rotated at the edge of the opening, scanning the interior. The van was empty.

Nobody appeared to be hanging about in the dark. The corners of the pole barn and the doorway of the wide-open sliding door, as far as I could see, were empty. It was a guess but, I thought, a sound one; the shooter, the second shadow, had followed Rudy inside. I wasn't certain if they'd retreated there to hide or stopped in for something specific. Were they collecting a hidden something or lying in wait?

I moved up the passenger's side of the van, took a deep breath, and readied to run for the corner of the big open door. A flash of movement stopped me. A projectile missed me by inches. This time it wasn't gunfire. It was a hurled object that hit the van's front grill in a blur with a familiar *thwack*. I dove near the tire for cover and heard somebody taking a whiz nearby. I looked up for the source and discovered it was the hurled object. A knife had been thrown with expert force and, thankfully, the tiniest error in precision. It protruded from the grill with its blade buried in the radiator. The radiator was relieving itself.

I looked from the murderous blade, to the gun in my hand, to the open door of the gloomy pavilion. I shook my head wondering exactly what kind of weapon a worn-out detective ought to bring to a knife *and* gun fight? No answer presented itself. I considered my options, decided I didn't have any, and ran for the barn in pursuit of Rudy and his shadow.

The Callicoat wagon pavilion lost its charm by night. Throughout the building's wide span only two overhead lights were lit, one in the corner to my left as I entered, and one catty corner the full length of the barn away. That left a lot of dark and, thanks to the oddly shaped wagons, a lot of shadow between for atmosphere. Creepiness had taken over as the bright reds, yellows, and greens of day melted into battling shades of gray and the painted smiles of clowns became knowing leers.

Damn it! Wagons, wagons everywhere (I couldn't see twenty feet in any direction). Among all those wagons were two stone-cold killers. But where? I needed to know. I needed to see them, if only for a moment. I needed a vantage point. A moment of thought and I realized that problem answered itself. Thank God, there were wagons, wagons everywhere.

I picked one, the tallest within view and likely the tallest in the building, an ornate monster of a circus wagon, a red and gold rectangle box with a huge blue half-globe of the earth (the continents painted in brilliant gold) decorating either side. On the right side of the wagon, the Eastern Hemisphere protruded; on the left, the Western. Along both sides of the top, and across the back, stood more than a dozen standard poles, each baring the flags of nations from around the world.

I ran for the front of the World Wagon and leaped to the team harness. I climbed it like a flight of stairs, driver's foot board, seat, back rest, wagon top, and dove for the roof. On my belly, I low-crawled to the edges, slowly, one at a time to listen. I reached the fourth side and, against my better judgment, lifted my head between the standards for Old Glory and the national flag of Spain to steal a peek below and see what I could see. I saw the tops of the other wagons, the lady Danita's vacant coffee patio at center, and all-around stark shadows with fingers of light stealing through. I didn't see the villains I'd chased into the building. Where were they?

As if in answer, I heard movement below and to my right. A caravan wagon with a little cupola on its roof shuddered and its rear door came open. A shadow, that must have been Rudy Ace, slipped out. What had he been doing in the wagon? Hiding? Lying in wait? Or had I been right? Had he and his partner returned to the pavilion for something specific? Something hidden away? He started to move and I foolishly lifted my head higher to follow.

A shot rang out.

I lost track of Rudy's shadowy figure. I was busy ducking. The round missed me clean but struck the light hanging behind me, plunging the front half of the barn, the top of my World Wagon, and me into darkness. I peeked again and, in the dim spill from the remaining light, saw what looked to be the shooter's shadow beyond the calliope.

I now had an idea where the killers were. All it had cost me was the revelation of my own precise location. I had to move. But to where? Where had Rudy disappeared to? Wondering took time and I decided not to bother. I leaped up and, without looking, hopped feet first over the side onto the wagon's Eastern Hemisphere. I stepped on Russia to stop my fall, dropped to my seat west of Mongolia, slid down India from New Delhi to Sri Lanka, and became the first human to fly over the Indian Ocean without a plane. Amazingly, I landed safely on my feet, smiling at Australia. Then again, safely may be too strong a word. Without warning, a thrown knife sank itself into Madagascar right behind my head.

I'd found Rudy!

I took off running, leaped to the back of the first coach across the way, the caravan wagon he'd just vacated, and grabbed the handle on its rear door. I opened the door and ducked behind as another knife came flying. *Thwack.* The door, a perfect shield, caught the knife. But I was far from safe. Rudy meant business. I ducked inside and pulled the door closed behind me.

I had little, if any, time and knew it. But I was there, where he'd been, and owed it to the case to nose all I could. The caravan looked to be the pavilion's improvised storage area. Circus junk of all sorts, banners, costumes, wagon parts, passed over extras, or items yet to make display. It looked... gone through.

I paused for an item that looked familiar; a circus poster. I unrolled it, turned it to catch the scant light slipping in through the tiny caravan window, and got an eyeful. I'd seen one before, exactly like it, at the circus museum. I thought of my coffee clutch with Mrs. Callicoat and recalled the space on one of the pavilion walls, a gap in the display that threw off the esthetics and made the place look one poster short. I was certain I held the missing one-sheet – and couldn't help but wonder why.

I looked closer, made out the bold legend on the bottom, and understood. Then I examined the whole, remembered it under lights in the museum, and understood even more. I saved it to the side.

Discarded in a corner, I found a gray metal box with a sprung lid. It was empty. If the box had held Rudy's stash, it had been reclaimed. That theory would be easy enough to prove. All I had to do was survive the night, gift wrap the chauffeur for Wenders, and search his pockets. A healthy wad of cash would be a feather in my cap.

But I was out of time to search. The door (and its meager lock) shook, causing the caravan to shake, and informing me someone wanted in. Or wanted me out. I decided to oblige. But, as was my habit, I did it my way. I leaped, grabbed a ceiling beam, pulled my ever-widening hind end up, and ventilated the wagon roof with a couple of hysterical kicks beneath the stylish cupola. It gave way. I climbed onto the roof and dove off the wagon. I darted for cover into the blackest shadows in sight.

Sometimes I'm my own worst enemy. In the dark, I tripped over Rudy's haphazardly coiled garden hose. I kicked, trying to escape its snake-like grasp, and stumbled ass over tea kettle into the nearest wall. I fell atop, rolled over, and dropped off the far side of a partially depleted pallet of fifty pound bags. Of what, I didn't know. They looked like construction materials, powdered concrete mix, if I had to guess. I wasn't a general contractor. All I knew was, as they looked as if they might slow down a bullet or stop a knife in flight, I drew my gun again and paused there for a breath.

The killer, I'm pleased to report, did not immediately follow with his knife act. Apparently, he didn't like the dark any more than I did. Or maybe he was giving me credit that, given the chance, I might defend myself. I sagged against the bags of – whatever – on the pallet and caught that breath. I took all the advantages of the time out. I listened, hoping to hear my opponents. I wondered, how in blazes I was going to get out of there alive? But the question was mute.

There came the sound of movement behind me and a murderous voice growled, "Got you!"

Chapter Twenty-Four

I spun in place giving the voice the business end of the barrel. I expected nothing but a knife from the shadows. That's all I'd gotten since slipping into the pavilion, lethal tag, creeping shadows and hurled projectiles. But this one, massive shadow and bass voice combined, was sinister in an all-too familiar way. There behind me stood Lieutenant Frank Wenders fat as life. What can I say? He'd sounded murderous to me. But then he usually did when we talked. I exhaled so loudly I sounded like a survival raft foundering, then whispered in anger, "You scared the crap out of me!"

"Yeah. Boo," he said. He stared. "Is that a gun you're holdin', Blake? I don't believe it. Why?"

"You'll find out if you don't get down."

A normal human being would have hit the deck, but not Wenders. He looked side to side like he was making to cross the street. Then it dawned on him what I'd said. Then it dawned on him I was hiding behind a stack of cement bags. Then – and only then – danger finally registered in his pea-sized brain and he dropped to his knees beside me.

As if I wasn't already a big enough target. At least, in theory, he was on my side. "How did you get here?" I asked.

"I picked Dave Mason up from the hospital; was takin' him home when I heard your parade on the squawk box. A high-speed chase with a circus van? That was a clue even without your butt-ugly Jag involved. Of course, now you've moved up to an air-conditioned Pinto you're travelin' in style. Who the hell you chasing? And why? What are you doin' here where rich people live? With a gun in your hand? And why in hell didn't you tell me you had somethin' cooking?"

"There was no time. It boiled over." I couldn't help it. Looking at the lieutenant crouched there like a frog on a lily pad, I had to ask. "How did you get here? Did you climb the fence?"

"Fat chance. I used the intercom out front. Told the house to open the gate."

"So where are your men?"

"They're not my men. Mason's in my car. The others are patrol officers saw you speedin' through their suburb. Two of their units are down at the gate. A third followed me back here so's we could figure out what you were up to. They're outside till I need 'em."

"You're going to need them."

"Why, smart guy?" Wenders demanded. "What new circus have you started?"

"Your killers are here, in the pavilion. Two of them."

That one dawned quicker. Wenders drew his gun too. "The Major?"

I shook my head. "Never again in this life."

"Huh?"

"No. We pulled a boner there. The Major was not our killer. He's hanging by his neck in the Big Top at Navy Pier, victim number four."

"Dead?" Wenders asked.

I did a take, amazed by the caliber of the question, then gave him the answer he deserved. "He thinks he is. The way he looks I have no reason to doubt him." The lieutenant looked at me like I was nuts. "The suspects stole his van. We followed them here."

"Where's here?" He nodded at the nearest wagon. "Who owns this menagerie?"

I stared, stupefied. "You haven't been here either? You're some investigator. Danita Callicoat, owner of the circus on Navy Pier. This is the back forty to her estate."

"Mrs. Callicoat? Are you sayin' she–"

"Nix that," I said, shaking my head. "She didn't kill her performers. The ones we're after, I'm guessing, hid something here in her barn. A nest egg probably. The killing's gotten out of hand and, it seems, they're ready to get out of Dodge. They thought they lost us at the Pier. They came here for their stash without expecting to be followed. They're cornered now and are acting like it."

"We're sitting ducks here," the lieutenant said, scanning the wagons, the shadows, and the darkness. He pointed with his pistol. "You circle that way, Blake. I'll go the other. Pin 'em down between us."

It was my turn to look at him like he was nuts. "You're a little confused. I'm the taxpayer here. Get Mason!"

"He can't do anything yet. Stitches."

I nodded. "I left my girl in the car too."

"Have a heart, Blake," Wenders said with a scowl. "The guy just got out of the hospital." He pointed. "You got a gun in your hand."

I did at that.

"'Course, if you want, we can both just forget it. These murders can still wear your by-line as far as I'm concerned. It's up to you."

"And I'm supposed to have a heart? All right." I nodded my acquiescence. "See you in the funny papers." I jumped up and ran to crouch behind the nearest wagon to the right. I turned back to see Wenders lumber left. Both of us edged forward into the dark end of the wagon pavilion.

Trouble was there were a couple of nasty killers somewhere ahead of us. Rudy, the chauffeur, who I'd discovered was a darned impressive knife thrower. And the shooter, whose identity I was now certain of, who I'd come to learn wasn't any good with a gun. My assessment of the situation did not bolster my confidence. Rudy's hidden skill was deadly. Had it not been for haste and anger marring his aim, I might already be cooling to room temperature. I had high hopes he stayed mad and in a rush for the next few minutes. The lack of skill on the part of the other was wildly dangerous. Even a blind hog found an acorn now and again. If the cat and mouse game kept up someone would likely wind up dead.

I thought it came to that when, a moment later, I heard Wenders cry out in pain.

I took off in his direction, hit the floor, rolled underneath a wagon blocking my way, and came up on the other side to see the fat police lieutenant in an uncomfortable and unenviable position. He was on his feet on the Western Hemisphere side of the World Wagon, bowed oddly backwards, with his ugly gut defying gravity, ogling the ceiling. Then I saw the hilt of a knife and read the situation.

Wenders was not star gazing, or looking for holes in the roof, or praying to God. He'd rounded the wrong corner, stepped out in front of Rudy, and had been forced to all but do a back flip to avoid the blade of a flying knife. He'd barely saved himself. The knife had nicked his Adam's Apple (and at least two of his chins), gone through his coat collar, and had pinned the homicide detective to the Atlantic Ocean directly over the spot where the Titanic went down. A stream of blood, fortunately for him a tiny stream, was messing up his poorly chosen neck tie.

I spun left, raised my gun, and screamed, "Don't!"

Rudy Ace had a second knife aloft, ready to throw and finish Wenders off. His tunnel vision in the lieutenant's direction had given me the second I needed. Now I had the drop on the chauffeur. Someone should have told him because he proved he could talk by shouting, "Back off!"

"Good advice," I replied. "If I were you I'd take it."

Rudy remained ready to throw. I stood ready to shoot him if he tried. We had ourselves a standoff.

But a woman's scream interrupted the mirth and commanded everybody's attention. There came a vicious sounding slap and an unmistakable cry – from Lisa (I would have recognized her voice anywhere). Before I could take a step, there followed a second slap, meatier and meaner, and a cry of pain and fear from someone else. A solid black object (that took an instant to identify as a handgun) flew out from behind a wagon, landed with a metallic clatter, and skittered across the floor.

Then Lisa hollered, "Knock it off, sister!"

An instant later, Alida Harrison appeared, stumbling gracelessly from behind the same wagon. Then I saw why. Lisa was on her heels driving the acrobat out into our group. She had Alida in an arm bar, like one of my mother's television wrestlers, and both girls looked like they'd gone several falls. Despite a scratched and reddening face my secretary had clearly come out on top. "Here, Blake," Lisa said with attitude. "Here's your second shadow."

Lisa tugged Alida to a stop, causing the pixie to cry out, and examined our standoff. Wenders, bent partially backwards (his gut offering a sight that could never be unseen), remained pinned by Rudy's knife. The chauffeur stood a few yards away with another knife at the ready. I completed the triangle with my weapon targeting Rudy's chest. I would have dished out a suggestion but Lisa didn't need one. She cranked Alida's arm like a viking wrenching a drumstick off a turkey. Alida screamed and rose to her tippy-toes. Rudy cringed and took a half-step her way.

"Drop the knife," Lisa demanded, "or I'll break her arm."

Wow. Get her, I thought. My secretary was going to be insufferably pleased with herself for weeks. I was delighted. I wanted to cheer, and would have, had it not been for the life and death situation. Even an uncouth washed-up detective can muster some decorum. I gave her a wink instead and turned back to the chauffeur. Rudy sneered and threw his knife to the floor.

Bless her heart, Lisa had saved me from having to shoot Rudy. I made up my mind then and there not to hold it against her that, in doing so, she had also saved Wenders' life. Sometimes you had to take the bad with the good; beggars couldn't be choosers.

Though I hated to do it, still targeting Rudy, I stepped up and unpinned Wenders. He caught himself from falling then made long work of groaning, stretching, coaxing his circulation back, catching his breath, and tamping his bleeding throat with a hanky. Then he made short work of calling the suburban patrol, and his slow-moving partner, Dave Mason, in from their lounging positions outside. He put a couple of guys on Rudy and asked the lone female officer among them to rescue Alida's arm from Lisa. The acrobat thought she'd be feisty but vetoed it when Wenders growled.

Everybody took a breath. Then Wenders turned to me like the village idiot in a tornado. "Aw-right, Blake. What the hell is goin' on here? Who are these people?"

"You don't know them?" I admit I was aghast. The list of people, places, and things Wenders didn't know would probably have stretched to the moon and back. But for the lead investigator, even one as slipshod and lazy as Wenders, to be unaware of all the possible suspects in a multiple homicide he was working; that I couldn't believe. "That's Rudy Ace. Mrs. Callicoat's chauffeur. And that's Alida Harrison, the aerial acrobat and contortionist. You really don't know them?"

"I seen her act from a distance," he said, jutting a fat thumb. "It was okay, if you like the circus. I don't. I read a report; one of my detectives interviewed her. It was a nothing burger." He turned the thumb on Rudy. "Him I never seen before."

"Some cop!" I shouted. "How were you investigating this case? With your television clicker?" I didn't know whether to laugh or cry.

Wenders reddened and gritted his teeth. "Yeah, yeah," he barked. "Like always, Blake, you're talkin' but you're not sayin' anything. What's the owner's chauffeur got to do with anything? And why's he throwing knives at me?"

"He's your murderer."

"Why? What's he got against circus performers?"

"I should have said one of your murderers." I pointed at Alida. "She's the other."

"Okay," Wenders said without enthusiasm. "She at least gets us into the circus." But as he stared at the acrobat, all one hundred and five pounds of her, rough but fetching in tight jeans and sweatshirt, he didn't appear convinced. Not that Wenders was seeing what I was seeing. Sexy to the lieutenant was a hoagie with melted cheese. And a killer, in our experiences together, looked like whatever I handed him. "My guys talked to her. Or tried to. They said she's always up in the air; at least her nose was. What's she got to do with a janitor and a couple of Freak Show performers? What have either of them to do with it?" He glared at me. "I'm askin'?"

"All right," I said. "I'm telling."

Chapter Twenty-Five

"The tale that needs to be told is remarkably twisted," I said. "To begin to untangle the murderous mess, we need to go back to another time, long before the Big Top came to Navy Pier; over three years ago. To another place, Cape Girardeau, Missouri; the north boundary of the southern circuit for circus entertainment. Back to the last days of the small, now defunct, Kessler Traveling Circus."

The chauffeur shot a quick hard glance in Alida's direction. "You see," I said. "Rudy knows the name." The acrobat didn't see the look or pretended not to. She continued to stare a hole through me. "So does Alida but she's keeping it to herself."

"Well I don't," Wenders growled. "So fill me in."

"The Kessler Traveling Circus is a name lost now to history. But once, for a short while, it had its own genuine claim to fame, a trapeze act featuring an acrobat advertised as 'Elegance in the Air' and known as The Canary.

"Her real name was Aurelia Marx Herman. She was an unequaled talent, a stunning beauty and, with her husband, Gunther Herman, made up an act known as 'The Hawk and The Canary'. They were a smash. But it didn't take a genius to see Aurelia was the reason for their success. The spotlight shown far brighter on her than her husband and Gunther, being a business minded fellow above all, chose not to fight it. The act remained the same but their name was changed. Soon they were wowing audiences as Kessler's star attraction, 'The Canary'.

"Gunther didn't mind. Both on stage and off it was a situation that came up occasionally; his taking a back seat. He anchored their act as he anchored their marriage. He was a marvel of physical strength and prowess, but he was also much older than Aurelia. From their first meeting the couple hit it off. They worked well together, enjoyed each other intimately, and had a great deal in common. Both were strong, handsome, dazzling performers.

Both were successful. They shared a similar world view. Both were narcissists. And both, they discovered, had severe kinks in their personalities, particularly in regard to their sexual tastes. Aurelia and Gunther were voracious sluts. It was a match almost made in heaven. I stress the word almost. Because it was this particular attribute, their lusts, that led to a crisis.

"Some of what follows is conjecture. But it is intelligent conjecture supported by fact. An event occurred; a bad thing happened... in one of three ways. Either Gunther did the bad thing. Or he and his wife did the bad thing together. Or Aurelia acted on her own. The third option is the more likely of the three. As mentioned, it's a matter of rumor and record the couple were sexually ravenous. But Gunther was two decades older and no match for his young wife in the libido department. Despite the will he had no way to keep up with Aurelia. He wasn't a fool. He recognized the situation for what it was and, as with the name of their act, knew better than to fight reality. When Gunther reached his sexual limit, he was forced to stifle his jealousies and temporarily bow out of the game. His wife played on without him. But, as surely as Gunther was the anchor, Aurelia had control problems. Things sometimes got out of hand; also a matter of record. On those occasions when Aurelia's activities got her into trouble, and there were several, Gunther had to come to her rescue.

"The circus didn't like it. They were a family entertainment. But she was The Canary. And Gunther was at least as good a fixer as he was an acrobat."

Wenders growled. "Is this history lesson about people we never heard of goin' anywhere?"

"It is," I assured him. "It's arrived. One of their playmates, Aurelia's last playmate, was an equestrian performer, a Russian trick bareback rider about her own age, and very much her own build, called Luna Blaženovic. Records show she'd only been with the Kessler Circus for a few weeks. At first sight, the Hermans thought Luna a tasty-looking morsel. They wanted her and they pursued her.

"As I said, the acrobats' marriage was a match made in heaven... until one day from hell. One day, when Gunther had taken himself out of the game, and The Canary was playing alone, Aurelia caught Luna. One way or another the two young ladies met for an afternoon of *sapphic amor.*"

"They met for what?" Wenders asked.

"They hooked up," I told him. "The girls, they got it on."

"Oh, that," he said dully. "How the hell do you know? And why do we care? Is this necessary, Blake, in mixed company?"

"The details of their encounter? No. They might make a juicy page turner of a novel, but they're not vital to our purpose. What is vital is the fact the encounter took place. Because it was during their tryst that Aurelia, as she had a tendency to do, lost control. Luna Blaženovic was accidentally killed."

Though by the looks a minor shock went around the pavilion, not a word was spoken.

"When she got control of herself and realized what had happened, as she always did, Aurelia called on her husband. He may have been alarmed by what he saw. He might even have been sickened. But ever and always he was devoted to (if not obsessed with) his wife and he did as she demanded. She demanded he get rid of the body.

"Gunther had to think quick. Thinking quick was part of his profession and he wasn't one to panic. He would protect his wife. But, as we already know, he was also a man of business and he saw an opportunity. Rather than make the body disappear, he would proclaim the death, put the body in the spotlight, and gain a chunk of change for the effort.

"Their profession made it necessary their lives be heavily insured. The death of either The Hawk or The Canary would set the other up for life. Aurelia and Luna had nearly identical body shapes and both looked superficially alike. If they fiddled the insurance company, if Luna – as The Canary – died in Aurelia's place... But Luna's body was already cooling. The next show time was quickly approaching. There was little time to plan.

"Still plan they did. The Canary would put on her heart-stopping performance as usual. A chaotic event would grab the attention of the audience and stop the show. During that diversion, a tragic accident would occur. With Luna providing the corpse, The Canary would die before hundreds of witnesses and nobody would see a thing.

"The glitch in the program was that Gunther and Aurelia, busy on the trapeze above, would need an accomplice to create the diversion and assist with the body switch. There was no way around it. There were few prospects from which to choose. And they had no time. Gunther found his answer in a long-time co-worker. His name was Michael Gronchi. Circus visitors knew him as Mickey, the Sideshow Geek. The upside was Mickey was desperate to keep his job and his loyalty could be cheaply bought. The downside was he spent most of his free time inside a whiskey bottle. He might not have been the best choice but there was no time to be choosey.

"Luna's body, dressed in a costume identical to the one to be worn by The Canary for that night's performance, was hidden in an ordinary trunk. It's a guess but, I have reason to believe, a good one. Just before the show, the ringmaster would be informed Luna was ill and would not perform. One of a half-dozen bareback riders in the show, the ringmaster would not have had time to check and would likely not have cared awfully. Message delivered, Mickey hurriedly dragged the trunk to ringside then made himself scarce. A trunk among the countless electrical boxes, props, and odds and ends at ringside? With the show ready to begin who would have noticed? Who would have guessed? The dead little trick rider was there for the whole performance; until she was needed.

"On cue, most likely a dicey and dangerous moment above, when The Canary would have had every eye under the Big Top on her, Mickey followed his orders and, unseen, created their diversion. He set fire to the straw in an empty animal cage on the far side of the tent. It went up like tinder. But Mickey didn't know. Without looking back, he was off to his next assignment – the trunk near center ring.

"One by one backstage personnel spotted the fire and began to perceive the danger. The tent crew shouted to one another, interrupting the show without caring, calling for water and help as the flames spread beyond the cage and caught a row of draperies. Within seconds, performers and animals became alarmed. The audience, mesmerized by The Canary's performance above, caught on slower and in waves, but they did catch on. Within minutes the fire, like the lady acrobat that had inspired it, went totally out of control. Panic erupted.

"No one actually saw the accident. How could they? They were all on the run. The ushers and clowns trying to move the crowd to safety. The performers trying to rescue their props. The animal keepers trying to herd their frightened charges away. The ringmaster trying with little success to organize the chaos. No one saw Mickey the Geek open the trunk, lift out Luna's body, and lay it in the center ring beneath the aerial rigging. No one saw Aurelia slide to the ground and fold herself up in that same trunk. No one saw Mickey drag the trunk away. And no one saw Gunther drop from above, fall on Luna's body, and begin to shout his lungs out that his wife had fallen. All anyone knew was The Canary was flying aloft, a fire erupted in the tent and, as they scrambled to escape the blaze, The Canary lay dead in the sawdust of the center ring.

"Gunther was, of course, too distraught to allow anyone else near the body. There is no record as to what he thought of Mickey's handiwork. There's no doubt the geek came through for them. But he overdid it. When the smoke cleared nearly one hundred people, performers and audience alike, had been injured. Several seriously. One person went missing, a trick rider named Luna Blaženovic. One person, Aurelia Marx Herman, was accidentally killed. The Canary died when she fell from the sky.

"The following day Gunther and Mickey identified Luna as the dead Aurelia. After a perfunctory Coroner's jury reached a verdict of 'Accidental Death', the body was cremated, and Gunther collected his insurance money. The Kessler Traveling Circus folded without another performance. Heartbroken, Gunther retired and, almost immediately, vanished from the face of the earth.

Chapter Twenty-Six

"Fascinating," Wenders growled with no sign he was fascinated. "But how does a questionable death and an insurance fiddle in Missouri three years ago lead to modern day murder in Chicago?"

"Because the principals in that tragic tale didn't really vanish from the face of the earth. They merely seemed to. Circus performers have always come and gone like gypsies. Small circuses have always done the same. No one batted an eye when, several years later, a tiny circus appeared out of the blue. It was owned and managed by its ring-master, Karl Kreis, a fellow nobody had ever heard of before. He preferred to be called The Major. He called his show The Major's Major Circus.

"After the fire, Gunther Herman had no trace-able future. He disappeared. Before the fire, Karl Kreis had no past. He didn't exist. Karl Kreis, The

Major, was Gunther Herman. He'd returned to the circus; no longer as a trapeze artist, those days were over, but as the head honcho. His new show was a rousing success. So much so it was acquired at a handsome price by a financial group owned by a Chicago entrepreneur. Herman had his second big windfall in less than three years and, out of it, the All New Callicoat and Major Combined Circus was born.

"Only one step remained in Herman's plan; the plan concocted in haste that fateful day of Luna's death. But a hitch came last spring, bringing with it several weeks of fear, when Herman's new partner and majority owner, Reginald Callicoat, was killed in a plane crash. What would happen to his circus? What would happen to the final step in his plan? But it sorted itself. The heiress and new owner, Danita Callicoat, was willing the circus continue. The Major breathed a sigh of relief and kept on keeping on. Not long ago, his plan came full circle. He hired a brilliant aerialist named Alida Harrison…"

Everyone, even Rudy, turned to stare at the pixie. Alida lifted a proud and defiant chin.

"It was quickly apparent she would be their headlining act. What no one knew was Alida, like The Major, had no discernible past. In short order, and in spite of their age difference (nearly two decades), and to the wasted tears of a pint-sized circus clown, The Major and the new acrobat became engaged.

"Nobody knew The Major and Alida were already married. Gunther Herman was back from obscurity and Aurelia Marx Herman had returned from the grave; both with new identities and new lives, The Major running his own circus, his wife performing a new solo act."

"You mean," Wenders asked, chucking a thumb at Alida, "this is Aurelia Herman?"

The little acrobat gnashed her teeth at the homicide detective. Wenders gave her a sneer in return.

"In the flesh," I said, going on. "They'd allowed things to cool off and reunited to resume the fun and games. Everything might have been jake except the little clown, Alfonso Valencia, a self-proclaimed second-in-command, took it upon himself – without his bosses' knowledge – to hire a down and out Sideshow geek to sweep up around the circus. Michael Gronchi had, by sheer coincidence, wandered into Chicago and the Callicoat and Major Circus.

"The crap hit the fan in no time at all. Gronchi, who'd performed with the Kessler Circus and aided in their insurance fraud, recognized The Major as Gunther Herman and Alida as Herman's supposedly dead wife, neither of whom he had ever expected to see again. He recognized – if not a gold mine – at least a pot of gold to call his own. After all those years on the circuit he saw a chance to stroll down easy street. He knew he was complicit in their original crime. He also knew, if his scheme went wrong, the worst he might face would be a charge of mishandling a corpse or conspiring to defraud. He had manslaughter to dangle over the Hermans. It was worth the risk. Mickey blackmailed the couple.

"The Major may have been willing to go along. He'd had a lot of practice giving in, especially where his wife was concerned, and might have parted with a little money to keep the old drunk quiet. Mickey wasn't a professional gangster, after all, just a bum with an opportunity. But Alida, then and now, lived for Alida. She knew her wants and desires and nothing else. She never gave in. She saw Mickey as a threat to be dealt with immediately and for good. If The Major wouldn't take care of it she had an easy way of finding someone who would. She's a talented performer but her outlook on life is a living embodiment of a Third Grader's joke. *'With one of these,' the little girl said, lifting her dress, 'I can get all of those I want.'"*

Wenders ogled the pixie and swallowed hard.

"That's what she did," I went on. "Using her God-given credit card, Alida purchased the aid of the circus owner's husky chauffeur, Rudy Ace." I turned to Rudy. "Isn't that right?" He didn't answer but he didn't waver either. He held his silence and a cold thousand-yard stare. I returned to Wenders. "On her order, Rudy hurled a knife into Mickey's back and shoved the old drunk into Lake Michigan from the deck of the submarine Silversides there on Navy Pier. That should have secured their secret and ended the problem.

"Should have. But Mickey hadn't kept the secret. He'd told a buddy of his from the old days of the circus, Gerald Lapinski, known to the world as

Sybil the Bearded Lady. Then Mickey disappeared and Sybil got nervous. When I hit the Pier talking about a floating body, asking questions, getting answers that hinted the body belonged to Mickey, Sybil's nerves gave out. She ran for her life."

"To Wisconsin?" Wenders asked. "Why Wisconsin?"

"Where does anyone run? Home, of course. To the winter quarters and the circus museum. Alfonso guessed it. The killers guessed it too.

"Alfonso got there first. He found Sybil and spoke with her. For how long, I don't know. But long enough for the Bearded Lady to tell him something of what she knew. He was still there, and Sybil was still spilling the beans, when – on Alida's orders – Rudy showed up. As he'd so expertly done with Mickey, he silenced Sybil with a knife. Alfonso saw the attack and heard the murder."

"Heard?" Wenders asked. "What do you mean heard?"

"Sybil was talking when the attack came. Alfonso sat listening on the far side of the Bearded Lady. Rudy never saw him. When Sybil took a knife to the back, the midget dove under the bed.

The killer came the rest of the way into the train to finish Sybil off – unaware he had a witness. Alfonso was there the whole time, too pinched by the bed frame to even turn his head, listening as the killer strangled her with her own pearls and hacked her to death. Alfonso heard the murder but never saw the murderer.

"How the midget got out after, whether Rudy turned his back or what, I don't know. But he did and ran like hell to find me. He was desperate to leave the museum but I wouldn't let him. I made him lead me back to Sybil. She was long dead by the time I entered the train car. All I could do was stare at her and wonder who'd done it.

"At the time, there were two favorites on my mind. Tommy Dagger was an obvious guess. He could throw a knife like nobody else and had a temper of historic proportions. But he seemed too pat. He looked and acted evil but felt innocent. The other was The Major of whom Alfonso was no fan. But the fact was I knew nothing significant about either or their motives. If, at that point, one or the other had a reason to kill it was still a secret from me.

"As I stood there staring at all that remained of Sybil, I was ignorant of one other important point. The killer, awaiting his moment to escape, was still in the train car – behind me." I touched the tender back of my head and nodded my respect to Rudy. "You did a fine job on my skull. Then you left me to take the rap and explain the Bearded Lady's untimely death to the Wisconsin authorities."

The chauffeur made no reply. He barely looked at me.

"Alfonso raced back to Chicago," I said, returning to my story. "He didn't know the killer's identity either but it's likely he had similar suspicions, Tommy or, my favorite, The Major. The little clown was afraid for his life, no doubt, but that wasn't what drove him. He was propelled by his love for, and fear for, the apple of his eye – an aerial acrobat who didn't know he was alive. When he got back to the dorm, he didn't even bother going to his own room. He headed straight for Alida. I don't know what Alfonso was thinking, he didn't make that clear to me."

"What?" Wenders asked, shaking his head.

Oops, again. I really needed to watch that. "Nothing," I replied. "I'm just saying I don't know what was on Alfonso's mind. I don't know exactly what Sybil told him or how he took it. Did she tell him Alida was Aurelia, Gunther's wife? That she was part of a fraud? Did he understand what that meant? He was in love with her. Love is a strong emotion and, to survive, can filter a lot of truth if need be. He may have been looking to hold Alida blameless or make her The Major's victim. Or, if he recognized her guilt, he may have wanted to help. To explain it away, reason may have gone out the window. All I know is, despite his own danger, Alfonso went to Alida's room. He planned to wake her and tell her what he'd learned from Sybil. That The Major was a fraud. That he'd hidden a suspicious death in the past and was behind two murders in the present to cover it up. That her life was in danger.

"He found Alida's room empty. That broke his miniature heart all over again because he assumed she was with The Major. By then it was the wee hours of the morning. Alfonso was afraid to confront The Major and he didn't want to embarrass

Alida. He was too exhausted to do anything more. He decided to wait, there, in Alida's room, and fell asleep. He was there when she returned early this morning."

"He scared me," Alida shouted. "It scared me finding the little creep there. I ordered him out." They were her first words since our arrival and, of course, they amounted to a lie.

"No, you didn't," I said, cutting her off. I told those gathered, "I had no idea when I reached the performers' dorm late this morning, with the circus owner's permission to inquire, how close I was to wrapping up the whole affair. Not that I'd done any detecting of note but because of my uncanny habit of stumbling in the right direction. I arrived intent on finally meeting Alida Harrison in the flesh and finding out what it was she had to say. We surprised each other in the hallway outside of her room. She was hyperactive, red in the face, almost breathless, she was so glad to see me. She'd heard about the nosy detective wandering around. She had to show me her new act. She champed at the bit to walk and talk and solve the mysteries of the universe together." I sighed. "If only I'd recognized her nervous energy for what it was."

"No, Alida," I told the pixie. "You didn't order Alfonso out of your room this morning. He stayed. He excitedly told you all he'd been told and all he believed; that The Major was a fraud, a criminal, and a murderer. That Mickey had been killed for blackmailing him. That Sybil had been killed for knowing too much. He told you that you were in danger. He'd have been wiser talking to his mirror."

"It's insane," Alida objected. "Why would I have anything to do with that midget? Why would I have anything to do with any of those Sideshow freaks?"

"You wouldn't normally. They were beneath you, pun intended. But they were talking too much about your past. That jeopardized your future. And The Major... Or should we call him Gunther? It's all so confusing. Your husband was too weak or trusting to deal with it, so you dealt with it. Alfonso foolishly came to your rescue and for his trouble you smashed a Tanqueray bottle over his head." I lifted my hand and waved my hastily bandaged finger. "You missed a piece of glass when you tidied up. You busted Alfonso's skull because in your twisted mind you had no other choice."

"Wait," Wenders put in. "You're sayin' this morning when you were outside of her room—"

"Yes. I'm saying this morning Alfonso lay dead behind Alida's door only a few feet away from me. But by then he wasn't alone. Alida had been calling her husband to clean up her messes forever. But he wasn't working out anymore. She'd had to cajole Rudy into killing for her. And The Major had begun to make a fuss about how she was dealing with their crumbling cover up. This time, she called Rudy. He was there, likely in the middle of rolling the poor midget up in her bloodied bed sheets, making him ready for disposal. And what a disposal they planned!

"I saw the Callicoat limousine outside the performers' dorm on our way out. I remember questioning it then, foolishly, letting the subject drop. Alida led me around the circus grounds like a dog on a leash. She showed me her new act. I learned she could fold herself into a business-sized envelope and mail herself anywhere in the world. It would occur to me later that a trunk would have been no sweat at all. We walked and talked among the animals, I pretended I knew something and she pretended she knew nothing, and in that time Rudy carried Alfonso's remains from the dorm. He didn't even need to hide it; just a bundle of linens and a blanket rolled up in his arms. I flirted with Alida, absorbed a new threat from Tommy, and was told to pound sand by The Major, while Rudy casually stuffed the midget's body into the trunk of his limo, whistling while he worked. Then he tipped his hat to Olive and Alfonso's dog as he drove past the ticket booth headed out; headed south."

"South?" Wenders asked.

I nodded. "For my apartment, where you were taking tea and lying in wait. Like I said their plan for getting rid of the body was a cold-blooded doozy of a frame. They knew I found Mickey on the lake."

"Yeah," Wenders blurted. "Yeah, you did."

"Excuse me. I wound up with Mickey," I said, rephrasing it and giving the lieutenant my best 'not now' look. "That looked bad for me. Later, I was over top of Sybil when the killer added to my troubles; knocked me out and left me napping with the corpse. A frame was taking shape by itself. Then came Alfonso. It made evil sense to complete the hat trick and sew me up. Rudy took the midget's remains to my place and folded him into my cupboard. That gave me a third murder victim from the circus I needed to explain." I eyeballed Rudy and Alida. "You're bad people."

"Thank God the cops in Chicago – with a few exceptions – aren't blockheads. Lieutenant Wenders knew I wasn't it. We knew the killer was at the circus. We thought, wrongly it turned out, the murders looked good on The Major.

"Like I said, Rudy thought I was in the bag. But Alida wasn't convinced. She wanted a backup; someone else to fall in case I didn't. And, as she had a new fixer, protector, and lover, and as The Major was starting to rub her the wrong way, it occurred her tedious husband would fit the bill. She conceived a new murder and a new frame.

"On top of being amenable to the suggestion of murder, Rudy had another nasty habit of which Alida was aware. He's not the first; lots of psychos share a similar fixation. He collects trinkets from those he kills. I don't want to think about why. He kept them in a cigar box – probably to visit on occasion. Had he thought of it, and if he could have parted from them, he might have brought the box to my place with Alfonso's body, and sealed my doom. He didn't. But Alida remembered the creepy keepsakes and, when she decided her husband was needed for a patsy, used the box for the same purpose – to frame The Major. She hid it in Gunther's dresser ripe to be found.

"The Major was to be killed and his death made to look like a suicide. Guilt after all those murders got him down. But Gunther Herman refused to go down easily. Rudy, and the evil Mrs. Herman, took too long in erasing him and were delayed in getting him strung up.

"In the meantime, I stumbled back onto the Pier. I found the cigar box in The Major's room and, though I should have known better, bought the frame. I convinced myself he was our killer. But by the time I got to the Big Top, and found Gunther hanging, and spotted The Major's suicide note…"

I looked at Wenders searching for words that wouldn't leave me sounding stark-raving nuts.

"Events… led me to know the idea of suicide was a lot of hooey, the box of mementos was a plant, and the suicide note a complete fiction. I stumbled into the center ring in time to know The Major had been murdered. I caught our killers at the scene of their latest crime and they had no choice but to try to kill me. My brilliant secretary rescued me and… here we are."

"But why are we here?" Wenders asked. "I don't get the chase here. Is Mrs. Callicoat somehow–"

I shook the idea away. "Mrs. Callicoat had nothing to do with the circus murders. Owning the circus is her only connection, that and having a killer for a chauffeur. We're here, I believe, because the time came for Rudy and Alida to fly the coop. He's been living here. His resources were squirreled away here. He visited a cash box hidden in a caravan intending to fill his pockets and run."

One of the cops guarding Rudy patted the chauffeur down. He jammed a hand into his front pants' pockets and, with a nod, withdrew wads of cash from each that could easily have choked a horse.

"Ahh," I said. "It's fun to be right on occasion. What Rudy didn't plan on was a parade of cops and detectives following them here."

That was the moment, sisters and brothers, Danita Callicoat appeared around the corner of one of the wagons. She'd been listening to us from the shadows. You couldn't call it eavesdropping, she owned the place and was the only person who actually belonged. But she'd been listening. Judging by the expression on her face the rich widow had not enjoyed a word of it. She stopped outside of our circle, her blazing eyes directed solely at Rudy, and she screamed, "You filthy rat!"

That was the last piece of another puzzle I'd been going over in my bruised brain. Danita Callicoat and Rudy Ace had been an item.

"I'm sorry, Mrs. Callicoat," I told her. "It's an old story. If you'll excuse my flipping the pronouns, it was old a hundred years ago." I was no Elvis Costello. For that matter, when it came to carrying a tune, I was no Lou Costello. But the situation called for it and I gave it the old college try. I started singing:

*"She'd fly through the air with the greatest
of ease,
   That daring young girl on the flying trapeze.
   Her movements were graceful, all boys she
could please,
   And your love she purloined away."*

The lyrics hit home, you could see that, but only the lyrics. Otherwise I might as well not have been there. Danita Callicoat wasn't seeing me. She wasn't seeing any of us. She only had eyes for Rudy, red, hate-filled eyes. She clenched and unclenched her fists. Then, spitting fire, she shrieked, "You rotten, stinking, no good cheat!"

That startled us. Then she startled us again. She moved – too quickly for anyone to react. In what would have been impressive for an athlete, forget a furious millionairess, Danita did a cartwheel. She came down on one knee atop Alida's dropped handgun. Nobody had bothered to pick it up. Until that instant, I doubt a soul in the building – cop or criminal – remembered the damned thing lay there. With grace and speed Danita scooped the weapon, leveled the barrel, and fired. I was too close. I only heard the first blast, the rest were drowned by ringing in my ears, but I saw three flashes.

They hit Rudy like three kicks from a mad mule – beautifully grouped – in his cold unfaithful heart. Blood spurted from the big man's chest to the gravel floor. Rudy coughed a matching red. His eyes became cue balls and he fell as dead as a whorehouse at dawn.

Chapter Twenty-Seven

My ears still ringing, I stared warily at Danita through the curling gun smoke. "Easy, lady," I said. "You did that in front of the cops." She looked from the lump on the floor that had been Rudy Ace, to me, then to Wenders standing stunned beside me. She stood and smiled.

The suburban patrol, in one startled if understandably delayed move, drew their weapons. I threw a hand up for calm all around. It's not that I thought I was in charge, I wasn't. Neither was I horrified at the thought of the rich widow being put down, though that would have been a shame. But I didn't want the too-close quarters turned into a circular firing squad. "If you're done, Mrs. Callicoat," I said, reaching slowly for her shooting hand. "I'll take that for you."

She spun the gun, dangling it from her trigger finger, and handed it to me. "Call me Danita."

I nodded, slid her weapon into my jacket pocket, and took a deep breath. Everyone in the pavilion took a breath, save for Alida. She'd fallen to her knees and was still there. Aware the jig was entirely up, that her lover was dead, but that she'd been spared the same judgment, the dam burst and she began to cry uncontrollably.

Wenders, who hadn't moved a muscle through the whole gory moment, pointed at the acrobat and told Mason, "Get her out of here." The junior detective looked happy to oblige, happy at least for an excuse to leave the barn. He yanked Alida to her feet, pressed a supporting hand to what must have been a pang in his stitches, and hustled her outside. No one played 'A Gift for Caesar'.

Ogling the widow now, the lieutenant said to me, "I got two questions. How did she do that? And why did she do that?"

"There should be a law, Wenders, prohibiting your pay." I stepped to the caravan, opened the back door, and withdrew the rolled circus poster I'd seen earlier. Coming back, I asked, "Question. Where did Chicago businessman, industrialist, and entrepreneur Reginald Callicoat III develop his love of the circus? Answer: He didn't. His supposed obsession was crap fiction. One fateful day he found among his holdings a small and insignificant entertainment, The Major's Major Circus. He didn't knowingly buy it, he'd acquired it.

"He couldn't get rid of it at a profit – circuses, I'm told, are not in high demand – so he went to see it instead. And though he didn't give a rat's rump about the circus, at first sight he fell head over heels in love with one of the performers. That was his obsession; a mid-level performer whose headlining days were behind her, a once-famous rope spinner and trick shot artist."

I unrolled the poster, a boldly colored one-sheet from the Buckets & Barnes Circus (unlike my secretary, I did not say "Ta dah!"), and showed Danita. Uninterested, she turned away. I showed it to Lisa and Wenders, a print identical to one I'd seen at the World Circus Museum, a cartoon likeness of Danita Callicoat, in western garb, over the heading Dead-Eye Danny 'Greatest Trick Shot Artist of Them All'.

"Danita Sawall," I told them. "Her maiden name. Known in the circus as Dead-Eye Danny. A one-time star but, by then, merely a member of The Major's troupe. Reginald loved her, wooed her, and took her out of the fading limelight. He gave the circus his name, then did likewise for Danny."

"Call me Danita," she said through gritted teeth.

"Not long after, Danita," I told her. "Your husband noted that, despite his millions, you appeared to be unhappy. He thought you missed the circus and, to cheer you, built this pavilion. It wasn't the circus you were missing."

I shook the poster. "Before the Major Circus, before Kessler, there was the Buckets & Barnes Circus; your headlining heyday when you performed on the same bill with knife thrower Rudolpho Acciai." I pointed to the banner across the bottom of the one-sheet, reading: 'Plus Rudolpho the Great'. "Your long-time lover."

"When your husband bought the circus, you brought Rudolpho here and put in a pitch for him. But your husband refused to hire him. His circus already had a knife thrower. So, to keep him near, you hired Rudy Ace as your chauffeur and valet.

Life was good again. Now you had money and the rooster of your choice. What you didn't foresee was Alida Harrison popping up, twisting herself into inviting shapes in front of Rudy, stealing your lover away, and involving him in murder."

"I don't blame her," Danita said. "She's a rotten slut. But the world is full of sluts." She looked at her former lover in a heap on the floor. She spit on him. "He should have resisted. He owed me."

"Okay," Wenders told the rich widow, halting the proceedings. "That's murder one, Mrs. Callicoat. You're gonna have to come along with us."

Danita shook her head. "You'll never prove murder. You won't even make the charge."

The lieutenant stared. "We got a barn full of witnesses." He chucked a nod at the corpse. "Saw you fire three bullets into him."

Danita nodded her agreement. "But he didn't exist."

Wenders turned his confused bovine face my way, asking without asking.

"She makes an interesting point," I told him. "Before he was Rudy Ace, he was Rudolpho Acciai. Rudolpho the Great. Before that, if you chase the circus records down he was Chandu the Magnificent, another Impalement Artist, and was paid under the name Tedaris. His real name, God only knows."

"He wasn't," Danita said stiffly. "His driver's license was a forgery. He had no papers. No green card. He didn't even have a birth certificate. You can't prove who he was... because he wasn't. He was an illusion. You can't murder a man who never existed."

"You–" Wenders stopped, looking like a deer in the headlights. "You can't just walk out of here."

"Have no fear, Lieutenant," Danita said as if he was a child. "I'll go quietly. Go through the motions, if you like, it makes no difference. Put me on trial, if you're able. I'm a grieving widow, a paragon of society, seduced and made a fool by a manipulative gypsy. A criminal foreigner with no identity. A three-time murderer, who started a gun battle in my back yard and who, at the time he was shot, was threatening not only me but all of my guests, including yourself. Murder, bargained to manslaughter, becomes justifiable homicide. Before it's over, Governor Thompson will take me to dinner and Mayor Byrne will give me a key to the city."

"You got it all figured out?"

"If I don't..." Danita shrugged her shapely shoulders. "If they don't... I'm rich, attractive, and can afford the best lawyers in the country. Extreme emotional disturbance; that is a hung jury over and over again. The thin gold plating on the watch they'll give you at retirement, Lieutenant, will turn green before I spend a minute in a cell."

Wenders examined it, his face running the gamut of emotions, annoyance, anger, disgust and, finally, despite his best efforts, confusion.

Lisa put the question. "Could she get away with that?"

I screwed up my lips and shrugged. How the hell did I know?

"Well," my secretary went on, "that's Wenders' problem. You captured the murderers you were after."

"Dummy up," Wenders barked.

"Don't sweat it, Frank," I told him. "Lisa means well. She's just wrong."

"Wrong? How am I wrong? What do you mean?"

The time had come for a confession (I hated confessions). "I mean," I said, unbagging the cat. "We unwound four murders without solving the murder we intended to solve."

"Blake," Lisa exclaimed. "What are you talking about? Rudy's there!"

"And," Wenders added. "Mason took the acrobat out in cuffs! What game are you playin'?"

"It's no game," I told him. I turned to Lisa and reminded her, "This started when you set out to find the victim in my vision. I tried to solve his murder; the murder of the drowned man. But I got my psychic wires crossed because I can't control..." I waved at my own head. "...this thing. I conflated images from two separate visions. I didn't solve the murder of the drowned man. I solved the murder of the guy you pulled out of the lake."

"Huh?" Lisa twisted her lips and poked her glasses off the end of her nose. "You're saying Mickey the Geek wasn't the drowned man?"

"Lisa," I said with a sigh. "Did he drown?"

"Well, yeah..." She stopped herself. "No. No, he didn't. He bled to death in the cold water from a stab wound we didn't know he had."

"Right. But I'm here to tell you, and make no mistake about it, I saw a man who was drowning. A man who drowned."

"So it wasn't Mickey?"

I shook my head. "No."

"And my finding Mickey in Lake Michigan really was just a coincidence?"

"I'm afraid so." I smiled, but only because Lisa looked so dejected. "There was a connection, but only coincidentally. The bottom line is, we solved the circus murders, but we've yet to solve the murder of the drowned man."

"Aw-right, you two!" Wenders growled. "Enough of your babblin'. Enough of your nonsense about visions, and ESP, and drownin' men. I'm sick of it! Do either of you two geniuses got a suggestion for how we proceed with Mrs. Callicoat here. She committed murder right in front of us and now she's blowing raspberries at justice takin' a hand."

Wenders definition of justice had never walked arm-in-arm with mine. That didn't mean he didn't have a point. I stepped past Rudy's body, crossed the space to the circus owner, and looked Danita in the eyes. I held the look, taking every ounce of amused contempt and superiority she was laying on me, then called for my secretary over my shoulder.

When Lisa arrived at my side, I asked, "Your car. Not the Pinto, your car, the roller skate. It broke down while you were tracing our vandals?"

"Yeah," Lisa answered. She shook the question from her voice, cleared her throat, and answered again. "Yes. It's in Des Plaines. Both of our vandals live on the same block in Des Plaines."

"That's where I thought you said." I nodded my appreciation.

It's a character flaw of mine, sisters and brothers. I'll often go on with something, in spite of a huge likelihood of making an ass of myself, if there's the remotest chance I'm right. The last time I'd gone through this nonsense, during the Reverend Delp murders, the excruciating visions had come to an end when the killer died and his accomplice was hustled off to the hoosegow. The appeased murder victims, for want of a better way to express it, got what they wanted and shut up. Here, the case was solved. Alida and the late Rudolpho had done it. But I'd messed up and something told me not to let it stand.

"Your husband," I asked Danita. "He was an Ivy League graduate?"

Her beauty disappeared as her face twisted. She couldn't figure me out and, clearly, had grown tired of trying. "Yes, you poor, sad, amusing little detective. Princeton."

I reached for Lisa, telling her, "Take my hand." She hesitated among so many strangers. Then, as it was me asking, interlaced her fingers with mine and held on.

"Forgive me," I told Danita. "This will either annoy you or add greatly to your amusement."

The rich widow yelped as, with my free hand, I clutched her by the neck beneath her left ear. She and everyone else in the pavilion, probably, reacted in shock to one degree or another. I didn't see it. For several painful seconds, I saw nothing at all. I was being thunderstruck.

There were no instructions to go with my lovely affliction. I'd never succeeded in initiating a psychic vision at will and was as surprised as anyone in the barn. I gritted my teeth and took it as the heat and pain shot through my head, the colored lights exploded behind my eyes, and the hallucinations came.

I expected another trip through the valley of the shadow of death (forgive the Biblical flowers). I expected to again experience the demise of each of the recent circus victims; Mickey's stabbing and a shove into the drink, Sybil's stabbing and subsequent mutilation, Alfonso's bludgeoning and a nap in my spacious kitchen cabinet, The Major's being hung like a Christmas goose. I expected all the pain and terror of each as, over and over again, I entered the Undiscovered Country. But it didn't come.

What came instead was a fiery flash of hell on earth. Holy balls!

I'd never been mistaken for a philosopher. Chroniclers were not beating down my door. Those few who knew me knew that, if asked, only if asked, I could dispense a cynical word about life on the mean streets of Chicago. But that I'd as soon keep it to myself and let you carry your own load. That said, I had on occasion, if only fleetingly, contemplated the meaning of life and the eventuality of death. No one that has been dragged to the edge as often as I, without falling off, would claim any different. But I'd never obsessed on it or arrived at any answers profound enough to warrant a speech in the town square. Sadly, I still operated under the basic belief that, regardless of family, friends, love, or lust, we puny humans come into the world alone and, owing to the laws of nature, go out the same way. But, holy balls, I'm telling you, in the next few seconds I learned there are times when death was anything but lonely. Sometimes death was a spectator sport.

My ears buzzing, my brain flashing, my neck flushed with heat, my noggin ready to explode, I found myself standing in the middle aisle of a passenger plane. Yeah, I know, but I'm telling you. Despite the fact my body was physically in the Callicoat wagon pavilion, glared at by Wenders and company, in a human chain between Lisa and Danita, my mind and senses were on a commercial jetliner.

A quick glance, coupled with the hum of several hundred voices, told me the plane was full. The vibration in my feet told me we were already hauling ass down the runway. Experience told me we were nearing take-off speed. Then, above the din of the passengers, I heard a loud snap and crunch; the sounds of metal coming undone. I looked up and to my left, through one of the windows overlooking the wing and, in a twisted reality where everything moved in slow motion, I saw a three-foot piece of the leading edge of the wing rip away. The plane's port engine – torn from its moorings – flew forward as if it had lift, then up, then back and over top of what remained. The engine and chunk of wing vanished behind us. Other than a few passengers near the window, who raised their heads in confused curiosity, nobody aboard appeared to notice. They were still chatting amiably. The plane was still rolling forward – and lifting off.

We cleared the ground, went airborne and, seconds later, the plane began to roll hard to the left. The happy chatter stopped. An excited, then frightened, murmur rose in its place. The plane rolled over. I hit the ceiling of the fuselage, now the floor, with my head and shoulders. Forward, near the lavatory, two stewardesses did the same. Between us hundreds of passengers buckled in their seats hung like bats, shrieking and screaming madly, while their carry-on baggage and personal effects flipped and fluttered through the confined space. We were flying upside down.

Flying is too strong a verb. And no adverbs or adjectives come to mind that might better describe the situation. You can either imagine it or you can't. The flight was over in less than a minute; fifty seconds according to the record books. Fifty seconds – then the lives of all aboard would end in a horrific crash. Their short nightmare would be over. Mine would only have begun.

Upside down, we hit the ground. I was crushed and ripped apart, like the others, as the world burst into flames around us. Yet somehow, I was still there, taking it in and feeling it. Tearing metal, splashing fuel, fire, screams, rended bodies, blood, and death. And then, from among the screams came individual cries aimed, not at the horrifying situation, but at me. One, then another, then another, until there were hundreds of tortured souls yelling directly at me.

As quickly as it had started, the vision ended. I was back in the pavilion. Back on my feet, at least for an instant. Then, shaken and trembling, I released my holds on Lisa and Danita and fell to my knees. "Not there," I screamed. "He isn't there!"

"Nod," Lisa called. "Nod, are you all right?"

"What's not there?" Wenders demanded.

"He isn't," Danita insisted, pointing at me. "He isn't all there. He's obviously mentally ill. He had one of these attacks before, right here on this spot. There's something wrong with him!"

"There is something wrong with me," I said, fighting for breath in order not to puke. Lisa helped me back to my feet. Holding tightly, I took a deep breath. "I'm sick. Murder makes me sick."

"Grand. Me too." Wenders sneered. "So tell me, smart guy, if you're done crying and sweating, what are you trying to prove? What ought I do with our trigger-happy socialite?"

"Arrest her. Murder in the First Degree."

"We've been over that," Danita said with disdain. "Take me in, for all the good it will do you. My attorneys will have me out before you've finished your reports. Nobody will be shedding any tears over a homicidal maniac."

"No," I agreed. "They probably wouldn't. But you're going to jail for murder all the same, either for life or to await your day in the death house, whichever the People of the State of Illinois choose."

Now everyone was talking at once, Danita denying the charge and calling me mad, Wenders defending a rich taxpayer and calling me a fool, Lisa confessing her confusion and begging for an explanation. They were making my battered head hurt. "Stop. Stop!"

The pavilion went quiet.

"What are you talkin' about?" Wenders demanded. "If you agree we won't tag her for this." He pointed at Rudy's cooling corpse. "And you insist she had nothin' to do with the circus murders. Then what the hell are you talkin' about?"

Lisa nodded – which made me pause. I'd never seen her agree with Wenders before. I didn't blame her this time. "Nod," she asked, "who did she kill?"

"The drowned man."

Chapter Twenty-Eight

"Good," Wenders shouted. "Clear as mud. Who, for the love of Mike, is this drowned man?"

"Danita's husband," I said. "Reginald Callicoat III."

"What are you…" Wenders was so beside himself there were almost two of him. One was plenty. "The whole world knows her husband died in a plane crash. The worst crash ever, fer cripes sake!"

"They do," I agreed. "And it was. But he wasn't aboard."

I stepped unsteadily away from the women, still shaken by my last vision, got my bearings and addressed the group. "The Callicoats were not getting along. By then the new chauffeur had settled in. Rudy wasn't just taking care of the limousine, he'd gone off-road and was doing the driving in Danita's bedroom as well. Reginald may have caught on to that fact. Or he may simply have grown tired of an expensive wife that didn't love him anymore. He said as much to a number of friends and talked about it at length with at least one attorney."

I turned to Danita. "Do I have that correct?" If looks could kill. But they can't, not by themselves, so I moved on without an answer.

"Danita returned the feeling. She was as tired of her husband as he was of her. But divorces are messy, unsettling and, most of all, expensive. Danita's position could be summed up using simple math; divorcées get a settlement, widows get it all. Reginald Callicoat had to die."

I wandered the circle, avoiding what remained of Rudy. "The plan, equally as simple, went like this. Reginald would board a commercial airliner and fly out of her life."

"That's a plan?" Wenders asked with contempt.

"That was it. He would fly away and never be heard from again. He would be reported missing, the authorities would search (spending oodles of tax dollars), and find nothing. Many rumors would be collected, a few theories would be developed:

he ran away with another woman, he was kid-napped and something went wrong, he changed his identity for his own reasons and vanished, he suffered a mental breakdown. But the complete answer would never be known and the millionaire would never be found. Like I said, simple.

"Of course, there was a bit more to it than that. When an appropriate number of days passed and Danita *learned* her husband had disappeared, the plan called for her to report the loss with mixed fear, grief, and embarrassment. She would have no idea where he'd gone or why. She would be unable to say whether he was a victim of depression, dis-enchantment, or foul play. She would be aghast at the suggestions he'd run away or had a secret lover somewhere. But, when all was said and done, how could she know and what difference would it make? Reginald had gone on a business trip and never returned. She would eventually accept the fact, get over it, and move on. So would the au-thorities.

"To that end, the most important part of Danita's plan required her to remain under the radar, to act like an abandoned wife, and patiently wait until the required number of years had passed and Reginald could be declared legally dead and his estate and life insurance become hers. Four years? Or is it seven in Illinois? What's the difference with millions waiting and drawing interest? She had her trust to keep her in brandy and a chauffeur on the premises to keep her in shape. She's pragmatic. She's patient."

I paused speaking directly to Danita. "You killed your husband. You reserved a First Class ticket for him aboard Trans Air Flight 191, non-stop from Chicago O'Hare to Los Angeles. You put Rudy in one of your husband's best suits and sent him to the airport the morning of the flight. You had him pick up your husband's ticket and present it at the boarding gate. But, instead of boarding, Rudy came home to you. The plane took off with Reginald Callicoat III listed as a passenger."

"Minutes later," I told the group, "in an unplanned and unexpected twist, the business world, the banking world, the circus world, and Danita and Rudy – in particular – got the surprise of their lives. A shock that, once the vibrations ebbed, as far as Danita was concerned, became the handiest stroke of luck. The DC-10, supposedly carrying her escaping husband, had suffered a catastrophic mechanical malfunction. It lost an engine on take-off. It was airborne less than a minute before it flipped and hit the ground in a fiery crash that killed two by-standers, all 297 persons aboard, and – at least on paper – one wealthy entrepreneur not on board."

"Is that true? Can you prove any of it?" Wenders asked. "Even if you can, where's the luck?"

"Every word is true. I can prove it. As for luck… The crash altered the legal criteria of her situation and made Danita instantly rich. Exposed to imminent peril, a plane crash, without returning, neither Callicoat's body nor years of waiting were required to file a petition for a 'death in absentia' ruling. Only seven bodies came out of that disaster intact. There was no question of Callicoat being aboard, no reason to suspect he wasn't among those who would never be identified, or that he might have pulled a fast one and been alive somewhere else. The court had no cause to deny the petition."

"*Not here! He isn't here!*" I heard them again, in my memory, as I'd heard them in my vision, all two hundred and ninety-seven souls wiped out in an instant in that field, screaming at me that Reginald Callicoat was not among them. "Not here!" I said, repeating the phrase in a whisper. "He isn't here!"

Wenders roused me from my ghostly reverie. Not with applause for a case well-solved, I assure you. He was screaming at me, as usual, if not with slightly more vitriol. "That's enough! Boy, that's more than enough! You're spewin' accusations all over the place, but you ain't sayin' nothin'. Proof, Blake. Have you got any proof of anything? You lay out a fancy insurance scam based on Mrs. Callicoat being a murderer. But you ain't said squat about a murder. If Callicoat is a victim of homicide it's time to spill it. And prove it! You called Callicoat the drowned man. Who drowned him? How? And where? And where's his body?"

"Nearby," I told Wenders. "So close even you ought to be able to find it."

I stepped to Danita's raised lounging area and turned to take in the wagon barn. "This pavilion was erected three years ago," I said. "There's a building permit recorded in the county clerk's office. In the same office, same file, is a permit taken out six months ago for the construction of this center ring." I pointed. "Technically it's a deck, so she needed a permit. Danita's charming breakfast circle."

"The remains of what used to be a full pallet of fifty-pound bags of concrete mix still sit beyond that calliope. I know," I told Wenders. "And so do you. We were cringing behind it only a few minutes ago hoping not to be shot or stabbed."

Wenders sighed, hating me. "Get on!"

"A check of bank accounts, going back no further than eight months, will produce all the evidence anyone needs to confirm certain incriminating purchases and secure search warrants. Survey maps of this estate, as with every property in the county, are also a matter of public record. Consult them as I did. This new concrete slab is laid over top of the property's original well. You know, the old-fashioned kind we used to holler into as a kids to hear our echoes, or throw pennies into to make a wish, or haul up buckets of fresh cold water to sip from a tin cup."

"Blake!" Wenders barked. "You got diarrhea of the mouth again. What are you babbling about?"

"Listen, will you! Reginald Callicoat didn't go out in a blaze of glory, with 297 others, when a DC-10 fell from the sky at the end of its runway and exploded in a ball of fire in a nearby suburb."

"You say!"

"I do!" I gave up on the tub of lard and turned on the rich widow. "You murdered your husband, Danita, for his estate and his life insurance. You scammed the court and the insurance company. Rudy helped you with the killing. Your husband's class ring was the first bauble in his little cigar box of collectables. You didn't loan Alida a practiced lover, you passed on an experienced killer. But, a few minutes ago, you relieved everybody of the need to care about his involvement. You're the only one left to fall for it. You incapacitated your husband. Then, while he was still alive, you chucked him into the old estate well.

"To his terror, Reginald came awake in the dark bottom of that well, choking and spitting up filthy water. While he struggled unsuccessfully for a way out, you rained fresh water and cement mix down on him from above. When he became cognizant enough to kick up a fuss, you shot him. I imagine you'll claim you did it for him, to put him out of his misery. But you were doing it for you, to put him out of your misery. Funny thing is, you missed."

I wandered away, putting space between us, enjoying a laugh at her expense. "Dead-Eye Danny missed a simple shot like that. I shouldn't criticize; I would have missed too. It was black as pitch down there. You hit the wall beside him. The ricochet caught your husband in the head." I touched my left temple. "It didn't kill him. It stunned him and shut him up but didn't spare him the agony as his bronchi choked with dirty water and wet cement. All it did was spare you the noise, left you in peace and quiet to drown him and bury his corpse at the same time." I shook my head. "Your mother-in-law doesn't need a medium to search for her son. He isn't in the great beyond."

I turned to Wenders. "He's entombed there, beneath that decorative cap, eighteen feet down if the County plat books are accurate, under several feet of concrete. He drowned in a filthy oatmeal of cement and he's waiting to be found."

Still dabbing a handkerchief to his throat, Wenders waddled over and, hesitantly at first, then with growing confidence, informed Danita he was arresting her on suspicion of murder. He recited her Miranda Rights. She seemed not to be listening. She was staring holes through me instead. Wenders finished his speech and asked the rich widow if she understood her rights. Ignoring him, Danita told me, "I knew the moment I met you at that séance… I knew my life was over."

I opened my pie hole, to respond, but Wenders cut me off. "Don't feel bad, honey. Everybody meets Blake ends up feelin' the same way."

Chapter Twenty-Nine

For the drowned man, the waiting would soon be over. The experts would move in, wreck the hastily erected deck that served as his tomb, and return him to the mother that still had things to say to him. Reginald Callicoat III would find a safer rest in friendlier confines. For everyone else, the waiting had just begun.

We'd all slipped into different groups, in separate sections of the Callicoat estate, based upon our duties, intended destinations, or various depths of despair.

Lieutenant Wenders, as he would, had retired into the Callicoat mansion with the lady of the house to await a Chicago patrol unit. They would take custody of Danita, shuttle her into the city, and book her for murder. Though it was against the rules, and bad policy, Wenders allowed the self-made widow to while away the time sipping fine brandy. Dispensation had been granted because, while he couldn't honestly appreciate it, the fat lieutenant liked brandy too. The two suburban police officers, watching Danita from a quiet corner of the room did not partake. They were on duty.

In the drive outside, Alida Harrison sat handcuffed in the back seat of Wenders' car waiting for the Chicago paddy wagon ordered on her behalf. She may have been a star headliner, but she was not a millionairess circus owner. Her First Class days were behind her. From that point on, she would travel the route of all perps.

Mason leaned against the rear quarter-panel of the same car, guarding Alida, holding his abdomen and wishing the prescription in his pocket would magically morph into pain pills. I mention it but that's as far as my sympathy stretched. (Being allergic to most pain killers, I felt worse than he did and had no prescription. So nuts to him.) Besides, Mason complained out loud. He hated the wait. He wanted to go home. He didn't trust the pixie contortionist and fully expected her to pull a vanishing act of some kind. He was whining, if you asked me. Aurelia Herman was boxed in and couldn't twist out.

One of the suburban units remained at the estate's front gate, waiting to let the police scientists in and preparing to keep the media out. The second unit had come up from the gate and the officers now stood guard at the wagon pavilion. Whatever romance the Callicoat's barn had once held was gone. The gateway to the glories of the circus past was now just a crime scene – and a temporary morgue.

Inside the pavilion, Rudy remained face down on the bloody gravel, awaiting the arrival of the coroner's van and his penultimate ride. Reginald awaited the jack hammers. Neither of them minded. The dead were patient.

Willie, Lisa, and I sat in the soft grass of the manicured lawn hanging out like Woodstock hippies. Willie hugged himself, supporting both his newly shot and his partially healed shoulders, whining about the pain and waiting on the ambulance the cops had insisted on calling. They were too short-handed to take the slug to the hospital themselves and wouldn't let us do it. The rented and wrecked Pinto was part of the crime scene and couldn't be moved. That was just as well. With its shot-out windows and skinned doors, the poor little Ford didn't look like it wanted to go anywhere.

As for us... Lisa and I had statements to make and questions to answer. Many many questions, I suspected.

Emotionally exhausted, Lisa had so far been holding her tongue. I appreciated that. Physically done in, I ached from tip to toe and held my head hoping it wouldn't explode and mess up the pretty yard. The hopeful part of my mind roamed through a dream involving my next life; a life in which murder was something you visited in museums and read about in history books. The darker chunk of my brain, on the other hand, the part that directed most of my days, slogged its way through a mire of depressing questions I couldn't help but ask myself.

"Nod," Lisa said, touching my shoulder and shaking me from my dream. "What are you thinking so hard about?"

"Oh. I'm just curious about this… What do you call it? This… head thing. Would we have solved Reginald's murder sooner, would we have saved Alfonso's life, or Sybil's, or The Major's, or even Rudy's, if I'd just touched the poster of Dead-eye Danny instead of Mickey's picture?"

"You can't do that to yourself. There's no telling what, if anything, would have happened. The circus murders and the Callicoat murder were connected, you said so yourself. How were you supposed to un-jumble the flashes? You're too hard on yourself."

"I just wish I had a handle on this–"

"Head thing?"

"Yeah. The head thing."

"You got it to work today when you wanted it to. You controlled it. That's big, isn't it?"

"I don't know. It was a wild guess. Now it's a guess whether or not it really worked."

"Nod," Lisa said, getting that gleam in her eye I really, really hated. "There's this professor I've read about. He's some sort of psychologist or psychoanalyst, but he's also a spiritualist. He's doing this lecture at one of the local colleges."

"Lisa, no."

"I was just thinking he might..."

"No, Lisa. Every time you try to study my head, I wind up in a sea of crap. I'm going to chain you to your desk."

"What kind of thing is that to say to your confidential secretary? Your faithful dogsbody? Your sometimes partner?"

"You're not my partner!"

"Sometimes!"

"Not ever! I don't have a partner. I work alone."

"You're missing the point, which is, what kind of thing was that to say to me? Come out of the Dark Ages, Blake! It's 1979! Haven't you ever heard of Women's Lib?"

"No. I've heard of Women's Lip. You've got more than your share of that."

"No, this is different. This is with a 'b'. Women's Lib. You should check it out."

"I'll do that."

We were interrupted by the arrival of the paddy wagon for Alida and a shiny squad for Danita. Behind came the police scientists in an impressive parade and Willie's ambulance. As the ladies were led, Danita from her digs, Alida from Wenders' car, to their official conveyances, the picture takers, finger print lifters, blood samplers, and distance measurers unloaded and went to work. Organized chaos ruled then settled into a rhythm. Wenders reappeared, barking my name and demanding our "little talk."

"You're hurt again and I feel responsible." Lisa said, helping me to my feet. She ducked under my arm and supported my weight.

"Well, don't go out on a limb. What do you mean you feel responsible?"

"I'm saying, I guess, in a way, this was partly my fault."

"Are you kidding?" I asked, ogling her like the Two-Headed Boy in, forgive me, a circus Sideshow. "The whole thing was your fault, Lisa. The entire case from front to back."

"That's not fair!"

"Fair? I was in the hospital because of the Delp case, which was your fault. You insisted I get my head scanned, your fault. You dragged me to a phony medium to talk to the dead. That was your fault. And who, asked the bleary-eyed detective, told you to go to the harbor and find a body? No-body. You did it on your own. It's your fault!"

"Well, I don't feel that way."

"That's because you've forgotten the first rule of detecting: The facts don't care about your feelings."

"That's ridiculous. There is no first rule of detecting."

"How would you know? You're not a detective."

"I'm going to be! Someday soon."

"Over my dead body."

"See," Lisa said, assisting me toward the scowling police lieutenant. "We agree. And, at the rate you're getting beat up, that'll be in no time at all. Gosh, I'm going to be a detective even sooner than I thought." Lisa smiled wide beneath her goofy glasses. "I better get ready."

I sighed a ton. "I think I better get ready too."

Dear reader,

We hope you enjoyed reading *Red Herrings Can't Swim*. Please take a moment to leave a review in Amazon, even if it's a short one. Your opinion is important to us.

Discover more books by Doug Lamoreux at https://www.nextchapter.pub/authors/doug-lamoreux-horror-mystery-author

Want to know when one of our books is free or discounted for Kindle? Join the newsletter at http://eepurl.com/bqqB3H

Best regards,
Doug Lamoreux and the Next Chapter Team

About the Author

Doug Lamoreux is a father of three, a grandfather, a writer, and actor. A former professional firefighter, he is the author of eight novels, a novella, and a contributor to anthologies and non-fiction works including the Rondo Award-nominated Horror 101, and its companion, the Rondo Award-winning Hidden Horror. He has been nominated for a Rondo, a Lord Ruthven Award, a Pushcart Prize, and is the first-ever recipient of The Horror Society's Igor Award for fiction. Lamoreux starred in the 2006 Peter O'Keefe film, Infidel, and appeared in the Mark Anthony Vadik horror films The Thirsting (aka Lilith) and Hag.

Other books by Doug Lamoreux

- The Devil's Bed
- Dracula's Demeter
- The Melting Dead
- Corpses Say the Darndest Things: A Nod Blake Mystery
- When the Tik-Tik Sings
- Seven for the Slab: A Horror Portmanteau

Books by Doug Lamoreux and Daniel D. Lamoreux:

- Apparition Lake
- Obsidian Tears

You might also like:

Looking For Henry Turner by W.L. Liberman

To read first chapter for free, head to:
https://www.nextchapter.pub/books/looking-for-
henry-turner

CPSIA information can be obtained
at www.ICGtesting.com
Printed in the USA
BVHW040227040520
579143BV00002B/176